CADY HAMMER

Chasing War

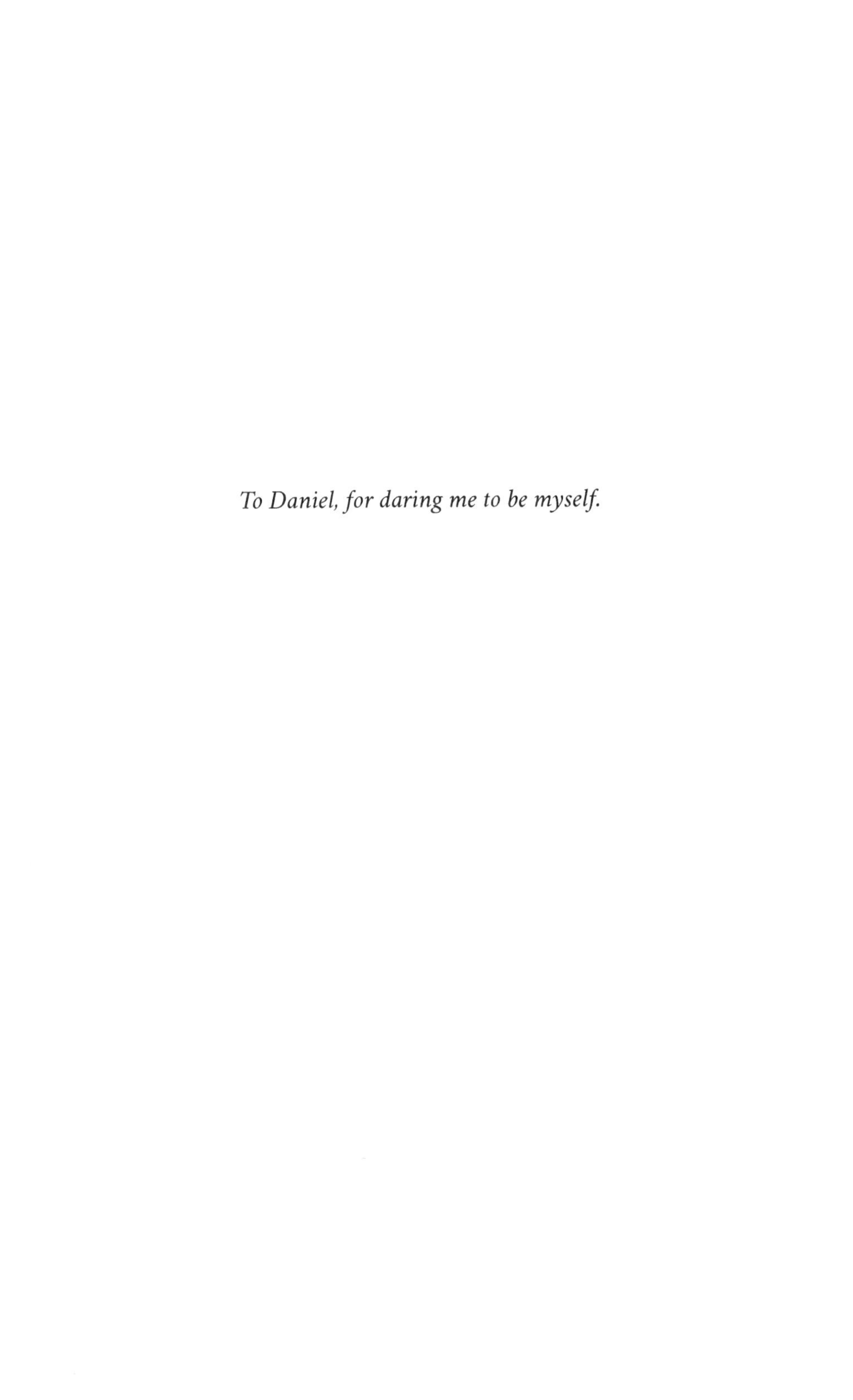

To Daniel, for daring me to be myself.

Author's Note

Things My Beta Readers Said To Me While Reading (and Revising!)
Chasing War

Draft #2
Explain the levels and tiers of magic! Explain the skills and how they build! OMG this should have been done already.
Neil's character needs more development. I want to see more anger out of his character.
I'd love to also see more of [the House of the Wind] here.
Whoopsies, just took over the realm. Don't do this. This is not... poof... realm domination.
Stupid choices lead to stupid deaths.

Draft #4
I LOVE that you opened with [the violin] - not only do I relate very much, but [it] really got me hooked in the first few seconds and created an image in my brain.
Oh, I love this. Further isolation of Grace and emphasis on the fact that anything she wants here, she must get for herself.
The jealousy of my OTP.
Suspicious... wooooooo.
YAY THE SHIP IS A SHIP.

Enjoy.

Chapter One

There's something grounding in the consistency of a well-tuned violin. Once the player has tuned the string to exactly where they want it to be, they can create their music by following a simple road map. The third string without any fingers pressed down will always play one note, and pressing the first finger down on the second string will always be another note. Even if another player tunes that same instrument to a different key, those notes created will always be in the same place if you put your fingers in the right place. But from player to player, nothing is consistent. When one plays notes in a sequence, even in the same sequence as another, they never sound the same. Each musician makes their own music, takes a song and transforms it into something new and exciting.

I draw the bow slowly across the violin, drawing out a soft pure note. My first finger vibrates on the second string to gradually build up the note to its richest sound. For the ten thousandth time since I picked up my first violin, I fuse notes together into a beautiful melody that starts quiet and builds to a swelling crescendo. The music sweeps me away from the room, and I am transported home once more. I play for myself and myself alone, and as I breathe it all in, I feel calm.

When I finish the last note, I open my eyes. The soft lavender music room greets me once more, illuminated by the fading light of the day. The light casts long shadows across the tile floor and the baby piano in the corner. I place my violin down on its stand and carefully lay the bow across its top compartment. The silver strap holds the instrument's neck in place.

In the two weeks I've been here, I have practically been holing myself up in the music room just trying to stay out of everybody's way. While the little girl, Analise, may be a fan of mine, I can't say the same for the rest of my father's family. If looks could kill, Neil and his mother would have put me in the ground ages ago. The attendants aren't much better. I can't tell if they hate me or fear me. Every time I come across one, they give me quite a wide berth. It's strange, being in a house with so many people moving about. Something is always happening, whether it's nobles dropping by for a business conversation or servants moving about their daily chores throughout the castle.

Before the duel that changed everything, I was gallivanting across the Upper Realm with Aiden, looking for answers surrounding my brother's death. I'm not even sure I got all the answers I wanted. I know how he died and what for, but not how he knew what he was dealing with. How did he understand the significance of black obsidian? Did he know something that I didn't? Part of me misses the chase. I mean, I thought I had problems on the road as a mortal in a Fae's world. Try being a half-Fae in a world where your very existence is an abomination.

I miss my mother. I sent word to my uncle with an envoy on its way to negotiate a trade deal with my home city. While I was told that the message was delivered, I received no reply. Not even a verbal message. At first, I doubted it had been sent. The Fae have no reason to do it for me. But if they had… I can't blame my uncle for not replying. He would have been in shock hearing my name tumble from a Fae soldier's lips. *The way Leo's did after he passed.*

My body has been changing the longer I stay in the Upper Realm.

Minor characteristics have been manifesting. My eyes have turned a brighter shade of blue; my jawline is getting sharper. When I push my hair back, I see my ears are elongating. The palace physician said that because my magic was suppressed with no training and no knowledge of its existence for so long, the traditional physical signs of being a Fae weren't visible. Now that my magic is manifesting openly for the first time, my body is recognizing the change and adjusting accordingly. I have spent hours upon hours staring into the mirror at night and wondering what Leo would say now if he saw me like this. I wonder: when he died, did he know that I was half-Fae?

On the good days, I hear him tell me to carry on and be strong like the tides and move along as they do. On the bad days, I doubt he would love me as I am now. I hate those days because I don't know if those thoughts are wrong.

"Miss?" A soft voice comes from the doorway.

I turn over my shoulder to see a housekeeper with her hand at the door. "Yes, Jeanine?"

"Your father insists that you come down for dinner tonight."

"No," I answer quietly. "Not tonight."

"I'm sorry, miss. He says you've had long enough, and it's time to sit down and be a part of the family." My scoff causes her to glare at me. "His words, miss. Not mine."

I groan loudly and lean my head back to stare at the ceiling for a moment. "Fine. I'll be down."

"I am to escort you to your room to change and then downstairs to dinner," she says flatly. She waves me over, and I have no choice but to comply. I rush down the palace halls behind her. I can barely keep up. Past the paintings and the occasional large mirror hanging on the wall, I am ushered into my room to get dressed. I slip on a simple, long blue dress and tug on a pair of black heels. It's a bit of a struggle as the dress usually requires help. But I am uncomfortable with asking Jeanine, so I sort of rig everything together myself. Why an individual should ever have to wear royal dress to a family dinner, I will never understand. When I open my door again, Jeanine is still there waiting for me. She beckons for me to follow her towards the stairs. "You're running late, miss."

I straighten, readying myself. "How late?"

"Just come now," she snaps at me over her shoulder. Her eyes flash briefly with fear before she turns away from me. "Try not to frustrate your father any further." My heels keep catching on the carpet before clicking down the tile-covered staircase behind her. When we reach the dining hall, before I have a chance to brush myself off, the housekeeper swings open the door. To my dismay, my father and family have already been settled at the table for a while now and are staring back at me like I'm something the cat dragged in. "May I present Lady Grace, High Lord," Jeanine introduces as she ushers me into the dining room. I don't know whether to curtsy or bow or anything, so I stand there awkwardly and wring my hands.

"Grace," the High Lord… my father says. "Join us."

I don't think I will get used to referring to him as my father. I slowly make my way around the table to the side on the left-hand side of my father. His wife and my new half-brother, Neil, glare at me as I walk. I stare at Neil as I take my seat until he's forced to look away. Then I turn my attention to the mother; her eyes dart away much faster than his did. The only bright spot in this room is little Analise, waving at me discreetly from her family's side of the table. She almost makes me want to smile. But I need to stay focused. I have no idea why my father chose now to pull me into the family, but whatever is coming, I need to be ready for it.

One of the things that has struck me the most about being a noble's daughter is the abundance of wealth. The kitchens here are astonishing and so much fuller than those back in the Middle Realm.

Back home. I feel a slight twitch in my chest that's there every time I dare to think of Lisden. I must admit, my heart may pine for home, but my stomach is full for the first time in years from hearty meat and fresh fruit. Several servants enter the room, bringing in the roast beef, potatoes, some sort of green salad, rolls, plum sauce, and at least three different varieties of wine and set them out on the table in front of us. The smell is heavenly. Another housekeeper serves everything to us one plate at a time. And yes, maybe I do dive into my meal a bit more vigorously than the rest of these nobles, but honestly, I couldn't care less what they think of me.

The room is quiet except for the silverware clinking against porcelain plates. I can sense the others at the table looking at me. I try to ignore them and sit tall in my chair. *By the Lady, let this dinner go by quickly.*

"Grace…" I look up at my father across the table who gestures toward me. "What have you been doing this week?"

"Playing violin," I answer steadily.

"The whole week?" Neil interjects. His eye roll infuriates me.

"For the most part," I emphasize as I glare at him.

"Daddy, she plays wonderfully. You should listen to her." *Thank the Lady for Analise.* "She plays me lots of songs."

My father turns to me with a hint of surprise in his eyes. "You've been playing for her?"

I shrug. "Whenever she asks."

He laughs. "Well, I'm impressed. Analise isn't one to listen to somebody for a long time. Does she sit still for you?"

I stifle a chuckle. "Yes."

For the first time since the day I arrived, I hear Alexander's wife, Elise, address me. "I have never seen her sit still for anyone longer than ten minutes. I suppose you must be commended for that."

I nod in thanks.

"Are you liking your room?" My father brings my attention back to him.

I nod again. "It's nice, thank you."

"Well, do tell Jeanine if you need anything," Elise gestures to me with her fork. "We weren't prepared for a long-term resident." I see Elise glance sideways at her husband and I inwardly cringe. I might be thrown off by being here myself, but I can't imagine a husband dropping in with his bastard child unannounced to his family. The table falls silent for a while, aside from Analise's swinging legs and the occasional clinking of silverware.

"There is something we need to discuss, Grace," my father finally breaks the silence. Before I can ask what that something is, we are interrupted by Neil violently slamming his glass down on the table and storming out of the banquet hall.

"Analise," Elise stands and puts a hand on her shoulder. "Why don't we step out and find a story in the library for bedtime?" She ushers the little girl out of the room. Now I face my father alone.

"Grace," my father hesitates before standing and pacing. I can't help but feel like I'm on trial in my dining chair. "It has been two weeks since you arrived here. And I have tried to give you space to adjust. But it is time for you to step up and take your place as a Lady of the House of the Evening."

"I am not ready," I answer immediately. "You have to give me more time."

"There is no more time," Alexander stops and leans on his hands against the table. "It is time you started your education. You are very far behind comparatively to the others, and our House should not suffer for that."

I cringe at his wording. "Isn't that a little harsh, Father?"

He shrugs. "Grace, I'm sorry, but it's time. There will be tutors arriving in the next day or so, and you will begin the most intensive noble training program that has ever been seen. No expense has been spared."

"Father, it is too soon," I protest. "I am not ready for—"

"We don't have a choice, Grace." The High Lord reaches across the table and takes my hand softly. "I am sorry. You have been thrown into the Fae world with little time to prepare, but the time for resting is done. It is time to get serious about becoming the heir to the throne. The rest of the realm is watching us to see if you will succeed or fail. And for the future of the House of the Evening, you must succeed." He squeezes my hand and then turns around to leave. "Be in the library first thing after breakfast in the morning. And please don't try to stay in bed all day. I will send someone for you."

Once my father is around the corner, I sink back into the chair with a groan. This is going to be a disaster.

Chapter Two

Originally, I had hoped to hide out in bed for as long as possible the next morning. But unfortunately, the maids have a key to my bedroom, and I was rudely woken up at some un-Ladylike morning hour with the rough opening of curtains. I mean, the sun had been up for a while, but getting it shined in your eyes abruptly makes any hour un-Ladylike. I try to stall my way through breakfast, taking my time to slather my pancakes in syrup and savor every bite. But it isn't long before one of my father's buttoned-up attendants finds me hiding out in the dining hall. "Miss Grace, your father is waiting for you in the library," he says shortly.

"I'll be there in a few minutes."

"Miss Grace," the attendant repeats. "The High Lord would like to see you now."

I sigh and stand up, leaving my dishes where they are. "Fine," I groan as I get to my feet and brush a stray crumb or two off my shirt. "I'll go."

"Actually, your father would like me to escort you."

"He doesn't believe I'll get there on my own?" The attendant doesn't answer, but the stern expression on his face confirms my suspicions. I begrudgingly follow the young man as we climb the stairs to the library. "This is ridiculous," I mumble to myself. Whether or not my father's attendant heard me, I don't know, but I'm not sure that I care.

The attendant pulls open the library door, and I walk over to the table where my father and another tall older man are standing. The stranger looks like the more tired version of Aiden's tutor, Master Xavier. He has a very gaunt face with silver glasses perched on his nose. His pinched expression is unnerving. "Grace," my father starts, "I would like you to meet Professor Roland. Luckily, you have a strong general education, so he will be focusing on the areas of House of the Evening law, customs, and politics. You will meet with him every day and spend dawn to dusk learning this material until your magic tutor can be arranged. Then you'll transition to a fuller schedule."

"Dawn to dusk? You want me studying all day?"

"We are pressed for time, you know."

Resisting the urge to sigh, I offer my hand to the professor. "Hello, Professor Roland." He barely shakes my hand before jerking his own away like he had been burned. *Great, another Fae who can't stand mortals.* I look at my father pointedly. *Did you see that?* I try to say with my eyes.

The High Lord ignores me as another attendant comes in to give him a message and therefore, completely misses my signaling. "I will leave you both to it," the nobleman nods to the two of us as he exits.

When he is out of the room, Professor Roland scoffs at me. "So you're the half-mortal brat?"

At first, I'm taken aback that he came out swinging as soon as my father disappeared, but I end up chuckling at the ridiculousness of this grown man. "I'm guessing you didn't tell my father you hate mortals."

"Here's how this is going to work, miss Grace." Roland's voice takes on a hint of a growl. "I am putting up with you because your father is paying an exorbitant amount of money for you to be educated. You are going to sit at that table," he points to the table in the corner, "and read whatever I give you. I am going to sit over there," he then points to a table on the literal opposite side of the room, "and work with my own texts."

"So... there won't be much actual teaching going on?" I snark.

"If you read, you'll figure it out," Roland snaps. He pulls a book off the shelf and practically shoves it into my hands. I notice that he avoids touching my hands again as if he can catch some "mortalness" from me. "Take this and go." Without another word, he spins around and leaves me standing awkwardly in the middle of the library. I peer around the corner to find him rummaging through some of the back shelves.

I'm not going to gain his favor right now, it seems. He's going to be of no help. Part of me wants to bail now and just find something else to do for the rest of today. I don't have to put up with his bigotry. But I do want to learn something. I want to learn what I need to know to lead this House, for my father's sake and the people's. And I don't really know where to start, and maybe this professor does. I crack open the book and flip to the first page.

* * *

Not even an hour goes by before I'm bored out of my mind. I take a sideways glance at my so-called instructor who has been ignoring my presence rather effectively. He has not moved from the other table or looked up to see if I'm still there. Meanwhile, I've poured over these books, trying to make heads or tails of them. I'm puzzling over information about naming customs in noble families and oaths that are sworn during various stages in a young noble's life, most of which I have missed. I'm not sure how starting with this is supposed to help me understand anything.

Besides, the more I read, the more I feel like an anomaly. According to these texts, a baby is inducted into Fae society by their very first week of life. The parents remain sequestered away from the rest of their extended family with their baby for three days. It is a bonding period for Fae of all classes and an important time to discuss the baby's name and what kind of future the parents imagine for them. At the end of the three days, the family comes out before the community and does an ancient protection ritual invoking the name of the child. Then there is usually a large community feast, and for a noble child like me, it would have encompassed the whole House.

I lost out on an entire magical curriculum with a gradual introduction to the skills and concepts of my magic types starting at age seven. I would have been able to build skills over years instead of what will end up being months. I was never presented to the House as the next heir; I never got a chance to meet the people and understand the society that I was born to lead. The more I think about it, how is the House of the Evening supposed to accept me as their leader with no exposure to the kind of person I might be?

It's strange to think about what life could have been like had I been raised Fae. The fanfare, the luxury, the power. It would have been like something out of my wildest childhood dreams. To be full, to be safe, to not have to worry about every little change in the wind. But then I would have missed out on a life with my brother, and I would never give up that for anything.

I look up again to see that my supposed mentor has fallen asleep in the middle of his book. I have no idea why my father thought this was the person to teach me the ways of the Fae. *I am not sitting inside all day and reading five hundred years of House of the Evening tradition while this guy sleeps. I gotta get out of here.* With a soft exhale of breath, I slowly close the tome until the pages softly rush against each other. I push myself up from my chair with my fingers on the table. When the professor doesn't wake, I run from the library.

I would love to run out the front door and not look back. But in the interest of starting off on the right foot, I feel like I should at least speak to my father about the situation first. *There's a first.* I make a right out of the library and half-run, half-skip down the hallway. Jogging down the stairs, I whip around into the throne room where my father is waiting with a handful of other officials. He stands up immediately when he sees me. "Grace, what are you doing down here?"

"The professor you hired is asleep upstairs," I chuckle.

"Asleep? What do you mean, asleep?"

"He handed me a book, told me to sit down and teach myself, went clear across the room and started doing his own reading. And then he fell asleep."

My father shakes his head in irritation. "How could you have managed to scare off the one person I could get to come out here and teach you?"

I laugh out loud. "You think it's my fault? He's prejudiced towards mortals. Did you not see how quickly he shook my hand before having to wipe the mortal disease off his hand?"

He holds up a hand to stop me. "Just… go back upstairs, and try to work with him. Just try! I'll attend to Professor Roland in a bit. Please, Grace. I have things to finish." Before I can say a word in protest, he ushers me out of the room and shuts the door in my face.

I stand in the hall for a few moments in shock, resisting the urge to slam both hands into the door as hard as I can. This is ridiculous. I have barely started to learn what it means to be a Fae, and my father is already writing me off without listening to me. *I am not going back to that library.* Frankly, I don't want to be in the palace right now. After a few minutes of reflection, I can't ignore it. I need to feel some sort of freedom. I need to be outside. I dash up the stairs to my bedroom.

Removing my dress, I slip into one of my few pairs of casual Fae wear that the palace has deemed to give me. I leave the room, make a few more turns, and finally rush down the back stairway and slip out the back door by the servants' quarters. The sun hits my face, and I grin. I sprint down into the gardens and away from the palace grounds. The dark-colored hills roll underneath my feet as I rush toward town.

Just being out in the crisp fresh air is intoxicating. I haven't been out of the palace since I arrived a couple weeks ago. My circumstances made me feel trapped, but it is quickly becoming clear that I have been trapping myself. Until someone forcibly puts barriers around me, I am going out into the world.

* * *

The town of Silvervale glistens in the melting snow as it slips off the rooftops onto the street. The water travels through the cracks and grooves in the cobblestones and trickles its way to the vents down the hill. Despite it being early afternoon, it's quite gray out. The overhead streetlamps are on, shining a soft glow over the wood and brick structures. It's a peaceful sort of quiet. Only a few Fae are out and about now, making them easy to avoid.

My cloak shields my face as I wander down Main Street. At night, things around here are much livelier. I often listen to the music playing from the streets below on my balcony. If I had felt more comfortable, maybe I would have snuck down here earlier. But for now, I'll stick to the streets and the alleyways.

Part of me wants to wander aimlessly through town and take a moment to breathe. But my body hasn't fully transitioned out of survival mode, and what I need more than anything is news of what's outside of here. News from the House of Darkness, news of war, perhaps even news of the Middle Realm if I can get it. The best place to do that is a tavern. Ships are always moving in and out with the latest shipments of goods, and sailors come in to drink and talk. They bring news to each other from all over the realm, and they're often too drunk to care who hears it. Therefore, the tavern is one of the best places to find information without looking too hard for it.

I turn down a left side alleyway and head towards the sound of clanging ship bells. A few moments later, I make my way around a brick building and set my sights on the open river. There are a few small skiffs on the nearby docks and a few taller trade ships with a handful of sailors sitting on crates or walking into a rowdy pub where the docks meet the town. I pull my hood up and walk over to the swinging door, making my way inside.

Sailors, bartenders, and barmaids fill the building wall to wall and from floor to ceiling past the second story. The chatter is boisterous, and I am bumping into Fae left and right as they make their way to tables or to lean against walls in some unknown dance. A few Fae throw sparks at the chandeliers dangling overhead, causing them to spin in dizzying, swinging circles. I throw a couple copper coins on the bar and take a stein of beer from one of the bartenders before stashing myself at a table by the back wall. I keep my ears peeled.

It doesn't take long before the opportunity presents itself. A tall gangly man wanders into the bar to raucous cheering from the table next to mine. "Phil!" The man laughs and comes over to the table, shaking hands and patting others on the back. One of the sailors at the table yanks Phil down and slides him a beer. "How have you been, Phil?" he says. "I haven't seen you since *Glory*'s last shipment."

"Doing fine, doing fine, Ravlen. Got a job working on *Firestorm*," Phil answers. "Taking shipments of crops to the House of Fire."

"House of Fire?" another man pipes up. "How many shipments have gone to them this season? That's the fourth one I know of in the last month."

"They got some kind of party going on," Phil scoffs.

"It's about time," he shouts before taking a swig of his drink. I angle my head ever so slightly to hear them better. *Alright, House of Fire is importing more supplies. Stocking up... for their army? What's next? An invasion?* Unfortunately, I don't learn anything more from that group. Their conversation devolves into idle chatter about their families and girls back home. I angle my body to try and overhear another table. I can only hear flashes of conversation, a few words here and there. "House of the Day…. spring solstice… Sun… amulet… House of Darkness… traders… House of Earth… quiet." Nothing quite comes together in my head. Even after several cycles of sailors moving in, getting their drinks, and heading back to the docks, I don't gain anything else relatively useful. It angers me.

After I have wasted away most of the afternoon, I leave a few more coins on the table and make my way outside. I haven't even turned out of the dock area before a familiar voice startles me. "There's only a few more weeks until the spring solstice, and we're hoping to have the new processional ship ready for then." I look up to see one of my father's advisors coming towards me… with my father following right behind. I have nowhere to go. I panic and tug my hood further down, keeping my head lowered to the ground. I keep walking forward hoping to pass by without confrontation.

"That should be just fine," my father said. "I'll be in touch about the final arrangements for its launch. A visit to the House of Water would be a nice maiden voyage." "Do you want to take a tour of the facilities, High Lord?"

"I am unable to now. I'll need to reschedule." As I move alongside him, giving him a wide berth, a cold force washes over me and holds me in place. "I have other things to attend to," my father says. I close my eyes and grimace. *Caught.*

"Let me know when the best time is, High Lord, and we'll be ready for you." The man shakes my father's hand. His footsteps click across the stone as he continues towards the water.

The cold sensation leaves me. I raise my head slowly to see my father's eyes boring into my head. He makes a singular motion: *come.* I resist the urge to shrug as I follow behind him dutifully. "What do you think you're doing out here?" my father hisses to me.

"Why don't you ask Professor Roland?" I counter. "I bet you he didn't even notice I was gone."

To my surprise, he sighs and stops in his tracks. He turns to look at me. "I admit… I was wrong about Professor Roland. I went up to check on your progress, and you were right. He has prejudices that will inhibit his teaching of you. I have sent him home."

I chuckle softly. "You want someone to teach me what I need to know, you're going to want to do a lot better than him." Our eyes lock, and we are in a standoff.

After a while, my father simply nods once and continues walking back into town. "You'll have better. I'll make sure of it." I doubt his words, but I don't really have a choice but to follow him back to the palace. On the bright side, though, he won't be able to keep me holed up anymore. I've tasted the world outside those walls now, and there is no way I'm turning back.

Chapter Three

Professor Roland was out of the palace before we even made it back inside, and my father set me up with an advisor of his back in the library. Advisor Underell is a much kinder, gentler man who takes the time to sit with me and answer my questions. Under his guidance, I slowly begin to pick up the laws and customs of the land. There are so many documents to go over and codes to memorize. There are plenty of rules regarding trade; merchants need the proper paperwork and visas to move between Houses and sell their goods. There's even more paperwork if one wants to trade with the Middle Realm, months and months' worth of procedure. I learned that most magic is legal in the House of the Evening, except when used to murder another Fae or fundamentally, permanently change nature. Each village, town, and city have their own separate criminal and civil courts, but magical capital crimes are taken directly to the noble family.

In other words, it is all way too much to try to memorize at once.

After a few days of drilling customs and concepts, my father allowed me to join in one of the recurring ones, the Day of Petition. About four times a season, the House of the Evening hosts this town hall with the people of the surrounding villages and towns. Here, the people can petition their grievances to the High Lord, and he can respond and come up with some sort of solution or assign a member of the court to assist.

The troubles of the people are diverse. Most people come to resolve trade disputes, some involving money and others involving barter. Each presents their case to my father one by one. If both sides of a debate are present, each has a chance to speak. If not and the other party is located within the House of the Evening, that person is sent a summons for the following Day of Petition and the matter is put on hold until then. If it involves members of other Houses, it is up to the High Lord's discretion. After listening to the issue, my father then asks questions and ultimately decides what should become of the dispute. It's a very similar process to court. The High Lord's decisions are certified with the court system as final say. It is quite interesting to watch how careful and thoughtful my father is with each case.

A handful come not to argue, but to ask for the High Lord's blessing in a marriage. "A blessing from the High Lord," my father explains to me in between rounds, "is as close as getting a blessing from the Lady herself. It is said to bring about good fortune." Couples from all over the lorddom come to speak to him for such a blessing. I find this to be a sweet little tradition. Rumor has it the High Lord's blessing can even strengthen a couple's magic. As the day goes on, I can see why my father wanted me to sit in with him. This lesson is much more about application of the law rather than the bare text that I have been reading.

"Lady Grace," my father interrupts my train of thought. "Would you like to take this next one?" The murmuring of the people in line suddenly drops to a dead silence. Their nervous eyes make *me* nervous, but my father's eyes make it clear this isn't a choice. He's looking to me to show what I have learned so far, what kind of leader I might be. And the people are watching too. This is a critical moment for them to see the type of person I am and who I might become.

I look up to see a young man in front of us who can't be more than a few years older than me. He carries a satchel over his shoulder that rests on his hip. His clothes are a little dusty, a little ragged. My heart pangs a bit as his haggard, but determined face reminds me of my brother.

"Yes, High Lord," I answer. I beckon for the young man to step forward. "What is your name, sir?"

"Caleb, Lady Grace," he answers with a slight bow to his head.

"What is your request?"

His throat bobs a little as he gulps. "Lady Grace, I am a fish trader between here and the House of the Day. Some of my catch often makes it to the Middle Realm. I usually make a handsome earning off the combination of these sales. Over the last few weeks, I have been continuing my trips down to the border. Now there is a standard tax at the border for transporting goods. But the new regiment posted at the border is charging arbitrary fees depending on who is coming through. And… see, one of these border guys… well… we got into a bit of a struggle, and I may have punched him."

I try to cover a small chuckle behind my hand. My father gives me a look, but I do see a hint of a chuckle in his eyes too. I can understand why the people feel so comfortable talking to the High Lord in such an informal tone; he does make people feel like they're talking to a friend. "Go on, Caleb," I manage to say.

"Now they're charging me double and triple the fee of the posted prices. I can barely keep up with them; it's taking too much of my monthly income. I have tried speaking to their commander, but he won't give me the time of day. I'm too young to be respected. I need a solution." He meets my gaze. "Are you able to help me?"

I take a deep breath before rising out of my throne and reaching to shake his hand. Caleb takes my hand and grips it in a firm shake. "I…" I start before looking over my shoulder to see my father's reassuring nod. "Thank you for your story, Caleb. Let me start by asking, have you apologized to both the man you punched and their commander?"

"No!" Caleb blurts out before looking down quickly.

I chuckle lightly. "Okay. Well, you're going to need to apologize first if you want to get anywhere. However, I have questions about the validity of their unit, so I'm going to send one of the advisors out with you the next time you head out that way to speak to the commander. He will report back to me, and we will see what the next steps should be. Will that work for you?"

Caleb bows low to me. "Yes. Thank you, Lady Grace. May the Lady bless you," he says before bowing slightly to my father and exiting the room.

I rejoin my father on the throne beside him. "How did I do?" I whisper to him.

My father chuckles. "You did just fine." Strangely, I feel a sense of pride well up in my chest. I settle back in my chair and wait for the next party. My father and I work together all day to cycle through every man, woman, and child. It was a long day, but I felt like my father and I got to understand each other a little more. There are moments I catch him considering my verbal thought process with a careful eye. And there are equally as many times when he says something or gives advice that resonates with me. I found the day to be quite enjoyable after all.

When it's all over and all the officials and citizens have left the room, I can't help but sink back into the throne. I look around the empty hall, and I wonder what it would feel like for it to be mine. It's a strange feeling because I have no idea how to lead a land or even if I want to. Of course, that's what I am meant to be studying for, but looking up at the mountain of lessons to learn, it doesn't quite seem attainable yet.

The soft clicking of heels turns my head to the opposite hallway where my stepmother is walking slowly into the room. She carries herself with such poise, made more striking by her tall figure. She wears another long formal dress, and I realize I have never seen the High Lady out of noble dress like my father or her kids. As she crosses the parquet floor, she looks me up and down. I can't quite figure out her mood. She just stands there and stares at me. She studies me like a statue she plans to analyze the construction of. It's a bit unnerving.

After a while, I break the silence. "Were you watching me? The High Lord and me?"

"Yes," she answers. "For a while."

She returns to staring at me blankly. Part of me wants to try reaching out to her as a noble and try to speak to her on her level. I am going to have to deal with her for as long as I live in this realm, so I might as well be polite and try to learn from her. "High Lady Elise, do you have any advice?" I ask carefully. "I mean… for leading. I have been trying to study as much as I can, but it all somewhat runs together. Do you have any insight you could share with me?"

"Yes, I do." She stops pacing, standing right in front of me and locking our eyes. "I would suggest you leave."

I sit up and forward. "Excuse me?"

"Leave," she enunciates. "You don't belong here. You don't belong in this castle, you don't belong in this House, and you certainly don't belong in this realm."

"We agree on that. But I'm here, and I have to make the best of it."

"You can dress up as much as you want, but you are not an heiress," she spits at me.

"You may not like me, but I have been nothing but respectful and courteous. I just need more time to adjust—"

"Adjust?" the woman raises her voice. "You can adjust all you like, but you will never be worthy as a High Lady. You have taken the throne away from my son. He was the eldest child, and he was destined to be High Lord!"

"Well, in case you haven't noticed, Madame High Lady," I finally snap, "I didn't ask for this. I didn't ask to be born first."

"You could have said no!" *I'm not sure how to argue with her there. I could have gone home.* "You should have died in that duel like you were supposed to. Now you are just the half-Fae bastard child sullying the name of my House, my pride and glory. Your name will forever be intertwined with mine, and I have fought too hard to get where I am to let you blacken me and my family's legacy."

My chest heaves. *So many words about her and her family and not a single thought for who I am and what I have been ripped from. What it would have been like to grow up without a father, without half of my identity.* "You know what, *Elise,*" I use her first name callously. "I don't owe you anything. I don't owe you an explanation of why I'm here, and if you keep pushing me, I may not owe you a home when this is all said and done." I regret the words as soon as they leave my mouth. The High Lady's intense glare may just strike me down where I stand.

She walks close to me and jabs her finger in my face. "You will never be a part of this family. You will never be enough for this House, and I will fight you every step of the way if I must. By the Lady, I swear it."

Her long braid slaps me in the face as she storms off, her heels pounding hard enough against the floor that I swear it would break. I am left in the throne room alone, wondering exactly where everything had gone so horribly wrong.

Chapter Four

The following afternoon after a session with the tedious law books of the House of the Evening, I head into the library to meet my magic tutor. He finally arrived at the palace late last night. I have yet to catch a glimpse of him and am unsure what to expect. My father says the man comes highly accredited from a well-known school of magic, but after that awful professor, I'm not sure I can entirely trust his judgment. Besides, what do I know about magical education? I have been trying since that day in the arena to replicate that surge of magic that I felt in my bones. But no matter how many times I stare at my hands and *will* something to happen, it never does. What if that was it? What if that was all the magic I have?

I try to shake these thoughts off as I round the corner. To my surprise, I find a younger gentleman in a seat at the library table. He doesn't look much older than me. His shirt and vest hang loosely on his frame. As I approach him from behind, I notice a couple stray scars trailing down his back and left arm. I clear my throat as I reach the table. The man stands up to greet me. His brown wavy hair hangs in his eyes as he bends over in a bow.

"My Lady." He rises and extends a hand to me. His voice is deep, but has a youthful lift to it. "My name is Talon Khane of the House of the Sun's Magical Conservatory. The High Lord has asked me to teach you the art of magic."

"Wonderful." I have a hard time keeping the sarcasm out of my voice as I shake his hand.

To my surprise, Talon takes a moment to study me. "I've heard quite a bit about you, my Lady."

"Nothing good, I imagine."

Talon chuckles. "I've heard just about everything from you're a demon in disguise to you're a brat who can't be taught. Actually, that's why I'm here."

"Because you think I'm a demon?" I raise an eyebrow.

"No. Because I want to know if a half-Fae can be taught. And I'm the first one who jumped at the chance. Others saw the potential, but they hesitated when it came to coming out here and actually teaching you."

I start to understand the man better. "You want to know if my magic is different."

"It's the greatest unanswered question of the magical world," Talon leans in, "and I plan to find the answer with you."

"You're gonna put me through my paces then?"

He laughs and waves off my concern. "Oh, relax." He leans back in his chair. "I'm not a formal professor. My true teaching style is a little eccentric. Most students I teach are younger, so I am often obligated to teach them in a certain way per their parents' instructions according to my contract. You are quite different, as I'm sure you have realized."

I sit down across from him. "So you're a child's tutor?"

"Yes… technically." He taps his hands on the table. "But I've worked with people up through age fourteen."

"Are you saying my father thinks I need a child's tutor to teach me the complex art of magic?"

"Yes… I mean… no…" the man stutters. "I mean, not exactly. Look, this is new for me, it's new for you, it's new for everyone. I'm not gonna pretend I know what to do with you. You're the first mortal I've ever taught, so… this promises to be interesting."

"Half mortal," I correct him. "If most students you teach are under their parents' thumbs, what about me?"

Talon tilts his head from side to side. "You're a special case. Your father wants you to learn whatever is needed for you to be a strong High Lady. Most of that is up to my discretion, though there are a few boundaries he has made." He reaches under the table and picks up a small rough leather bag. "Before we can talk about that, however, I need to know what I'm working with. Time to test your magical capacity."

"How are you going to test me?" I ask carefully.

"Nothing crazy." Talon fumbles through his bag and removes a small vial of liquid and a needle. "I'm going to need a bit of your blood. Your hand, please."

I pass my hand over, and he takes it lightly. "Only a high level of sensing magic can give you an indication of what types of magic a person has. Blood tells all." He jabs my finger quickly. I wince at the sharp sting. He takes my hand and pops the vial open. He squeezes my finger to let a drop of blood fall into the vial. I take my hand back as he corks the bottle and swirls the liquid around.

"Whatever happens here," Talon says as he places the vial on the table, "will determine what kind of magic you've got. There should be some sort of colors or swirls or patterns that emerge in just a moment. Has anyone explained to you how magical ability is broken down?"

"No."

Talon looks up at me in surprise. "No one has talked to you about that?" When I shake my head, he leans back into his chair. "Wow… I'm shocked. What about the High Lord?"

"We've barely talked."

Talon's uncomfortable expression amuses me somewhat; he looks like he walked into something he didn't mean to. "Oh… okay, well… well, let me clear things up." He fumbles for his bag and pulls out a sheet of paper. "Let me draw this out for you." He sketches out a few lines. "Each magic type has three main levels, and each level is broken into five tiers. At each tier, you step up the strength of each type of magic. At each level, you also increase the strength. Every magic ability follows this pattern. Regular old Fae like me are born with a few abilities while you should have a few additional gifts on account of your noble blood. In a moment, we should see where you're at."

As he finishes his sentence, the liquid turns a vibrant shade of purple. Then blue. Then green. Suddenly, swirls and sharp lines and suspended bubbles begin to emerge. Talon's eyes grow wide as he writes frantically on his scroll. The vial in front of him violently fizzes and continues to change colors. I tap my foot nervously as he continues to write for what seems to be much longer than the minute he promised. *What could be taking so long?* Just as I decide to lean in and try to read the scroll, he sweeps it off the table and away from my gaze.

"Okay…" Talon breathes. He leans back again. His mouth attempts to form words, but no sound comes out. I wait for him to gather his thoughts, and eventually he does. "I have never seen this before, Grace, and to be honest with you, I am not quite sure how to proceed."

"Is there something wrong?" I ask.

"Not wrong, per se. Just…" he breathes in a rush, "highly unusual. In all my studies, someone with your capacity for power has never existed. Except in legend or cataloged in some of Professor Xavier's studies. Xavier, he's a well-known—"

"I've met him," I interrupt. "He's very articulate."

Talon's eyes snap up to mine. "You met Professor Xavier? By the Lady, it is a dream of mine to talk to him someday. He is the leading expert on the Lower Realm and how Fae magic interacts with demonic magic. What was he like? Did he talk about the magical history of demon magic? His texts are like diamond mines—"

"Talon. The magic."

"Oh, right. Exceptionally high," he gushes. I let out my own sigh of relief. Talon runs a hand through his hair before setting the scroll back on the table. "Here's what the vial shows. You have high levels of elemental magic, fire and wind. You have exceedingly high levels of energy magic; it's going to take me several hours to pinpoint which subtypes. The colors of each subtype are so specific that they can be hard to decipher. I'm seeing disintegration magic, flight magic, glamour magic, and possibly weapons amplification magic in varying medium and high levels. And psionic magic in unusually high levels regarding empathetic magic, telekinesis, and telepathy. This is wild."

I reach across the table and pull the scroll out from under Talon's hands. My eyes scan the page with fervor. *How is this possible?* One day, I have no magic, and then suddenly, I have more magic than I could have imagined. As amazing as that feels, all I can think of is how much work this is going to be. "What… what do we do now?" Where do we start?"

Talon clicks his tongue. "I start with your father. We have to get a good training plan in order."

"Wait!" I shout.

Talon starts. "Is there a problem with that?"

I bite my lip. "Look, as I'm sure you can imagine, being a half-mortal in a Fae's world is difficult enough without being potentially more powerful than the people in this household. Have you ever had family trouble?"

Talon laughs shortly. "You could say that."

"Well, my family trouble involves a pissed off stepbrother who should have been the heir, but now isn't, and a stepmother who has made it very clear that I can never be welcome here. Telling my family about the magic I possess may risk my presence in this castle." I gulp and tap my fingers on the table as I try to think. "Why don't we make a deal?"

"What kind of deal?"

"You want to know how magic interacts with me and my blood. I need you to teach me, but you could use what you learn from observing me to change the magical field as you know it." Talon's eyes grow wider, and I know I've got him hooked on the prospect of research. "Here's my offer. You tell him about most, but not all the magic I possess. And I promise to be your most attentive student. You can run whatever tests you want to run with me, make any notes, show me whatever you want to show me. And when I become High Lady, I'll make sure no one comes after you for publishing your findings. You'll get no trouble from me."

Talon studies me as he contemplates my offer. After a few moments of silence, he nods and reaches out to me once more. "You have got yourself a deal, Lady Grace." I clasp his hand firmly, and we seal the deal with a tight grip. "Buckle up. We've got a long way to go. Your training starts in the morning. I need time to make a plan, speak to your father, make some notes." He fumbles for his bag and dumps out an array of notebooks and writing instruments. He waves me off distractedly. "You're free to go." As I leave the library, I take a glance back at my tutor making furious notes about what he's just witnessed. *I don't know what he has planned for me, but let's hope he doesn't let my father in on all of it. I could use an ally around here.*

Chapter Five

To my annoyance, Talon decides the best course of action to wake me just before dawn with a loud pounding on my bedroom door. My eyes spring open, and all I can think is *by the Lady, please make it stop.* Unfortunately for me, the knocking doesn't cease the entire time I am trying to wake up enough to get out of bed. When my head clears, I scramble for my robe before pushing it open a crack, weary-eyed. "Hello?" I groan.

"Come on!" Talon says in a way-too-chipper tone. "We've got places to be."

"The sun isn't even up yet," I protest.

"We have a lot of ground to cover, and much of it is time sensitive," he replies.

"Ground to… to cover?" My brain does not work well when I am tired. "But what about breakfast?"

"We'll eat on the way back. Now get dressed and hurry up." Talon leans against the wall. "If you're not out here in three minutes, I'll just keep knocking until you come out here. Trust me, I've been told I can be extremely irritating. And bring a jacket!" he calls after me as I rush back into the room. I wish I could go back to sleep. My eyes and head are heavy, but I am in no mood to hear more of that knocking if I don't hurry up. I throw on the first shirt and pants I can find and snatch a jacket off a hanger, knocking a few things down on the way.

Once I learn magic, I can't wait to be able to wave them all back to their place. But for now, I just leave them there.

Talon gives me a once-over. "That'll do." Without another word, he takes off towards the stairs. I struggle to keep up with his long strides.

"Why are we starting so early?" I ask as he traipses down the stairs.

"You'll see," Talon insists as he swings open the front door for me. When we're outside, he leads me from the palace courtyard towards the forests on the edge of the palace grounds. I thank the Lady that I had the forethought to wear some boots. He leads me up the narrow path through the inclined woods. I trudge forward as I try to wake up. It's freezing outside, and after last night's rain, freezing drops fall from the pine trees and into my hair.

After we have been walking for a while, I'm not sure whether I should be starting a conversation with my companion. Before I get my first words out, however, the woods open and we reach a clearing. Wildflowers litter the grass. The wind creates small ripples on the small creek cutting across the west side of the field. The sky is beginning to lighten up, enough so that I can see the outline of several large boulders scattered across the field.

Talon stops short. I crash into his back. He looks back at me with an amused quirk of his lips. "Are you awake now?"

I glare at him and reply, "I'm fine."

"Good. Go stand in the middle." He gestures towards the center of the field. I trudge my way to the spot, my boots dragging against the damp grass.

I turn around and throw my hands out. "What now?"

"Elemental magic," Talon paces in front of me, "is the most funda-mental form of magic. Its simplest forms are the easiest to master. To begin learning them, we need to be in a location where the elements are readily accessible. This means you won't have to summon an element to begin; it will already be present." He gestures to our surroundings. "The wind is strongest here in a wide-open space on top of the mountain. This area several years ago suffered from a forest fire started by magical means. The grass regrew, as you can see, but tests done around here have shown that the earth absorbed the fire magic. Because of that, you will be able to will the field to ignite, and the creek allows me to douse the flames before you inevitably torch the forest." I cringe slightly at his implication.

"Why do we need to be up here so early?"

"The early morning is the best time to practice elemental magic. Something about the dawning of a new day resets the elements in the realm a bit." He walks forward so he is across from me. "Wind is going to be the easiest for you to harness right now." Talon holds out his hands parallel to each other. "Hold your hands out like this. This is going to prepare you to move elements for the first time. When you're more advanced, you won't need to start at this base position. But as a beginner, I like to start off with something that is easy to return to and visualize each of the movements." I move my hands up according to his instructions. "I want you to take a deep breath and tap into your magic. We're gonna start slow. I want you to feel the wind around you, feel the power in it. Then capture a breeze in your hands."

"Just… capture it? That simple?" I contemplate my rough hands.

Okay, I guess we're doing this. I look at the space between my hands before closing my eyes. It takes a moment before the wind starts again. The cold breeze rustles my hair. If I focus close enough, I can feel each individual hair move. I lean into that feeling a bit more, letting the cold seep inside of me. Reaching out with body and mind, I am grasping for something… something I can't quite understand. Then I feel something rush over my head, my shoulders, and down to my arms. It moves quickly with some force behind it. I imagine capturing the energy between my hands, feeling it, manipulating it.

That's when something shifts. I slowly open my eyes, and I see that I have captured the wind. The dust in the air makes the outline of the element visible to me. It is a clear, tightly swirling ball of air contained perfectly in between my hands. I feel the energy flowing through the wind into me and vice versa. "That's it, Grace!" I startle at Talon's shout of pride, losing my concentration. The wind ball breaks apart and flies out in all directions. The breeze is strong enough to knock me over and send Talon back. He plants his back foot in the dirt with a sharp motion and whistles softly.

"Did you have to shout?" I ask as I push myself up off the ground.

"Hey, it's not like I was trying to make you lose concentration," Talon protests. "Do it again."

For the next hour, Talon makes me run drill after drill capturing wind and sending it out to different areas deliberately. I took down branches, swirled water from the creek into a mini water tornado, and even knocked Talon over on his backside. "That's the way!" he shouts at me as he scrambles back to his feet. "Fire next."

Unfortunately, fire was much more unwieldy as an element. When I approached it the same way I approached the wind, I nearly lit the forest on fire. Talon was quick to douse the flames with a wave of water from the creek. Fire felt different in my hands than wind: hot, but not quite enough to burn. There is a volatility in the substance that feels like the magic could leap out of my hand on its own at any second. Fire took more concentration to keep it with me.

By the end of the session, I hadn't even figured out how to send out a fireball.

"Dammit!" I shout as the fire dissipates in my hands for the umpteenth time. "I can't get it!"

Talon chuckles. "Grace, it's day one. Give it a rest. We'll be back up here tomorrow."

"Another early morning?"

"Get used to it, Lady Grace. This is your new morning ritual. Two to three lessons from dawn until mid-morning. Then you can eat."

I groan. "Are we done now?"

"Almost, almost. I want to take note of something that we're going to need to know for tomorrow's lesson." Talon circles me. "I want to explore flight magic with you next."

My heart flutters a bit at the prospect of flying. "Oh really?"

"Yes," my teacher replies. "Now what is important to understand is what type of flight magic you have. There are two main types. There's wind manipulation and winged flight."

"I must be wind manipulation then?"

"Not necessarily," he counters, to my surprise. "The presence of wind magic in a person is not a guarantee of wind manipulation flight."

I gesture to my back. "Well, last time I checked, I do not have any wings."

"Well you wouldn't see them," Talon explains. "Fae wings are only active when flight magic is intentionally being used. They're a force of energy that become solid under your force of will. Won't even tear a hole in your jacket." He takes a step back. "Go ahead and imagine the feeling of flight. Imagine what it feels like to move through the air, light as a bird and free." At my look of skepticism, he urges, "Just try."

I close my eyes once more and take a breath. I remember what it felt like to fly through the air in the Middle Realm with my grappling gun. What it felt like to fall from the ogre fight as the Lower Realm exploded around me. By the Lady, what I wouldn't give to feel that free again.

Then I feel something roll over my back. The feeling rolls out from the center of my back out to my shoulders and past. As I shift my eyes over my shoulder, I see two long, slightly pointed purple wings with black edges. The length is covered in pink and blueish-purple stains like watercolor paint dripped into water. They move against me with every breath I take in. "Whoa," I sigh.

"Would you look at that?" Talon claps once. "That's what I'm talking about. Wings are so much more complex to work with." I grin at his excitement. "What do you think, miss Grace?" he asks.

"I think they're beautiful," I say as I try to turn my head far enough to see more of the wings. "Can I try them out?"

Talon laughs a deep belly laugh. "You're gonna need a lot more training before you get up in the air. For now, we're gonna need some breakfast. Follow me." He offers me his arm politely, and we make our way back toward town.

Chapter Six

Over the next few weeks, I dive into the most intense education program that I have ever experienced in my life. Honestly, I'm surprised I haven't collapsed already. After dawn every morning, Talon drags me up to the top of the mountain to practice elemental magic. There we stay until we make some progress on both fire and wind. Talon doesn't like to waste time; every moment has a lesson to be learned. Then we head back down for breakfast before he sends me off to meet with my father's advisor once more to continue my lessons in law, diplomacy, and tradition. Just recently learned that dueling is an acceptable and legal form of formally airing out one's grievances against another person. I am hoping I don't get caught up in one before I can defend myself properly.

In the afternoons, Talon returns to tackle magic lessons in a variety of subjects. At this stage, we have dabbled in almost all my magic types. I take to psionic magic, essentially mind magic, right away. Turns out my skill on the violin can be amplified by empathetic magic. I love being able to practice the instrument outside and seeing how far my empathetic pull can reach. Talon has me practicing off the violin too in other areas of psionic magic. My telepathy skills come naturally although my telekinesis could use some work. I'm enjoying using energy magic between siphoning energy from Talon's spells to fuel my own and walking through the town square to practice sensing who has which magic. And *flying.* I can't even begin to describe how it feels. I haven't quite gotten a handle on the mechanics though. Understanding wind patterns and how to manipulate my body and wings to take me where I want to go is next to impossible.

I'll get there though.

The only thing I can't understand is why Talon refuses to show me how to weaponize the magic types that I have. I keep asking him to give me a chance to try something on a larger scale, to physically use this magic to defend myself. But he doesn't know what's coming. He isn't clued in like I am on impending war in the Upper Realm. Every time I try an advanced movement with intent to destroy or eliminate, he stops me and changes the subject.

Hasn't he figured out yet that I am not a Lady for display? I need to be the real deal.

Or there's a high probability I'm going to end up the *dead* half-Fae bastard child of the House of the Evening.

On a random afternoon after an intense week, Talon sends me a message offering me a day off. He plans on meeting a sailor friend in town for drinks before he leaves for another merchant trip. I don't mind losing a session; it finally breaks up the monotony of the new status quo in the House of the Evening. Plus, I welcome the chance to practice my magic on my own. The days have been so packed, I have had no time to assess my growing skill by myself.

I head down to the arena to give myself a nice open space to practice. When there is space, one can use it to their advantage, fire bigger spells, and push harder. Moving myself to the center of the field, I start by sending out waves of fire from my hands. They move with a newfound ease, creating black circles against the dirt. It's small, but to me, it means so much. There is *power* in knowing my own magic.

I fool around with my magic for a long time. A servant comes by once and offers me lunch and a drink of water. I imagine my father sent him down to make sure I didn't overdo it. Even though Talon doesn't recommend using too much energy all at once yet, I'm feeling creative. I build myself a tall maze out of fire, building high walls and then flying through it using my new wings. Though I must admit, I may have come way too close a few times to singeing a wing. With a wave of my hand, it all vanishes again. Then I change elements; I use the wind to move dirt to build walls before forcing my hands towards it and bursting it into a million tiny particles.

"Hey!" a male's voice comes from the top of the stairs of the arena. I turn around wildly and look up to find Neil staring down at me menacingly. Even from down here, I can feel the irritation radiating off him in waves. "What are you doing here?"

"I'm practicing," I call back.

"Well, I want to use this space, so you need to leave."

I roll my eyes hard. "I'm sorry, but you're going to have to wait until I'm finished. I was here first."

Neil storms down the stairs, his feet clomping and banging with every step. When he hits the dirt, he storms over to me. His light brown hair bounces on top of his head. If he wasn't so irritated, I might have been amused. "I don't think you heard me. This is not your place. I want you gone." He gets up in my face, and I automatically take a step back. I get the feeling we're not just talking about my presence in the arena.

"I have a right to be here, Neil." I try to keep my voice level. I have no idea why after weeks of not speaking to each other, he is here to challenge me. "I will move out of your way shortly. Now leave me alone."

Suddenly, I feel my body lift off the ground and wrench backward violently. I go flying across the arena and land flat on my face in the dirt. Spitting out particles, I rub my eyes free. "What the hell?" I shout at him.

"I told you…" He breathes heavily. "Get out." I rise to my feet slowly. Now he has pissed me off. I throw my arm out and send a wave of fire his way. But he blocks it with a sharp and rapid breeze. It dissipates as quickly as I summoned it. How he does it, I have no idea. He pushes forward with a gust of wind, hoping to trap me again. I push back with one of my own, but his is much stronger. I go flying again, slamming into the ground. I push back up, but he has become hellbent on making me pay for this unseen sin.

Moving quickly, I send a fireball Neil's way. It fizzles out a little faster than normal. Having practiced all those tricks that may have been a little more advanced than what I am used to, I'm tired. My stamina is shot. I try to run to the exit, but Neil's next gust of wind sweeps me up again and holds fast. The wind tosses me left and right, up and down. With every move, my skin breaks apart. A cut here, a gash there. My head throbs. I'm trying to shield it with my arms, but the gusts are forcing them apart. I try to summon magic to fight back, but I can't hold my concentration well enough to cast a spell. *By the Lady, please don't let this be how I die.*

"NEIL!" I hear a high-pitched voice squeal. The hold Neil has on me breaks, and I drop like a stone to the ground. A groan slips from my lips as my head collides with the dirt. My head is swimming, but my eyes can barely make out the small frame of Analise. "What are you doing to her?"

"I… Ana…" Neil stutters for the first time ever. If I wasn't in pain, I might have summoned enough energy to be shocked.

"I can't believe you!" I hear a body running into another and an outrush of breath. "Were you going to kill her?"

"No, Ana, of course not!" *Another minute though…*

"Are you gonna help me get her to the infirmary or not?" Analise sounds so much older than she is. I almost imagine her with her hands on her hips. I open my eyes for a brief second and realize that she has her hands on her hips and is giving my stepbrother the tongue-lashing of his life. I lose phrases and words in the ringing in my ears. "Finally have a sister…"

"… mortal… heir…"

"… family!.. doesn't that matter to… Should… guards…"

"No!.. handle… ourselves."

After a while of trying to decipher the conversation, I decide I can't stay on the ground any longer. I push myself up slowly to my knees. Analise rushes to my side. "Don't get up! You're bleeding."

"I'm alright, Ana," I say quietly. "I'll be fine." I rock back and sit down hard. My head spins from the effort.

"Neil, don't you have something for her?!" I wince as my stepsister practically shrills in my ear. "Oh!" She lowers her voice. "Sorry!" she whisper-shouts. I chuckle lightly.

"I'll get something from the apothecary on the second floor," Neil responds frantically. "Don't move! I'll be right back." He takes off towards the palace. If I was more alert, I might wonder how the fear of a little girl's wrath could make him move so fast. But every step of Neil's on the stairs pounds like a drum in my ear. I bring my knees up to my chest and press my head to them. I desperately want to lie down, but I'm afraid I may have a concussion.

"Why were you fighting our brother?" Analise asks, still trying to stay in a hushed tone.

"He was fighting me," I mumble. "Got mad. Started a duel."

"He shouldn't have hit you so hard." The girl sits down next to me. *Can't say I don't agree with you there.* I don't answer her because I don't have an answer. "You're just learning," she changes the subject. "It won't take you very long. I learned how to use my elemental magic within a few months. You're bigger than me; I'm sure within a week or so, you'll be able to beat him."

My lips quirk up unconsciously. *I wonder if this is what I sounded like to Leo. Perky, eager to please, eager to compliment.* I wince as the smile hurts my face. "Oh, you're still hurting." I look up to see Analise looking quite distraught. I reach up to touch her arm to reassure her, but before I can lay my hand on her, her face lights up. "Wait! I can do something! Hold still."

She takes my face between her hands. Her skin is surprisingly cold. I try to pull away. "Ana, what are you doing?"

"Just hold still!" Her eyes close as she begins to whisper under her breath. Her whispers have a slightly musical quality to them, and I feel her hands turn as cold as ice. Ana's magic brushes across my cheeks in slow steady pulses, and small wounds all over me close. My head still hurts like hell, but my face is clear of any injuries.

"That was very helpful," I tell her with a now less painful smile. "Thank you."

My stepsister breathes out a heavy sigh as she plops down next to me. "I'm sorry I can't do more. That's the most I've ever done before."

I am surprised. I can't believe she would try something advanced to help me, a practical stranger in her life. Shaken, I reply, "Well, take a breath and don't worry about me. Neil will hopefully be back soon with that—"

I am interrupted by the man running back down the stairs to the arena. "I found it!" he calls out.

"Good!" Ana stands up to go get it, but I pull her back down.

"You, sit," I order. I motion for Neil to come over. "Give me the bottle."

"This is the strongest I could find," he says as he passes me the blue liquid. He looks down with an unreadable expression on his face. I look at the bottle before uncorking the vial and throwing it back. Though I probably should have been more observant and checked that it wasn't poison, I doubt Neil would murder me in broad daylight in front of his little sister. It takes a moment, but finally I feel my body start to right itself again. I could almost cry in relief as the pain in my head recedes to a dull ache and then to nothing.

"Thank the Lady," I breathe as I set the glass bottle next to me. I nod once at Neil. "Thank you."

"Are you gonna tell Dad?" he blurts out. I am taken aback by this question. I hadn't really considered what I should do in the aftermath of this fight. I could make him regret the day he decided to thrash me. Or I could bide my time and get stronger to fight him a second time and see who can take who in a fair fight.

Before I can answer, Analise chimes in. "She should tell Dad! You could have killed her!"

"Quiet Analise!" Neil hisses.

"I will not be quiet!"

I hold up my hands to stop them both as I get to my feet. "I have no need to tell our father about this little incident. I can take care of myself." I walk up to Neil and poke him in the chest. "But don't you dare attack me again, or I won't hesitate to mention it to whoever I need to. I believe attacking the heir results in swift execution." His eyes widen, and I am reveling in the fury and forced acceptance in them. "I hope you have gotten that out of your system. Do not touch me again. And don't forget, now your sister knows exactly the kind of man you are."

I turn to Ana and ask in a much softer tone, "Would you like to practice elemental magic with me upstairs?"

"Yes!" she answers brightly and comes to take my hand. I brush past Neil, and the two of us stroll up to the palace hand in hand. She beams at me, and I smile back at her. *A small victory, but a victory nonetheless.*

Chapter Seven

I don't end up speaking to Talon about Neil's attack. I'm not sure what I would say to him. *"Hey, I need you to teach me magic faster so I don't get killed by my stepbrother?" Talk about an awkward conversation.* Besides, I'm embarrassed by the whole thing. Back in the Middle Realm, I was always able to hold my own. Even in this realm, I did a damn good job. But now I feel weak and underprepared. All I can do is work to learn as much magic as I can. Talon can see a shift in me; I beg to stay just a little longer at lessons each day to learn one more spell or try a complicated motion one more time.

After a particularly difficult and exhausting day of training under Talon's laser eye, I wind my way through the hallway headed for the stairs. *A hot bath and an early night sounds like a wonderful idea.* "Lady Grace!" a soft voice calls to me from further down. I turn around on the second step, exasperated. A young maid approaches me with a small box. "Miss, I'm sorry to disturb you, but this just arrived for you from the House of the Sun."

I freeze. "Did you say the House of the Sun?

"Yes, miss." She reaches the stairs and holds the parcel out to be. I take it from her quickly, but with care.

"Thank you," I say absentmindedly as I rush up the stairs, my eager questions driving my steps. All the while, I turn the box over in my hands, trying not to disrupt the contents inside. When I reach my room, I push the door closed with my foot with a soft click. The lock latches shut, and I sit at the foot of the bed, box in my lap.

Aiden. It's been ages since I saw him at the Winter Solstice. I haven't heard a word from him since then. Not a letter, not a messenger. Nothing. Despite all the chaos happening inside the palace, I have been worried about him. I've been missing his sarcastic, steady presence. I'm dying for another adventure out on the open road with nobody to answer to, no one to hold us accountable. I wonder if he had missed it too. Or if this was some sort of sign that he didn't want to talk to me.

I'm overthinking this. I need to open the box. When I lift the lid, a glint of glass catches my eye. Nestled in a bed of silk, a glass ball stares up at me, swirling inside with individual strands of purple and red magic. I run my fingers over the smooth surface curiously. I slip the tiny note out from under it. "Wait until it gets dark," Aiden's narrow handwriting reads. "Tap this ball three times and think of me." I chuckle. *How straightforward.* Out the window, I see the sun beginning to set. It won't be long now before the day turns to dusk.

I hide the orb among my clothes in the back of a dresser drawer before heading downstairs to suffer through another family dinner. At least this time, my father is more focused on Analise and her recent music lessons rather than my training. I manage to get out unscathed. All I can think about is Aiden. *What exactly is supposed to happen? Will I see him? Will I hear him?*

Finally, the sun sinks down over the valley. I practically leap into bed and roll onto my back, settling the glass ball on my stomach. It moves up and down slightly with the deep breath I draw into my lungs. With a light touch, I tap the ball three times. I focus on my memory of him: the way he looks, the way he smiles at me when I'm telling him what to do, the way he felt to have his hands in mine.

"Grace?" I hear Aiden's voice in my head. I start violently in bed, barely managing to keep the glass ball from tumbling off the bed and shattering. "Calm down, Grace; don't fling the ball across the room." I hear his warm chuckle directly in my ear, and I can't help but smile.

"Aiden? Is that you?"

"Yes, it's me. Who did you expect?" I can sense Aiden's smile. Imagining the warmth of it makes me feel all tingly.

"How is this happening?" I can't help but grin.

"The glass ball I sent you contains a condensed form of telepathic magic. It's an expensive little item, and it only lasts for a little while. So let's not waste any time."

I feel something warm resonate in my chest. "How are you?"

"I'm good." His smile grows brighter in my head. "How are you?"

"I'm… I'm fine." There's a moment of silence where I just revel in the fact that I am hearing Aiden again. Before I get too caught up, however, I cut to the point. "Why haven't I heard from you until now?"

"I'm sorry, Grace." There's a genuine tinge of remorse in Aiden's voice. "My father has been extra secretive lately. He's become super paranoid. He put out an order to start screening mail that came in and went out of the palace. I don't know what he's looking for, but I couldn't exactly send you a letter. Then when I came up with this little plan, I needed time to get the funds together for the orb. I found this old merchant on the outskirts of the House who could get his hands on one. Took ages. But believe me, I haven't stopped thinking about you since you left."

"I've missed you, Aiden."

I sense his smile again. "I miss you too." We sit together, entire lands apart, reveling in each other's company for a moment. Too soon, Aiden speaks again. "We have to keep talking, remember?"

"Oh yeah… right." I blush. "Have you heard anything on your end from the House of Darkness?"

"Yes," Aiden sighs. "The High Lord of the House of Darkness has been here a couple times in the last couple months. He always comes in the very, very early morning and is out before dawn. I have stayed up a couple times to watch him and my father take their meetings in the library, but I haven't been able to get in close enough to hear what's been said." I nod slowly to myself. "I'm sorry, I wish I had better news."

"No, no, it's okay," I quickly respond. "You're doing the best you can. You'll let me know if something changes?"

"As soon as I can. Probably gonna need to find an alternate mode of communication." There's a slight pause on his end. "So." I can hear the smile in Aiden's voice. "How is the training going?"

"The heir training or the magic training?"

"Both."

"Oh, by the Lady, it is a hassle," I groan and flop back on my pillows. "There are so many statutes and codes to remember. My memorization skills are only so-so. And my magic tutor is a menace; he's been putting me through my paces. Nearly every day, from sunrise until sundown, we train. I've conjured more fireballs and breezes and water spheres than you can possibly imagine. But finally, *finally*, we are getting into some more complex magic."

"Hey, a slow and steady start lays the foundation for—" I groan louder to interrupt him, and he laughs. "Alright, alright, do you like it at least?"

I consider the question for a little while. "I do, actually." I run my fingers over the glass ball as I think. "There's something about being able to master the elements or move something from one place to another or make people feel that is... quite beautiful."

"I knew you'd like it once you gave it a try," Aiden teases. "I remember my first time trying my magic full out. There's nothing like it, is there?"

"Oh," I drag out the word before grinning. "There really isn't. When I'm not being pushed to my limit, I like practicing spells on my own.

The power feels… intoxicating."

"Good, good. Enough about the magic lessons," Aiden's voice suddenly gets a little more insistent, "how are you?"

I sigh softly and pull one of the many pillows on the bed into my arms. I hug it to my chest. "I'm tired," I answer. "I'm very tired. Of everything. Everyone here expects so much of me. I'm not ready to be an heir. And my family… I am alone here. Except for Analise," I add after some thought. "The little one. She's been friendly the entire time. I owe her a lot. I squeeze the pillow tighter. "I wish you were here."

I hear Aiden breathe in my ear. If I concentrate hard enough, I can feel its warmth on my cheek. "I wish I was there too."

"If I wish hard enough, will you appear next to me?"

Aiden chuckles. "Not quite. Magic won't give us that. Not at this distance at least."

"So if you came closer, I could wish you here?" I raise an eyebrow.

"Sure."

"Then I'll need you to take a carriage here."

"Oh, you know I would love to, darling. But you know I can't do that," Aiden lets me down gently.

I sigh and pull the blankets up over my chest, running my hand across the pillow in my arms. "I know." We sit together on opposite ends of the Realm in silence. I feel his presence in my mind, soft and comforting. I stifle a yawn.

"Someone sounds tired," Aiden teases.

"I have another early morning," I stretch and snuggle further into the sheets.

"Then close your eyes. I'll stay until you fall asleep."

"Then I'll try to…" I yawn again, "stay awake."

"Go to sleep. We'll talk soon." I hear the soft blow of a kiss and a light feather touch on my cheek before I drift off into oblivion. "Good night, Grace."

Chapter Eight

When I wake the next morning, I look to the the glass orb. My heart sinks when I realize the magic inside has dissipated. The orb is a useless glass centerpiece now. It occurs to me to ask Talon if it could be re-enchanted. I'll have to come up with a vague way to ask so I don't need to explain why I'm communicating with another Lord heir secretly. I set the orb on the table before settling back into bed. Last night was one of the better nights that I have had since I got to the palace. But now everything is quiet again. I can't stand being in a quiet I did not create.

Life returns to a never-ending cycle of magic lessons and law seminars. Every lesson is a stepping stone for this grand role I don't know when I'll be able to fill. But whether I'm ready or not, things are moving quickly around here. Before I knew it, the Spring Solstice crept up on the realm, and similarly to last winter, a ball was to be held at the House of the Day. The celebration rotates among most of the Houses every season, and it was our responsibility now to travel as a family to celebrate the coming of spring. This solstice is seen as a symbol of rebirth and new beginnings, and as such, I am to be presented as a Lady for the first time. My father tells me the solstice is a great time for the revelation of a new heir. Usually, it is done when a child is much younger, but of course… everything with me is different.

On the day before the Spring Solstice, the castle prepares for our departure. Multiple carriages full of supplies and attendants will be guided by almost two dozen guards on horseback. My father's right-hand man, the court vizier, arrives to watch over the House of the Evening while we're gone. "High Lord Alexander, I will keep things running smoothly in your absence. Is there anything that I should keep an eye out for?" he asks my father as he takes his last satchel down to the luggage carriage.

"Watch for the next shipment of building supplies in from the House of Earth," my father says. "Make sure they are moved immediately to the construction sites for the new boat on the river. They are due in any day now."

He nods curtly. "Understood. Best of luck to you, High Lord."

My father then turns to me. "Come down then. We need to get going. It's more than a two-day ride from here to the House of the Day."

I rush down the stairs and join my stepmother and her kids. Neil shoots me a short frown, but to be honest, it lacks a bit of its usual bite. Analise takes my hand and beams up at me. "Aren't you excited?" she asks, only barely managing to contain her bouncing. I chuckle and nod. When I look above her head, the High Lady is scowling at me.

"Come, Analise," she snaps as she practically yanks the little one out of my grasp. She protests as they rush out to the carriage. Neil lets out a short laugh but follows. I pause for a moment, alone in the hallway, before mentally shrugging and heading out to load up. To my surprise, there are two riding carriages instead of one.

"You will ride with me, Grace," my father says as he opens the door to one of them. A quick glance at Elise lets me know that the reason there are two may have something to do with her not wanting me anywhere near her perfect little group. Better to banish me to a separate vehicle.

Good on my father for not letting her.

"Looking forward to it." I smile sweetly over at my stepmother before climbing into the carriage.

My father follows after me and shuts the door. Then at a flick of the reins and a quick shout from the driver, the caravan departs.

Thus ensues an agonizing two-day journey down the mountain range and through the countryside. I mostly sit in silence with my father. He wisely has packed a book and reads it as the carriage rumbles along. I'm surprised my father doesn't take much time to teach me or even speak to me, but when I work up the courage to ask him, he only says he isn't a fan of long rides out of town and prefers to stay quiet. Resigned to a wordless trip, I stare out the window and watch the scenery change as we move from House to House. I don't think I will ever get used to the brightness and the perky atmosphere of this side of the realm. As the flowers start to bloom with the new season, I am filled with a bit of hope. For them, a new beginning comes along every spring. This Solstice is mine.

Whenever we stop to eat, my stepfamily joins us at the same table, but they do not speak to me. Well, except Analise. She is still as animated as ever, telling me about all the word games that she and Neil have been playing. I try to turn all my attention to her and ignore the obvious glares coming from my stepmother and stepbrother.

When we stop in the evenings to sleep, the inns go out of their way to accommodate us. According to my father, these inns have been assessed beforehand by the captain of the guard himself to ensure our safety. An entire floor is cleared out with a room set aside for each of us, and we are served a hearty dinner. When we retire upstairs, guards take turns patrolling the floor that we are in to keep an eye out for danger. They make me nervous. I don't like knowing I'm being watched.

On our second overnight stay, I am feeling especially suspicious.

The air in this room, even with the window open, feels stale and tense. As I lay back in my bed staring straight ahead, my heartbeat steadily thumps in my ears. If I stay perfectly still, I can hear very faint footsteps walking across the floor outside my room and then away again. I tap my fingers against the sheets lightly. *I really need to go to sleep.*

Just before I decide to get up to go to sleep, my door lock clicks. I sit up. The door swings open a crack. My hand reaches blindly for my side table where my dagger is stashed. When a guard's head peeks around the corner, my hand stills. "Yes?" I ask.

"Has anyone been by to see you tonight, Lady Grace?" the man asks in a hushed voice.

"No, sir," I sit up. "Is there something wrong?"

"Has your father come by recently?"

"No, he should be in his room; he said he was turning in early. Is there a problem?" The guard steps into the room and shuts the door behind him. When the lock clicks closed, alarm bells are going off in my head. My hand begins creeping towards the side table again. "Is there something else you need?" I ask again, a little more insistently.

His hand flashes white, and I hit the floor just in time for a shot of disintegration magic to slam into the wall where my head was. It explodes the wall into plaster and dust. As it rains down on me, my heart leaps out of my chest. *By the Lady, this is it!* Thinking fast, I set the floor under his feet on fire. The flames creep up around his ankles. He jumps away with a scream and fires off another spell. I roll to the side to avoid it.

"Hey!" I shout towards the door. *How are there no guards hearing this?* I blast off the lock behind him and pull a breeze from the window to swing the door open. "HEY!" When another disintegration spell zips towards me, I jump to my feet and put up a force field. The shield absorbs the magic, but I struggle to keep it up. But before the rogue man can aim at me again, he freezes in place and falls face-first into the floor with a loud groan. His face presses deep into the burned wood, so forcefully I worry it will cave in. I raise my head up to see my furious father with a glowing mass of magic keeping the man on the ground. I breathe heavily as he stares at me. "What happened?"

"He attacked me." I want to elaborate, but the words won't come out. The adrenaline is slowly fading from my body and leaving me shaky and uncertain.

"Can I get the alternate guards here, please?" he snaps to the man behind him who swiftly waves over another small group of men. They rush into my room and wrench my attacker off the floor. "Get him outside. I want to know what the hell is going on here." He looks at me, and his expression softens. "Are you alright?"

I get to my feet and sit back on the bed in shock. "Yes... I'm fine. He didn't get me."

"Stay here. I'm leaving Warren with you, alright? I will be back shortly." He places his man outside my doorway and leaves the door open so I can see him. The High Lord then rushes for the stairs with a flourish of his robes. Before I even have a minute to process what just happened, my father is gone.

I sit in silence on my bed once more with a thousand thoughts running through my head. In the wake of the attack, I am reminded how dangerous the Upper Realm truly is. In the palace, I had snide looks and quick comments, but no one dared to strike the next High Lady. Well, except for family, of course. But out here... I feel no different than I did when I was a mortal playing pretend. Except this time, the world knows I'm a fraud and will stop at nothing to take me down.

My father knocks quietly on the door frame several minutes later. "Grace?"

I look up quickly. "What did you find out?"

He sighs and motions towards the bed. I move over, and he takes a seat next to me. "The man was an imposter. Swapped out for another guard of ours during our first leg. He was hired by the House of Fire to take you out in one hit. However, they were under the impression you hadn't been trained nearly enough to hold your own."

"I got lucky, Father. Nothing more."

"That is certainly true. You were lucky." He faces me. "I'm going to assign guards to watch you specifically when we are out in public and a smaller detail for the palace."

"Father, don't do this," I stand up and groan. "I hate being followed. I can't stand it."

"This is not negotiable, Grace…" The High Lord stands. "You are my daughter and the heir to the House of the Evening. You must be protected. I'm stationing two men here for the night. We'll discuss more when we return to the palace." He walks over and places both hands on my shoulders. I try not to falter at his steely gaze. "You should get some rest. The Solstice is still tomorrow. We must present a good face and show them we will not be shaken by anything." With that, he turns and leaves the room. As the door closes, I am left with a growing sense of dread and an inability to close my eyes and rest.

Chapter Nine

As we arrive on the edges of the House of the Day, I see the effects of the Solstice celebrations on the lorddom. The outer villages are a bit more decked out than the ones I walked and rode to at the beginning of my journey. There are decorations across buildings and banners welcoming the incoming guests of honor. Buildings have been patched up and repaired. When we reach the center of town, the marketplace is in full swing. Everything is loud and bright, just as I remember it, but with even more people. They cheer at us as the carriage rolls by. As I lean in closer to the window, I can see a surprising array of merchandise. The silks are more expensive, the fruit more exotic, and the drinks flow faster. To me, it looks like the House of Day has prepared for a show of pageantry. They want the other houses to see their strength and consider them worthy.

When the carriage approaches the palace, the knot in my stomach grows larger. I wipe my palms on the front of my dress. I look at my father who is glancing out the window with a soft smile at the scenery. "Father, I don't think I'm ready for this," I say quietly as we rumble up the spiral cobblestone street. "Not after last night."

"I think you are, Grace." He turns his head back to me to reply. "You have done remarkably well in the last couple months. I am pleased with your progress, particularly with your magic. And remember, not a word to a soul about last night's events."

"Why not?"

"Because I imagine they are all watching for us to break."

"Do you think other Houses were involved?"

"No. But many of them will be aware by the end of the day, no doubt."

I take a deep breath. "Do you think I will need to showcase any… skill… or magic?"

"Oh no," Father shakes his head. "There shouldn't be any need to showcase any magic. Although I can't promise no one will ask you for something. Noble Fae are very traditionalist, and you… my child, break all their rules."

"Their rules? Aren't they yours too?" I look down at my hands.

"They are. But I'm not sure how much I agree with them anymore." My father looks out the window with this faraway expression as if reliving a moment from a long time ago.

"What changed your mind?"

"Meeting you did."

I look down as I feel an odd rush of pride flood my body. After months of having my heritage not being acknowledged, my new stepfamily denying me, and trying to find out who I am essentially alone… to hear my father see anything of value in me is something I have craved for a very long time. Even before I knew who he was. I grasp his hand as he pulls it away from my cheek. We sit silently for a few minutes before the driver taps at our roof.

"That's our cue," my father nods to me as our carriage falls in line with a multitude of other carriages containing other noble families. Each has been decorated with the House's crest and colors, and their finery sparkles in the sunlight. He removes his hand from mine and reminds me, "We are third in the line-up this time around because the House of the Day is hosting. First is the House of the Sun, then the House of the Moon, and then us. Remember after I step out with

Elise and the kids, you will be announced. This is standard procedure for a first solstice as a Lady. You should have been so much younger for this…" he trails off.

"Dad…" I use the unfamiliar moniker once. The man looks up at me with a quick snap of his head. "I'm going to be fine."

"Good."

I look out the window and pull the curtain back slightly to see a tall glittering castle of glass and white and gold stone rise up in front of us. The sunlight streams down and makes it shine, casting a brilliant light on the courtyard that we are making our way towards. Blue and yellow banners of the House of the Day fly over our heads, welcoming us to the city. As the nobles were greeted at the Winter Solstice, important officials and wealthy members of society clap for us on either side of the street. We finally arrive at the courtyard where the High Lord of the House of the Day and his family are waiting for us.

When I catch a glimpse of the front door, I watch the back of High Lord Çaelic of the House of the Sun disappearing inside. I groan internally. *That means I just missed Aiden.* But I don't have much time to dwell on that thought before I realize the House of the Moon family is getting out of their carriage.

"By the Lady, we're next."

"Yes." My father's voice startles me. I didn't realize I said the last sentence out loud. I flush. "Take a breath," he says as the carriage pulls up to the center of the outdoor space.

"Presenting… the House of the Evening!"

My father nods to me solemnly before he steps out of the carriage with a smile and a cordial wave to those waiting to greet him. The people cheer as he shakes the hand of the High Lord. Out the window, I see the High Lady and my stepsiblings step out and move to join him. "And for the first time, the House of the Day welcomes Lady Grace

Andrea Faelie, the new future heir to the House of the Evening."

That's my cue.

I stand and slide around to the door. Lifting the layers of my long lavender dress, I exit the carriage down the small steps. My head raises to lock eyes with the High Lord. I need something to focus on to keep moving forward. The crowd falls silent. Or maybe it's the ringing in my ears; I can't quite tell.

I slowly make my way across the flagstones of the courtyard. I feel the curls bouncing on my shoulders, and I pray they're holding. The ruffles of my dress flow behind me as the designer said they would. He said it would make for a dramatic moment, and wow, don't I feel it. Everyone's eyes are on me. But with every step I take, I grow a little more confident. This is my moment, my era. My amulet sits lightly on my neck as I meet my father at his side. Lady Elise looks at me with shrewd eyes, but I ignore her as I reach out to shake the hand of the High Lord of the House of the Day. He smiles at me warmly, to my surprise. "Welcome, Lady Grace," he nods to me.

"Thank you, High Lord," I reply cordially. With a nod, he holds his hand out to the staircase. My noble family moves to enter the palace, and I quickly follow. The herald announces the next family group, but I am searching for one that has already arrived. When we reach the front hall, I have to bite my lip to keep my mouth from falling open in awe. I wonder if I'll ever stop being mesmerized by the grandeur of these balls. The hall is lit by these beautiful major skylights shining down to light up the white glass floor. The room glitters.

As we enter the ballroom, I search frantically for the House of the Sun's family. Despite half of the Twelve Houses being outside, the room is still packed full of nobles, attendants, and other guests. I stay with my family as we maneuver our way through the crowd. Suddenly, a bit of dark green and a flash of blond hair catches my eye from across the ballroom. The man looks up, and I can see that it's Aiden.

I separate from my father, but his hand jerks out and grabs my arm. "Father, I just want to see—"

"You can't run off wherever, Grace," he scolds. "There is etiquette."

"Etiquette until after the dinner and then the ball is almost a free-for-all, Father," I protest. "I just want to see my… friend."

"You may see him after dinner, Grace. Let's go." My father tugs me away in the opposite direction from Aiden.

"What happens now?" I ask.

"We wait here until the High Lord has formally introduced everyone into the palace," my father leans in and speaks into my ear. "Then he'll give a little speech, and we will congregate in the banquet hall for dinner."

"And then?"

My father smiles and offers me his arm. "Then we dance."

Chapter Ten

The banquet itself was lovely. The banquet hall is much bigger at this palace than at ours, and it can encompass the whole of the nobility class and several tables for those officials and allies who rank high enough to eat in the main room. One long table seats the High Lords and Ladies while I am relegated to the heirs' table. I am sandwiched awkwardly between the two sisters from the House of Light. Neither makes a move to speak to me. Aiden sits on the opposite end of the table. We lock eyes, but don't try to communicate while the dinner is ongoing. Instead, I engage in light small talk with Lord Demetrius, the heir to the House of the Earth. He's quiet, but I appreciate the attempt to engage with me.

As soon as the ball begins, Aiden and I reunite on the edges of the ballroom. I rush to his side in hopes to snag a hug, but Aiden halts me with a hand. I'm a little taken aback, but when he takes my hands and smiles, I relax. "Hey…" he says. "I want to hug you, but we both have eyes on us. My father is very concerned about the optics of you being discovered in our palace right under his nose. Let's not break too many protocols yet. We'll save that for later." He shakes his head with a soft breath. "Look at you. You look beautiful."

I chuckle lightly and squeeze his hands. "And you look handsome. I can't believe you're here. We have a lot to talk about," I adjust my tone to a more serious one. "Alright." Aiden looks out to the dance floor. "Let's talk out there." He offers his hand to me. "May I have this dance, Lady Grace?"

"Yes, Lord Aiden." Aiden smirks and moves a hand to my waist. With one hand on his shoulder, we are off to the dance floor. As the music plays on, Aiden's adept hands make me feel light on my feet. As we twirl along the dance floor, he leans into my ear. "What do you need to tell me?"

"I was attacked on my way here," I whisper under my breath.

"What?" his voice hisses loudly. At a raise of my eyebrow, he brings the volume back down. "Sorry. What happened? Are you alright?"

"It was a hit from the House of Fire. No injuries. I fought him off for a while before my father sent him to the ground. It was… crazy."

"An assassin hit? Are you serious?"

"Do I look like I'm making things up, Aiden?" I scan the room. "We're going to need to be on our guard now more than ever. Keep up appearances as much as possible."

"Well, in that case, I suppose I'm just going to have to keep asking you to dance."

"Is that wise?"

He shrugs. "Everyone out there is expecting it anyway. Let's deliver. It's not a scandal if everyone knows it's happening. Besides, I don't want to let you out of my sight." We take control of the night, the two of us. Song after song we spend moving around and around the room. We alternate partner songs with large formal dances in the center of the floor. When it feels like we have been dancing for too long, I stay close to the edges of the room while Aiden takes a turn with another of the heirs.

Eventually, my aching feet give me a sign that I need a break. We applaud the band with the rest of the nobles before I pat Aiden on the arm. "Could you go grab me a drink? I need to sit down." Aiden nods and with a slight ruffle of my hair, heads off to flag a servant. I lose sight of him in the crowd.

Making my way over to a small bench, I sink onto it, rubbing my ankles. I take a moment to look around the ballroom and take it all in for the first time. The House of the Day's palace shines in gold and blue. The moonlight shines in through the tall glass windows and carries one's eyes to the beautiful painted ceiling. Everyone here is dressed impeccably in reds, pinks, purples, and greens. I catch a whiff of various floral perfumes practically everywhere I turn. It's giving me a bit of a headache. One could spend hours sorting through the details of this one room. But for once, I'm not here to stay silent and observe. I'm here to take part in the game.

When Aiden doesn't return with my drink right away, I get up and wander through the ballroom searching for him. Without his presence, I feel out of place again. Every move I make is another opportunity to embarrass my father… or myself. It takes me a while to weave through the crowd of nobles, but I finally find myself a side door. *Thank goodness.* I speed up and head for the door. Before I can make my way through though, the door suddenly closes in front of me.

"Tsk, tsk, tsk…" a tongue clicks behind me. Spinning around, I face a rather unwelcome sight. "Well, what have we here? The brand new heir to the House of the Evening breaking tradition once again at her very first official function?"

I stifle a groan as I turn around and face the heir to the House of Darkness. "Lord Faolan."

Faolan smirks at me as he straightens up. "Soooo…" he drags out his words. "The famous heir deigns to recognize little old me…" He's certainly laying it on thick tonight; he does clean up nice. A black dress coat is draped over a deep red shirt with silver buttons adorning the cuffs. The leather pants fit against his frame tightly, leaving little room to the imagination.

I raise my eyes to his in defiance. "Is there something you need, Faolan?"

"I'm here to see how the little half-blood is faring in this world," he smugly replies.

"Don't call me that," I hiss. "I have nothing to say to you."

"Oh, darling, you're not going to try to hold a little swordplay against me, are you?"

"You tried to kill me."

To be fair, it was tradition. An absurd one, the duel of the heirs. But nevertheless. You're a Fae Lady now. Should you not be proud of your heritage?" he smiles devilishly. His sarcastic tone makes me cringe.

"I don't have to stand here and listen to this. When I reign, the House of the Evening will no longer be doing business with the House of Darkness; I can promise you that."

"Oh, how naive you are… as if you could control such things." To my shock, he extends a hand to me. "How about a dance, milady?"

"Absolutely not." I start searching for Aiden's blond hair in the crowd.

"Oh, someone hasn't been reading their etiquette books carefully," Faolan teases. His voice is starting to piss me off. "On an heir's first coming out event, it is expected of him or her to dance with all of the heirs of their alliance. That, my dear, includes me. And I'm cashing in my dance now."

I curse at him, to which he only chuckles. His hand takes mine against my will, but I have no choice but to comply. "Fine." I stomp over to his side. "Let's get this over with."

He stops me for a moment. "There's more. There's a little game."

"A game?"

"Yes." Faolan leans in. "The heirs take turns asking each other questions. The objective is to learn all we can about the other person without giving anything important about our House away. Lying is forbidden, but asking direct questions about inter-House policy is as well. It's a game of cat and mouse, so to speak." His grin only grows. "I tend to enjoy it more than most."

I frown. I have no knowledge of this tradition. "I have never heard of that."

Faolan waves off my concern. "It's more of an alliance tradition. Your father should have mentioned it to you; you wouldn't find it in any of the books."

I slowly take a step back and look around to see if I can feasibly slip away. "I'll have to ask my father about that."

Faolan takes a step closer and blocks my exit with a hand on my wrist. "You can ask, but he'll only confirm. And it will make a scene that will only serve to embarrass you before you inevitably do what you are supposed to. It's your choice."

Well, it doesn't seem like the man is going to take no for an answer. "Fine. One dance."

Faolan offers me his arm, and I take it roughly. He chuckles. "No need to be rough. I'll be gentle with you."

Not thinking, I slap his arm. Hard. I gasp as I bring a hand to my mouth, but looking around, no one seems to have caught it.

Faolan laughs out loud. "You, Grace Faelie, might be the second most interesting thing in this room."

"Second?"

"After myself, of course."

"Focus on the dance, Faolan." *The sooner this is over, the sooner I can get out of his grip.* "You get the next song, and that's it. And it's Grace Richardson," I emphasize.

"Still haven't taken your father's name?"

"It's my name; it's my choice."

He smiles. "Is it though? We shall see how long that lasts."

To my horror, he starts leading me away from the edge of the room. "What the hell are you doing?" I whisper-shout as I try to pull his arm back.

"You didn't think I was gonna let you hide from this, did you?" Faolan grins, and I know I've been had. He pulls me toward the center of the ballroom, and I'm not strong enough to pull him back. The nobles surrounding us are noticing the pairing, and whispers begin to permeate the room. My face turns redder and redder as we move closer to a clear space, and I still can't find Aiden. A waltz begins, and Faolan pulls me along.

"Why is everyone staring?" I ask quietly.

"They're curious how you'll act."

"What are they expecting?" Faolan shrugs. "That depends. Many different people want many different things out of you."

"Including you?"

His lip quirks. "Perhaps."

"Has the game already started?"

"You tell me." He spins me into a turn. "Have you adjusted to noble life well?"

All the questions he could ask, and that's what he chooses to lead with? "It's going fine," I answer cautiously.

"And how are your newfound siblings?" His eyes bore into mine like he knows something.

I look over Faolan's shoulder, scanning for Aiden. "Neil doesn't like me very much. After all, I took his heirship."

Nodding dismissively, he replies, "I'd be shocked if he took it calmly. And your father?"

"Why are you asking all these questions about my family?" I snap as I purposefully step on Faolan's foot with my heel. "When is it my turn?"

"Whenever you please, my Lady." Faolan smirks as he drops me into a sudden dip and brings his forehead way too close to mine. "Though your refusal to answer my question is quite telling."

I mask my surprise by leaning into the dip before stepping forward and spinning us into another turn. I am hyperaware of the eyes continuously watching. "You tried to kill me only a short time ago. Why are you so curious about me now?"

Faolan looks over my shoulder. "I don't like when people lie."

"I had a good reason, and you know that," I protest.

"I. Don't. Like. Lies."

There's clearly no arguing the point with him. I didn't want to waste my breath. The music plays on as we waltz around the floor. "People are still staring!" I hiss at my partner. "When will this song be over? Aren't there other heirs to dance with?"

Faolan chuckles. "Oh, this party will be many hours yet. Do you truly wish to cut our time so short?" He leans into me. "Besides, I paid off the conductor. He'll play until I'm ready to stop." My jaw drops, and Faolan laughs. "See, there's a lot a man can learn if he's got the mind and the resources to. Including stories of a young girl asking questions about a human mercenary in Fae lands."

I spin. "You didn't do background on me, did you?"

"Didn't take long," he teases. "It's not everyday someone is asking a lot of strange questions."

"How much do you know about me?"

"Tsk, tsk, tsk," he clicks his tongue. "No direct questions, remember? But I'll allow you another question."

I growl. "How is it being the heir to the House of Darkness?"

"Rather pleasant." Faolan leans me down to the right slightly.

"Is that so?" I bring my face close to his, trying to intimidate.

"It rather is. I get to dance with beautiful women as I please. All I need to do is make up a tradition."

I stop dead in my tracks. "You did WHAT?" I whisper-yell. All

Faolan does is whip me back into the dance. I am horrified. The entire court has just watched me dance with the House of Darkness heir for what feels like hours. *What have I done? How will that come across?* I growl. "You have made me look like a fool."

"No," he scolds as he pulls me close. "I made you look like an heiress. Not a starstruck lovebird who fawns over the heir of the House of the Sun."

"I do not fawn—" I protest.

"You don't know what these people see," he interrupts. "You look as if you've already pledged marriage."

The music shifts and slides into a new tune, a swing song that I recognize from the high society mortal parties I used to play. Faolan swings me around and pulls me in tight, his hand on my waist. He sends me into a spin, and I don't have a moment to hesitate before he launches into dancing me across the floor. His steps are precise; with every move, he flourishes. I hate the way he smirks at me like he's enjoying watching me squirm with embarrassment.

Well, two can play at this game.

I summon what little courage I have remaining and think back to Leo's dance lessons in the living room on those turning-of-the-year nights when we could hear music pouring out from windows all over the city. I outstep my partner, pushing him back and swinging around him in a turn. He catches my hand, and I force the lead into another turn. His eyes flash for a moment before he steels himself. He yanks me closer, and suddenly we're moving together. The dance is an intricate back-and-forth, both of us fighting for dominance. I don't think I've danced harder in my life, but I'm not letting him win this, Lady be damned.

It isn't until near the end that I realize that we've ended up in sync, and he's smirking at me. I realize this was his plan all along. He wanted me to dance with him, to get close to him without a fight. Just as I come to this realization, he swings me into a dip; my leg comes up to his hip and he grips my thigh as my hair drops to the floor. The music stops, and the Fae nobles around us have no idea what to do. There is no applause, yet there's also no silence. Sort of a mild din as people try to turn back to their individual conversations without showing their intrigue at watching us dance.

Faolan raises me up from the floor slowly, his hand sliding from my thigh to hold my hip as he sets me down. "Now wasn't that fun?" he smiles coyly at me.

I quickly take a step back. "What did you gain from all that?"

He shrugs. "Entertainment of a sort. And perhaps answers."

"What kind of answers?"

"How well you'll fit in this society and how well you can cover your tracks." He comes in close again. "Let me give you some advice. It took me a day to know your name, birth city, goals and journey. I even know you traveled to the Lower Realm. So what could you have done differently?"

My heart nearly stops. "You know I've been to the Lower Realm?"

Faolan raises an eyebrow, but breaks out into a grin. "I do now."

I want to slap him, but there are too many people nearby. I curtsy in a semblance of politeness and say through gritted teeth, "This isn't over."

Faolan bows graciously. "Until next time. Be more careful with your reactions."

"I'll be wary of con men," I spit.

"We are the ones to be wary of," Faolan says softly. "But you'll find the need to embrace us if you want to survive." He brushes a finger across my cheek. "Keep in touch, Lady of the Evening." He backs away and disappears through a congregation of nobles.

A familiar hand grabs my arm. I whip around to see Aiden's alarmed face looking at me, drink in hand. "What was that?" he says to me under his breath as he passes the drink to me.

I take a long slow sip and gulp before responding, "I honestly have no idea, Aiden. He lied to me about some tradition where I was supposed to dance with him. I haven't exactly finished reading all the etiquette books."

Aiden turns me to face him, his smile replaced by a stern expression. "You need to be exceptionally careful around him, Grace. He has more tricks up his sleeve than there are in the book, and he is probably the most dangerous noble in the Upper Realm. With the exception of his father." His hands squeeze my arms. "Promise me."

"I promise," I soothe him with a brief kiss on the cheek. "Now no more about Faolan tonight. Let's dance." Aiden's smile returns, and handing off my empty glass, we return to the dance floor for another spin.

The ball goes on for hours as the nobles revel until the early hours of the morning. Then the lot of us wander off upstairs, some to drink and some to sleep. I kiss Aiden goodnight when no one is looking with a promise to meet in the morning.

As I drift off to sleep in a way-too-big-for-one-person bed, I can't help but muse to myself…. *What a beautiful night…*

Chapter Eleven

I wasn't expecting to wake up to the shattering of glass.

It's such a distressing sound for me. The streets could be rough in Lisden. When I was younger, every so often, gangs would rule the streets for the night and you would have to pray your windows didn't get taken out by a rock or a hunk of metal. All around us, glass would shatter into the early hours of the morning. My mom would tell me to go to bed, but I would lie awake and listen to it. The sound reminded me of some twisted version of wind chimes.

Inside a Fae palace? That spells trouble.

Before I can even process where the sound is coming from, there's a harsh knock on my door, startling me further. "Lady Grace!" I hear an unfamiliar female voice shout before the door swings open violently. A maid flies into the room. "Lady Grace, your father needs you downstairs immediately," she says matter-of-factly. She opens my wardrobe and pulls my valise out. "There's a problem. I am here to pack your things."

I quickly push myself out of bed. "What kind of a problem?" I ask as I wrap myself in a blanket and catch the dress the maid throws at me.

"You need to get downstairs," she repeats.

"I'm not moving until you tell me what is going on!"

"They're talking about war!" she snaps at me.

"War?" I freeze in my tracks. *Is this the moment the Coven foretold? Is this the war?* "What do you know about it?" I throw on the dress and shove my nightgown into the suitcase.

"Nothing, Lady Grace. I'm just the maid," she answers with a slight edge to her voice. "I caught the news on my way by the Great Hall before your father stopped me and asked me to send for you."

"Who's in the Great Hall?" I ask.

"Everyone."

With a flick of my wrist, I summon my amulet and my shoes over to me. I awkwardly run down the hallway while trying to put them on. When I reach the stairs, I get a snapshot of the chaos. From the stairwell into the Great Hall and around the other corner as far as I can see, it is wall-to-wall people pushing and shoving and shouting. Servants carry cases and valises, trying to make it out the door, while others dart through with what appear to be messages. Noblemen in various stages of dress shout at each other. Several soldiers from different Houses try to clear the people and direct them outside as they try to exit themselves. There is a general air of confusion and frustration.

I rush down the stairs and shove my way into the crowd. It is then that I catch the first words of what is going on. "Are you saying they invaded? They actually invaded?!" one soldier shouts to another while frantically trying to button up his jacket.

"They bombed the hell out of the town hall," he replies as he pushes past me. "The House of the Earth is in shambles."

I startle at that and grab the man's arm before he can exit. "What do you mean the House of the Earth is in shambles?" He goes to move his arm before his eyes flash in recognition. He and his companion do their best to stand at attention in the moving crowd. I wave them off. "No, no, no, no need for formalities. Tell me what you know."

"Lady Grace." The man dips his head in acknowledgment. "The Houses of Darkness and Fire just invaded the House of Earth." My mouth falls open slightly. "High Lord Carron, High Lord Halden, and their families exited in the middle of the night and met up with their armies stationed in the House of Fire. They mobilized overnight; no one can figure out why intelligence didn't pick the information up. In the early hours of the morning, they swept through and took out no less than six villages before hitting the main town. No one knows how many casualties yet. We're supposed to be meeting our captain to figure out what our House wants us to do. No one has any idea how to respond. We have to join them."

I pat both of their arms. "Yes, of course. Go. Good luck." With a quick salute, the men are on their way. I push my way through the crowd toward the Great Hall. The scene there is even more packed and inaudible as the High Lords and their families appear to be debating over what to do now. There are shouts to call more soldiers to aid the House of the Earth whose High Lord and family, I notice, are already missing. They must have left to see what was left of their lorddom to salvage. I don't see my father in the congregation, nor can I find Aiden.

My body is suddenly pulled back by a hand. I whip around, ready to push away whoever it is. My father's panicked face stops me. "Grace, I need you to come with me." He pulls me along back towards the palace entrance. "We are getting in the carriage right now and heading to the House of Peace. Neil is waiting for us with the driver. There has been an emergency War Council called to discuss next steps."

"A War Council?"

"It is an organization designed to keep the alliances in agreement on what needs to be done in the presence of wartime. I had no time to prepare you for this, but the House of the Evening runs the Council, and we have to leave. Now."

I nod in affirmation. "I'm ready."

"Good. Let's go." We fight our way to the courtyard. Spinning away from two carriages that nearly run over my feet, I grasp my father's hand who pulls me up to the steps of the carriage. He moves to speak with the driver, and I step up on the carriage steps to get a better look at the scene around us. I have to see Aiden before I go. Who knows how long it's going to be until I see him again. But to my disappointment, I can't find him.

I'm tempted to rush back inside and find him, but a soft breeze over my shoulder catches my attention. I smell the characteristic sweetness of elemental magic mixed with something acrid like heavy smoke. When I look up, I see a figure perched up on the lower courtyard wall. My eyes squint as I move closer to the window, trying to make out the presence.

Another breeze teases my neck, and I catch a whiff of cologne. In an instant, I know who that man is. My hands grip the windowsill in a vice. I can just make out the quirk of Faolan's lips. He raises a hand to me in a lazy greeting. He looks way too relaxed for a man whose father started an entire war. I'm not sure what I'm supposed to do here. I turn my head back to the crowd and open my mouth to say something, to alert someone to the House of Darkness's continued presence here. But when I glance over my shoulder again, he's gone.

"Grace!" my father snaps behind me. I startle and turn to find him and Neil waiting. "Get in." I slide in quickly, and the two men join me. Neil shoves in next to me. He doesn't say a word and only stares out the opposite window.

"What the hell is going on, Dad?" he asks as my father slams the carriage door closed and hits the front wall to signal the driver. I am thrown back into my seat as the carriage moves out at a much quicker speed than before.

"War, son." My father's voice is quiet. "It's on its way." For the next hour or so, the only sound that can be heard is the frantic clicking of wheels on paved and gravel road.

Chapter Twelve

When we arrive several hours later, the atmosphere is so different from the last time I saw it. It's an overcast day, and the gray shadows cast over the buildings make the normally bright landscape look sullen. The lamps that are on create an eerie glow that makes me shiver. As we roll past the marketplace, I peer out the window to see the Fae staring at us. There's an apprehension in the eyes of the people, a fear of what is to come. News travels fast. They know why we're here. And although the House of Peace is a gracious hostess, the people are afraid of what the recent events could mean.

The House of the Peace's palace resembles the temples around us with its tall, textured columns that span the base before branching out into tall towers with column-framed balconies that wrap around its entire length. But the brightness and the life I had seen during my first trip here is now a shell of its former self. The air is heavy as we approach the entrance. Before we can get any closer though, we are met by a gridlock of carriages. Nobles and other important officials are abandoning them with their drivers and making their way to the palace on foot.

"We should get out here," my father says as he taps the front wall again. The driver pulls to a stop, and we climb out. He throws an arm in front of Neil and me to keep us from being run over by another carriage's wheels. "Come on. Quickly now." We rush up to the palace.

The doors have been thrown wide open, and for the first time, there is no one attending them. Just like the House of the Day was, the hallway is packed with people, a mixture of those from the Spring Solstice celebration and other officials from the House of Peace. My father pushes forward through them, clearing a path for me and my stepbrother to follow tightly behind. We rush into the Great Hall where a large table is set up for the High Lords to discuss what to do next.

The High Lord turns around and places a hand on both our shoulders. Neil and I both glance sideways at each other. "Stay here. Listen, and absorb what you can. You should be able to hear us once the town hall begins, but you'll also hear how the people are reacting around you. Take it in, and be ready to report back to me when we get home. This is extremely important, do you understand?" We both nod. "Good. Be good."

My father leaves Neil and me off to the side as he approaches the other High Lords near the head table. By my account, not all of them appear to be here yet. Depending on when the crowd dissipated at the House of the Day, it could be hours before everyone who is supposed to be here arrives. We could be waiting for quite a long time. "Come on," I say distractedly to Neil.

"Where are you going?" he snaps while grabbing my arm and pulling me back.

I roll my eyes and face him. "Look, this could be a while. We're going to want to be near a wall to lean against as this drags on. Come on," I repeat and push his back along. We aim for a spot of white catching our eyes against the sea of colored clothing.

"Grace!" Aiden's voice comes from behind me. I spin around, leaving Neil, and dart behind a small group of people to reach out for his hand. Aiden grabs me and pulls me into his chest. "Thank the Lady," he whispers into my hair before pressing his lips to my head discreetly. "I couldn't find you anywhere."

"My father pulled me away before I could find you," I answer as I hug him tight. "I'm so sorry."

"No worries, you're here now." Aiden pulls away and holds me at arm's length. "What have you heard?" he asks in a hushed tone. "Do you think this is it? Is this the prophecy starting?"

"Yes," I breathe. I think this is it." I grab his hands and pull him toward the wall. "Come here, stand with us."

Aiden nods his head to Neil. "Neil."

Neil eyes him suspiciously. "Aiden."

I wave for them to be quiet as the High Lords take their seats and my father motions for quiet. "Alright, can we get quiet in the room, please?" His voice calls out over the general crowd. "I need everyone who is not an heir, a family member, or the handful of designated officials to leave now." A group of servants ushers the others out of the room. The doors close around us, and the room sinks down slowly to quiet. "I want to thank High Lord Gabriel for allowing us to congregate here at the House of Peace to call this emergency meeting of the War Council. As High Lord of the House of the Evening, I preside over this council, and I am formally calling it to order. Can we start by taking stock of what we know?"

"I would like to speak on that point," High Lord Aaron of the House of Light raises his hand. "I was with High Lord Adam when he heard word from his people. I probably have the most complete timeline of events."

"By all means, go ahead," my father says as he sits down.

High Lord Aaron sits forward. "Just before dawn this morning, the House of the Earth was invaded by the House of Darkness. High Lord Carron led the charge, having snuck away from all the festivities only a few hours prior. The messenger that High Lord Adam spoke to said that the main village was nearly decimated. The town hall and the noble family's home have burned to the ground. High Lord Adam left shortly after hearing the news to attend to his people and attempt to regroup his troops. As far as I know, no one has heard any updates from him since. The speed at which this took place is unprecedented, and we should be very concerned about the outcome."

"Any intel on what's happening on the ground in the House of the Earth?" my father asks.

High Lord Aaron shakes his head. "We've heard nothing."

My father nods. "How would we like to proceed from here? In my opinion, it is important that we send aid immediately to the House of the Earth to join High Lord Adam in hopes to liberate his territory."

High Lord Dylan of the House of Water raises a hand. "It is of my honest opinion that we should not get involved in this." I am a bit taken aback by this, and by the looks of the man standing next to me, so is Aiden.

"High Lord Triton, you would say no?" My father's brow furrows.

"Look, none of you have been in the western Upper Realm region for a while. The House of Darkness is a big player, and there has been talk for years about increased military spending and supply hoarding. We all know that High Lord Carron is a power-hungry bastard, and his land is infertile. He imports more food than any of us and pays through the nose to get it. And he and the House of Fire have been cozy for decades. Recently, there have been more and more diplomatic missions between the two of them, too many."

High Lord Dylan continues. "I live in that region. I have no energy to go toe-to-toe with the two of them nor the resources. If the two of them will be satisfied with the House of the Earth territory to feed their people, well, that's something I'm willing to live with."

High Lady Morgana points her finger in the man's face. "You would let your fellow High Lord lose his home and his lorddom to protect your own interests?"

"Absolutely!" he bellows. "And if you really look deep down into yourself, you will realize it too. The House of the Earth is the smallest of us. We cannot move to defend it; we would have to be on the offensive. The House of Darkness is too strong for us to oppose without proper planning. We can stand and defend the rest of the realm as nine. Maybe we'll even get something done with three less voices chiming in!"

The head table dissolves into murmurs and whispers between men. To my horror, many people seem to be agreeing with the head of the House of Water. I keep my eye on Aiden's father, the High Lord of the House of the Sun. He is engaging in the conversation just as fervently as the others, but his eyes tell a different story. He is content to watch all of this fall apart around him. It's driving me mad.

When my father calls for a vote, the House of the Evening, the House of the Moon, and the House of Wind stand alone in a desire to aid the House of the Earth. All of the others choose to give up the fight before it has even begun, including the House of the Sun. *Traitor. Aiden's father is just sitting up there while allied with Darkness and Fire and pretending nothing is wrong.* I feel Aiden tense up beside me. I can't believe I am watching this go down in flames.

Chapter Thirteen

The crowd dissipates after the High Lords reach their decision. "Stay here," I order Neil. He scoffs, but I don't stick around to argue. Aiden and I rush towards the front of the room, pushing past Fae left and right. I dodge a few rogue arms and shoulders while Aiden blocks the rest. *Thank the Lady for tall Fae men.* We fight our way to the head table where I grab my father's arm.

"Father…"

"Grace, grab your brother. We need to get back home now," he interrupts me.

"But Father, Aiden and I need to…"

"Grace, go get your brother now!" He scolds me and turns to speak to High Lord Gabriel in a hushed tone. "Meet me outside in five minutes." When I don't move immediately, he shouts. "Go!" Slightly startled, I look over to Aiden and pull him aside as we walk back toward Neil.

"I'm so sorry," I apologize quickly to Aiden. "Neil, he wants us outside in five," I call across the room to Neil who nods once and then disappears towards the front hall. When he turns his back, I pull Aiden over to the hall, gripping his arms. "I'm sorry, I'll talk to my father when we get going. Maybe we can work something out; maybe I can meet you somewhere."

"It's alright." Aiden squeezes my arms as he looks around us. "My father is going to be looking for me; I have to go."

"Can't you come with me?"

He smiles softly and pulls me into a tight hug. "You're going to want me in the House of the Sun for now. I need to see what the next phases of this are. I'll report to you as soon as I know, I promise."

Breathing hard, I hold on to him tightly. I don't want to let go. Right now, everything is so uncertain. But I can see that my father is wrapping up his conversation and preparing to leave. Gulping, I reluctantly pull back and kiss Aiden briefly. "Don't die."

Aiden kisses my forehead once, lingering for as long as he can. "You too." With one final hand squeeze, we pull away from each other in opposite directions: me towards the front hall and him towards the head table to grab his father.

I make it through the crowd and meet up with Neil outside before my father joins us. I get an eye roll from Neil, but he turns back to the window to continue ignoring my presence. "Let's go," the High Lord says shortly. With a quick wave to the driver, he ushers us forward and inside the carriage. As we take off toward our homeland, my father finally takes a breath. He sinks back into his seat with that non-lordly air that I had seen right before the solstice, but with much more melancholy rather than relaxation. "I apologize for being short with you, Grace. I needed us to leave as soon as possible. We need to go home and prepare for the House of the Moon and the House of Wind."

"They're coming to the palace?" Neil asks. "Why?"

"We plan to pool our resources and send aid to the House of the Earth right away."

"But the official decision of the War Council was—"

"It doesn't matter," our father interrupts, "what the decision of the War Council was. Each House has the right to act as they see fit outside of that Council as well. To be frank, I am appalled that we were the only three Houses to vote yes on aid, and I am disappointed in my fellow High Lords today." He sighs as he bangs his fist on the window three times. "If you both will give me some time to sit here in silence so that I can think, it would be greatly appreciated."

We have no choice but to oblige.

It takes another couple of days to arrive back home at the House of the Evening. This journey was much quieter and more solemn. The three of us barely spoke the entire way other than idle pleasantries and questions about lodging for the evening. When we arrive back at the House, High Lady Elise and Lady Analise come out to greet us. Although the High Lady seems irritated to see me, I do get a surge of pride when the little one runs up to me first. My father walks up and embraces his wife, whispering something in her ear. She smiles before her expression changes to a more serious one at my father's words. The two of them move inside, presumably to talk.

"You're not ready for this, you know?" Neil says matter-of-factly out of the corner of his lips, trying to keep Analise from hearing. I ignore him and make my way inside. "Hey!" he calls after me. "Where are you going?"

I chuckle lightly and call back, "To prepare for company."

* * *

It takes several days for the House of the Moon and the House of Wind to arrive. My father told me the plan was to return to our homelands, pull resources together, and meet at our palace to figure out how best to distribute those resources. He keeps me extremely busy during those days. He cuts off all my Fae noble training and slashes my magic training time in half for me to assist him in these movements. "Everything you need to learn about ruling, you can learn at my side from here on out," he said. He was right. I learn more from him in this interim period than from any other mentor.

We took to the streets from the afternoon we arrived home. My father sends me by carriage to nearby villages to speak directly with farmers while he takes care of the larger merchants in the city. Working with other local officials, we gather pledges of a steady supply of food to later be arranged in package form. Then we turn to the apothecaries to collect medicine, bandages, and as many healers as we can pull together. Some of those healers are permanently conscripted to the palace. We are building an army on the home front in every locale. My father also alerts our current army to stand ready. Who knows if we will need to go to battle in the near future.

The citizens are now clearly aware of the danger that is lurking, and I have been quite amazed at how many people are taking the time to join the rescue effort. Left and right, Fae bring supplies, expertise, and manpower. When I look back to my mortal life, I can't imagine the Lisden community coming together during a time of crisis at this scale. It's not that we didn't want to; we just had very little to give, very little to share.

On a bright crisp morning, I watch from the balcony as two distinct congregations move toward us. The House of the Moon descends from the north, and the House of Wind rises from the south. They ride into town with scores of Fae of every profession like our gathering of people. The three groups intersect in the courtyard of the palace with the armies spilling over down the hills, onto the grounds, and even into Silvervale itself. My father greets them with the same magnanimous air that I am growing accustomed to seeing from him in official settings. As soon as he shakes both the High Lord's and the High Lady's hands, I make my way quickly downstairs to hear the latest plans.

This time, I don't need to stand and listen from the doorway as my father spots me and motions for me to come in to listen. He waves me off from the second throne, however, so I stick to the wall.

"Now that we are here, High Lord Alexander," the High Lady of the House of the Wind speaks in a sharp, yet kind voice, "what do you propose is the best move?"

"I've gathered a bit of intel," my father responds. "I sent a few soldiers in secret to scope out the conditions of the House of the Earth, and it is not good. Most of the farms have been commandeered on behalf of the Houses of Darkness and Fire. We need to send humanitarian aid to that region as soon as possible."

"Have we figured out how we are going to ship aid in?" High Lord Daniel questions. "And get the aid distributed to the right people? We don't want it commandeered by their armies.

"I want your commander to discuss that with mine and the High Lady's commanders. Between the three of them, they should be able to come up with something that will be satisfactory to the lot of us. Additionally, my soldiers have told me that it appears the House of the Day may be the next target. I have already sent High Lord Michael a message, and he is embracing a small party of military assistance for the time being."

"Only a small party?" the High Lady asks with a raised eyebrow.

"You know how he is," my father sighs. "He'll agree for the precaution and because it may make his people feel better, but he honestly doesn't believe this is coming to him."

"Old fool."

My father chuckles before turning to address me. "Lady Grace, will you show High Lady Morgana what we have been able to pull together in the healing department so that we can combine her resources with ours? We'll get you both an escort," he waves to two of his guards.

"Yes sir," I respond as I offer the High Lady my arm. She smiles at me.

"Lady Grace, I have not had a moment to speak to you since the

Winter Solstice. May I ask you for your story? I would so much like to hear more about your journey through the Upper Realm concerning your brother. And your experience in the Middle Realm would be quite interesting." I try not to be too overwhelmed by the idea of recounting *most* of those details. Though I am excited that someone finally wants to listen to the mortal side of this story.

"Yes, of course," I answer as confidently as I can as we exit the room.

Chapter Fourteen

Now that the palace is crawling with the Houses of Moon and Wind, my father has been taking many meetings upstairs behind closed doors. Every time I try to reach out to my father about the subject matter, he brushes me aside with a few mindless words before he's off to the next meeting. It is honestly a bit frustrating. I thought we were bonding. Perhaps he's too busy now. I don't know what to try to get him to talk. Besides, I really need to know what's happening in that meeting room.

In the meantime, I turn my focus to preparing for war. And for that… I need to speak candidly to Talon. When he returns to the palace for our lessons, I struggle to find the courage to tell him what went down with Neil all those weeks ago. Part of me is humiliated that I even got mixed up in a fight with him in the first place. The rest of me is furious for the exact same reason. And if I do tell him, I can't ensure that he won't immediately go to my father with the news. But I absolutely need to be learning combat magic. I may not survive… no. I won't survive what is to come without it.

It's clear my tumultuous internal feelings are affecting my magic. I have caused more magical mishaps today than on any other day of my training, from misplaced fireballs to very tiny explosions from lack of focus. "What is wrong with you today?" Talon finally stops me after I nearly light another wall of the arena on fire *again*. "You know all of these spells, Grace; now it's like you're back to being a new Fae. Are you alright?"

"I…" I groan in frustration. "I'm sorry, Talon. My head is just in other places today." Gathering my strength, I continue to speak. "Something happened a few weeks ago. I need to tell you about it."

Talon raises an eyebrow. "What exactly went down?" The look on his face makes me even more nervous than I already am, so… I back off. *I could ask for something slightly different and never have to tell the whole story.*

"Talon, you have got to teach me some combat magic, please," I beg. "We have barely touched the spell books. I'm tired of creating simple forms; I need to be able to defend myself."

"Unfortunately, Grace, I'm not authorized to teach you combat magic right now," Talon counters. "Come on, let's try that fire spell again."

"No!" I throw my hands down, sending a line of fire down into the grass. With a wave, I snuff it out before the burning spreads. "Who am I not authorized by? You?"

"Your father." Talon sighs. "I'm sorry, Grace. It is the one form of magic the High Lord asked me to hold off on. And because he's controlling the silver, there are a few lines we can't cross."

"This is different. If it's silver you want, I can get you more silver. But I need to learn combat magic."

"Why is this so important to you?"

"Because I was attacked by an assassin before the Spring Solstice! Because there are dangers everywhere for a High Lady, especially a half-Fae!" I shout. "And because I got my ass kicked by my half-brother, and he would have killed me if Analise hadn't stumbled upon us in the yard!"

Talon takes a step back from the force of my shout. He looks at me curiously. "Neil tried to kill you?"

I grit my teeth and repeat myself. "I need to learn combat magic."

"That's not important, what's important is—"

"Grace…" Talon warns.

"Okay, yes! Yes!" I finally cave and start pacing. "Neil tried to kill me. It was several weeks ago before the Solstice. He had his magic wrapped around my limbs and my head, and there was nothing I could do to stop him. I need to learn combat magic to protect myself and prove to the realm that I am worth my salt as a Fae. As a mortal, I learned to fight to do what needed to be done. As an heir… I will need it." I take a deep breath. "For what is coming… I will need it."

Talon looks at me with an unreadable gaze. I feel vulnerable under his eyes. For a moment, I think I shared too much with him. Then he nods slowly. "You're right. You do need to learn some magic for self defense. I should have taken that into account." I sigh in relief. "We'll start right away," Talon says. "Come with me."

I follow him from the side of the field directly into the center. After looking around to make sure no one is looking, Talon stands across from me with his arms clasped in front of his chest. "I told you that conjuring magic requires focus on intent. For simple magic, intent is enough to conjure what you are looking for." He summons a small sphere of fire.

"However," Talon fiddles with the fireball. "When in combat, you need to use that power in more complex fashions. That requires force of will along with intent. I know you can create all kinds of shapes and entities with your magic now, but that is not enough. You have to land your magic precisely where you want it to go and control the spell the entire way through." He throws his hands out, and the fire shoots across the field and lights one of the seats in the arena on fire. With another wave, the fire vanishes. "Alright, it's your turn. I want to see you try this."

The first few times I try, I can hold the fireball in my hands and throw it, but it doesn't stay lit or combust. "Try thinking about exactly what you want your spell to do," Talon suggests.

I ponder over his words carefully. "I'm having trouble visualizing."

"Think about the state of the object, think about the moment when the fire hits it, and then see it in the state of destruction."

I turn back to look at the seats at the arena. I pick one nearby and focus on its shape, its material, and its distance from me. Moving my hands, I summon another fireball, this time containing it in my hands. When I push the sphere forward, I see the journey as it is happening from myself to the arena seat. The seat ignites, and I pump my fist into the air. *There it is.* The fire burns out quickly, but I am thrilled that it landed. "There you go!" Talon praises. "Now let's do it again."

The tutor has me drill combat magic using both fire and disintegration for a couple hours. He creates things with fire and water for me to destroy before moving on to having me break items he is tossing at me. I love the thrill of being unsure whether my magic is going to land, and it drives me to keep getting better. I imagine Neil's face and the terrible feeling of being slammed into the ground. The moment when the assassin shot his first spell at me. When I was surrounded by demons in the Lower Realm, hoping to the Lady I would have the strength to make it out. I use that fury to grow stronger.

When I'm panting and sweating, Talon decides to switch tactics. "Alright, your technique is looking good. Now I want to try out the one power we haven't tried yet: weapons amplification." He throws me a sword from his pack. I catch it with one hand.

"Finally," I sigh. I love the weight of the sword in my hand; I haven't handled one in a while. "This feels good."

"You'll like it more when I tell you what your powers can do to enhance it." Talon disappears for a moment into one of the tunnels under the arena. After a few moments, he brings out a stuffed manikin and wheels it over to me.

"What is that?" I ask.

"This is a mechanized dummy that is designed to react to your movements and magic. Most of the palaces have a few of these for their soldiers to practice on. I'm sure they won't miss this one temporarily. You wanted to spar; now you'll have a shot at it." Talon backs away from the dummy and moves behind me. "I've heard you're good with a sword. Here's what you're going to do. You're going to take all that knowledge of the physical sides and apply those same principles to your magic. I want you to take your instinctive reactions and feel them with your magic core as well as with your mind. Weapons Amplification magic begins with feeling your magic combine with your physical abilities. Both need to be present for you to succeed."

He pats my shoulder. "I've got to step out to take care of some things in town, but I want you to stay here and practice. Keep an eye out if anyone comes this way."

"Alright," I say, lost in thought. He chuckles at me and leaves.

It takes me a few minutes to get started. Talon didn't instruct me on how this would work. I reach out with my sword and whack its chest lightly. The dummy shivers to life. It reaches out its sword and swipes at me. I jump back. "Ooh," I breathe. The next time it swings at me, I am ready to parry it away with the flat side of my blade. I feel the shiver of magic in my fingertips. I roll with it, and soon the dummy and I are in battle.

Every movement is coupled with a flow of magic through my hands, and I can actually tell the difference. My movements are more assured, the tip of my sword cutting the air itself. With each move, my magic starts to settle in more seamlessly with my physical movements. It feels like two souls moving as one entity. We spin around in this delicate dance of some kind as I battle this inanimate mage until I run out of energy and shut the dummy down. With heaving breath, I grin. *I might have a fighting chance now.*

Chapter Fifteen

Over the next couple of weeks, combat training intensifies. Together, Talon and I learn how my weapons amplification magic works with various types of fighting styles and weaponry. A sword works better with the magic type than a dagger, and in hand-to-hand combat, the increase in strength is minimal. With a bow, the arrow flies straighter and more precisely toward its intended target. Sneaking around to learn magic is even more fun than learning out in the open.

One morning, I wake to bright sunlight streaming in through my window. At first, I panic, thinking that I've overslept. Talon will be furious with me. We have so few mornings dedicated to magical study as it is now that my father has me entertaining our High Lord and Lady guests during mornings more often while he works on domestic affairs. But then I spot a small note slipped under the door. When I pick it up, I read that Talon has graciously allowed me to take the morning off, and he would like to meet him in the arena after a leisurely breakfast. And... *by the Lady,* he has finally asked me to spar.

Finally. I have been begging Talon since we started working on combat magic to let me test my skills in an actual fight. But he was insistent that I master the basics and have some intermediate skills up to par before getting into a fight. I guess after hearing about how terribly Neil trounced me in our encounter, he is feeling protective. Despite my protests, he wanted to make sure I was ready before having me take him on. My hands are clammy, and my nerves pulse in anticipation. I hope I live up to what I have been training for.

I rush downstairs and snag the last bit of breakfast before the table is cleared. Then I hurry off to the arena to meet Talon. He's standing at the end of the stairs waiting for me. His smile lets me know that my timing is alright. "Are you ready?" he calls up to me.

"Yeah," I yell back. "Are you ready to lose?"

Talon laughs. "Feeling confident today, are we?"

I chuckle. "Trying to be. I'm ready to use some of these techniques in an actual fight."

"Now, I'm going to go a little easier on you since it's your first time," Talon warns.

"Do you have to? I told you, I'm ready for this."

"And I told you, I'm not going to risk actually injuring you. This is to practice your reflexes and apply your recent lessons."

"Fine…" I draw out the word and bounce on my feet.

He nods and paces around me. "Alright, when you're in a sparring match with someone, you need to be constantly sensing their next moves. In a magical sense, that means keeping your eyes on your opponent's eyes and hands. That is where you are going to be able to detect when a spell is being cast. Your sensing abilities need some developing, but with time, you'll get there."

He moves over to the arena wall and picks up his sword. "One thing I don't know about is how your physical condition is in a fight. So let's start with that."

I laugh lightly before reaching out my own hand. "Alright then." My own sword flies from the same place, albeit a little shakier, and I catch it. I grip the hilt tight. It just feels right in my hand. "Let's go." Charging forward at Talon, I take my first swing. Our swords connect. From there begins a back-and-forth dance of blades. Every time I move forward, Talon pushes me back. When he moves in for a stab, I parry him and give it right back. He fights like my brother Leo did, professionally but with just enough spontaneity to make things exciting.

"You're good with a sword," Talon praises with a stab to my left shoulder. "Where did you learn?"

I lean back to avoid it before jabbing at his stomach. "My brother taught me."

"Was he a soldier?"

"He was." I hit his sword hand with a sharp whack, and he drops the sword. He quickly summons it back to his hand.

"Good," he says. "Now I want to see some of your amplification magic used. Channel it into your weapon."

It takes some concerted effort to get my magic coordinated with my physical moves when I first attempt it during a fight. Once I connect with my sword though, everything grows much easier. The sword feels lighter in my hand. Each move is sharper or quicker. And Talon can tell the difference; I can see him pushing himself more to keep up with me.

After a few rounds, he holds up his hand to stop me. "Well done." Talon shakes his head and climbs up gingerly from the dirt. "Your swordplay is brilliant. Your weapons amplification magic is coming along nicely." I reach over and help him up with a grin. "You physically fight well. Now I want to focus on your other magic." In a blink of an eye, he throws out a hand, and a line of water shoots out at me. I have no time to move before I am drenched in freezing cold water.

"Hey! What the hell?!"

Talon shrugs before giving me a smirk. "Always be sensing."

"I didn't know this was part of the fight!" I say incredulously.

Talon smiles. "Everything is part of the fight. You watch your back. You got that?" I nod. "Alright, let's go."

When he sends the next wave of water, I'm ready. I block it with a barrier of wind and manipulate it, flinging it back to him. He dodges and makes an approving sound. He tries fire next like a whip. It takes more than a couple seconds for me to decide what to do, but I quickly fling out my own rope of fire, intertwining with his. I siphon power off the spell and use it to pull him towards me. I don't wait for him to strike the next blow; I send a gust to his feet to flip him over. He counters by using that gust as a jumping point to launch himself at me. I flick my wings out and launch into the sky to avoid him.

"Hey!" he shouts up to me. "Who said you could fly?"

"Everything is part of the fight," I tease him. He laughs and shoots a dome of water above me, forcing me out of the sky. The fight moves fast. He fires off more spells at me than I can keep up with. Despite the intensity of it, underneath is an educational air. Talon encourages me to experiment with all of my magic types. Every move he makes is deliberate, and I can tell he is studying my reaction patterns. Which spells I'm using, which physical movements I make. I can tell he's impressed with how far I have come to date, but he doesn't hesitate to trip me up. By the end of the sparring match, I am laying breathless on the ground after one too many hits to the chest.

Talon pants with heavy breath as he walks over to my prone body. He offers me a hand. "Good run. Be ready tomorrow for more."

I grin and clasp his hand. "Wanna grab lunch?"

Talon shakes his head as he pulls me to my feet. "Oh no, Grace, I gotta breathe. I gotta recover for this afternoon." We laugh and shake hands. "Meet me back here when you finish eating." With that, we go our separate ways.

Chapter Sixteen

The following day, Talon cancels lessons. He says it's to give me a day off, but I think he needs it too. My body feels like it could lay in bed all day, but I know that I would regret that decision later. I sleep in a little and then get up to take a light walk around the palace grounds and some intentional stretching in the gardens. The sun is way past its peak in the sky by the time I make my way back to the front hall.

As I make my way toward the staircase, I catch a hushed conversation coming from the throne room. "With all due respect, I don't think we can sit back and wait for the House of Darkness to make their next move!" a voice projects a bit louder over the others. Curious, I hop off the bottom step and move over to the door frame. I lean against the wall to listen.

"High Lord Daniel, I respect your opinion, but we have no information about their movements. Strike too soon, and we could wipe out our own resources before something bigger comes along," I hear my father respond. Another voice chimes in, one I recognize as Lady Morgana's. "Alexander is right, Daniel. Confronting the Houses of Darkness and Fire head-on at this stage would be a mistake. But I do agree that we need to consider making an offensive move."

"What information *do* we know? Do we have anything?" Daniel asks.

"Very little," my father responds. "The people I sent in are coming up short. They can't seem to get close enough to the House of Darkness's camp to glean any usable information. All I know right now is that most of the people in the House of the Earth are hanging in there. The battle killed about one hundred fifty soldiers and another fifteen civilians at the town hall. The villages lost dozens when trying to defend themselves. Unfortunately, the entire noble family of the House of the Earth has been taken prisoner." My heart drops. "Additionally, there are issues with our aid. It is getting to them in segments, but the invaders are stealing some of it before the people can consume it."

"Should we be sending more then?" Morgana asks. "Or less? Or perhaps redirecting it so we can avoid our supplies being taken by the enemy? And what about High Lord Jameson? We can't just leave him and his family there. Can we attempt to save them?"

"Well, I think we should…"

Somewhere in the middle of High Lord Daniel's spiel, I zone out. *The House of Darkness hasn't made any more moves yet? Why not? What could they be planning? From what I saw with Aiden at the House of the Sun, I suppose it's plausible they could be satisfied with just taking the farmland. But High Lord Carron seems more the realm domination type than the one-and-done takeover type. I wonder…*

"… you for your time." My father's voice interrupts my thoughts. "We'll reconvene later this evening." I jump as I hear footsteps coming towards the doorway. Panicking, I throw a quick glamour over myself. With the wave of a hand, my red hair takes on a blonde hue and my clothes transform into those of a traveler. I don't really have much time to think about my appearance as the men breeze past me. I stand off to the side and try not to look too conspicuous.

My father comes out of the room. I duck my head a little more. When he bursts out laughing, I realize that I've been caught. When I look up, this man, this buttoned-up High Lord, is bent over, gasping for breath as his lungs force him to keep laughing. It goes on for so long that it starts to make me uncomfortable. When he finally gets some air, he speaks. "Oh, Grace. If you're going to put up a disguise, you have to remember to concentrate on a singular image. Your face…" He laughs. "You need to look in the mirror." He gestures to the mirror behind me.

When I turn around, I groan. "Oh, by the Lady…" My eyes are mismatched colors, one primary blue and one neon green. My hair is fully blonde, but my reddish roots are shining through on the top of my head. The skin on my neck is two different shades of white. I drop the glamour and watch my features return to normal. "Well, you caught me, I guess," I concede as I turn around to face my father.

"How long were you listening?" he asks.

"For a while," I answer honestly. "I don't know how long you were talking with the others. I came inside and I heard you and wanted to know what was going on."

Father looks at me curiously before giving me somewhat of an amused smile. "Come with me, Grace." He beckons for me to follow him up the stairs. I comply. He leads me up to his private floor, an area of the castle I have yet to explore. He unlocks the main door with a key before leading me down a short hallway to a set of double doors. With a flick of his hand, he swings them open, and for the first time, I enter my father's private office.

As he moves towards the back wall, I stand by the door, hands tightly clasped behind my back. I resist the urge to bounce on the balls of my feet. Instead, I take a moment to look around the room. It's a beautiful office filled with fine cherry wood furniture and paneling along the lower half of the room. The bookshelves along either side of the wall are filled with thick, heavy books that span from end to end, and the big windows behind the desk bring in so much sunlight. I would have loved to study in this room growing up. I wonder if Neil ever got to work here.

My father moves to a cabinet in the corner of the room and opens it. To my surprise, he pulls out a tall glass decanter of wine. He sets it on the large desk and follows it with two glasses. They clink together softly. "Sit down, Grace."

Intrigued, I pull a second chair over from the side of the room and sink into it. My father doesn't say a word, only methodically uncorks the decanter and pours the wine into each of the glasses. He settles into his chair and takes a slow careful drink. "This is the finest wine in the House of the Evening. Try a sip," he urges.

I bring the glass to my lips and drink. The flavor is sweet and rich. I wish I knew the right words to use as my father looks expectedly for a reaction. I settle on saying, "It's pretty good."

He nods absentmindedly. "Grace, I'm going to cut to the point." I tense up. "I need you to trust me and know that I will give you the information that you need regarding this war."

"I can't do that, Father," I respond quietly. "I can't. This is too important."

"Grace…" He sighs. "You may be the heir now, but there is so much you don't understand."

"Then tell me. Don't keep sending me off to other people to teach me. I should be in the room, hearing what you hear."

"Customarily, meetings of war are conducted between High Lords and High Ladies, the heads of the Houses. Heirs are not informed; they often take care of the daily issues while the leader focuses on the war effort."

"Then why haven't I been taking care of that?"

"Because you're not ready. Your training is coming along well, but I'm not so naive to think you can take on everything right now." I have no response to that because unfortunately, he is right. I glare at his chest.

My father chuckles at me. "You have a spark in you, my child. I've been watching you over the past season. Sneaking out of your political lessons, from what I hear, demonstrating some significant power in your magic lessons, and spying on your father in the middle of a meeting?" He laughs out loud. "I was just like you as a kid."

I bite my lip and study the man across from me. Behind closed doors, he's lost his stoicism. A soft, peaceful smile tugs his face as he reminisces, and I can't help but smile a little. His body is relaxed, leaned back against the chair, and his grip is loose on the glass of wine. The man's entire aura is completely different from anything I have seen thus far. *Is this bonding? Is this what it is supposed to be like between a father and daughter?*

"Do you really see a lot of yourself in me?" I find myself asking.

"Quite a bit," he answers immediately. "You have my eyes. You have my curious nature, my swift processing. I see it in you every time you step out into the noble world. Or lurk outside of it."

I chuckle but bite my lip again before daring to ask another question, "Father?" He nods to me as he takes another drink. "If you had known… that you had a child with my mother… would you have come back for me?"

The High Lord falls quiet. His eyes look far away to a time long gone now. Then he drains the entire rest of his glass and pours himself another one. The wine tinkling into the glass is the only sound in the room. My father takes one more drink before finally answering. "Grace…" He sighs. "I would like to think I would have come for you. I would like to think that I would have thrown out what my family wanted for me and brought you into my home, half-mortal and all. I certainly would have told you who I was and prepared you much earlier for what life was going to be like. No matter which way it had gone. But we can't change the past."

"No, we can't." I sip my drink and look up into his eyes. "But I would like to think… that I would have loved you." I see a warmness in my father's eyes that I haven't seen before. He reaches over and pats my head lightly. I summon the courage to blurt out the burning question in my chest that I have had ever since I arrived here. "Tell me about my mother?"

He looks at me with the most appalled expression I have ever seen on a man's face. I openly cringe. "I… I'm sorry," I quickly interject. *Great. I've ruined the moment.*

"No," my father says gently. "No, it's alright. The question was just unexpected. What would you like to know?"

I swallow loudly. "What was she like when she was younger?"

My father leans back against his chair. "Amelia… she was so bright. She was one of the most creative people I have ever met. Her paintings had such emotion to them; the colors practically jumped off the page and touched your heart. Does she still paint?"

"Yes," I answer quietly. "A little. Less since my brother died."

"Ah." My father looks down at his lap. "I'm sorry to hear that."

"When you met her," I begin slowly, "what made you choose… her?"

The High Lord chuckles. "You mean what made me sleep with a mortal woman?"

I blush. "Not in so many words."

"Everyone has been asking me that question since that day of the duel. And I haven't been able to give them a good answer. All I can say is that… mortals, as much as we have tried to separate ourselves from them… many of them are positive, constructive members of society. They have creativity and fire… and we can't discount that." My father reaches over and brushes my cheek. "I wouldn't have you, now would I?" We smile at each other. As he settles back into his seat, he changes the subject. "Is there anything in your lessons giving you trouble?"

"Flying is rough."

"Ah yes, flying," my father chuckles. "That used to happen to me when I first started learning. Try to think about moving with the wind as you would with wind elemental magic. Let me tell you about this one time when I first started using my flight magic…"

As he recounts his childhood mishaps, I smile and take another sip of my drink. Perhaps if I listen closely enough, I can find something of myself in my father. Something to hold on to as we navigate this war.

Chapter Seventeen

Although my recent connection with my father kindled some small progress, it isn't enough for him to take me under his wing. Talon and I continue with our war training instead. Luckily, with my father holed up in the palace most of the time, we can use the arena often. We alternate between specific magic lessons and all-out brawl sessions. Each spar gets more intense, for me at least. I'm getting my ass kicked. Talon is quite the warrior. I'll have to pick his brain sometime on how he learned those skills.

The catch on all this is that while Talon agrees to keep giving me sneaky sparring sessions, I must take part in some specific experiments he wants to run on me and my magic. That time finally arrives when I receive a note slid under my door one morning. *Meet me upstairs at midday. Far west attic.* Seeing as I didn't even know this palace had an attic, let alone multiple attics, it takes me a while to find it. I wander upstairs through a winding set of staircases and empty passageways until I see Talon's head pop out of a doorway.

"Where have you been?" he says, waving a hand. "Get in here."

I rush over. "Couldn't find this place to save my life. Why are we up here?"

Talon motions for me to take a seat at a chair that he has set up over by a small round window that faces off the side of the mountain. "It's private, it's tucked away, and we are less likely to be caught."

I raise an eyebrow. "Should I be concerned?"

"No, no, it's just… frowned upon. Not illegal."

"But dangerous?"

The man shrugs. "A little." He motions to the chair again. "Sit, sit." I sit down and spin around to look at him, but he spins me back around to face the window. He crouches in front of me. "Alright, this is how this is going to work. I want to test your magical endurance. Every Fae has their magical limit using a particular skill. Magical exhaustion can come quickly when a lot of magic is used at once or when one skill is used over an extended period." I nod slowly, trying to take all the information in.

Talon's eyes light up. "But you… you have mortal blood running through you. If the legend of the Half-Fae Coven is accurate…" *Oh, my friend, we have things to talk about,* I think as I remember my time in the Lower Realm. "Half-Fae blood is significantly more powerful. It is possible you could have a higher capacity for maintaining magical strengths. So I want to run a test on that. I have been wanting to try this for a while, but I needed to come up with the proper experiment given your magic. Are you comfortable with that? "

I chuckle a bit. "It depends on what you want me to do."

Talon shakes his head. "Oh, right. I want you to try to maintain an environment of wind around you. I thought that was probably better than trying fire. Try keeping a steady breeze around you: not too strong, not too light. I will monitor your progress and make some notes as time goes on."

"How long do you want me to maintain the spell?"

"As long as it takes."

"For what?"

"I'm not sure. I'll know when I see it." Talon moves behind me and stands back by the door. "I'm gonna keep guard over here. You focus on you and your magic. Go ahead!"

I'm a little skeptical. I am not exactly sure what's going to happen here, but hey, if Talon thinks it will reveal something about half-Fae, I could use the information myself. Shifting in my seat, I focus my gaze out the window at the blooming landscape. With a soft puff of breath, I gather myself and summon a reasonable breeze. The cool air moves around until it is a self-contained space of swirling wind. Then I wait.

At this stage in my training, it doesn't take much to keep the wind sustained. It feels very much like a windy day outside. I can then shift to looking out the window. I don't think I'll ever get tired of the view from the palace. Everything is bright and colorful in the sunlight, and something about it feels wondrous. I draw on the strength of the environment to fuel my magic. Eventually, I slip into a bit of a trance.

I am comfortable here, reflecting on what I can see and absorb and feeling my magic flow around me. As I mentally soar high above the space, I am at peace. I have never felt this relaxed. My magic and my mind work together to keep me in some sort of stasis. I am aware of the environment outside and the magic flowing through me, but nothing else. Minutes go by like seconds.

Grace.

I think I hear Leo's voice somewhere in the distance. It breaks my concentration a bit, but the wind only dies down slightly.

Grace!

That's not Leo's voice. Why do I feel faint?

"Grace!" Talon's voice and a hard shake of my shoulders jerk me back to the present. I sink into the back of the chair as a wave of exhaustion descends over me. When I look up to the window, I am shocked to find a dark sky. My head pounds.

"What…" My voice is weak. "What happened here?"

"Here, drink this." He presses a glass of water into my hand, and I drink it greedily. It soothes my dry throat.

"How long was I under?"

"Twelve hours," Talon says with this unfamiliar reverence in his voice. "You lasted twelve hours." I feel a brief prick of a needle against my finger and vaguely watch Talon drop my blood into a vial of clear liquid. The substance turns a pale shade of lavender. "And your magic still isn't depleted fully. You have so much more power than I previously thought. I have so many questions I can't—"

I want to listen to what he has to say, but if I don't lie down soon, I feel like I am going to faint. "Talon," I manage to force out. "Can you… I don't think I can stay upright."

Luckily, he sees my distress and pulls me up from the chair. "Oh… right. Sorry. I'm an idiot, by the Lady. I gotta take you downstairs." I chuckle but let him fuss over me for a while. He forces me to drink the entire glass of water before getting me another. Then we hobble down the few floors to my bedroom where he tells me to stay hidden until I have fully recovered.

By the Lady, I'm tired.

Chapter Eighteen

I sleep for almost two days after the experiment. Talon makes excuses to cover for me for both our lessons and family meals. He told my father that we went a little too hard during one day of practice, and I was injured. He got an earful and was nearly thrown out. Luckily, he was able to talk the High Lord down by swearing on the Lady to be much more careful with me. I'll have to ask him how he managed that sometime.

When I wake again, my body throbs as if I have been run over by a carriage. Getting up takes as much energy as I have. Talon later tells me in the library that it is possible we went too far. "Your magic lasts longer in a hypnotic state than anyone I have ever read about," he praises as I eat my first meal in a while. "However, when it is over, you need a significant recovery time. I haven't determined yet whether or not it is longer or shorter for you; we would need to run more tests." At my incredulous look, he reassures me that we will be taking a little time off before trying again.

When I feel stronger after a few more days of light studying, I go searching for my father. I want to speak to him a little more about playing a bigger role in domestic affairs. I scour the upstairs floors in search of him. But he's nowhere to be found: not in his bedroom or the library or any of the various specialty rooms upstairs like the theater or the gallery. I make my way down to the first floor. No one in the throne room or the banquet hall, so I try the little garden off the tearoom. Occasionally, my father told me, he hides out in here for a quiet afternoon with a cup of tea and a pastry of some kind.

But when I enter the room, all I find is Neil sitting by himself at the table outside. I stop short as soon as I cross over the threshold. "What are you doing here?" he scoffs at me.

By the Lady, I do not want to get into it with him today. "I'm just looking for Dad," I answer shortly.

"Well, he's not here," Neil snaps.

"Do you know where he is?"

"No idea, now why don't you fuck off?"

I grit my teeth. "Fine." I turn to leave, but I just can't help myself. He makes me so angry. "What is your problem? I've been here for months at this point. Get over yourself and your petty grudges. In case you haven't noticed, there's a war going on."

"Do you have any idea what it has been like since you have been here?" Neil asks me incredulously.

"Has it been rough? Has it been rough for you, Neil? What do you think it's been like for me trying to become a Fae in less than three months?" I cannot believe the audacity of this man.

"Try getting your entire life ripped away from you by somebody you don't even know, a sister who you have never seen!" Neil shouts. "Try preparing your whole life to be the perfect heir for your father to find out that he's decided, you know what, fuck you, my bastard daughter is older and therefore Fae law says she gets to be High Lady!"

"At least you had a father," I hiss. "At least you grew up with your family complete. You knew exactly what you were getting into from birth. I had no father. I had my brother and my mother, and I lost them both. One's dead, and one doesn't even know I'm alive!"

"Oh boohoo," Neil mocks. "You're going to be a Fae queen. Everything you could possibly want was just laid out in front of you."

"Neil, I am so tired of telling you that I didn't ask for any of this." I chuckle dryly. "I fought to get into this realm, and then I fought a bunch of heirs trying to get out of this realm, and then I shot fire out of my hands and blew up an arena. You knew magic. You knew you had magic from the moment you were born. I had to find out at 19 that I have it, I'm a Lady of the House of the Evening, and heir to a lorddom."

"Don't flip this around on me, Grace." He pushes a harsh breath through gritted teeth before continuing, "You have to understand. I was going to lead this world. I needed to lead this world. And now you have taken everything I have ever wanted and everything I have ever worked for and now it is… I don't know what to do now!" He throws his hands up and walks a little way off from me, shaking his head.

I take a moment to think over what he is saying. On one hand, I'm pretty sure he's an asshole. I mean, he's done everything he can to sabotage my ascent. He fought with me, nearly killed me when I wasn't prepared. He hasn't given me one ounce of support in this family; he is nothing like Leo. And he hates me for something I can't control. I didn't even want this fucking title! But if I really dig deep, I can find a shred of compassion in my bones for Neil. I can't imagine what it must feel like to be the heir and then some bastard child comes and takes it all away. Before all of this, before I even came to this realm, I couldn't see any future after my mission to avenge Leo. My brain was so goal-focused. How can I blame Neil for being the same way?

When it comes down to it, maybe he's just protecting his interests. And I am very much in the way.

"Look…" I finally say. "I can't apologize for what I didn't cause. If you have a problem with the way I was thrust into the heirship, take it up with our father. Better yet, take it up with the fucking law.

Because I agree with you in principle: this is some fucked up shit. I don't belong here. But I'm stuck here trying to play politics because I can't go home. I can't go home again." I tighten my jaw as the words sink in. *I gotta refrain from saying that out loud.*

"Why can't you go home?" Neil snarks. "What's stopping you?"

"Our father says that my uncontrolled magic is dangerous for my mother. That I could kill her by mistake just from a… a simple motion. I can't be held responsible for that, Neil. I won't be. Not after everything we've been through."

"Did you kill your brother?"

"No!" I shout at him, my fury blowing past my will to hold it back. "How dare you say that!"

"Do you really think your mortal brother would approve of you abandoning your mother to pretend to be a Fae?"

"He would have understood." I barely restrain myself from lunging at him. "He would have been proud of me. He would have supported my magic lessons; hell, he would have joined me here himself. And he would have told me to run with it and revolutionize the House of the Evening in any way I wanted because it was my fucking lorddom to command. And you had better hope that I don't take his advice from beyond the grave."

We glower at each other in a standoff. Neither moves until a voice comes from the doorway. "Excuse me, Lady Grace?" I glance sideways to see one of the front entry attendants standing by the door.

I look back over at Neil, who still looks quite irritated, and take a deep breath. "What is it?" I manage with some semblance of politeness.

"There is a package for you." He holds out a small box to me. I instantly recognize the shape and practically snatch it from the man's hands. *By the Lady, Aiden.*

"Thank you, sir." I reply quickly. He nods and exits. I move to follow him out myself, but Neil suddenly slides in front of me and blocks the door. "Neil, get out of my way."

"No," he says firmly.

"Neil, move! It's important!" I shout at him.

"This is the second package you have received in the last week. What is in that box?"

"What, are you spying on my mail now?" *Who does this man think he is?* "Neil, if you don't move out of my way, I'm going to…"

"You're going to do what? Throw me? Curse me? You may be getting better, but you're still nowhere near in control of your magic. Now you can show me what's in the box, or I can force it out of your hands. Take your pick."

I grit my teeth and weigh my options. I don't want him to know everything that I know, but I also don't want him to see what's in this package. He could break it. I take a deep breath. "I need you to keep this a secret. It could get people killed."

Neil crosses his arms. "Maybe. No promises."

I resist the urge to growl. I break open the box and pull out another telepathic orb. Neil's eyes widen somewhat. With a bit of hesitation, I grasp the ball and concentrate hard.

"Grace, you have got to get your father to call off the aid now," Aiden's frantic voice booms in my ears so loudly I almost drop the ball. "My father has been briefed on every movement of your alliance by a rogue operative. The House of the Sun had a spy in the House of the Moon. He knows, Grace. He knows every movement your family is about to make. They're planning a massive scale attack and an ambush; you've got to reroute now."

The glass tumbles out of my hands, only being saved from shattering by Neil who dove to the ground to catch it. I start and stare at him down on the ground underneath me. We lock eyes. "What just happened?" Neil asks. "Something happened. What did you—"

"The House of the Sun had a spy," I blurt out. The truth seems like the easiest thing to say now as a million thoughts race through my head. "There's going to be an attack," I speak fast. "Aiden just told me. The House of Darkness is lying in wait."

"You gotta tell Dad." He shoves the orb into my hand and takes off down the hallway, shouting for our father. I run after him. We sprint towards the throne room. At that moment, we are unified in our efforts, holding doors for each other and shouting at people to get out of the way.

"What the hell is going on, Grace?" he hisses at me as we navigate the palace halls.

"Look, I'll tell you what I can when we find Dad, okay?" Since we're somewhat on the same page now and he is helping me stop this movement, I suppose I can tell him a couple things. Or at least enough that he won't ask too many other questions. Gripping the glass orb in my hand, I reach out to Aiden telepathically again. But this time, he doesn't answer. Panic grips my lungs. *What if something happened to him? What if he got caught?*

When Neil and I reach the throne room, I curse loudly at the emptiness. Neil runs out to the hallway. "Grace! Over here!" My heart leaps in my chest as I dare to hope, but it immediately drops to my stomach when I round the corner to see my stepmother.

"What is the problem here?" she says shortly.

"I need to talk to my father," I insist.

"The High Lord has been gone for a couple hours now," she replies while glancing sideways at her son.

"A couple hours?" Neil interjects.

No. I rock back on my heels. "Where did they go?"

"There was a change in plans," Elise snaps at me. "The High Lord and the others went to meet a delegation from the House of the Day to discuss military affairs. What does this matter to you?"

I can't take her tone anymore. I turn around and storm back into the throne room. "Mom…" I hear Neil admonish her lightly from the hallway. "It was important." I don't hear anything else after that as they walk a little way from me to have a private conversation. I sit down on the steps to the thrones and drop my head into my hands. I have no idea what to do now.

"What should we do?" I hear Neil walk in. "We have to get the information to him."

"Are there any telepaths in the palace?"

He shakes his head. "No one with a high enough level for that distance of telepathy."

"Then there's nothing we can do but wait," I answer quietly. We wait for a long time, sitting there in silence. I don't think either of us had any idea what to say. But an answer does not arrive.

* * *

I try to contact Aiden via telepathy all night. It doesn't work; I don't even get a flash of emotion from him, let alone a word. I don't sleep. Instead, I sit up in bed with my back against the headboard turning the glass in my hands repeatedly, hoping for a change. I hate how it makes me feel. Aiden can certainly hold his own in this realm, but it doesn't make it any easier. I hope he's alright.

And I hope my father is alright. It takes a full three days for any news to arrive, much longer than it should have taken for the High Lord and the soldiers he took with him to return to the House of the Evening. Neil spends the entire time in the throne room pacing back and forth. I wait in the front hall. After our fight and the ensuing madness of the war, I'm not taking any chances that Neil's walls around his volatility will slip and we'll end up in another brawl.

Eventually, the front door opens wide, and a multitude of people rush inside. I leap to my feet from sitting on the stairs and Neil runs into the hall. I hold my breath, and I can feel Neil holding his breath behind me. My father walks inside, surrounded by officials on either side, and we both take several steps back in relief. The man is haggard, but his face retains its color, and he moves towards the throne room with purpose. Everyone in the hall smells like sweat and dirt. Several of the officials file into the throne room behind my father, and Neil and I follow quickly behind.

"Father, are you alright?" Neil speaks up first and reaches the man before I can. Hand on his arm, he guides our father into his throne. The High Lord sinks into it in exhaustion.

"Dad?" I move over by his feet. "Are you alright?"

He waves off the officials, mumbling something unintelligible to them. They leave the room.

"Yes," he finally answers. "I'm alright."

"What happened?" Neil and I ask almost simultaneously.

Our father takes a slow breath, rubbing at the bridge of his nose. "We were blindsided. The House of the Sun came up from the west to meet us at the bottom of the mountain. We thought they were coming to join us too. But… but the soldiers started to attack. We had no choice but to flee."

Neil runs a hand over his face, settling it on the back of his head, before taking a step off the platform and taking a lap pacing around the room. I take a deep breath and squeeze my eyes shut. The thought of watching an ally supposedly come to our aid and turn on us causes me physical pain. "How many did you lose?" I ask softly.

"Not as many as we could have. We fell back in time."

"What about the delegation from the House of the Day?" Neil's voice echoes from the other side of the room. We both look up at him, and his face is twisted in this strange contortion.

"I received word from a messenger as we arrived that the House of

Darkness swept in while we were distracted. The House of the Day has fallen."

"So that's two." Neil raises his voice in a heightened sense of panic. "Two houses under the House of Darkness's control?"

"Five," I breathe.

My father looks down at me. "What do you mean five?"

I stand up and move in between them, looking to either side of me as I speak. "Five under the *leadership* of the House of Darkness. The House of Fire and the House of the Sun may be allied with them for now, but… we all know that the House of Darkness won't just split their haul lightly." I remember the maps and contracts that Aiden and I found in the secret library room. "My theory would be that even if there is some sort of agreement for a fair split, it comes with a promise of loyalty to High Lord Carron. So that puts five under his purview: House of Darkness, House of Fire, House of the Sun, House of the Day, and House of the Earth."

The High Lord leans back in his throne, slumping. Judging by his expression, I sincerely wonder whether I have made things ten times worse by pointing that out. "You're right," he says quietly. "It's going to get a lot worse."

"It's almost half of the realm." Neil slowly comes around to the realization. "Maybe this will convince the others to join us now."

"We're going to have to," I agree. "There is no way we can make it with just us and the Moon and Wind. We should send word to the others."

"Can you and Neil start that?" My father pushes himself out of his throne and to his feet. There is a little more color in his face and much more drive in his eyes. "Go to my study and write letters on my stationary. Neil, you know where the wax seal is?" Neil nods. "Send notices off to the other Houses, and I'll have my people ride out tonight to get them delivered. Can I trust you two to work together for once?"

Neil and I lock eyes again. "Yes," he says as he nods to me begrudgingly.

"Yes," I echo.

"Alright. Get going then. To my office."

Neil and I take off towards the study to get to work.

Chapter Nineteen

The next few weeks are more chaotic than I've ever faced in the Middle Realm. Neil and I worked through the night on that very same day the House of the Day fell and got notices out to every other House outside of the House of Darkness's alliance. Within days, word began pouring in that the High Lords and their attendants would be on their way to the House of the Evening to formally instigate the full War Council. All I could think was *it was about damn time.* I could not understand why they decided to delay action after the House of the Earth fell. I hope we haven't screwed ourselves with such a time delay.

One by one, we get official caravan after caravan as each of the Houses arrives. The castle is soon packed with foreign nobles and servants. I will never understand why one High Lord requires so many attendants. The influx of people has changed so much about the way things operate in the palace from day to day. It has caused quite a confusion down in the servants' quarters with regards to who is supposed to be attending to who and who is in charge. I try not to call for anyone unless I absolutely have to. They have enough on their hands as it is. Each visiting group of servants is trying to attend to their own High Lord while also supporting the general household while the House of the Evening's servants is taking care of us and everyone else.

I wait for something to happen, but the Council drags their feet. Of course, only the High Lords sit in on these meetings, so I don't know all the details. But from what I can glean from my father, no progress has been made on battle plans or where to send aid. In fact, nothing eventful happens until… well… until Aiden arrives.

After trying to make sense of magic theory in the library, I come downstairs to the front hall and make my way towards the entrance to take a walk into town. I nod to the door attendants as they pull the door open for me. But before I can get out the door, I see a man on a horse galloping up the road to the palace at top speed. The guards stationed in the courtyard shout at him to stop, but he doesn't. They ready their weapons and their magic, and I start to back up into the palace. But then I catch a glimpse of blond hair and hear a familiar shout. "Asylum!"

I run outside, screaming. *"Hey! Don't touch him! Don't touch him!"* Aiden reaches the top of the courtyard and jumps off his horse. The guards rush him, firing off a round of assorted magic, elemental and energy. Reacting on instinct, I throw a desperate force field at the Fae man, and to my surprise, it lands and holds. The magic bounces off harmlessly. I would have been impressed with my newfound abilities if the guards had not physically rushed through and grabbed him. Holding him by his arms, they drag him towards the palace as he struggles.

"Let go of him!" I shout as I run up to them. "Aiden!" I reach out for him, but I am sidestepped and circumvented by the men. I rush behind them all the way to the throne room where my father sits in discussion with several of the other High Lords. They scatter to the edges of the room as Aiden is roughly brought in.

My father's guards drag Aiden before him, and I rush to his side. "Aiden!" I yell. Angrily, I turn to the guards. "Let go of him now!"

"Grace, it's alright," he insists. "Don't worry about me."

I whip around to my father. "Father, I need to…."

"Not now, Grace," he interrupts me. "I want to hear the young man speak." His tone seems much harsher than usual, that voice that tells me that this idea isn't up for discussion. I don't know if I agree, but I will keep my mouth shut for now. With a quick squeeze of Aiden's hand, I step back and stand next to my father. The High Lord doesn't even look at me. "Why have you come to the House of the Evening, Lord Aiden?"

Aiden gulps as he raises his head to look my father in the eye. "High Lord Alexander, I am here to formally request sanctuary from the House of the Evening."

"On what grounds?"

"On grounds of war refuge."

My father nods. "State your case."

Without missing a beat, Aiden speaks passionately. "My father and brother have fallen in line with the House of Darkness and the House of Fire. It violates everything I believe in about the spirit of the alliances, the spirit of fair play, and what I know is best for my House. I do not want to be anywhere near that fallout. I want to be here on your side offering my skills to help your war effort."

"What evidence can you bring that we can trust you?" the High Lord then asks. "How do I know that you're not going to take whatever you hear in these walls and send it back to your father?" I watch Aiden's eyes carefully as I am also interested in how he is going to answer this. But the flicking left and right of his eyes alerts me to the fact that he has no idea how to respond. As his mouth slowly shifts to a grimace, I suddenly grasp that he didn't realize exactly how much his father's actions could taint him.

"I…" he stutters.

"I'll vouch for him," I blurt out. The guards, Aiden, and my father all stare at me. My father's face is unreadable.

"That's not protocol, Grace," my father responds sternly.

"Actually, according to the texts you keep so lovingly pushing me to study, any person who comes before the High Lord and pleas sanctuary can have a witness speak for them," I retort evenly.

The room falls silent for a moment. I see a hint of a smile on my father's face. "No Lady has ever pleaded the case of a refugee before."

"I don't mind being first."

I get a chuckle from my father for that. "Go ahead then." He motions for me to step in front of him. I move down alongside Aiden. He gives me a little smile of reassurance.

"Aiden is one of the most valiant soldiers of the House of the Sun's army. He knows the other soldiers, their generals, how they operate, and what their tactics are. Aiden and I have worked together on several infiltration missions. We fought our way through hell and back again. He also fought to get me a message from the House of the Sun to here, warning us that they had betrayed us and sided with the enemy. If you hadn't left already, it would have been he who prevented it." The people around us murmur. I continue, "Is it not more of a testament to the fact that he can be trusted not to bring information back to his father that he escaped the House of the Sun and traveled all the way here to be put on trial through House of Darkness conquered territory?"

When I see my father slowly start to tilt his head, I know I've got them. "I would vouch for him any day, anywhere," I finish strongly. "I trust him, and so can you. He won't betray us or our army. He should be granted sanctuary not just for his benefits, but for ours." I wave off the guards again, and finally, they let go of Aiden. "I ask that you grant him asylum."

The High Lord studies us carefully for what seems like an eternity. Finally, he nods. "Aiden Çaelic, I will grant you asylum in the House of the Evening. You will stay here in the palace and assist us in the war effort, particularly alongside Lady Grace. I will require every bit of information from you that you can give me about the House of the Sun and your father's intentions with the Houses of Darkness and Fire. If I find that you have been hiding anything, I will immediately revoke that offer and you will be a prisoner of this House."

I sigh in relief and drop a slight bow to my father. "Thank you," I insist. "Thank you, Father." When I look over to Aiden, he gives me a quick flick of his eyes toward the ceiling. I send a telepathic message to him to follow me upstairs. I turn to leave, and he takes a few steps to follow.

"Don't take him away just yet, Grace," my father interrupts. "I would like to speak to Aiden and learn what he knows first." I hesitate to leave Aiden alone to weather the officials, but his little nod and smile reassure me. I acknowledge my father and then leave the room.

* * *

I don't know how to take up the time between when I leave Aiden in the throne room and when he eventually makes his way to me. I contemplate going to the library to study as a distraction, but I know it won't be enough. I could go to the music room and bury myself in some music. But it wouldn't calm the swirling thoughts in my head and the pounding in my chest. Instead, I decide to go to my bedroom, shut the door, and just… wait. Hours pass. I wonder if I should get up and do something else, but I can't bring myself to be somewhere else in case Aiden arrives. I play my violin, I keep in my room, I run a bath, I walk onto the balcony and watch the day roll by. Time moves so slowly.

When the knock finally comes at my door, I am more than ready for it. Rushing over, I flip open the lock and throw the door wide open. Aiden wastes no time in storming into my room and into my personal space, sweeping me off my feet in a passionate kiss. My heart tries to leap out of my chest. I barely have time to kick the door closed and flip the lock before he pulls me down to my bed, me on top. Our lips break apart as he rolls me over before finding mine again. We kiss for a long time: sometimes heated and passionate and other times slow and methodical.

I have never seen Aiden this excitable, but I can't say I mind.

When we break for air, my heart melts a little at the sight of his thoroughly ruffled hair. "Hi," I whisper.

Aiden smiles at me. "Hi."

We embrace and lay together for a long time. I rest my head on his chest, and he presses his head against mine. Aiden doesn't leave my room that night; instead, we relish some time alone away from the chaos of the war outside these walls. After he falls asleep, I lay awake on his chest, tracing softly over his skin. I have no idea where we're going from here. I don't know what my father needs from me or Aiden or what the war needs from us. And that damn prophecy keeps playing on repeat in my mind the more the war develops. All I know is that Aiden is here beside me, and nothing here, not in this realm or the next, is going to break us apart.

Chapter Twenty

When the sun streams in through the window, I open my eyes slowly and roll over to look at the man beside me. A tiny smile crosses my lips as I study Aiden's beautiful sleeping face. After the Spring Solstice, I felt like we had been ripped apart before either of us was ready. To see his chest breathing now beside me feels like the biggest weight lifting off my shoulders.

Aiden shifts onto his side to face me and opens his eyes. A warm and somewhat smug smile spreads across his face. "Hi," he whispers.

I resist the urge to giggle. "Hi," I whisper back. Aiden grins and leans forward to kiss me. I hum lightly against his lips.

When he pulls away, he presses a soft kiss to my forehead. "Hell of a night, huh?"

"I'm just glad you're here now," I answer.

"As am I, Lady Grace." He smirks.

I groan. "By the Lady, please don't call me that in bed." Aiden laughs at my misery.

"What happens now?" he asks as he slips a hand under the covers to caress my hip.

I roll my eyes at him. "No more of that. Not now at least." I ignore Aiden's little pout. "We need to sneak you out of here before anyone knows we spent the night together."

"You're not ready to show me off?"

I chuckle. "My father just offered you asylum here; I'd rather he not throw you out on the first day. Besides, we need to talk strategy in the library. Can you meet me there in an hour?"

"Why an hour? We could go there right now."

"I want breakfast. And a hot bath. Not necessarily in that order."

Aiden laughs out loud as he stands up, looking quite proud of himself. He gathers his clothes and slips them on. "I might do that myself. But in my own room. Unless…"

"Out!" I scold him and point him toward the door. With a little wink, he exits my room.

I can't help but smile at his antics before climbing out of bed to pick up all the clothes off the floor and turn on the bath.

After a bath and a solid breakfast, I make my way to the library to meet Aiden. He's already sitting at a table, looking much fresher and more awake than when he left my room. "Did you make it to your room alright?" I ask with a smile.

"Oh yeah," he assures me. "Didn't get spotted by anyone. Even messed up the sheets a bit to make it look like I slept there."

I chuckle as I take a seat next to him. "Let's get down to it. What did you share with my father?"

"Essentially everything you and I found in that room in the library," Aiden says as he settles back into his chair. "I told him how long the alliance had been going on, the ins and outs of the House of the Sun's palace and troop movements in general. Talked about my time serving with them and what a few outposts looked like in other Houses. Told him about everything except the prophecy."

I nod once. "Good. That all sounds good."

"It was rough, actually." Aiden's eyes gaze off into space. "I felt like I was betraying my friends, my superiors. I gave him what he needed, but I don't feel good about it."

"I'm sorry, Aiden." I pat his arm lightly, not knowing what else to do.

"What exactly is the plan in terms of the prophecy? Have you made any headway on who the other members might be?"

"Well, I've been a little busy learning magic and House of the Evening diplomacy," I call down from the library's ladder as I pull out a small notebook from in between the highest shelves. "So I haven't really had much time to figure that all out." With a push, I slide the ladder over to the edge and climb down. "But I do have a few ideas," I answer now more quietly. I sit next to Aiden at the table and open the notebook, sliding it over for him to see. On one page, I have written the entire prophecy in divided lines. On another, I have a few brief notes on the Houses and what magics may be associated with those places. Amidst my studies, I have been attempting to compile this information whenever I find it. It's not a complete list, but it's a start.

"We need eight members, right?" I continue. "And we know we are two of them. Which two is unclear. But I figure, we're looking for people with some serious power and some type of special quality that puts them into one of these eight categories."

Aiden nods. "I'm thinking you're the ringleader, the Enchantress."

"Oh no, I'm praying to the Lady that it is not me. I can't lead this group into battle, I'm not even fully Fae!"

"What if that's the point?" Aiden proposes. "You are one of the most powerful mages in several generations of noble Fae, right? Sure, you can't control it yet but…" He laughs as I punch him hard in the arm. "But you've got something special in you. The Enchantress is the one who is supposed to "unite the mages". You're the one finding all of these people. Then once they're here, I think you're going to be the one to organize us."

I sigh loudly. "Let's leave that conversation for another day. Can we pick out somebody who might fall into one of these descriptions? You know these families a lot better than I do."

Aiden falls silent then and scans the page. He flips it over to show the next set of notes. He taps his fingers against the table. "What about Aira?"

"Aira? Lady of the House of Wind?" I flip over to my notes on her. "What kind of magic does she have?"

"Uhhh… off the top of my head, I can remember wind, flight, healing… a little empathetic magic. I can't remember all of it; it's just what I can remember her showing off."

"Hey," I whisper softly. "The House of Wind is the only House with a High Lady."

"Yes, the first generation of solely High Lady leading."

"The lost child… the strongest of the women's breed… Aira doesn't know who her father is, does she?"

Aiden rubs the back of his neck. "Be careful bringing that up. It's kind of a taboo subject in the Upper Realm. Bastard children don't really… become heirs." I give him a pointed look. "No offense," he quickly adds.

"Uhuh…" I trail off. *Another bastard heir, huh... this, I want to see.* "So what should we do about her? How should we contact her?"

"I think we should head up there," Aiden suggests. "High Lady Morgana mentioned in our little meeting yesterday that she is planning on going home for a day or two to take care of a few things at home. If we talk to your dad and make up an excuse, we might be able to hitch a ride with her."

"What would we say?"

"Diplomatic show of strength. Reassure the people of the House of Wind that this alliance for aid is worth it."

I nod. "Alright. Let's do it."

Aiden reaches over and takes my hand. "We can present the plan at dinner tonight. For now, can I interest you in a walk around town, Lady Grace?"

I chuckle. "Why, of course, Lord Aiden." He pulls me to my feet and sweeps me out of the library.

Chapter Twenty-One

As High Lady Morgana's carriage rumbles up the steep path, I'm grateful that Aiden is next to me to stop me from sliding to one side. He grips one of my hands tightly in his, partially hidden by our sleeves to create a semblance of noble propriety. Though from the High Lady's continuous smug smile, it appears that she wouldn't mind public displays of affection from the two of us.

My father approved of our plan to visit the House of Wind to spread morale from the House of the Evening. Aiden's idea worked perfectly; I think the High Lord was quite impressed. I went ahead and let him present the plan himself because the Lady only knows he needed as many points as he could get after requesting asylum. He needed to establish himself. I silently curse Aiden's father for even putting him in the position of having to do that in the first place.

As the carriage shifts to a more level path, I look out the window to see the outskirts of the House of the Wind. The peaceful atmosphere relaxes me. I can hear a soft whisper of the wind through the slightly opened window; it moves the light-colored grasses and brightly colored flowers as we ride toward the city. We drive through mountain passages. I spot deer and wolves around every turn. Their eyes follow us as we pass by. When we reach civilization, bright buildings line the sides of the cobblestone street, short and colorful specialty shops interspersed with apartment buildings. There are open and airy squares and circles every so often throughout this stretch of road where traffic is diverted, and foot traffic takes precedence. Beautiful fountains and park areas sit in the middle of these places. The whole scene makes me smile.

The palace at the head of the street is quite striking to look at. The white base rises to an impressive height, blending in with the mountain it is sitting on. The royal blue towers stand out against the pale sky with matching streamers catching the breeze. If I squint my eyes, I can just make out glittering silver trim around the windows. The grounds extend out to the edge of a crystal lake, marked by similar white towers and structures. With a wave of High Lady Morgana's hand, a long glass drawbridge lowers out over the lake. We follow it all the way up to the palace door.

High Lady Morgana smiles graciously at us. "Welcome to the House of Wind, heirs. I hope you enjoy your stay." The driver opens the door to our carriage, and the woman steps out. Aiden and I follow and look up in awe at the beautiful smooth palace facade. It is much grander up close.

When we enter through the doors, we are greeted by a tall, rounded glass wall in the Great Room overlooking the mountains. The windows bring so much light into the room and illuminate the purely white tile pattern with pops of silver and blue tile intermittently. The hall is vast and open. The whole place is beautiful in its simplicity.

If I ever become High Lady, perhaps I'll redo the palace to be like this.

"Mother!" A young woman rushes into the room in a flash of silver hair. She wraps her arms tightly around her.

"Hello, darling," the High Lady replies affectionately as she hugs her daughter.

"You didn't send word you were coming home."

"Oh, I wanted it to be a surprise. I'm only here for a quick popover anyway; High Lord Alexander is expecting me back at the House of the Evening before long. Besides, I have brought people for you to see." The High Lady indicates to us over the woman's head.

When the daughter turns around, I am instantly drawn to her startling violet eyes. Her face is as pale as the tile around us, and it makes her eyes stand out even more. She seems shy, but curious as she grants Aiden and me a soft smile. "Oh!" She blushes. "Lord Aiden, Lady Grace, hello. I'm sorry I didn't see you."

"That's alright, Aira," Aiden says warmly before taking her hand and kissing the back of it gently. "It is wonderful to see you again."

"Of course," Aira smiles at him with a soft blush. I raise an eyebrow. *Is there something that used to be there?* She then turns to me. "Lady Grace, it was so unfortunate that I didn't get to speak with you at the Spring Solstice. I wanted to apologize for the debacle of the *previous* solstice. I..."

I wave off her apology. "It was a different time. I was an intruder; you were an heir tasked with taking care of the problem. Don't worry about it."

She smiles at me gratefully. "Well, we welcome you both to the House of Wind. How long will you be staying?"

"Only for a day or so." The High Lady walks towards the stairs. "I have a few things to arrange with my advisors." She makes her way upstairs and disappears around the corner. To my surprise though, she pokes her head back out... *through the wall* to continue talking to her daughter. "Aira, so why don't you show Aiden and Grace upstairs to the observatory? I'm sure you can keep them entertained until dinner, yes?" At my dropped jaw, Morgana only chuckles. "Quantum tunneling, dear. One of the rarer forms of magic. I'll show you what I can do sometime."

With a fluid movement, she exits once more.

"Yes, Mother," Aira calls to her mother before turning back to us with a smile. "Neither of you has been here, have you?" Aiden and

I shake our heads. "Oh, then you're going to love the observatory." With a beckoning hand, she motions for us to follow her upstairs.

We wind upstairs for more than a few floors; I count ten. Then we reach a point where the staircase splits into regular stairs and some sort of empty channel with bars on either side and wind supporting the space underneath. "Do either of you have wind magic?" I nod while Aiden shakes his head. "Grace, you might love this. This is the air lift that wind magic users can hop onto. It's mostly for my mom and I, but occasionally guests are able to use it." She steps into the open air, and the wind magic acts as a platform, gliding her up to the next floor. With a glance over my shoulder at Aiden, I step onto the breeze myself and laugh as I immediately begin moving up after Aira. Aiden grumbles as he is forced to jog up the stairs after us, much to my amusement.

We reach the highest point of the palace inside one of the towers. Aira leads us to a big set of heavy wooden double doors with silver engraving. With a grin, she pushes them open with a shove. When we step inside, the room is illuminated by a stunning glass mosaic dome ceiling with intricate gold metalworking in between each pane. It covers the entire span of the tower. The room is simple with a few shelves around the outside walls and two small benches on either side of the center of the room. In the middle of those benches sits a large map of the stars, only partially filled in. When I move closer to it, I notice it looks hand drawn.

"Whoa," Aiden breathes beside me. "This is incredible, Aira."

"This is my favorite place in the entire castle," Aira muses.

"Is this yours?" I indicate the map.

"Oh, yes." Aira tucks a curl behind her ear. "I've been working on my own atlas of the sky. I want to see if I can put it together myself before referring to the accepted version."

"Why is that?"

"I've always been fascinated by the stars. They are constantly moving, yet we can chart course by ship with them. I don't know exactly what I'm trying to find by doing this, but I'll know when I get there."

"That is amazing," I say. "How long have you been working on it?"

"Several months now. It has been such a fascinating project. I work up here most nights."

"How do you get things done around the castle?"

"My mom is very accommodating." Aira smiles. "She often lets me sleep in in the morning, and we work more on domestic issues in the afternoon and late evening."

Aiden whistles. "Man, I wish I had that option growing up. Dad was always trying to get me up to decide on policy at the crack of dawn."

"Oh no," Aira moans in sympathy. "My mother hates to be up at dawn. She likes that I'm a night owl like she is. Sometimes when she doesn't have work to do at night, she'll come up and sit with me while I chart, and we'll swap stories. Have you guys ever heard the legend about the founder of the House of Wind?" Both Aiden and I shake our heads. "Ohhh," she breathes. "I have to tell you."

She beckons for us to sit around her, and we oblige. "The House of the Wind was built by a simple mage with a piece of the souls of the Lady's children that she split during the Great War." It takes me a moment to put together where this fits in with the legend the Half-Fae Coven told Aiden and me in the Lower Realm. "He liked to build beautiful things with his own two hands, and his wind magic was soft and subtle. He fell in love with a high-born woman at first sight. She was a beautiful Fae whose wind magic was powerful enough to bring about thunderstorms and hurricanes with one flick of her finger. But as soon as the man got close to her, he lost his breath to her winds. He struggled to build up his own wind magic to be strong enough to get close to her, but no matter what he did, he was blown back. After months and months of attempting, he finally got fed up with waiting and forced himself through her magic to her. He fainted at her feet, clutching a letter that told of his feelings for her. When she read his words, she forced her magical life force to quiet, and she revived the man by putting the air back into his lungs. They became the first High Lord and Lady of the House of Wind."

"What a beautiful story," Aiden finally says after a moment of quiet.

"Yeah…" I echo.

The Lady of Wind smiles. "Now it's your turn. So… how exactly did you two meet? I have been wanting to ask this question ever since I found out you were a mortal. Or… I guess mortal blood now, right."

"Well, I got caught by him actually," I answer. "I was running from a group of soldiers who would have discovered my identity and ended running directly *into* a soldier who saved me from them, but discovered my identity anyway." I look over my shoulder at a smirking Aiden. "He listened to my story about why I was in the Upper Realm, to find answers about my brother's death, and he basically forced me into accepting his company. From there, the rest was history. We traipsed across multiple realms, gathering different pieces along the way. And… well, you know what happened at the end when we got caught. And all of that is what got us here."

"Wow…" Aira breathes. "What an adventure."

"Speaking of adventures…" Aiden looks pointedly at me. He indicates the Lady with a quick flick of his eyes. *Oh… right.*

"Yes," I shift my train of thought, "Aiden and I need to talk to you about something."

"Oh?" Aira takes a seat on one of the benches. "What about?"

I quickly take a seat in front of her. "Do you believe in prophecies?"

"Of course. They're like the foundation of all the best legends. And divination as a magic form. Why do you ask?"

"Well… what I'm going to say may sound a little far-fetched." I look at Aiden and he nods reassuringly at me. "During my time in the Lower Realm, Aiden and I heard a prophecy. It states that a group of eight mages with considerable power will team up to lead the Houses against the House of Darkness and its alliance to victory. These mages each have their own role and magical and personal attributes that make them uniquely suitable to the task. Aiden and I are two of those members. And we think you are one of them too." I pause there to give Aira time to process. Judging by the expression on her face, she needs it. There is a mix of confusion, fear… and what looks like intrigue.

"Which one do you think I am?" she asks tentatively.

"We think you're the Spinner," Aiden chimes in.

"The Spinner?"

"Spinner of tales and spinner of winds. She's a lost child… the strongest of the women's breed," I recite the prophecy line.

"Lost child? I'm not a lost…" As Aira trails off, I can see the recognition coming to her slowly. "And how could I be the strongest of the women's breed? There are so many other women who could fit that role better. But… I am a daughter of women like my mother. Maybe that's what it means. Lost child… I have no father. I see…" she muses to herself while tapping her fingers softly on her knees. "Do you have a copy of the prophecy with you?"

"Oh, I… we actually haven't written it down. We're not sure who to trust at this point. We can make you a copy, though you would have to keep it hidden."

"That's alright," Aira says quickly. "Well can I at least hear the rest?" I recite it to her briefly. When I finish, her eyes look like her mind is blown, but her lips contort into a determined shape. "Alright then… What a prophecy…"

"Yeah," Aiden breathes as he lets out a wry chuckle. "It's a doozy."

Aira stares down at her feet and at the large map in between us. I can practically hear the wheels turning in her head. I imagine she's feeling just as crazy as I felt when I heard it for the first time. I reach out to her and place my hand on top of hers. She looks up at me, slightly startled. "What do you think?"

Aira breathes heavily. "I think… I think this is crazy… I mean, why me? Why you? Why now?"

"I want to answer your questions, Aira, but…" I sigh. "Even now, I'm still struggling with it. You're the first person we could pin down."

"But a woman of a prophecy? Are you sure it's me?"

"We're fairly sure," Aiden reassures her. "Come on, Aira. Join us."

Aira stares at the ground for a while. I watch emotions play across her face rapidly. I see apprehension, curiosity, determination, and finally acceptance. When she looks up, a smile creeps across her face. "Alright… I'm in. What do you need from me?"

I sigh in relief, and Aiden pumps his fist in a small victory celebration. "Stay here. Continue to supervise the palace for your mother as you have been. And then… we'll call for you when it's time. Until then, lay low. And tell no one. Not even the High Lady."

Aira nods. "I can do that. Will you call for me soon?"

"I'm not sure," I answer. "We're still looking for others. Actually, you may be able to help us with that. If you could think of other people who might fit the other descriptions, write me a letter, and we can try to come back and meet up somehow. Or we'll bring you to the House of the Evening. But in the meantime, we have to keep this to ourselves. Keep any letters coded if you can."

"Understood," Aira agrees.

Aiden pipes up. "Now that that is out of the way, Aira, why don't you show us the rest of the palace?"

The Lady practically leaps to her feet with a grin. We exit the observatory and leave the prophecy conversation in the room where it happened.

Chapter Twenty-Two

We spend two days in the House of Wind, getting to know the area and getting to know Aira. After a whirlwind tour of the palace, she and the High Lady escort us down into the city. After a promenade down Main Street, we find ourselves in the main courtyard where we are greeted by a delegation of Fae from all walks of life in the House. Although they are here to greet us in a formal setting, the High Lady invites them to join us for a meal. There, I have a moment to interact with the Fae one on one. Each of them has a story to tell, and I have all the time in the world to listen. One old man tells me about his time traveling the realm as a merchant. Another young woman tells me about starting her jewelry shop fresh out of school. A mom tells me about the first time she took her babies to the palace for the Solstice where fireworks lit up the sky.

Aira is such a brilliant woman. I've never connected with another woman my age. Her magic is beautiful. She can breathe underwater and heal, and her knowledge of wind-based flight magic is impeccable. There's an art to the way she casts her spells. I wish I could look that skillful. My spellcasting is still choppy. I am sad when we have to go home and leave her behind.

As we depart for the House of the Evening, we bring with us an entire new round of army recruits. It breaks my heart to see so many young men saying goodbye to their mothers and girlfriends. I see so much worry and pain about leaving their loved ones behind, but also a determination to keep the realm from imploding. It reminds me so much of Leo, it hurts. I hope for their sake, the war ends quickly. Before the carriages roll away, I take a moment to take a breath and enjoy the scenery for a moment. Who knows when the next time I'll be able to do that is.

The High Lady, Aiden, and I return home far sooner than I would have liked. My father welcomes us home, and Aiden and I get back to work figuring out the prophecy. We sort through names, research the core magic in each House, and pore over each line of the text in excruciating detail as we search. I introduce my partner to Talon as I continue both my magical and physical training once again. They are strangely wary of each other for a while until the two of them try sparring. There's an element of respect there that I don't quite understand. *Boys are weird.*

When Talon isn't training me, Aiden and I spar. He shows me a few techniques with elemental magic that Talon was unable to, and we throw down in the arena a few times. The current count is 9-2 in terms of wins. Those two wins were hard fought, but by the Lady, did it feel good when I saw Aiden on the ground breathing hard. With more practice, I can make it a more fair fight. His fighting style is quick, faster than Talon's. It is certainly a challenge to go head-to-head with him. As the days go by, we do whatever we can to wait for information to come in about the war. It's a waiting game.

One morning when I am leaving my room for a late breakfast, I am confronted by one of my father's personal attendants. "Lady Grace? The High Lord requests your presence in the throne room."

"Is everything alright?" I prod lightly.

"The High Lord wants to see you now," he repeats.

That's not worrying at all. I move forward and close my door quickly. "Alright. Let's go." I follow him through the palace and down the stairs.

He waves me towards the throne room, and I make my way inside when we separate. My father is with several local officials, signing a stack of documents and talking quietly. When he sees me, he waves a hand, and the people disperse. We are left alone.

"How did you know it was me?" I wrinkle my eyebrows.

My father chuckles. "Every other person in this house either wears quiet shoes or practically tiptoes down the stairs. You, my dear, wear loud shoes and take those stairs quickly. I can always tell when it's you."

I blush. *Note to self: find quieter shoes and sneak around better.* "Was there something you needed from me?" I change the subject.

"As a matter of fact, there is." My father motions for me to sit next to him. I take my place accordingly. "I need your help with something concerning the war effort."

Finally. "Yes, sir. Whatever you need."

My father stands up and begins to pace in front of me. "What limited intel I have has led me to believe that the Houses of Darkness, Fire, and Sun are planning on consolidating their forces and taking out the House of Peace next. I am putting together a regiment, and we are going to join the House of Peace to help protect them. The High Lord never believed in having a standing army, and now he's in trouble." He shakes his head. "Ridiculous man." He puts his hands on my shoulders. "I need you to step up and take care of administrative things here. Can you do that?"

I nod. "Yes. Yes, of course. How long will you be gone?"

"I'm not quite sure. Could be a few days, but most likely closer to a few weeks. High Lord Gabriel wants my army to help train people to protect the city when we eventually move to help with other territories. I feel that I should be there to oversee the process, at least for the time being. I should be long gone from the territory before the enemy strikes." My father smiles warmly at me. "You don't need to worry."

My lips quirk up. "I'll do my best. Is there anything in particular I should be keeping an eye on here?"

"First, make sure no War Council meetings are held in my absence." My father looks very solemn. "High Lady Morgana and High Lord Daniel should be able to keep the others in line, but in case they fail, you are the next line of defense."

"Do you really think the other High Lords would try to make a move without you?"

"Absolutely." I chuckle as he shrugs with a secret smile. "You have to understand, Grace, we have not worked together on this scale in absolute centuries. We hope that each other will stay in line, share resources, and agree on a plan, but we have often been allies in name only. Primarily for trade purposes."

I nod slowly. "Maybe this war will change that policy."

"I hope so." My father takes a seat again. "We were nowhere near as prepared as we should have been to mobilize." We sit next to each other, reflecting on those thoughts.

"When do you leave?" I break the silence.

"Tonight."

"That soon?" I wish I had a little more time than that to prepare or even process.

"It will take several hours to reach the House of Peace's borders. We want to get there as soon as possible to ready defenses. That being said, I should get going. I want to see my wife before I go."

"Wait." I lay a hand on my father's arm. He looks back at me. I press my lips together tight. "I need to know more."

"Grace." My father addresses me with a solemn look. I bite my lip and drop my head. He reaches over and pats my shoulder affectionately. "You will know more when it is time for you to know more. In the meantime, take this as a trial run. Damien will assist you in my absence with whatever you need, okay?"

I nod. "I'll keep the place together for you."

"Good. Keep it in one piece, alright?" When my father smiles, I smile back.

I won't let you down... Dad.

Chapter Twenty-Three

As soon as my dad left for the House of Peace, it was like an entire avalanche of responsibility dumped on my shoulders. I take over all day-to-day operation business plus the issue of the war on my shoulders. I meet with dignitaries in the morning and hash it out with merchants and foreign trade officers in the afternoon. At night, I have barely enough time to catch Aiden in the library to discuss prophecy measures before catching a wink of sleep and doing it all over again. Every day brings new challenges and new problems to tackle. One day, it's a trade deal with the House of Light nearly falling through. *And yes, I find it ridiculous that we're somehow still negotiating trade deals when we can't agree on what to do with the war.* Another day, it's making sure to approve the new purchase orders to keep enough food, linens, and soaps to keep this place in order.

I don't know how I feel being in charge. Sitting on my father's throne, it feels too big and too grand for me. I prefer my smaller throne off to the side. I don't know if I'm exactly able to switch them at this point, and I'm worried that it would be wrong to ask. The more I follow in the High Lord's footsteps, the more I am unsure of my position as a future high Lady. This is chaos right now managing the bare minimum of leadership; I can't imagine trying to take over during wartime in full capacity.

Three mornings after my father left the palace, my father's right-hand rushes into the throne room while I'm speaking to one of the officers overseeing the reserve troops about current supplies. "Lady Grace, I apologize for the intrusion, but I need to speak to you immediately." His face is troubled and a bit manic. I nod and apologize briefly to the man before dismissing the officer.

"Damien, right?" I ask and he nods. "What's going on?"

"Lady Grace, the House of the Darkness and the House of the Sun attacked the House of Peace early this morning," he answers, hands clasped in front of his chest.

I sit up and forward in my chair, slowly to not show just how startled I am by the news. "What happened?"

"There was an ambush in Craine two days ago by the House of Darkness and House of Fire. Not only an ambush, a large-scale attack. The House of Peace wasn't prepared, even with our help, and fell almost immediately. The entire area is in chaos. A messenger for our army just arrived. All I know is that a portion of our troops managed to retreat; they are only a few hours behind him. The details are unclear. The poor man collapsed before I could get anything else out of him." Damien shakes his head. "I'm sorry."

I am frozen for a few minutes. There is nothing I can think of to say or do. But I jump to my feet anyway and motion for Damien to follow me into the front hall. I wave over to a servant. "Get medics ready," I order. I motion to the other people in the room. "I need the High Lords and High Lady down here as soon as possible; I need to brief everyone. Damien, can you get Aiden and Neil please?" The people around me scatter, and I am left alone in the hallway for a moment.

There is a sense of dread welling up inside of me. *Will the people have been able to get in place in time to defend the city? Has it officially been annexed? How many injuries have been sustained? And by the Lady, how many deaths?* As people begin to make their way downstairs, we all end up waiting out by the front door, packing in wall to wall. Aiden and Neil make their way to the front.

"Hey," Aiden says as he embraces me quickly. "What do you know?"

"Not much," I mumble. "The House of Peace has been attacked; we don't know the outcome yet." He nods and takes my hand discreetly, squeezing once.

I look over at Neil. "Did Damien inform you of everything?"

"Yes. Are you sure there's nothing else?" Neil holds his hands down by his sides, but I can see they are shaking.

"I'm sure. There's murmuring around the palace, but no one knows anything more. It's all speculation." I reach over and try to offer him some comfort, but he violently pushes me off. I decide not to press him further. We don't bother to sit down, only stand there and wait.

When we hear the galloping of horses in the distance start to rumble and shake the palace, I motion for the front door attendants to throw open the door. The packed hallway funnels out into the courtyard as we collectively hold our breaths to see what happens next. Our regiment comes up over the hill, and my stomach sinks when I realize that our troops are significantly depleted. There are fewer soldiers on horses, and more being carried in carriages and on stretchers in trailers being pulled up the road. The general shouts to us for aid, and medics rush forward to assist. We part ways to let the injured through, scanning the faces for familiar ones.

The uninjured members of the regiment file towards the arena as the others flood into the palace. Aiden, Neil, and I get swept up in the thick of it. I fight my way through the throng of people, searching for my father, one of his officials, someone who can create some kind of order. There is so much shouting and pandemonium, I can't get a word in edgewise. But then I hear Neil break into a wail. My heart stops dead in my chest. I shove through the crowd more violently; I have probably bruised several soldiers' arms and heels on the way. Finally, I reach the stretchers.

My eyes skip over the wounded soldiers and land on my father. My insides twist up into tight little knots. His face is so pale; the life has been drained out of him. His body lies so rigid on the stretcher, and his chest moves up and down very slightly. Neil is collapsed by his side, crying and clinging to his hand. I reach for my father's shirt, but he is being pulled away from me faster than I can reach him. I cry out for them to wait, but there is no time. They rush him off to the hospital room while Neil and Aiden follow. They don't even notice that I am not there with them; they must think I am following right behind.

The truth is that I don't know if I can.

Instead, I slip back through the crowd and off into the side door of the throne room. I leave the door open in case someone is looking for me, but likely no one will be in here for several hours. As I sink into my throne, my head drops into my hands. The silence is both chilling and comforting at the same time. It allows me to sort through my thoughts in peace.

I have seen too much death already. First, my brother, whose death started off this entire journey for me. Then the soldiers we lost over the last couple of months. I have stood by at so many funerals to honor men I have never met, but who all look like my dear Leo. It's like feeling the pain of his passing over and over again. And now my father is lying upstairs somewhere, unconscious, possibly worse. And I have no idea what to do now. If he dies… life is going to get very difficult very fast.

And there's still a war going on outside.

I hear the soft tap of shoes walking into the throne room behind me. I almost don't want to face whoever has just walked in and send them on their way. "Grace?" A stoic voice changes my mind. I turn around to see Aiden with a solemn expression on his face. There's a quiet pain on his face that I recognize well. It's a softer version of the pain that I had when I found out Leo was never coming home, a more respectable expression.

I gulp and steel myself for the impending news. "What is it?"

Aiden closes his eyes in a very long blink before staring at me. "He's in a coma. They can't revive him."

There's a simultaneous relief in knowing he isn't dead yet and a deep seeded rush of pain and hurt in the fact that he may never wake up. I clutch at my chest and turn back around to press my hands against the wall. In a rush of anger, I slam them forward. There's a sharp sting on my right palm and a tiny trail of liquid. I wipe the blood off on my pants as I face Aiden again. Whatever I had an idea of saying has escaped me.

He moves towards me, and I throw my arms around his neck. He presses one hand to my back and the other to my hair, rubbing the back of my head lightly. "Oh, Grace," he hums quietly as he kisses the top of my head. When I pull back, he places both hands on my shoulders. "You're going to be interim High Lady now… you know that, right?"

"I know." I can only just get out the words.

"Someone is going to be in any minute to tell you."

"I'm sorry," I breathe. I don't know what I'm apologizing for. Aiden pulls me back into his chest, and I hug him tightly and let a couple tears fall.

Another set of footsteps comes from the hall into the doorway of the throne room. "Lady Grace?" Damien's voice asks tentatively.

I raise my head and pull away from Aiden regretfully, standing in front of him. I level my eyes at the man. "Yes?"

He gulps and takes a short breath. "As of now, High Lord Alexander Faelie is incapacitated. The healers are unsure when he will emerge from his coma or whether he will emerge at all. As such, this is formal notice to you that you are now interim High Lady Grace Andrea…"

CHAPTER TWENTY-THREE

He hesitates at my last name. "Faelie," he finally finishes.

I bristle at the Fae name being forced upon me. I open my mouth to replace it with my mortal name, but with a look from Aiden, I hesitate. *Is my mortal name truly what is needed now? Would using it make things worse? Could I be taken seriously using it?* As much as I hate it, the answer to that question is no. I know that the people of the House of the Evening and the War Council are going to need a sign from me that my leadership would be strong and decisive. Anything less than a show of strength right now and the whole operation falls apart.

"Grace?" Aiden says my name gently.

"High Lady?" Damien echoes. The name sounds so foreign in the air.

I gulp. "High Lady… Grace Andrea Richardson Faelie. Make sure they get the name right." Aiden lets out a rush of breath behind me.

"Will do." My father's right hand reaches out to me. I shake his hand. "What would you like to do now?"

Frankly, sir, I have no idea how to answer that question. Aiden chimes in before I can speak, "Damien, we will find you when we figure out a plan. But with all due respect, give the woman a break. She just found out she's a High Lady." I look down and nod, squeezing his hand gratefully.

"Yes sir." Damien leaves the room.

I let out a sigh and lean back into Aiden. I shut my eyes tight. His hands come around my body and pull me closer to his chest. I take brief comfort in his arms. "What are you going to do?" he finally asks me.

"Aiden, I…" I start to snap at him, but when I see the genuine concern in his eyes, the heat dies on my tongue. "I don't know yet. There is so much to take care of and… oh by the Lady, the War Council."

"You're going to be fine. Let's take it one step at a time. Let's do some planning up in the library tonight."

"Aiden, I don't know if I can do that tonight. By the Lady, how am I supposed to pull all of this together? I have to run the entire—"

"We can figure it out, I promise," he interjects. "You need a plan, and you need one tonight. I have a feeling none of us are going to get much sleep tonight anyway."

He's probably right. I nod sharply. "Alright, let's do it." As we stand there together in reflection, I pray to the Lady that we all come out of this relatively unscathed. I pray my father wakes up soon and saves me from this craziness I am about to put myself through.

Chapter Twenty-Four

Aiden and I spend the entire night in the library working through my father's to-do list for the next few months and diving into the war efforts. He has me studying each of the High Lords' histories that sit on the War Council so that I know how to effectively deal with each of them. Though they each have their own quirks, they are unilaterally stubborn and tradition rooted. Except for High Lady Morgana. I hope I can get her on my side early. Aiden tells me stories about his limited interactions with them and fills me in on how they have acted in meetings so far. Unfortunately, it's not looking promising.

In the wee hours of the morning, we hone defense magic down in the arena as the sun rises. He pointed out to me that it may be very important to be able to defend myself now that power is shifting hands. Assassination attempts could be far more frequent now. *Great.* Finally, Aiden drags me upstairs and puts me to bed before the emergency War Council meeting I called for later this afternoon.

When I wake up, the news of my father's coma hits me all over again. There's a heaviness in my chest when I recall our last conversation where he promised me that I would understand more about this war in good time. *Who knew that time would come so soon?* Despite all the prep work of last night, I still feel entirely lost. I look around my bedroom. It is a mess of clothes and papers. I must remember to leave the door open for the maids to come through and put everything back in its place.

If only there were maids of life. But there is no one to come in and straighten all of this up and get pretty much the entire Realm back on track. Except...

Wait... that's my job.

By the Lady, that's my fucking job.

I scramble out of bed, slipping and landing on my knees hard. There is no time to waste here. The Council is going to want answers and a plan, and for them to take me seriously, I need to look the part. I call down the hall at the first maid I see. "Hey! Excuse me? I need some help." At my panicked face, she comes running. "I need to be a High Lady today," I manage to explain through my panic-attack-level breathing. "More... formal."

Luckily, the woman understands exactly what I need here. Within a few minutes, she summons a group of women to come dress me up. My hair is pulled up and tightly pinned to the back of my head. I'm wearing more makeup on my face than I have worn in my life, and this dress has been fitted, pinned, and tucked as tight as it can be. It feels uncomfortable and somewhat itchy in certain places. One of the maids finishes my hair with a bejeweled silver hairpin. When I look in the mirror, I see someone foreign: a figurehead with only a glimpse of the person underneath.

But the other High Lords need to see a High Lady. And not a girl.

There's a soft knock on the door. When one of the women opens the door, Talon stands there with a nervous expression. His eyes widen when he sees me. "Grace?"

I bite my lip nervously. "Do I look alright?"

He shakes his head. "You don't look like you." At my raised eyebrow, he quickly adds, "You look fine, I mean... you look the part," he stumbles over his words. To make him stop, I shoot him a half-smile. He's not wrong, after all. I don't look like myself. "Are you ready? I'm here to escort you."

I stand up slowly and brush the front of my dress. "As ready as I'm going to be." Talon offers me his arm, and he leads me down the hall toward the conference room. My heartbeat races.

"Do you remember what you're going to say to everyone?"

"I have a plan."

"Don't lose your head in there, okay?" I give him a little glare. He chuckles softly. "Unless someone tries to circumvent you." As we reach the door, Talon turns me to face him, his hands planted firmly on my shoulders. "If they do… burn it all to the ground." There's a fierceness in his eyes that I haven't seen before. "Whatever happens in that room is going to set the course for how this war goes. You're in charge. Act like it."

"I will," I say quietly. He gives me a pat on my arm before cocking his head towards the double doors of the conference room.

I take a deep breath and nod to the gentlemen at the door. They pull the handles open, and the High Lords at the table instantly turn to see me. My shoes click against the floor as I stride toward the head of the table. Their eyes follow me all the way. Aiden's are the only ones that give me some comfort. The room is deathly silent and way too cold. Another servant pulls out the head chair, and I take a seat. Unsure of what to do with my hands, I decide to intertwine them together and set them on the table.

"Alright," I start off loudly, perhaps a little too loud before backing off. "I know you were informed yesterday by the officials of this House, but my father is incapacitated after the annexation of the House of Peace. As such, I am taking over all of his responsibilities, including the leadership of the House of the Evening and this War Council."

"What gives you qualifications to lead us?" High Lord Michael Gerald demands.

I am slightly taken aback. "I'm sorry, what?"

"What gives you any qualifications to lead us?" he repeats himself. "You have barely been a Fae for more than a season."

"My father left the heirship to me," I argue. "And according to Fae law, the House of the Evening takes on leadership of the War Council. It has been this way from the beginning."

High Lord Aaron Blake of the House of Light laughs harshly. "You are a half-Fae bastard *brat.* I say we take a vote on a new Council leader." High Lord Gerald seconds the motion with a hand motion. The other men grow uneasy. In contrast, High Lady Morgana Swift is looking at me with raised eyebrows and a certain smirk across her lips. Her eyes are saying *You really going to let them walk all over you like that?* I am reminded how much I like her.

I stand up. "According to Fae law, the usurpation of the leader of the War Council can only be done by a unanimous vote of the current seated members of the Council. And you're never going to get a unanimous vote in this current state. So why don't we sit down and talk business unless you want to continue to waste our time with petty drivel?" The High Lady lets out a chuckle, and Aiden shoots me a secret smirk. High Lord Blake scowls and sits down.

"Alright…" I decide not to sit back down and begin to circle the table. "The House of Peace has fallen. High Lord Gabriel DiAngelo is out of commission for the time being, and the House of Darkness has continued their invasion of the Upper Realm. I don't see them stopping any time soon. We need a new strategy."

"I don't think it's about a new strategy; I think it's about strengthening our defenses and holding the positions we have," High Lord Daniel of the House of the Moon chimes in.

"Absolutely not, we need to be on the offensive," Aiden counters. "The House of Darkness will not stop here."

"Well who exactly do you think is going to defend our own Houses if we're all up here playing politics and congregating for half-assed attempts at liberation." High Lord Aaron Blake slams his hands onto the table.

"Aaron," High Lady Morgana warns. "I know tensions are running hot in this room, but let's take a breath. I believe what Lord Aiden is saying is that we need to make a concentrated hit so that we don't have to defend our own territories."

"Exactly." I nod to the High Lady. "It's time to band together and stay banded. No more going back to home territories to regroup. It's time to put your seconds in charge and stay here."

High Lord Dylan Triton from the House of Water stands up. "I'm not abandoning my House. Not for anyone or any reason."

"If we don't stick together, there won't be any of your House left to save," I shout. The room dissolves into chaos. There are arguments for and against banding together and a lot of arguments about my competency as a leader. Aiden and High Lady Morgana are among the biggest allies whereas High Lords Blake and Gerald are the angriest opponents.

"I refuse to take orders from a little girl!" High Lord Blake snaps.

"If we don't pool our resources, the Houses of Darkness, Fire, and Sun will take everything!" Aiden yells back.

"You're one to talk, your father is leading the lot! Why should we trust a word you say?"

Aiden rises to his feet. "Now listen here you pompous—"

Statements and insults fly around me like I'm in the middle of a swirling storm. The noise builds slowly under my skin, ringing in my ears. The men talk in circles, trying to ignore me and come up with their own plans. *This is never going to work.* And at that moment, I know what I need to do.

I get up out of my chair and lean over the table. "Everyone, sit down!" I shout. "I want quiet now!" At my raised voice, the nobles around me stop and stare. While a few sit, High Lord Aaron and Aiden remain standing. "I said… sit down," I repeat. After a few moments, they finally comply. I take a deep breath. "Look… this clearly isn't working for anyone here. We are fighting to find the balance between what is best for our Houses and what is best for the realm. We have to do both. We have to accomplish both."

I turn to High Lord Aaron. "I know your heart is with your House. And frankly, your head is as well." As he opens his mouth to retort, I quickly add, "There's nothing wrong with that. But it doesn't make for a good Council. I propose that you return to your Houses and send your heirs here instead. You continue to make the day-to-day decisions at home, and your heirs can coordinate the larger war effort. If something goes wrong at your House, you'll have protected its future by sending your children here." As I look around the table, I see genuine contemplation on the others' faces. Aiden looks proud.

"What about those of us who would like to stay?" High Lady Morgana asks. "I would be interested."

"High Lady, I would like it very much if you did choose to stay here. I could use your experience and advice as an advisor to the other heirs." To my relief, she nods and smiles at me in response. I scan the room. "What are your opinions of my proposal?"

High Lord Daniel slowly nods. "I'll second it."

"I'll third," High Lady Morgana chimes in. "Shall we have a vote?"

After a few moments of quiet debating between neighbors, the table eventually goes around and indicates their vote. My proposal passes unanimously, and my first Council meeting adjourns with the members in reasonable spirits. With a nod of respect to High Lady Morgana and a silent mouthing of 'later' to Aiden, I exit the room with my head held high.

To my surprise, Talon has been waiting outside this entire time. And judging from the look of awe on his face, he's been listening from the door. I can't help but admire him for it. It's exactly what I would have done. As I walk straight past him towards the hall, he stops me with an arm. "What did you just do?"

I chuckle. "Like you said. Burned it all down." I offer him my arm. "Care to help me start again?" Still looking at me with an incredulous smile, he takes my invitation. Arm in arm, we leave the rest of the room behind us, dumbfounded.

We build again. My way now.

Chapter Twenty-Five

It doesn't take long for word to spread that the new interim High Lady of the House of the Evening isn't playing around. The High Lords pack up their things within the next few days and leave the palace with our political relationships intact. Aiden later tells me I earned some begrudging respect from some of the more stringent High Lords for offering my compromise. High Lady Morgana leaves as well to make a brief trip back home to pick up her daughter and install one of her advisors in a temporary authority position. I could not be more grateful that she decided to stay and offer her assistance. I send each of the leaders with a formal request for their heirs' presence at my palace. Then it's just a matter of waiting, and luckily for me, the continual movements of the Houses of Darkness, Fire, and Sun make my summons a more urgent affair.

I hope the heirs get on board with the idea of making decisions for the realm themselves. Aiden spends several hours telling me about them, and from what I can tell, most of them are going to be much easier to work with. Young, bright individuals with an openness to change. At the very least, we can have some reasonable discussion.

It takes a couple weeks for everyone to arrive. Nearly every day, a new line of carriages rolls into the front courtyard. And each time, I meet them with a swarm of the palace's attendants and servants. We greet them and help people out and inside. As each House sends their

heir and accompanying delegation, more and more guest rooms begin to fill up. The servant quarters are completely full by the time the last House reaches us. Thank the Lady for the servant passageways that keep foot traffic moving reasonably smoothly.

When the Houses of Water and Light finally arrive, I gather all the other heirs into the front hall to welcome them and make a grand opening speech. Not exactly my forte. As I descend the stairs, the noise is deafening. It's chaos; everyone is talking over each other and trying to sort out what to do. I spot Neil in the middle of the crowd, trying to create some semblance of order. It is the first time I have seen him since our father landed in the hospital. He looks so tense, every muscle tightened. I can tell he is only here because he feels obligated to be. Sense of duty can be a hellion. He doesn't seem to be having much luck calming everyone down.

"Hey," I say loudly. To no avail, though. "Hey!" I try to call out louder, but only a handful of the palace's employees notice me. Eventually, I just shout over the crowd. "HEY!"

Servants, soldiers, and nobles alike fall silent. They look up at me with a mixture of emotions: concern, determination, and a few with slight irritation. "Alright. Now that I have your attention, I'd like to start things off with a brief roll call. I want to make sure everyone is here now or if I need to start sending search parties." I get a few chuckles for that comment, and I am satisfied. "House of the Sun, Lord Aiden." I indicate his presence with a hand. "House of the Moon?"

"Lady Luna, present and prepared." Luna's light, lilting voice raises above the crowd. When I look over at her, she raises her hand insistently and gives an exaggerated bow to the floor. I barely manage to stifle my laugh.

"Thank you, Luna," I bite my lip hard. "House of the Day, Lord Jason." A nod from a dark brown-haired man lets me check him off the list. "House of Light representatives, Ladies Aurora and Alena

Blake."

"We're here." The two blonde women step forward and give a slight head bow. If it wasn't for their pink and purple amulets, I wouldn't be able to tell them apart.

"Welcome." I bow slightly in response. The two of them step back into the crowd and whisper to each other. I wonder what their father told them and whether that makes them feel prepared to do better than he did. Or like a target of mine. *Better keep an eye on them.*

"House of Water, Lord Tristan," I continue.

"Here!" A gloved hand waves to me from the courtyard. "Am I late?" he shouts.

"No!" I shout back and try not to flush in confusion. "You're… right on time." I shake it off. "And lastly the House of the Wind."

"That would be me," a voice comes down from the stairs behind me. The woman, dressed in a shimmering silver dress, begins to descend toward the ground floor. Aira trails behind her dressed in purple.

I dip my head into a slight bow. "High Lady Morgana. Lady Aira, how nice to see you again."

The Lady gives me a little wave as her mother speaks, "Thank you for bringing us here, High Lady Grace." It takes my breath away hearing my title on her lips. "Heirs, please take note of my daughter, Lady Aira. She will be the speaking member of the House of the Wind on this War Council. Although, I have agreed to sit in an advisory role and occasionally as an additional voting seat for the most important issues."

"Wonderful," I say. "Thank you, High Lady Morgana. Alright, that's everyone. For the Houses of Water and Light, you can make your way upstairs. The maids will direct you towards your sleeping quarters while you are here. Get settled, get unpacked, and then be down in the banquet hall for dinner. Our first War Council meeting will commence then. Thank you." I step down the staircase as the crowd begins to disperse. Some take the staircase I was just on while others divert down either side of the hallway to take more direct paths. I meet Aiden at the door. "How was that?"

"You're doing well. Better than most of the people here probably expected." His lips curl up into a smile as I roll my eyes at him. I can't help but feel a little hurt by his comment. I may be new, but I'm still a Fae, and I'm doing my best and I'd like some support when I ask for it, dammit! But when he leans down and gives me a quick kiss, I accept it.

"Lady Grace?" I turn around to find Luna looking at me expectantly.

I smile at her softly. "Call me Grace, Luna. I'm tired of all of these formalities."

"Grace, then." Luna smiles a secret smile. "I need to talk to you and Aiden immediately."

"Can it wait until tonight's Council meeting?" Aiden asks. "Grace and I have a lot to get together to make sure things run smoothly."

"Well, it can, but I think you'll want to hear it for yourselves now," Luna replies. "Why don't we step into the throne room?" She indicates the door over her shoulder.

I nod to Aiden. "Let's hear her out. Come this way." Luna leaves her attendants, and we move into the throne room. I close the door behind us to give us some privacy. "Alright, Luna," I press my back against the door. "What do you need to share?"

"Don't be alarmed when I say this, okay?" Luna starts. Aiden and I exchange a somewhat panicked look.

"Is there an issue with the House of the Moon? Do you have intel about the House of Darkness's movements? Do we need to be mobilizing?" Aiden fires questions one after the other.

"Oh, no no, nothing like that. I just wanted to let you know that I'm a part of the prophecy."

It takes everything in me to keep my jaw from hitting the floor.

"Excuse me?"

"The prophecy? The members of the new Coven of Eight that you have been looking for?"

I stride towards Luna. "How do you know about that?" I am panicking. *If the word is already out and widespread, we are absolutely screwed. We have already lost the war if they know we're coming.*

"I'm the Soothsayer," she says matter-of-factly. "Divination magic. In the House of the Moon, there are certain channels to increasing powers of foresight, and I know all of them by heart." Luna turns to me. "I had a feeling about you the first time we met, Grace, and you accepted my offer of assistance in the duel of the heirs. Sorry about that by the way." I stare at her, bewildered. "As soon as it came out that you were half-Fae, I took the first full moon to see what information the Lady could give me about your future. And that's when I heard the prophecy for the first time."

Aiden shakes his head and runs his hands through his hair. "Is your divination magic really that powerful?" His jaw is practically on the floor. "I mean, to hear a prophecy from the Lower Realm without black obsidian is unheard of."

"Do you need proof?" Luna asks. "I can provide proof." She takes a deep breath and begins to recite in an even tone. "The Lady has foretold to us the Coven of Eight; That shall overturn impending war; To shift the balance of an impossible fate; Even an uneven score. The Bringer of Light burns the longest and the brightest, for his sacrifice for the greater good shall not be the lightest. The Soothsayer shall bring clarity to that which is blurry; But a sharp word of warning, as her words cannot be hurried. The Potioner will craft her potions like her spells. Intensely pure, combating those who rebel. The Deliverer shall bring more than sheer strength and power; he will bring in the last known ally to usher in the final hour."

At this point, Aiden and I are mesmerized as she continues. "The lost child shall be the Spinner, the strongest of the women's breed. Spinner of tales and spinner of winds, only she can commence the final deed. The Witch and the Conjurer, knights of the red; upon darkness and shadow will they always tread. But in the light, what the others won't expect: The Witch is to serve, the Conjurer to protect. The Enchantress shall unite the mages, and rewrite every inch of the realm's history pages. With untapped power that spans both mortal and Fae, she is the only one who will call night to an endless day. The Coven of Eight must protect the many, from mortal and magic, both and any. With a bond that's stronger than the fabric of magic, to override the destined to be powerful and tragic."

When she finishes, that serene smile returns to her face. "Is that proof enough?" I am at a loss for words.

Aiden stutters and finally manages to get out, "How long have you been sitting on this?"

"Since right after the Winter Solstice," she answers calmly. "But the Lady told me that it wasn't time to step in yet. Not until you summoned me." Unable to take this news, Aiden walks clear to the other side of the room, muttering profanities to himself.

I shake off my confusion and nod. "Alright then, Luna, you clearly.... know what you're talking about. You're one of us." Luna holds her hand out, and I shake it quickly. "After the formal meeting tonight, I am planning on running an impromptu meeting of the prophecy members in the library just before midnight. Most people should be asleep by then. That's you, me, Aiden, and..."

"Lady Aira," Luna interrupts. At first, I think she is showing off her knowledge again until I see the woman in question was actually walking through the door.

"Hi Luna, so nice to see you again." The two Ladies embrace.

"Nice to see you again, Aira." Aiden makes his way back over to us and gives Aira a quick hug.

"Aira, we have just learned that Luna is another member of the prophecy," I fill her in.

"Oh," Aira breathes and squeezes Luna. "Glad you could join us."

"Happy to help," she replies.

"Alright, Aira." I glance over at the door as I hear people above us descending the stairs, most likely to explore the castle or the town. "I want you to meet us up in the library just before midnight. I want to talk about our next steps and group up for the first time, alright?" She nods. "Alright, let's get out of here. I move to the door. "Remember, keep this under wraps for now." We part ways as I go to escort the other visiting nobles on a personal tour of the palace.

Chapter Twenty-Six

When dinner rolls around, I'm a bit nervous. Despite the new faces, there is still a palpable uncertainty in the air. In the eyes of the heirs, there are so many unknowns about the war: where it's going, what's coming next, and why I asked for their assistance rather than their parents'. I'm not even sure if they are okay with my presence in the Upper Realm to begin with. At the Spring Solstice, of course, I noticed the apprehension and the unwillingness to speak to me. It might take some time to persuade them that I belong here. I'm just hoping it doesn't interfere with the Council's planning.

Tonight is a big night in terms of setting the tone for the rest of my relationships with these people. I request semi-formal dress rather than formal dress from the heirs. I don't want this to be purely business; I hope I can get to know people a little more tonight. To me, that objective might be even more important than what war issues we tackle. I need to understand how these people tick to know how to interact and negotiate with them. So instead of having the maids put on my face again, I spend some time pampering myself and slipping into a nice shirt and pants. This feels so much more comfortable to be in than what I wore with the High Lords.

The Lords, Ladies, High Lady Morgana, and I take dinner in the banquet hall. The mealtime is filled with idle chatter and disjointed conversations between people sitting with each other. Things feel very fragmented as little groups splinter, much like the Solstice. Aiden, High Lady Morgana, and Aira are the only individuals who speak to me. *Oh, we have such a long way to go.* It isn't long before we are moving upstairs to the conference room. I take my seat at the head of the table, and once everyone is settled, I open my mouth.

"Hello everyone." My voice sounds strange against the walls of this room. "Thank you for joining us here at the palace. On behalf of the House of the Evening, I would like to welcome you to the table." I slowly rise to my feet. "This is an unprecedented motion to bring the noble youth of the Upper Realm to the forefront and put them on the decision team for the war effort. The High Lords of your Houses have agreed with me that they needed to return home to protect their lands personally. Therefore, you will be the ones making the calls for the whole realm. No pressure." Spattered chuckles echo throughout the room. Aiden gives me an encouraging smile.

I chuckle lightly with the rest. "I don't believe in tradition trumping all. I can imagine you can understand that seeing that I am the half-mortal bastard child turned Fae heir." I take note of the awkward grimaces and sideways glances taking place around me. "What I am looking for is innovation in leadership. Innovation in magical and physical war tactics. And I want an actual strategy to win this thing. Cause the House of Darkness is not going to stop with the House of Peace. They will be coming for your Houses and they will be coming for mine. So I want to hear ideas."

The table erupts into rapid-fire conversation. Everyone has ideas to share. All of their sentences blend, and I hold my hands up to pause them. "Whoa, whoa, whoa. One at a time."

Luna chimes in first. "I think we need to be combining forces and putting them in a singular place."

"I agree with you Luna, but I'm not sure how that is going to work," Tristan adds. "I don't think I can send the House of Water's troops anywhere past the House of Fire territory. They're too close, and I know their eyes are on us."

"What about the waterways?" Aiden chimes in. "I mean, it seems obvious right?"

Tristan chuckles dryly. "I am literally the Lord of the House of Water; of course, I already thought of that. But to move the number of people by sea would be so obvious, I'm afraid we'd get into a battle with no backup."

"What if you didn't bring them over with the big ships?" Aira pipes up. Everyone turns to look at her, including her mother. The High Lady looks intrigued. "What if you sent them with merchant fishermen, a handful at a time with supplies? They dress like civilians; they don't call attention to themselves. It may take a while, but it could be done."

"We are going to need to think very carefully about this," High Lady Morgana responds. "Right now, what the Houses of Darkness and Fire need are supplies. Sending merchant ships, even smaller ones, could be an automatic target."

"She's right," I concur. "I like the idea a lot, but it needs more fleshing out. Let's put people on planning that out. Luna, Tristan, I want you two in charge of that. Now I think we also need eyes on the House of Peace. The House of Darkness's movements are still way too unclear, and I think we need to see what is happening on the inside now."

"Well you can't just send a few spies in," Jason of the House of the Day immediately counters. "Over half of the people sent so far from your House and from others have not returned. You lost contact with another two in the House of the Earth, did you not?"

I wrinkle my forehead. "I'm sorry, where are you getting this information from?"

"I've been down in the barracks since I got here speaking to the soldiers. I also have information from my friends here and in my father's court." This makes me wary. I don't like that the first thing he did was spend time in the House of the Evening's barracks. I make a mental note to keep an eye on him. "You need to send someone powerful who actually has a chance of getting out," he continues.

"Who would you suggest?" I ask.

"Frankly, I would say Aiden," Jason offers as he turns to look at the Lord in question. My heart skips a beat. "He has the magical ability and the military experience. You can get in, check some things out, and then get out. Your intel would be invaluable to the war effort."

"I would be happy to make the trip, but I need someone with glamour magic to accompany me. We'll need clever enough disguises to fool the guards."

"I'll do it," I answer quickly. *Truth is, I want to keep an eye out for Aiden.* "Besides," I say out loud, "I want to take a good look at the House for myself."

"Are you sure you're up for it?" Lady Alena asks. "I mean… no offense, but you just became a Fae."

"Talon can vouch for her," Aiden says quietly but firmly. "We can bring him in if you need to hear about her progress. I have also done quite a bit of sparring with her in the last few weeks, and she's doing better than you would think. Additionally, she and I adventured alongside each other for quite some time. I think she's brilliant without the magic. With the magic, I'm sure we'll be fine." Alena looks skeptical, but the others around her are starting to look reasonably optimistic.

"Let's take a vote," I say. "All those in favor of running with the two ideas we proposed so far tonight?" Hands go up, and it's a unanimous vote. I grin. "Great. Let's start getting down into the details now." The conversation moves on late into the night, but I feel pretty good about where we are now. *Finally… we may have a shot.*

Chapter Twenty-Seven

Aiden and I settle on leaving the palace just before dawn. The War Council agrees that we need to see the House of Peace in the daylight to know what is going on. My glamour magic, now better developed with more practice, should be able to shield us once we're there, and in an emergency, Aiden's shapeshifting should be enough to get us out. After a very early evening to bed, Aiden and I meet in the stables when it's still dark out. We want the twilight to cover us as we ride out.

"Hey," I say quietly as I attach my satchel to the side of my horse.

"Hey," Aiden replies before kissing my cheek. "Are you ready?"

"Yes." I smile. "It feels good to be going on another adventure together isn't it?"

Aiden chuckles and teases, "You were always good at getting me into trouble." He shoots me a quick wink. "At least now you can use magic."

"Hey, I had some solid moves as a mortal woman. Even you had a hard time keeping up with me."

Aiden chuckles. "Oh, of course." I roll my eyes at the hint of condescension in his tone. But you're a full-fledged Fae Lady now. Your adventuring style may have changed in the last several months."

I place my foot in the left stirrup and swing my leg over my horse. "Well, let's find out, shall we?" As Aiden climbs onto his steed, we ride out of the stables and towards the House of Peace.

Riding with Aiden feels like old times with the wind in our hair and the world at our backs. Because the sun hasn't risen yet, we are able to ride right down the main streets of the town. It's like seeing the world again in a whole new light. The buildings are empty and quiet, yet I can almost sense an inkling of what life looks like inside of them. Every once in a while, I spot a lonely bartender cleaning up the tipped-over beer mugs and broken wooden remnants of a wild night out. They don't look up to see Aiden and me, which is all the better.

When we leave the House of the Evening behind, we take the country roads and small village streets toward Craine. It takes nearly two days to reach the edge of the House of Peace. We camp outside in a forest on the outskirts of the House of Wind to avoid being seen. Stopping inside any town or village now could alert the enemy to our movements. When we finally approach the city, Aiden pulls his horse alongside mine and motions for me to slow down. I pull the reins to slow my horse to a trot. "We should get ready now; we're almost on top of Craine," he urges. "Are you sure your magic is strong enough to hold a glamour over both of us?"

"Of course it is," I assure him. "I wouldn't have agreed to the plan if it wasn't. I'm not going to put you at risk. Though, remind me why you can't just stay in your shapeshifted form."

"My other magic isn't as actionable when in animal form. My energy all focuses on shapeshifting, and I have to shift out before I can cast something else."

"Fair enough."

Aiden nods. "Alright… put it up." I reach over and glide my hand in front of Aiden. His blond hair shifts to a brown, curlier variety and his clothes change to those of a traveling merchant rather than a noble soldier. When he turns to look at me, I notice his eyes have changed to a soft sea green.

"Done." I sit back and admire my work. "You look good."

"Good, now fix yourself," Aiden replies. I quickly slip a hand over myself. Red hair changes to blonde, and blue eyes change to violet.

"I never imagined you with red hair," Aiden comments with a light chuckle. "It's cute."

"Thank you. Now keep the talking to a minimum, just in case. I haven't quite mastered masking voices yet." We both fall silent as we approach Craine. As we round the corner, Aiden holds a hand up. When I peer through the trees, I see the entry road to Craine surrounded by armed guards. A procession of carriages and horses move with a steady pace towards the road, and soldiers appear to be stopping each group and chatting with them. "Oh no," I breathe softly.

"Don't panic yet," Aiden hisses to me. "We're merchants who live here. We're going to Craine to meet back up with our children and their grandmother who we left here while on a trip to the House of Light. Okay?" *Quick thinking, Aiden.* I give him a short nod, and we get in line.

I worry silently as the line moves slowly forward. I try to keep my focus on keeping both of our glamour spells up. My heart pounds in my chest. This is the moment that decides the fate of this mission. We either get in or the whole ruse falls apart and we probably get arrested, detained, maybe even murdered. I try to smooth my face out when we reach the front. The guard looks at us with a menacing glare. "Names," he barks.

"Tom and Elena Carrow," Aiden answers confidently.

"And your business here?" This time, the soldier looks at me, expecting me to answer.

I work hard to keep the magic stable as I answer, perhaps slightly more forcefully than necessary. "We are returning home from our merchant trip to the House of Light to reunite with our children. Their grandmother is watching them now." The soldier studies me.

Blood rushes in my ears as I struggle to keep a handle on the glamour magic.

"You may go." The rush of relief is euphoric. But the ruse isn't over yet. Aiden and I ride side by side past the checkpoint and into the House of Peace. The streets are almost completely empty despite being mid-morning now. The few people that are out are being ushered from place to place by soldiers. They travel in small groups around the city, swords raised and prepared for anything and everything.

"Keep your eyes open," Aiden mumbles to me. "How are you doing on the glamour magic?"

"Struggling…" I whisper back. "I haven't tried holding it up for this long." My energy is draining quickly. The magical pressure feels like a heavy wave bearing down on me and forcing me under. I try to breathe through it, but each breath feels harder. Though I press on, the magic is shaky.

"Have you tried zoning out with the spell? Has anyone taught you that?"

Oh, that's right. "I got it." I let myself slide back into a magic-induced haze. The pressure releases a little. *Thank the Lady.*

"We'll duck behind somewhere soon. Don't worry." We continue riding up the street. Disappointingly, there is not much to take a look at. Every street we move down brings fewer people and more soldiers. As we get closer to the palace, I can sense more trouble ahead. There are some powerful mages at the gates.

As my magic shudders once again, I motion to Aiden. We start to turn down an alleyway to rest when a group of soldiers on horseback ride across our path. I count six. They pull their horses around us. The head of the pack is the guard we spoke to at the gate. Their faces stare at us with grim amusement. My palms grow sweaty, and I scan for escape routes. Aiden speaks out to the lead soldier, "Excuse me? What seems to be the problem here?"

My hands began to shake; the glamour magic is not going to hold for much longer.

"After further research, I can't find a Tom and Elena Carrow on the city's registry," the man muses. "Care to tell us who you really are?"

"We just moved here," Aiden answers. "I don't know why we're not on the—" The conversation is interrupted as my glamour magic falls. Aiden's and my true forms are revealed. There's a split moment of confusion as our appearances change, then a rapid recognition. "Hey… who are you?" the guard begins to ask. But Aiden and I don't wait to see what else goes down here. Aiden throws a forcefield up, and the two of us jump off our horses, abandoning them. We take off down the street. I fire fireballs behind us in hopes to slow them down.

Unfortunately, with the sheer number of soldiers in the city, we get cornered pretty fast. The air becomes thick with flying spells in all sorts of colors. With one look, I grab Aiden and we move back-to-back as we did in the Duel of the Heirs. Aiden alternates between throwing fire with me and blocking other spells with sharp tendrils of earth and rock. Whenever he can, he captures soldiers' spells and converts them into pure energy to fuel his fire. I'm not even thinking about what magic is coming out of my hands. I throw absolutely everything that I have at these guys: fire waves, violent windstorms, force fields, telekinetically knocking them down with their own swords. Everything I can think of at the moment that it is happening. Telepathy guides me to communicate my motions directly with Aiden.

Aiden gets knocked down with a sudden succession of blows to the head. I grip his arm and keep him upright, although dazed, and fight with my other hand. But we are quickly backed into a fountain surrounded by guards. I can only be so strong against forty men. As they close in, I'm sure this whole thing ends now.

Suddenly, the ground shakes underneath us before exploding up from the center in a spraying of stone and dirt. Aiden and I put our hands up to shield ourselves from the debris. In a flash of black, a man drops down in front of us. He sends up a massive flash of light. It blinds all of us, including Aiden and me. A hand grabs my arm and pulls me out of the gridlock, taking us airborne and separating me from Aiden. I thrash around in hopes to escape the man's grasp, but it is tight. When we land on the other side of the guards and out of the light, the man turns around to reveal a familiar face. *Faolan.* His face is determined, eyes alert. His hand tightens around my arm. "You good?" he asks sharply.

I can only nod as I see Cary drop in from above and press her hands into the ground. The entire courtyard lights on fire. House of Darkness soldiers ignite. It's a horrifying sight to behold, but I can't focus on it as Cary zips over to us in a blink of an eye supporting Aiden with one arm. Even in his disoriented state, Aiden looks about as shocked as I feel.

"Are you two just going to stand there or are we going to get out of here?" Faolan shouts as he yanks me along. The four of us take off down the street. The soldiers have regained their sight and begin chasing us. I have no time to process whether Faolan and Cary are on our side. We just keep running. I move alongside Aiden with the House of Darkness twins on either side of us. There are spells shooting off around us left and right. Faolan yanks my arm down in time for a fireball to miss my head. I flick my eyes over, and he nods, accepting my silent begrudging thanks.

"Through here!" Aiden shouts as he points to the massive temple in front of us. We dash through the middle in an attempt to reach the other side. But in a horrifying turn of events, I hear a massive explosion behind us, and the columns begin to topple on top of us. When I look up, I see the roof begin to cave in.

"Look out!" I shout. As the rubble falls, I feel someone's arm around me, covering my head as we are all taken to the ground.

Chapter Twenty-Eight

My ears ring as I come to. There's a steady pounding that shakes my senses loose, and I can feel a raised bump sitting against the back of my head. My fingers twitch against the floor where I'm lying; I think it's some sort of smooth tile. Then I remember. *The explosion. Faolan. Cary. Aiden!* I think I'm jumping to my feet, but I'm only twitching helplessly against the ground. And the heartbeat in my head is only getting louder. A groan slips from my lips.

"Don't move," a low voice mutters behind me. A hand lays across my back, holding me firmly down. "Come on, Grace." A vial appears before my lips, and through my blurry vision, I see the characteristic light blue swirl of a healing potion. "Drink."

My basest instinct is not to drink. I tighten my lips and try to pull my head away. Which turns out to be a mistake as my breath is ripped from my lungs at the pain in my head. I let out a soft sound. "Come on, just drink it. It'll fix you." The vial presses insistently, but I keep my mouth shut. "Grace." The voice gets softer now, almost pleading. "Drink."

Finally, I let my lips part. I take a swig, choking as the liquid slips down my throat. "There you go. Alright, lie here for a second. Don't try to get up right away. You hit your head pretty hard."

As the pain slowly begins to recede, I groan softly in relief. "Aiden?"

A soft chuckle with a hint of sarcasm echoes in my ears. "No, darling."

No.

Ignoring the hand on my back trying to keep me down, I push myself shakily onto my hands and roll over quickly. Faolan's face glows in the ball of light he's created. I scramble backward and press myself up against the wall. Well, to call it a wall is a bit generous. The whole space we're in is crumbling around us. It's a disaster zone. The ceiling has caved in on top of us and is imposing on our heads. There's just enough room for the two of us to sit up straight. Pieces of destroyed timber jut out in the little alcove separating the two of us now as I press back against a jumbled stack of wood.

"What the hell's going on? Where's Aiden? What have you done with him?"

"What do you mean what have I done with him?" Faolan asks incredulously. "In case you don't remember, the building exploded and crashed down on top of us! I don't know where the others are. Don't accuse me of shit."

I breathe heavily, trying to remember how we got here. Flashes of fleeing from the House of Darkness's army, running into Faolan and Cary, and the building's collapse finally break through the slowly clearing haze surrounding my head. I scoot further back against the wall to keep my distance from the man sitting in front of me. "It was your army who blew the building."

"Look, you don't have to like it, but Cary and I saved your asses. If you two hadn't wandered in here with zero backup, we would not have been in this situation. Besides, we are not with the House of Darkness army."

"Bullshit," I hiss. "You expect me to believe that?"

"I don't care what you believe. It's the truth."

"I don't believe you. You've been an asshole ever since I met you, and I don't trust you one bit." I don't know why I'm so hostile toward him right now. He just saved my life. But after everything we have been through together, I don't trust that there is not some sort of ulterior motive here. "And don't think you can get in my good graces by healing me. For all I know, that draught was poisoned and I'm going to suffer in horrible agony later."

"Grace, if I wanted to kill you, you would already be dead," Faolan growls.

I say nothing and instead start searching for a way out. This is about the point where I realize just how…. small this alcove is.

In all the fuss, I forgot to be afraid, but my brain was certainly making up for lost time. That soft dizziness that comes with a rapid heartbeat and heaving breath began to creep up, and I double my efforts to find a way out, moving around in the tight space and trying to find spaces in the debris to crawl out.

"What are you doing?"

"Looking for a way out."

"Grace, we're well trapped in now." Faolan moves forward a bit and grabs my arm. "Besides, it serves us best to stay down here and let the generals think we're dead. There is enough space and enough air to linger here until things have calmed down. We can find a way out in a few hours when everyone should have moved away. If I can figure out where the weak points are, I can get us out of here."

I jerk backward violently, smacking my already sore head on a plank. It aches, and the panic begins to build. "No, I'm not staying in here a second longer with you than I have to."

"Grace, stop it. You're gonna bring the whole thing down on top of us," Faolan warns. I ignore him and continue scrambling for a space I can fit through, a piece I can move enough to escape this space.

"Grace," his voice grows softer, but stricter. "Dammit, you need to stop!" He grips both of my arms and pulls me forward away from the corner. His grasp sends me into a frenzy. I try to push him back with my magic, but the panic is stalling it. I wrench backward, smacking my back against a plan. I switch directions and smack my forehead into another one. I'm trapped. I don't know where I am. When he lets go, I am spinning around on my knees, trying to find the space that I know there is, but I keep running into more debris. I can't see, I can't breathe, and all I can do is scream.

Faolan's face looms in front of me, gripping my arms once again and pulling me forcibly to the center of the space. His eyes bore into mine, studying them. I flinch and struggle against his grip.

"Let go of me!" I try to sound angry, but my voice comes out quiet and weak.

"What's wrong with you?" he snaps.

"Please." I can't believe I'm begging him, but I don't care at this point; I need him to let me go so I can get back to the open space. "Please let go."

"Are you that afraid of me?" he inquires quieter this time. "I'm not gonna hurt you Grace. Do you want an oath on the Lady?"

It's too late. He's waited too long, and I feel the panic take over my faculties. I collapse against his grip, convulsing and gasping for breath. I can't pull enough oxygen into my lungs. *He's gonna kill me.* I can't summon any shield to protect myself from my opponent. "Get away," I choke out. "Get back." I feel unbearably hot, but my body is shaking with chills. My vision blurs.

"Grace!" It confuses me that he sounds concerned. My body jerks up, and I find myself inexplicably seated in Faolan's lap. His large hand presses my head into his shoulder and holds it against him. His other hand presses against my back, locking me in place. "I need you to breathe, Grace." I shake my head, trying to dislodge him. He thumps against my back.

"Come on, Grace, breathe!"

I'm getting increasingly lightheaded, and I know I'm about to pass out. But then I feel a light but insistent presence on the edge of my mind, pressing inwards. Faolan's prodding at my mind, and I'm too weak to put up resistance. "Come on," he mumbles again. "Relax." I feel the mental presence slip in and grip hold of my panic. A soothing breeze of darkness wraps itself around the panic and breaks it, and suddenly, I can breathe again.

Faolan lets go of my head, an action which I am grateful for. "What the hell was that, Grace?"

I hate that he hasn't given me a chance to catch my breath, hoping to catch me off guard enough to answer his questions. "It's… nothing…" I respond with heaving breath.

"Bullshit," he replies with a scowl. "You're claustrophobic, aren't you?"

I recoil and try to escape his lap, but Faolan holds me fast. "Don't deny it; I was just in your head. I could see it."

"Maybe don't go poking around in people's heads!" *Weak comeback, Grace, even with the lack of oxygen.*

"I'm supposed to let you hyperventilate next time?"

"Yes!" I cringe immediately after those words. I shake my head and turn away from the man I'm sitting on. "That's… that's not what I meant…"

"You would rather die than accept help from me?"

"That's not what I meant, Faolan. Now will you please let me up?"

"No," he answers rather definitively. "You go over there, you're just gonna start panicking again and we'll be right back where we started. Oh no, you're staying right here."

"On top of you? Really?"

A ghost of a smirk crosses his face. "Best seat in the house."

I roll my eyes but can't help a sarcastic chuckle.

"I won't bite, I promise." Faolan's smirk gets wider.

"Like I believe that," I retort.

Faolan chuckles before snapping his eyes shut abruptly. I watch as he mutters under his breath phrases I don't recognize. It sounds like a different language, perhaps a magical one. I can't say I'm not afraid of what he's uttering. I'm in a vulnerable position without any backup and a basic understanding of how my own powers work. I curse myself for not training harder over the last few months.

Faolan opens his eyes as quickly as they closed and locks on mine. His expression softens slightly. I hope he doesn't see my apprehension. "I've established a telepathic connection with Cary."

"You had a way to communicate with her this whole time?!"

"No, no, I've been trying for the last hour. It's hard to pinpoint someone that you don't know where they are or if they're reaching out telepathically to you as well. Excuse me for not saying anything until it fucking worked," Faolan snaps while rolling his eyes.

A slight feeling of shame creeps up on my neck. I hadn't considered that his sister was trapped in here too, his twin no less. I would have been a nervous wreck about Leo. "I'm sorry," I surprise myself by apologizing quietly. "What did you find out?"

"Cary is trapped about twenty feet to our right with Aiden. He's unconscious, *but!*" he quickly interjects at my terrified look, "but he's alright. Cary thinks he might have a minor concussion, but she's dosed him up with a healing elixir and she'll let me know what happens when he wakes up."

I breathe a soft sigh of relief. "Okay." I hesitate. "Thank you."

Faolan studies me carefully before giving me a half-smile. "You're welcome." Our eyes lock in solidarity. His eyes don't give anything away, and hopefully, mine don't either. There's something strange about the way the amber in his eyes swirls with the little black streaks. It's almost like a hurricane, a strange dusty one wrapped in shadows. I suppose it's fitting for him.

I'm the first to break eye contact. "What are we going to do?"

"Rest. Get some strength back so we can attempt to break out of here."

"Alright. I'll take the first watch then." I climb off his lap, but I don't get far. Faolan stops me and makes a little space to his side. He pushes me down there this time. "What are you doing?"

He chuckles. "You're not going anywhere, and I'm taking the first watch."

"Um… I am not gonna be able to sleep in this environment, so you might as well get some rest."

"I can fix that," he says softly, and I see the ball of light begin to dim.

My hand lashes out and grips his wrist. "Don't!" I surprise myself with the force of my whisper-shout.

To my surprise, Faolan only chuckles again. "Don't tell me you're afraid of the dark."

"Of course not." I roll my eyes. "I'm not afraid of the dark. I quite like it." I bite my lip at his smirk. "Oh, don't be ridiculous. I don't want it… and the…" My voice trails off.

His eyes flash. "And…" he coaxes teasingly.

"And tight spaces," I finish begrudgingly.

"Well…" He pulls my head to his shoulder. I try to protest, but he shushes me. "The darkness can be soothing too, you know." There's a soft breeze that brushes my cheek and a soft shadow that presses in on the corners of my eyes.

"Don't think…" Faolan's soft husky voice whispers in my ear. "Just breathe it in."

Before I realize I'm being manipulated, I'm falling into the warmth of the dark embrace and eventually his embrace as well. I feel a cloak drape across my body, warming me through and drawing me deeper into the darkness, and Faolan's grip tightens on me.

"Sleep."

I knew no more that night.

Chapter Twenty-Nine

When I come to again, the first thing I feel is a mixture of anger and this odd sensation of a fulfilling deep sleep. It's a strange feeling: fury and peace at the same time. I can't believe Faolan had the nerve to knock me out. I take a moment to take stock of myself and where I am. Looking around our cramped quarters and casting a small ball of fire to give me some light, I see that nothing major has shifted while I was asleep. When I look down, I notice that I am all in one piece. Nothing appears to have moved or been harmed during my slumber. But unfortunately… I am still tucked in Faolan's side.

Faolan's sleeping face unnerves me. His features are smoothed out; his eyebrows are sitting normally on his face instead of in what appears to be a permanently raised state. His mouth is curved in a soft frown. Seeing him in a relaxed state is strange to me. Everything he does, albeit self-centered and sarcastic, is proper. He has a style that never fails to irritate or intimidate. I wonder if he's ever let anyone see him sleep. I wonder if he knows how peaceful and… well… non-Faolan-like it makes him look.

But I'm not going to sit here and stare at him much longer.

I shift to move away, but Faolan's arm moves quickly to trap me there. Faolan opens his eyes. "Going somewhere?"

"Yes." I struggle in his grasp. "Out of this collapse."

Faolan lets go of me, and I scramble away on hands and knees. "It's going to take more than will to get out of here. Let me wake up a bit, and I'll reach out to Cary. We'll work this out together, take a breath." I begrudgingly listen and take a slow breath. "There you go." I glare at Faolan menacingly. He chuckles. He shifts and closes his eyes. His sharp face and the lines indicate he's reaching out to his sister. I try to wait patiently.

After a while, he opens his eyes and looks over at me. "Aiden's awake." Relief floods my body. "He's still a bit groggy, so it's up to the three of us. You're going to use your wind magic to prop up certain sections of the rubble—"

""Wait, wait, wait," I interrupt. "How do you know I have wind magic?"

"I hear things." He waves off my concern cryptically. "Like I was saying, you're going to use your wind magic to prop up certain sections of the rubble, and I'm going to use a precise form of disintegration magic to tunnel our way out of here. Cary will keep an eye on her side and let me know which areas to focus on. Can you do that?"

I nod. "Yeah. Let's go."

Faolan and I situate ourselves under a segment of the broken building. When he nods to me, I push out a gust that keeps the pieces above us elevated as Faolan blasts us through. The weight pushes against my wind magic, but I put all I've got into it because *by the Lady I want to get the hell out of this debris.* The space gets cooler and cooler as we make our way toward the open air. We work above us and occasionally to the side of us where Cary and Aiden are trapped. It is slow going, but when we break through to the open night sky, I nearly cheer in relief.

Cary climbs out of the rubble first, dragging a dazed Aiden behind her. I rush to him. "Aiden?" I check his eyes and feel around his head and his upper body for wounds.

"I'm alright, Grace," he says to me quietly. "Need a healer, but I'm fine."

I look around us and take stock of where we are. In the distance, I can see a handful of soldiers, but far less than what we were facing before. We may be able to get out of here alive by sneaking out. "Thank you both for this. We owe you."

"We're here to collect," Cary interjects immediately, looking over at her brother.

"Already?"

"Yes. We want to come with you," Faolan says. "We have horses stationed a little way out of here; we can sneak out of the city and head to the House of the Evening. But we want to come with you."

"Why in the world would you want to come with us? Why..." Between the escape from the soldiers and the cave-in, I haven't had any time to process the fact that the enemy helped us, let alone wants to escape with us. "What is going on?"

"There's no time to explain now—"

"There has to be time to explain," Aiden insists. "For all we know, your rescuing of us is a trap to infiltrate the House of the Evening."

"Fine, fine," Cary snaps. She sighs in frustration and looks up to stare at me. "We need to get out of this town. Because despite having originally agreed with our father's general sentiments, he has gone too far." Her eyes sear into mine. It's unnerving.

"What we understood from his plans is that he wanted to take the House of the Earth for their farmland. Maybe expand to a few of the outer villages of other Houses, but otherwise keep it contained. We had enough men to hold those positions without much effort and judging by what went down at your original War Council, we weren't going to have much resistance." He sighs and shakes his head a bit. "But then Father had to get greedy. He saw how fast everything fell, and he wanted more and more. And with that, he's destroying the realm. He has taken so many lives unnecessarily, executing prisoners instead of putting them to work, random rage killings and the like."

"He's going overboard," Cary adds. "He's involved in some things we don't want to be involved in anymore." The twins exchange a pointed look, and I would love to know what they are saying to each other. It is clear they know a lot more than they are letting on. "Look," Carry continues, "I know it's not under the best of circumstances, and we do not agree with each other. But we have valuable information from our father's plans that we will swear to share with you, only once given extradition to the House of the Evening."

"We can get you out of here," Faolan adds. "But it will cost you our freedom as well. Do we have a deal?"

The four of us stand against each other, locked in a silent standoff. If I say no, we get stranded here and have to find our own way out with Aiden barely able to stand. If I say yes… I kickstart something that I have no idea of the scale of the consequences. As I'm turning over the idea in my head, I hear Luna's voice in my head repeating the prophecy in her tinkling voice. *The Witch and the Conjurer, knights of the red; upon darkness and shadow will they always tread. But in the light, what the others won't expect: The Witch is to serve, the Conjurer to protect.* Could Faolan and Cary be members of the prophecy? Is this the shift I have been waiting for?

Well, now what? There's no way I can just reveal that information to the War Council as my excuse for bringing them in. And what would I even say to the two people in front of me? Faolan and Cary aren't exactly the easiest people to trust. But they did save us from certain death. I suppose that at least entitles them to a chance.

"Alright," I finally agree. Aiden looks at me in alarm, but I telepathically communicate to him to *trust me. They have something we need. I'll explain later.* "I'll get you both an audience with the War Council. And I'll speak on your behalf. But that's the best I can do."

"Done." Faolan and I shake on it. Then the four of us depart for clearer skies.

* * *

We make it to where the twins have stashed their horses, and we ride to the House of the Evening under the cover of darkness. Faolan shows us to a safehouse in a remote village for the black market where we spend the night. Cary attends to Aiden and his injuries a bit more, but she informs me that he will need to see a physician as soon as we get back to the palace to make sure there's no long-term damage. As the sun rises on the second day, we arrive at the palace. When we hop off our horses, the courtyard floods with people.

Lords, Ladies, and servants alike are staring at our unlikely band: Faolan and I supporting Aiden between us and Cary holding out her hands, ready to wave off anyone who may come charging at us. And judging by the expressions on everyone's faces, it very well may happen soon. "Can you all stop staring at us and get him some help?" I refer to Aiden who gives a little wave with one hand. Some of the attendants rush to our sides and take Aiden from us. "Finally, thank you." The confused and apprehensive looks have not shifted one bit as I look up.

"Okay, okay, I will explain all of this in a few hours, but what you need to know right now is that Faolan and Cary are applying for sanctuary here. They wish to join our efforts."

"We're going to need a lot more information than that before we let those traitors inside!" Lord Jason shouts at me incredulously.

"In case you've forgotten since I've been gone, Jason," I snap, "that is my Lady-damned castle, and I will invite anyone I want inside. If you want information, get into the throne room and we'll have a nice War Council meeting. But I am going to sit the hell down while we do it." Faolan chuckles beside me. Cary smacks his arm. If I wasn't so stressed, I would have laughed. I storm towards the palace entrance, pushing through everyone. Cary and Faolan trail closely behind as do the others. I can feel the other nobles' eyes on me, burning with irritation and questions.

When we reach the throne room, I collapse into my chair and drape myself over it rather unceremoniously. I motion for an attendant. "Find some chairs for everyone." A group of men returns shortly after, carrying multiple chairs. While everyone gets seated, I fight off the exhaustion and sit up straight on the throne. *Gonna need to be on a strong front for this one.*

"Are you alright, Grace?" Aira asks tentatively.

"I'm fine," I answer with a chuckle. "Just exhausted. Let's get this over with as quickly as possible." I sit forward in my chair and fold my hands, elbows resting on my knees. "Faolan, Cary, stand before this War Council."

"Uh, you got us chairs just to make us stand up?" Cary snarks.

"The chair's for when I can trust your intel," I fire back. I may not sound very Lady-like at all, but honestly, this whole situation is more than I can handle at this point. I like to process my information one piece at a time. This is not my forte. With a roll of her eyes, Cary stands up along with Faolan. They cross to the center of this little circle we've created.

"What exactly went down in the House of Peace?" Lord Tristan asks. "Can we just… start with that?"

"Fair," I acknowledge. "Aiden and I made it to Craine. We tricked our way inside by assuming false identities and names when checked at the border, but we were unable to reach the palace before we were spotted. The House of Peace is now the new headquarters for the House of Darkness."

"No, it's not," Faolan interrupts me. "It's an interim camp."

"Do you know where your father plans to set up permanently then?"

Tristan stares at him.

"He would prefer to operate his base of operations from the House of Darkness when he finishes what he wants to accomplish." Faolan looks back, unfazed.

"In the city," I continue, trying to take the focus off them, "there were soldiers crawling everywhere. It's going to be difficult to take it back. Despite the disguises, we were discovered almost immediately and caused a widespread chase." Murmurs circulate around the gathering, a mix of sadness and horror.

High Lord Jason's eyes haven't left the House of Darkness twins. He speaks loudly over the rest of us, "Can you get to the traitors now?"

"You know, I resent that," Faolan starts to say. Gratefully, Cary smacks his arm again.

"Jason, let's keep the name calling out of this." I glare at him before continuing. "Aiden and I got cornered in the city square. We were trapped, Aiden was down, and we were likely about to be killed. Suddenly, those two burst up out of… I'm not even sure where, but they got us out of there. The four of us got caught up in a building collapse, but the quick thinking of the two of them eventually got us out."

Taking a breath, I continue a little more powerfully. "Lord Faolan and Lady Cary Infernos are offering concrete information about High Lord Carron's movements, troops, and objectives. In exchange, we offer asylum and allow them to act as heirs while they are here."

"What does that mean?" Tristan narrows his eyes at me.

"That means they serve on the War Council and offer their assistance and resources. Same as us."

The room dissolves into shouting. "You can't just let them in here and expect us to vote to allow them to stay with them standing here!" Jason yells. "Don't you know Cary has mind control magic?"

"It's not like it's a secret if I use it," Cary says angrily. "I can't keep it on someone forever. And if I don't do it exactly right, you can completely tell. The glassy eyes, the vacant stare. That shit is hard."

"I think we should give them a chance," High Lady Morgana offers sternly. Aira nods beside her in agreement. "High Lord Carron is a dark and twisted man. But I have always found the two of them to be made of something a little stronger. I'm willing to trust them for their information at this time."

"I disagree," Lord Tristan counters. The conversations continue like this, disjointedly and flying around the circle. It's giving me a wicked headache. I can't stand this. I'm exhausted, and I don't want to argue anymore.

"Alright." I get to my feet slowly, drawing everyone's eyes. "Everybody shut up and sit down." My low voice causes the room to fall silent. "I cannot believe I'm going to have to do this standing up, but you people are ridiculous. I get that there are a lot of questions and frankly a lot of problems with the Lord and Lady in front of us." Faolan raises an eyebrow at me but continues to listen quietly. "Lord Faolan and Lady Cary are two extremely powerful Fae. And right now, we need all of those that we can get. Faolan has black market connections all over this realm that can suit us and our needs." I get a little whispering for that comment, but nothing crazy. "And I have seen Cary in action, and her magic is stronger than most of the people in this room. I'm not saying we need to trust them right away, but I will vouch for them now."

I sigh and throw my hands up. "Look, we need something significant to turn the tide of the war." I point to Faolan and Cary. "They are our next big move. We're going to throw off High Lord Carron, and that little slip, that little moment of faltering might be enough."

As I look around the circle, I see mixed reactions. But everyone has seemed to calm down a bit. "I want to take a vote. Let's go." As we go around the room, Lord Jason, Lord Tristan, and Lady Alena are still vehemently against the incorporation of the House of Darkness twins. But I have managed to somewhat convince the rest.

"That's 5-3 without Lord Aiden's vote," High Lady Morgana confirms. "Lord Faolan and Lady Cary stay."

"On a trial basis," I add quickly. "But now it's time for you to share what you know." I look the twins in the eye. "Don't make me regret this."

Chapter Thirty

It doesn't take long for the War Council to coax out everything Faolan and Cary must share about the House of Darkness. Faolan recounts what he told me to the others. As a few others suspected, the original plan had been to take the House of the Earth to have better access to fertile land. That invasion was even smoother than previously believed. Faolan had some of his black-market connections keep any information about the impending attack and others who opened the gates to allow it to take place. As furious as the nobles in the room were about these developments, they couldn't deny his resources could do wonders for us.

Once the House of the Earth fell, the House of Darkness moved in very quickly. The farmland was gobbled up by the oligarchy, and the people finally went to bed at night with full bellies. But they all lay in wait to discover whether the rest of the Upper Realm would come for them the following morning. Weeks went by, and High Lord Carron realized no one was coming to confront them. The rest was history. The High Lord believed there was nothing he couldn't do. He wouldn't be stopped. He started taking more villages on the outskirts and eventually entire Houses. The House of Fire wholeheartedly agreed, and well… the House of the Sun has just been along for the ride ever since.

We learned two pieces of shocking news from the twins. Cary

informed us that the House of the Earth's family had been executed recently in the House of Peace. The High Lord had made an escape attempt, and High Lord Carron killed him and his family on display as a warning to other noble families who may think they can escape him. That sent a shockwave around the room. Lord Jason was sent reeling into his seat, shaking his head. The House of Light twins were brought to tears. High Lady Morgana bowed her head and said a few words on behalf of the Council, asking the Lady to grant the fallen safe passage into the afterlife. She looked the most shaken out of all of us.

The second involves the House of Darkness's potentially scary new approach to war tactics. "My father has been spending an awful lot of time with some of the best demonology scholars in the Realm," Faolan shared. "He kidnapped them from all over the Twelve Houses. I have spoken to him about it only once, but from what I can understand, he may be trying to channel demonic magic through various experimental methods." The comment sent the room into a panic. Aira and Luna were appalled and concerned by the idea that demons could play a factor in this war. Tristan doesn't even believe it is possible. We discussed for at least an hour what we know about the Lower Realm and what we could be facing. I give an account of what Aiden and I experienced in our time down there. Faolan watches me as I speak a little more closely. In the end, we make plans to call for our best scholars as soon as possible to research the issue.

When the Council disperses, I find Aiden coming down the stairs all bandaged up. Relief floods my chest. I run to him and give him the biggest hug I can muster. I am so grateful to see him after all we went through and not knowing if he was okay. He hugs me back tightly. When he pulls back, I can see him looking over my shoulder at the heirs. "What did I miss?"

"So much. We voted on whether to let Faolan and Cary stay, and we gained some important information about the House of Darkness's movements. I'll fill you in later, okay?"

"I can't believe you went ahead and held the vote without me." Aiden shakes his head.

"You were incapacitated, love," I soothe. "The heirs were restless; I had to give them some answers. Besides, your vote would have helped us more. Count was five to three in favor of them staying."

"I would have said no."

I blink and tilt my head slightly. "I'm sorry?"

"I don't think Faolan and Cary should be allowed to stay. I just don't."

"They saved our lives! They've already offered a decent amount of information into the High Lord's plans to—"

"I don't care if they saved our lives, Grace," Aiden interrupts me. "This is war. They are shady as hell, Grace. I would kick them out while we can with this information before they have a chance to betray us."

I'm a bit taken aback by his strong words. I never thought he would be so violently against keeping them under our eyes. "Look," I say quietly. "I didn't get to tell you this earlier. But… I think Faolan and Cary may be the twins of the prophecy."

"Are you serious?" he hisses. "There is no way they are involved."

"Think about it. *The Witch and the Conjurer, knights of the red; upon darkness and shadow will they always tread.* They come from the House of Darkness. *But in the light, what the others won't expect.* No one expected them to turn to our side. Too many things check out."

"They can't be prophecy members! They're the enemy! Their father is wreaking havoc on this realm. Why would they be the solution to the problem?" He huffs. "We never should have brought them here."

"Um, they *are* members of the prophecy. I would bet my power on it. Who else would it be? And what exactly did you expect us to do?

We made a deal."

"I don't know," he groans. "Lock them up until we needed them."

"And you thought that was going to work?" I raise my voice. "How would that convince them to fight with us? Would that not work against us? We need them whether you like it or not."

Aiden stares at me for a solid minute, unblinking. There's something in his eyes that is so unfeeling. It is frightening to witness. "I… need some time with this." He slowly turns and walks away from me. I watch him go with a sinking feeling in my stomach. This can't end well.

Chapter Thirty-One

A couple days later, Aiden still hasn't come by my room to speak with me. And I sure as hell am not going to his room just for him to be in a pissy mood. I have been trying to keep myself busy, but waiting for him is starting to mess with my head. I knew he was stubborn, but this is taking it to an entirely new level. As I walk briskly down the stairs and into the basement hallway, I can't help but let out a groan of frustration. "Men…." I mumble under my breath as the heels of my boots click against the tile. "Ridiculous…" I push the door open to the sparring room and sprint inside, slamming into one of the punching bags on the far side of the room with full force. I scream in frustration as I punch it a few times before flying past it and pressing my hands to the back wall. My heart pounds in my ears.

"Someone's in a mood," a smug, familiar voice speaks over my thoughts.

I whip around, hitting my back against the wall. "Fuck… What are you doing in here, Faolan?"

The man in question only chuckles. "Well, I was resting after a workout until I was so rudely awoken."

"You were sleeping in here?" I look down at the hard floor and then back up at Faolan. He nods. I take note of the stack of mats he's sitting on before giving him a shrug. "Any reason you're not sleeping in the room I gave you?"

"More convenient to nap here if I'm going to train more afterwards," he replies simply. "Plus, I was tired. I was busy taking care of things."

My eyes narrow. "What things?" Faolan doesn't answer, but I see a glint of something in his eyes, and I know in an instant what he's done. "No…." I groan. "You're not bringing black market people into my castle, are you?" When he smiles, I lose my cool. "I swear by the Lady, Faolan, I just vouched for you only a few days ago!"

"Oh please." Faolan sits up on his hands. "Half the servants in your castle work for me."

What the hell? "Are you telling me you have black market contacts inside the House of the Evening? In the palace?"

"Uhhhh, duh?" Faolan's lip curls upwards, and I see red.

"Who are they?" I demand.

"Nope."

I chuckle dryly. "Worth a shot."

"Not at all."

"Oh shush." I finally shut the conversation down as I turn to pick up a sword off the rack.

"Or what? What are you going to do?" Faolan eggs on.

"Faolan, get out. I need to train."

"Or what?" he repeats.

I groan and turn around. "Or else I'll throw you out myself."

He laughs. "Maybe if I fought without magic, a sword, or moving in general."

I spin around and point my sword at Faolan menacingly. "Let's not forget who bested you at the duel of the heirs. Sword to sword, I'm the better fighter."

Faolan scoffs. "Oh please, I underestimated you. I could have blinded you with magic if I wanted to, and I chose not to. I won't make that same mistake again."

"You know what, I am fed up." I storm closer to him and point my sword at his chest. "Get up. Get up! You and me, right now. Trial by sword. No magic allowed."

As if to further mock me, Faolan yawns and stretches his arms. "But I just woke up," he whines playfully.

"I think you're afraid to get your ass kicked again." I turn my back on him and walk toward the center of the room. "Either get out or get ready to fight." When he doesn't move and sits smirking at me for another thirty seconds, I resort to drastic measures. I fling my hand out and draw water from the sink in the corner with a gust of wind to douse Faolan from head to toe.

To my surprise, that doesn't drive him out of his seat in anger. Instead, he slowly rises to his full height and brushes his wet hair out of his eyes. He strides past me to the rack of swords. My eyes follow him the whole time. He picks up a sword. "Fine," he says quietly with just a hint of danger in his voice. "Have it your way."

Before I can blink, Faolan whacks me on the head with the sword. "Oww!" I shout. I rub my smarting head. "What the hell?" He smirks at me, and I move forward quickly to stab him.

He sidesteps me with a parry. "Cheater. I already won."

I don't answer him; I only lash out with my weapon, preferring to let my sword convey my anger and irritation. Faolan laughs and smacks my sword down before leaning in close and blowing a kiss. "You can't hit me if you go at me based only on your anger."

Ugh. He's right. I take a deep breath and take a step back, bracing myself before jabbing at his stomach. Faolan sidesteps me again, this time sliding the blade along my side. "Better. Though it's a shame. You'll lose anyway. I know your fighting style."

I spin and catch his sword. "Don't be so sure."

The second I make that move, Faolan grabs my wrist with his free hand and twists my arm behind my back. I curse. "You can't outsmart me, Grace. Not a second time. I didn't earn where I am by being slow to learn."

I whack his hand so he releases my arm. "You didn't earn shit," I scoff. Another swing crashes our swords together. "You were born into it."

Faolan laughs and surprises me with several quick motions. I am forced to take several steps back as I parry to keep him from slashing me. "I built the black market alone. I shaped our world in my hands. Hell, I own half of it. And you say I didn't earn it?" His voice takes a dangerous turn. "I have fought all my life."

"You built your precious black market off the backs of my people!" The further we get into this fight, the more real it feels. I haven't spoken about my mortal home in a long time. *I'm still calling them my people. Why?* I feel myself losing control of not only my physical movements, but my emotions too.

And Faolan is egging me on with every word out of his mouth. "Your people begged me for help," he taunts. "They live because of me. I am the economic support for your mortal realm."

I lose my patience.

I throw my sword to the ground and scream as I tackle the man to the ground. I am throwing blind punches and grabbing at him to strangle him. But it isn't long until my hands are wrenched behind my back and he presses me to the ground. His grip is tight, but not painful.

"Calm down," he orders softly but firmly in my ear. I want to tell him to shove it, but all that comes out is some sort of pained breath. Faolan holds me there for a while until I relax, at which point he slowly sets my arms down at my side. "You need some work. Your physical skills are running too much off emotion. I imagine your magic is the same way, given your performance during the duel of the heirs. When you hit your tipping point, you become blind. Emotion is only half the battle; you have to have the skill and the foresight to back it up."

"And I suppose you have all the answers?"

"I didn't always." He gets up and crosses the room back to his makeshift bed. "My sister taught me."

"Cary?"

"I was the stronger in magic by far, so to show me up, she became a swordswoman. She's truly skilled. I learned everything from her whaling on me. Eventually, I became more skilled. I learned to memorize moves by watching her once or twice. Then I could pick up sequences and the way her eyes moved when she made a decision." Faolan stares off somewhere over my shoulder, shaking his head. "You have no refinement. No follow through. And you could win if you learned how to use your magic."

"I've only been learning magic for a couple months," I argue. "Talon can only teach me so quickly."

Faolan scoffs. "Talon knows fucking nothing."

"You know Talon?" *What the hell, does he have ties with everybody?*

"I keep track of everything. I wasn't kidding."

I file that tidbit in my brain to dig into later. "Are you offering to teach me?" I change the subject.

"You would have to prove you could handle it."

"How so?"

Faolan's lips curl upward. "I'll let you know when I figure that out. Until then, don't wake me up."

I chuckle and roll my eyes. "There's a war to fight, Faolan. You are going to be awake sometimes."

"But not right now."

"Yes… not now." My voice trails off as I walk towards the door.

When I'm most of the way out, Faolan's voice calls out to me one last time. "You should take a nap too."

"A nap?" I turn back and look at him in confusion. "When do I have time for a nap?"

"Find the time." With that, he curls up on the mats and closes his eyes.

Rolling my eyes, I leave the basement wondering why he made the effort to state such a thing.

Chapter Thirty-Two

Aiden eventually comes to my room with a bouquet of white lilies and apologizes for his outburst and for ignoring me for all the days that he did. Although I'm still not quite happy with him, I'm glad he's back at my side. He sneaks us out to the palace gardens one night and takes me on a midnight picnic. It is nice to have some alone time while all this is going on. It's hard for me to recharge when there's another challenge to face daily.

We meet with Aira and Luna and share my suspicion about the House of Darkness twins. Both agree that they fit the lines, and we agree it's time to bring them into the fold. I ask the three Fae to wait in the library while I go seek out Faolan and Cary. I find them out in the courtyard engaged in a hushed conversation. Cary appears to be arguing quite passionately, arms moving around in all sorts of configurations to punctuate her words. Faolan's face is grim as he answers her in very short direct sentences. When I walk over to them, they immediately stop talking. "What do you want?" Cary snaps at me.

"Stand down, Cary," Faolan scolds lightly. He smiles at me. "You'll have to excuse her, Grace. She's a little worked up." Cary glares at him, and he chuckles. "What can I do for you?"

"I need both of you to come upstairs to the library with me. A few of us are having a private meeting, and we would like you two to be involved."

"A private meeting?" Cary's eyes narrow at me. "Why not a meeting of the full Council?"

Faolan smirks. "Are you up to something, Grace?"

I resist the urge to roll my eyes. "I'll explain everything when we get there. Just… please come upstairs." The siblings exchange a look, but Cary indicates for me to lead the way. We head back inside and up to the library. Aira, Luna, and Aiden sit around one of the round tables with three seats left open for us. While Cary and Faolan take their seats, I close the doors.

"Alright." I sigh as I sit down. "Thank you, Cary, Faolan for joining us."

"Did we really have a choice?" Cary raises an eyebrow.

"Why are we here?" Faolan asks me. "There's only a few of us in this room. Is this a task force of some kind?"

"No." I shake my head and look around the table, trying to find the words to start. But everyone is looking back at me, waiting for me to make the first move. "First, let me make it clear that nothing we say here can leave this room. It is not a good time to let any of the other Council members know."

"We'll see," Cary answers.

"It's not negotiable," Aiden snaps. I give him a look to tone it down while Cary gives a short chuckle.

"I'll work with that," I interject before anyone else can argue. "Let's get down to it. After I broke into the Upper Realm the first time and teamed up with Aiden, the two of us ended up taking my journey into the Lower Realm together." Faolan raises a perfectly arched eyebrow, clearly relishing the fact that he had guessed correctly back at the Solstice. "I was in search of the Half-Fae Coven in hopes they would give me more information about why my brother died."

"The Half-Fae Coven?" Cary interrupts me. "That's a legend. What were you doing going on a suicide mission?"

"No, they're real," Aiden and I say together. He gives me a little smile as I chuckle. "We met them."

"The Half-Fae Coven?" Cary repeats herself. "You actually saw them?"

"We spoke to them," I continue. "But instead of giving me the information that I was hoping for, they decided to share a prophecy with us instead. It spoke of a group of eight powerful Fae who would turn the tide of a major war in the Upper Realm. These chosen would come from different backgrounds and each play a specific role with unique magic types and power. At first, I thought it was something crazy, that it was distracting me from my goal. But after the Winter Solstice, I realized that they were giving a prophecy for me, specifically. And Aiden. And… everyone at this table." I turn to Luna. "Luna, would you…"

She nods and recites the prophecy for the twins. As she does, I watch closely for their reactions. For the most part, their faces stay very calm. Occasionally, I see a flicker of recognition or curiosity on Faolan's face. Cary seems more thoughtful, taking the prophecy in as each line is revealed. When Luna finishes, she smiles at the two of them. "We think the two of you are the Witch and the Conjurer. Or at least we're fairly sure."

Faolan and Cary look at each other pointedly and stay silent for a long time. I look up at Aiden, and his face is drawn and tense. He gives a small shake of his head. My heart drops. He's still not on board with them being involved, and I can tell he's thrown by their lack of reaction. To be honest, I am a little too. Everyone, with the exception of Luna, had some sort of question or panic or… something. They are concerned like I am that they will just blow right on out of here and reveal our secrets at their leisure.

Though as I look at the twins' eyes again, I sense a conversation happening telepathically. I can't believe I didn't think about it before. While we're all sitting here awkwardly, they're working out all their thoughts between the two of them before they speak. I clear my throat. Faolan looks at me. His upper lip curls and he gives me a little wink. *Dammit, I was right.* "We're in," he says simply.

"Just like that?" Aiden asks. ""No questions, no thoughts, just… we're in."

"Unlike the rest of you, we're kind of used to this." Cary laughs. "We're the first twins to be born in the House of Darkness in seven centuries, the first Lord and Lady of the House of Darkness forced to duel to see which one gets to be heir, and the children of the first High Lord in modern times to attack other Houses in the realm. A prophecy? It is not even on the radar of the most legendary thing to happen to our House."

"Also, our dad has been trying to find black obsidian obsessively for years to see what stood in his way of conquering the House of the Earth," Faolan adds. "And I suppose, in hindsight, the rest of the realm. So it's not out there that there would be a prophecy related to the war. Now I am surprised we're involved in our father's downfall, but hey," he smirks, "we'll be remembered."

"Remembered?" Aiden snaps at him.

"Yes," he snaps back. "Remembered. Our father is going to sully the name of the House of Darkness for hundreds of years all on his own. But we may have a chance to bring it back in the future. I'll be repairing a broken House when it's over."

"What makes you think you'll still get to rule after we defeat the High Lord?!"

"I am the heir, and I'm on the good team now, right? So why wouldn't I?"

"Let's not get into that now." I stop Aiden from exploding by holding up my hand. "We'll have plenty of time to sort out the logistics. Right now, all you need to know is that we meet most nights up here in the library after the rest of the castle has gone to bed. For now, we're looking to figure out who the remaining two prophecy members are. So… think it over. We'll chat again soon." When we part ways, I feel a little more hopeful than I did before. Though I don't know how valuable Faolan and Cary will be to our mission, I have to hope that they will bring us closer to winning this war.

Chapter Thirty-Three

When I call the War Council to order a few afternoons later, I can feel the tension in the room. This is the first meeting where Faolan and Cary will be present as representatives on this Council, and honestly, I'm ready for discussions to run hot. Aiden is already eyeing Faolan with a death glare that I would not want to be on the other side of. But if he's noticed, Faolan isn't showing it. He sits down beside me, opposite Aiden to my right. I probably should have expected this from him, but it's a little too late now.

"What's on the docket for today?" I start briskly.

"We need to decide what we want to do about the House of the Sun." Lord Tristan immediately leans forward.

"What do you mean about the House of the Sun?" Aiden asks.

"Look, let's be honest," Tristan replies a bit sheepishly. "Of the three allies that we're fighting against, the House of the Sun is the weakest link. We need to do something to take them off the playing field. We've been holding out for long enough, Aiden, and I'm sorry. But we have to make a judgment call now."

"What exactly did you have in mind?" Aiden crosses his arms.

Tristan looks over to Jason who has pretty much taken on the role of being the hard news bringer. He sighs and puts a hand out. "We need to put pressure on the people."

"What do you mean by that?" I see Aiden's hands tighten against his chair. I'm anticipating an explosion.

Jason looks Aiden dead in the eye. "Punish the people to force your father to see to reason."

"No." Aiden leaps to his feet. "Absolutely not! I refuse to take part in this discussion."

"Then you will be left out," Jason answers harshly. "Aurora, Alena, Tristan, and I are putting this on the table today. The topic is not up for debate, but if you want to be a part of the conversation, sit down." Aiden glares at Jason with so much fire in his eyes, but he does return to his seat. Jason then turns to me. "Will you approve this issue to be discussed, Grace?"

I feel put on the spot. Aiden is looking at me intently as if staring at me hard enough will make me agree with him. But unfortunately, since there is a significant faction that wants to discuss the issue, I have no choice. "Yes." I avoid Aiden's eyes. "Let's throw ideas out."

"We could send troops in," Aira shares. "Try to take the area one village at a time?"

Alena shakes her head. "I don't think that will work. We shouldn't divert any of our troops at this stage. We need every soldier we can get for the main event. I think we should put all our focus on preparing for battle. No alternate strategies."

"I don't necessarily agree with my sister's idea, but I do agree with the sentiment," Aurora chimes in. "I don't think we should confront the House of the Sun because it might just anger High Lord Carron more. We could be opening ourselves up to more attacks.

There is a hush of silence that falls across the room as everyone considers the issue at hand. Then surprisingly, Faolan's husky voice rings out over the quiet. "Cut off trade."

"What?" Jason and Aiden ask in unison before glaring at each other.

"Cut off trade," Faolan repeats. "It's the quickest way to bring a House's people to their knees. I have people in the House of the Sun.

One notice from me and we don't even need to stop trade from the outside. The black market can hoard the supply that is delivered. Small, highly targeted robberies could stall trade much better than cutting it off at the pipeline. It won't take long before the people will be begging for the High Lord to cut a deal and back out of that alliance."

"No!" Aiden bellows. I've never seen him this angry. "I refuse to let my people suffer because of my father's decisions."

"Well, I'm sorry, but that's how government works," Faolan snaps. "The people always suffer or survive at the hands of the ruler."

"I can't believe I'm saying this, but Faolan is right," Tristan adds. "Your father would only be reaping the consequences of his own actions."

"He's one to talk," Aiden shouts emotionally and points at Faolan. "Your father is destroying this realm! Where are his consequences?"

"He'll run into them. But your father's right alongside him. He's a willing partic—"

Faolan's lack of reaction is getting to Aiden because suddenly, he lunges at Faolan. Faolan dodges in the blink of an eye. No idea he had reflex amplification magic. But that doesn't faze Aiden who changes directions and catches him again. The two of them end up rolling around on the ground. Jason jumps up to grab the man off Faolan. I rush over to help. The room is in chaos as Aiden lands a good old sucker punch to Faolan's smirking lip. Faolan swings back and would have hit Aiden if I didn't grab onto his arm.

"Boys, stop this at once!" High Lady Morgana gets to her feet and shouts at us. "NOW!" The lords and Lady Aira manage to pull Aiden off Faolan. I stand between them, shocked. "Come on, this is ridiculous. We are not starting a brawl in this conference room, do you hear me?" Aiden at least has the gall to look sheepish. "Now…how does everyone else feel about this?"

"I'm against it," Aiden growls.

"I'm for it," Faolan counters as he wipes the blood from his mouth.

"I second with Faolan." Jason moves back to his seat. From there, however, no one chimes in. They look around at each other, waiting for someone to add another comment. But no one speaks.

Finally, High Lady Morgana prods gently. "Maybe we should do a blind vote."

"Good idea," I agree while trying to hide the relief in my voice. I pass around small sheets of parchment. "Write yea or nay and fold it up. I'll do the count." The shuffling of papers and writing instruments scratching against the page fill the quiet. I look down at my page for a long time before marking my vote down. After a few moments, I motion for the others to pass their ballots. The room is so tense while the High Lady counts them. When she is finished, she reads out, "8-3. The motion passes. We cut trade immediately." I don't have time to say another word before Aiden storms off. The doors slam hard behind him. *By the Lady....*

"Excuse me," I say as I rush after him.

By the time I get out of the room, however, Aiden is already gone.

It takes me half the afternoon to find him. I follow the advice of different attendants who claim to have seen him, but every time I arrive at a place, I find he's moved on. Eventually, I hear that he's gone for a long ride into town and along the countryside. I settle on waiting on the steps of the palace for him as the sun goes down.

When he finally returns on horseback, I see a man with all emotion fallen out of his eyes. I meet his eyes, and I don't recognize who I'm looking at. He stares at me like he's looking through me. Like I'm not even there, just a presence that he must find his way around to enter the castle. I break the silence. "I'm sorry."

"You could have stopped it."

"No, I couldn't have, Aiden. There was a vote—"

"You are the head of the War Council." He climbs off his horse and moves towards me. "I have seen you stand up to High Lords with your words when you thought you were just a mortal; you could have done that here."

"First of all, Aiden… I was never *just* a mortal. My mortal side was pretty damn powerful when I started out here, and that hasn't changed. And two, it wouldn't have been right for me to stop it. The War Council is supposed to work as a team. Just because I lead it doesn't mean I can run it completely." I reach out and touch his arms gently. He's tense in my grasp. I have never seen him this agitated before. I feel like I need to dance around him a little to keep him from exploding at me.

"You agree, don't you?" he asks me. He looks down at me with menacing eyes. I must have folded under his glance because he pulls away from me violently. "I can't believe you."

"Aiden, it was a strong idea, and it could end that factor in the war for us," I plead.

"Those are my people!" he shouts. "Those are my citizens."

"This is a war, Aiden! I know you know what the consequences of war are. We could get it done quickly. Few casualties. We can recruit your people and offer them a better life here. This is for their own good in the end, whether you can see that yet or not."

"You know my father won't cave, Grace; he just won't cave."

"He can't stand up to the will of the people forever. He's not that kind of monarch, he—"

"My father is not weak!" he hisses, leaning in closer to my face. I can't help but take a small step back.

"I never said he was. Not once." Aiden breathes heavily but walks backward before sinking down to sit on the ground in front of the stairs. I take a seat across from him on the step. When I set my hand on his shoulder, he doesn't push it away. I hold it there until he recovers enough to speak.

"I am so tired of Faolan being here."

"He just got here."

"And I'm already tired of him. He walks around like he knows everything; both him and Cary do. Why the hell would you allow him to sit on the War Council after everything he has done?"

"Because whether we like it or not, their information was useful, and they were promised an opportunity to be treated like heirs. Faolan is blunt, but he has been respectful."

"Why do you like him so much?"

"I don't like him! I tolerate the man. But he has connections, Aiden. He has men on the inside, people who are loyal only to him. He can get us information and smuggle supplies. Could you get that if we needed it now? Could any of the other nobles upstairs get that?"

"He has people loyal to his money."

"Maybe so. But loyalty is loyalty."

Aiden looks up at me, and we stare at each other in silence. There is a separation between us that is slowly starting to become familiar. I want to tell him something to make him feel better, but I have no idea what would help. After a slow deep breath, Aiden finally speaks in a monotone voice, "I need to go home."

My heart drops in my chest. "What?"

"I'm sorry, Grace. I have to go back and protect my people."

"How the hell are you going to do that?" Anger and hurt rise in my chest.

"I have friends in the military there," he answers quietly. "I think I can go back and take over the military to protect the people."

"You're going to usurp your father as the authority in the realm?" The incredulity in my tone is a little too obvious, judging by Aiden's glare.

"No… just the army. I need to be there to make sure Faolan doesn't hurt my people, trade cut or no trade cut."

"I can't stop the plan just because you want to…" I can barely get the words out. "To go back. It will go forward anyway. If your soldiers try to stop it, they could get hurt."

"It's a risk they will be willing to take."

"You can't just… go…" I have no idea what to say to make him stay. "We need you here. The… the prophecy—"

"Will be fine without me until I can return," he interrupts.

"You're being unreasonable."

"Grace, I don't expect you to understand what it means to feel a sense of duty for your people."

"Really?" I laugh shortly and stand. "You don't expect me to understand? I'm running a Fae House with no training, no knowledge, no loyalty from the people. I could have given that up. I could have rejected my father's name being tacked on to my own when they call me the interim High Lady, but I didn't. I'm fighting for a House I don't belong in, and you're telling me I don't know anything about duty?"

"You still don't feel like you belong here." Aiden stands with me. "It's been months, Grace. I do belong in the House of the Sun. And you are Fae whether you like it or not."

"I am also mortal. I grew up mortal, all I knew was how to be mortal. So excuse me if it takes more than half a year for me to feel like I belong in a world I despised for so long. I am doing the best I can as a Fae High Lady and as a fucking person." I close my eyes and struggle to keep my breathing even. "Aiden… you can't be by my side and back home too. You have to choose. You're leaving me at the hardest point in my life. If you leave now… I can't promise things will be okay between us."

A moment of pain flashes across his face, and I see a bit of the man I fell in love with on my adventure through the Upper Realm. He takes my hand and presses a soft kiss to my forehead. "I'm sorry, Grace."

The words fall from his lips, and my heart breaks. "I can't stay."

I close my eyes. "So you've chosen."

"Yes."

I gulp. "When will you leave?"

"Tonight. I only have a few things to pull together."

"Get someone else to." I flag down a lone maid walking down the hallway before Aiden can respond. "Please pack Lord Aiden's things and bring them downstairs," I tell her. "He'll need a horse from the stables as well." The maid bows before darting off to complete the tasks.

The two of us stand next to each other for a while before Aiden slowly moves to embrace me. I let myself sink into it because it might be the last time I get to for a long while. Arms around each other, we sway in silence. Each of us waiting for the other to say something first. Neither of us does. I don't know how long we waited before Aiden's departure was prepared, but I do know it was too short. He kisses me deeply, holding my cheeks in his hands. When he pulls away, I feel part of me leave with him. He gives me a little wave as he mounts his horse before turning away for the last time and riding off down the pathway. I watch him as long as I can before he disappears from view.

Goodbye, Aiden.

Chapter Thirty-Four

I wave off the small number of attendants around me and tell them to go to bed. I want to be alone now. Sitting back down on the steps, I drop my head into my hands. The thoughts in my head haven't sorted themselves out yet. Aiden… left. He left without any thought as to what I was going to do without him. And in saying goodbye, we truly said goodbye. I don't regret what I said. I can't wait around for him to make up his mind on whether the duty to a traitorous house is more or less important than supporting me and the overall war effort.

But now what? I am going to need a new right hand, that's for certain. *And by the Lady, the prophecy.* When is he going to come back? What if something happens to him? We could be one man down for no reason besides his foolish pride. Yet despite all this, I can understand the sense of duty within him. I can understand needing to go back to your homeland and take care of business. There are days when I miss the Middle Realm and wish I could go back and use my magic to help. There isn't a day when I haven't missed my home. But to have that duty supersede what is happening here is… is something I can't comprehend.

"Grace?" Luna's soft voice startles me from behind. When I turn around, she's leaning cautiously over the landing of the stairs. "Are you alright?"

I chuckle wryly but nod. "Yes. I'm fine."

"What are you doing out here? It's really late." She takes a few steps down and sits next to me. Part of me is irritated by the company, but I don't have it in me to tell her to go away.

"I am… trying to figure out some things." When she looks over curiously, I sigh. "Aiden left."

"Left?"

"Yeah. A little while ago."

"Where is he going?"

"He is going home. To the House of the Sun. He is hoping to help protect the people from whatever maneuver Faolan's people pull to reduce available product within the lorddom."

"Oh… I see." She perches her elbows up on her knees. "When is he coming back?"

"I don't know. It could be in a few days, or it could be in a few weeks. Either way, I am going to need another right-hand person. Someone who will stick around and take orders," I finish bitterly.

"Do you want some help with that?"

"You want to take the job?"

To my surprise, Luna laughs. "Oh, by the Lady, no. I have no desire to take that kind of authority position."

"But you're a Lady. You'll be a High Lady someday."

"I prefer to work in a larger group of officials and make ruling and decision making a much more collaborative effort. You rule differently. You like collaboration, but for you to have the final say and your second to help support and execute. You wouldn't like me as a second, trust me. But I can help you think of who would better suit the position."

I'm not sure what Luna may bring to the table in terms of helping me figure this out, but I am willing to try. "Alright, I'll take it."

"Great!" She perks up and turns to face me. "Well, who are you thinking of?"

"Off the top of my head? Maybe Aira."

"Aira is a great choice. But in terms of the War Council, you may want her to remain an individual contributor. With High Lady Morgana as your advisor, the others may worry that the House of Wind is having too much influence over the Council."

Oh, that's a good point. No one had made any specific comments to that effect, but I have heard some muttering around the subject from the servants milling around the palace. "Okay, I can see that. One of the House of Light twins?"

"Inexperienced," Luna replies with a shrug. "Their father only invested in a bit of training for his girls. He believes they should be much older and he, much older before he starts getting into more technical High Lady training. Some say he wanted to give his daughters a good childhood; others call him foolish. What about Lord Jason?"

"Oh no, I couldn't work with him one-on-one. He's a reasonable man," I add in his defense, "but our reactions are typically too confrontational. I want to work with someone who challenges me but doesn't argue for hours and hours.

"Tristan is out then too," Luna points out. "He has some amazing ideas, but he won't debate with you for very long. He'll acquiesce after only a little bit of pressure is applied."

I groan in frustration and tip my head back, looking directly up at the stars. "Then who in the world is left?" Luna remains silent, waiting for me to realize. When it hits me, I fly back up to my original seated position. "Oh no. No, no, no."

"I think it would be a good idea," Luna starts.

"A good idea?" I interrupt. "You think it would be a good idea to choose a House of Darkness twin as my right hand? Are you crazy?"

"It's likely," she laughs lightly. "But yes. Faolan specifically."

My eyes are popping out of my skull at this point. "Faolan? Why him? He would be my last choice!"

"Oh, don't say that. He has all the qualities you are looking for in a right-hand. He takes direction well but will challenge you if he sees major flaws in your plans. He's not generally confrontational, merely inquisitive, and direct in his criticism. You said yourself his resources are expansive and can be a real asset to this group. Why not put that under your purview? And your selection of Faolan would give him some legitimacy in the eyes of the people and the War Council."

I can't argue with much of what she's saying. But Faolan? "I don't know, Luna. I just don't know."

Luna smiles softly and pats my shoulder. "Well, I'm sure you will figure it out. I'll leave you to your thoughts. Good night." With that, she disappears as quickly as she came. I will never understand how she can just breeze in and out of rooms and leave all sorts of quandaries in her wake without another thought. Maybe she does it on purpose in hopes to throw people off their game.

Her ideas do have merit though. Maybe I have to honestly weigh the pros and cons of Faolan being my right hand. On one hand, Faolan has resources; he has allies. He isn't the easiest to talk to, but he would tell me exactly what was right and wrong about my plan. On the other hand, I can barely talk to him because he's playing around with my emotions and other people's emotions and just all around getting on other people's nerves. He's impulsive, and he has the potential to be destructive if handled the wrong way.

But if handled the right way… he may be the Realm's strongest asset. And how can I say no to that? As the night drags on and I stare up at the stars, I am left reeling in the possibility of inviting that dangerous man closer into my circle.

Chapter Thirty-Five

After my conversation with Luna, I spend the majority of the next day upstairs in my room. I cancel the War Council meeting, the get-together with the prophecy group, and all domestic affairs. I formally announce Aiden's departure and use the excuse that I need time to decide who will be taking his place as my second. That has been enough for most of the people in the castle. A few grumble, but I am not in a place to care. As I sit on my bed, I turn over the idea of Faolan as my second in my head. Luna made some excellent points, there's no getting around that, but… can I accept him as the best choice? Can the rest of the War Council accept him?

After hours and hours of agonizing indecisiveness, I send a note by servant to Faolan asking him to meet me in the courtyard at dusk. I wait there quietly, looking over the hill at the town below. Things are quiet tonight. The tiny lights strung between the buildings flicker in the brisk night air. Normally, the view would bring me peace, but I'm too nervous to enjoy it.

"You asked to see me?" I didn't hear Faolan creep behind me, but I'm not even surprised to hear his voice next to my ear.

I turn around quickly. His amber eyes sparkle amidst the shadow cast against his face by the moonlight. "Yes. I wanted to ask you something."

"Is this about what happened with you and Aiden last night? Are you going to tell me where he went?"

"He's gone," I say flatly. "He's gone back to take care of his people. Make sure nothing fatal happens to them as we make our next move with trade."

Faolan clicks his tongue. "I see." He passes me and walks over to lean against a tree. "I can't say I didn't see this coming."

"What do you mean?"

"Aiden has always been very protective of his people. He went to fight for them after he couldn't be the heir to rule over them, and now he sees an opportunity to take his place as their leader. When it comes down to it, Aiden's homeland will always matter the most to him."

"I don't blame him," I respond quietly.

Faolan chuckles. "You know it would be okay if you did."

"Maybe. Maybe not." I laugh dryly.

"But at this moment, it doesn't matter. Don't try to find something where there isn't anything."

"I'm not trying to read you, Grace. I'm trying to tell it to you straight so you can move on."

"I don't get a day to think about it before I have to move forward?"

"No, you don't." Faolan moves to stand next to me when he sees the perturbed look on my face. "Not outwardly anyway. You've got to figure out what to do next without him. You need another right hand, and you need one quick."

Damn, he's cut right to the point, hasn't he? Guess that means I should just dive right in. "Faolan, I am considering taking you on as my second." His eyes flash. "I have been advised that you have all the qualities I need in a right-hand man. Someone who can get things done, who understands the resources and movements that are necessary to take back a certain territory, and someone who knows how to make the tough decisions even if they personally disagree with them."

"You flatter me, High Lady," he says in a low voice with just a hint of a smirk. I roll my eyes.

"What I need to know is if I can trust you. If I can rely on you to execute what I need done. If you can do as I ask, take my lead and follow instructions."

Faolan raises an eyebrow. "Are you sure you want me? The Council won't like it."

"The Council will have to deal with my decision," I answer. "They don't trust you or Cary. And that needs to change if we want to move forward. As my second, you will be raised to a higher position of authority, and I will be able to keep a close eye on you much more effectively." Faolan's eye roll makes me wonder if that will help all that much, but I press on. "Do you want the job?" I don't know what I'm doing. Aiden's out the door, the War Council is looking to me for answers, and all I can do is stare at this man and ask myself… "Can I trust you, Faolan?"

He looks at me for a while with a piercing gaze. He appears to be considering the answer himself, which does not put me at ease. He steps closer, and my breath catches in my throat. "A leader has to be able to trust her right hand. May I show you that I can be trustworthy?"

"How do you plan to do that?"

"By showing you how to utilize your power. You have trouble with your flying, yes?"

"Excuse me?" I'm completely thrown.

Faolan laughs softly. "From what I can tell, your flying could be a lot smoother," he replies matter-of-factly.

"You're getting there, but not fast enough. In battle, you're going to need to be able to maneuver through enemy lines without tumbling out of the sky."

"What's wrong with my flying?" I still can't figure out what's going on. "Wait… how do you even know I can fly?"

"I told you, eyes and ears everywhere. Don't ask how I know; ask what I can do to aid you." Faolan's hand brushes across my lower back and pushes me lightly to the balcony at the edge of the courtyard.

"What are you doing?"

"I'm going to teach you to fly properly. And that starts with you jumping off this thing."

"You want me to—" I can't decide whether to laugh or punch him. I settle on turning around abruptly and stopping him with both hands. "You're insane."

"Perhaps. You decide. You can go back inside and fret and contemplate for another day about what to do next and who to choose other than me. Or you can do something useful with yourself, learn this, and get something accomplished tonight." I glance at him sideways. He gives me a soft smirk. "You're gonna be fine."

"This won't kill me, will it?" I finally acquiesce.

"Nope."

"And when I tumble?"

"*If* you tumble, Grace, I'll catch you." My eyes narrow at that, but he just quirks the corner of his lips. "Trust me."

"You know I don't do trust easily," I quip even as I'm moving to the edge again.

"Don't think about it. Just feel the air around and visualize yourself cutting through it." Faolan stands behind me, arms crossed. "Just jump."

I glance over the edge, immediately regretting my decision when I realize how far down the mountain extends. The height causes my head to spin. The wind rushes down from my head to my toes and down over the side. Faolan's presence stands behind me like a rock, and if I concentrate hard enough, I can feel him brushing lightly against my mind. He's pressing just enough to let me know he's there, but not hard enough that I think he's going to invade. *Strange... but comforting nonetheless.*

I force my eyes open and take a leap before I have too much time to think about it.

Bad idea.

As I tumble through the air, thoughts fly through my head faster than I process them. *This is bad. This is very bad. Come on, Grace, concentrate! Flying... wings... direction... moving through the air... come on, deep breath. Fly!*

When my wings launch out and engage with the air, I let out a whoop and shoot up past the courtyard balcony. They extend out to their full length as I clumsily make my way back down to the ground. "There we go!" I shout triumphantly.

Faolan had other plans though. "Don't come down here, Lady Grace! You need to practice!"

I hover a few feet above the grass. "What do you want me to do?"

As the smirk crosses his face, I know I'm in trouble. "Catch me."

Without warning, he launches past me and hovers above me. His wings unfurl, and by the Lady, they are magnificent. Long black feathers make Faolan look like a dark angel coming to lay out some divine punishment. He is ethereal, if such a dark-hearted man could look so innocent. He grins at me before he practically disappears into the distance.

Thrown by the sudden launch, I take off after him. My wings move shakily as I speed up. The balance shifts over left and right as the wind changes. Faolan flies effortlessly, spinning wildly, yet controlled through the night sky. He darts sharply downwards, and I dive after him. He speeds down along the treetops before shooting back up into the sky. As we race, I notice what he's trying to teach me. Switching directions requires mental and physical focus to combat the wind. Movements must be deliberate, but quick to stay in pursuit. I grin as I feel more in control of my movements. My abrupt turns are slightly wobblier than his, but I'm gaining on him.

When he darts back down once more, something shifts in me. I have no time to correct my steering. I lose control once again. My wings become a weight that drags me down. When my physical control leaves, my mental control leaves too. And suddenly, I'm tumbling out of the sky. I cry out as I try to regain my concentration and make my wings do what I want them to do, but it's no use. They curl around me and block my vision as I crash through the edge of the treetops.

Then I feel strong arms catch me just before I tumble into the forest beneath me, and then I just *know.*

Faolan.

He's caught me like he said he would, and I'm faced with this odd paradox of past Faolan and present Faolan that somehow mesh into a singular man who shows no indication of whether he's going to stay on my side or not. But he's caught me and as my wings sink back into my back, I look into those amber eyes, and I see a smile, I see protectiveness, I see satisfaction for having beaten me and for having caught me himself. I see a smug bastard who has everything and nothing to lose but saved me because he had said he would.

Faolan flies me down to the courtyard again, his black wings wrapped around us like a shield against the impending wind. He sets me down on my feet and smiles smugly at me. "Better. Much better. A little more practice, and you'll almost be able to catch up to me."

When I step back from the man, I give him a bit of a smile. "Thank you. That was… enlightening."

"Did you find the answers you were looking for, High Lady?" On his tongue, the words feel more solid than any other person who has spoken my title.

"That depends. Do you want to be my right hand?" I repeat my previous question. "Are you in this with me?"

To my surprise, he walks towards me until he's close enough that I can feel his breath against my lips. Our eyes have no choice but to lock in on each other. "Yes, I can take your lead. Yes, I can do as you ask unless you're being stupid, in which case I will tell you so. *Yes...*" he breathes., "I am with you. And the trust thing?" He brushes a hand over my cheek, brushing my wayward hair behind my ear. "That is entirely up to you."

I shiver and thrust my hand out, almost punching Faolan in the stomach. "My second then." Faolan takes my hand and shakes it firmly.

We don't let go for several moments after, and something in me shifts. *By the Lady, I hope this is the right choice.*

Chapter Thirty-Six

After the debacle of the last two days, I call an early morning War Council meeting. I officially elaborate on Aiden's departure, and to my surprise, most of the Council takes it in stride. Perhaps Faolan was right about Aiden; his sense of duty to his people seems to be something that the rest of the nobility know as commonplace. But when I announce Faolan will be taking his place as my second, you would think I was starting a brand-new war right there in the conference room. Jason was angrier than I have ever seen him, and Tristan looked like he might have a heart attack as he collapsed into a chair. I do what I did with Luna; I lay out the pros and cons as best as I can and try to smooth things over. Luckily, with a little aid from Aira and Luna, we were able to come to a shaky truce. We're not even close to unity yet, but I am hopeful that we will get there.

Eventually…

After the Council meeting, the prophecy cohort and I move upstairs to the library to discuss it. When we gather around the table, Cary breaks the silence. "Faolan, Grace? Really?"

"Thanks sis," Faolan snarks. "For that glowing endorsement." She cackles at him.

"I'm not going to continue to defend this choice again today, Cary," I groan.

"Oh, I'm just messing with you, miss High Lady." She laughs at me.

"I think you couldn't do better besides perhaps me."

"You hate procedure, Cary; you know you do." Faolan gives her a look.

"I do. Better you than me, brother."

"I can't believe Aiden is gone." Aira shakes her head. "I mean, is he coming back at some point? He has to come back to execute whatever his role in the prophecy is."

I practically slam my head down into the table, covering my face in my arms. "I don't know, Aira. This is still new to me too."

"Do we have a plan to contact him if necessary?" Luna chimes in. She and Luna conduct a smaller side conversation while I hide out in myself. Cary joins in intermittently as the talk shifts between Aiden's absence and Faolan's new appointment. I take a moment to lie there. I am really tired of being the leader. *Someone please, come take this job off my hands.*

"I have something to share," Aira pipes up suddenly. "Related to the prophecy?" I jerk up as her voice breaks my concentration. Everyone is looking insistently at me. Their eyes are so frustrating.

"By all means, go ahead." I stand and cede the floor to her, walking towards the back wall with my hands behind my head in exasperation. Aira stands up and moves to the head of the table. "So, I have been experimenting recently with my sensing magic along with Luna and some of the more complex magic books in the library."

Luna smiles brightly and chimes in. "We discovered that she is able to combine her sensing magic with my divination magic. Together, we were able to conduct a magical scan of the immediate surrounding area. We couldn't get the entire realm, at least not on a first shot. However, we did find something interesting."

"There's a large amount of magical energy coming from the House of Peace," Aira continues. "Specifically, the palace. A high-profile magical signature that puts the person in contention with any of us."

"Did you find anything else? Maybe something about the magic type?" Faolan's stoic voice rings out over the rest of the table.

"No, nothing specific about the magic type. It took a lot of energy just to get that far. The House of Peace isn't exactly around the corner."

"Fair enough." Faolan leans back in his seat.

Cary lays her hands on the table. "We have three daughters to consider, right? Seraphina, Kiara, and Lara. They're all fairly close in age. It could be coming off any one of them. Just because we're all technically the oldest heirs doesn't mean it has to be."

"And prophecies aren't usually perfectly linear," Luna corroborates.

"Let's take into account what we know about the prophecy players and who falls into which so we can think about which heir may fit who is left." I walk around the table, pointing to people. "Faolan and Cary are the twins, the Witch and the Conjurer. Luna is clearly the Soothsayer. Aira is the Spinner. Aiden is most likely the Bringer of Light solely based on House affiliation, and there's a general consensus around here that I am most likely the Enchantress…"

"Just accept it already, Grace," Cary snaps. "You're already leading us; it's not that hard to extrapolate to the rest of the prophecy. By the Lady…" she mumbles to herself as she picks at her nails.

I resist the urge to roll my eyes. "That leaves us with either the Potioner or the Deliverer."

"Prophecy says the Deliverer is a man," Aira points out. "So we're left with the Potioner."

"So we're looking for someone with plant magic or herb magic." Faolan leans forward in his seat. "Something with a high level and tier."

"The House of Peace nobility has inherited either plant or herb magic for as many generations since the beginning, right?" Luna offers.

Aira claps her hands. "That's right! Oh, I can't remember who has which, though."

"Doesn't matter." Cary smirks softly. "Kiara has both."

"She has both? Are you sure?" I ask.

"Yes. I used to tease her for her abilities when we were kids."

"She's also a healer, isn't she?" Luna offers another tidbit.

"That's it then," I summarize. "Kiara DiAngelo is almost certainly the Potioner and member seven of our little troupe here." There's a little joy and a whole lot of satisfaction reflected on everyone's faces around me. "Now, how are we going to get her out?" Those smiles fade quickly.

"We'll need to send a message to her," Aira says. "She needs to know we're coming for her."

"No, there is no way you are going to send a message in through traditional channels," Cary interjects. "There are too many soldiers in the city. Even nontraditional channels are going to be tricky."

"And we need a plan to communicate to her as well," Faolan adds. "Don't forget that." I roll my eyes at his obvious point.

"Do any of us have telepathic powers?" Aira asks. "We could communicate with her that way."

"Across a span of what distance?" Cary clarifies.

Faolan taps his fingers together. "There's a place in the forest outside of the House of Peace. It's along the western wall; it backs right onto it. We could station a mage there with enough power to conduct telepathic communication."

"Who has strong enough magic for that?"

"Grace does," Luna reveals before I can answer. When I look at her, she gives me a little shrug. "The Lady showed me." Everyone else turns to look at me expectantly.

I sigh under my breath and nod slowly. "I can do it."

"Good," she replies perkily. "We should probably get moving on this as soon as possible."

"You're right," I concede. "Faolan and I can head over there as soon as we inform the War Council of the plan."

Faolan shoots me a slightly confused look before his features smooth out and he nods his agreement. "Should we inform the rest of the War Council?"

"The idea will need to be presented to them as something that is necessary," Aira says. "We don't want to let them know all the details. Just enough to say yes."

"Why don't you present it, Aira?" I sit back down in my chair. "You're one of the most articulate here, and frankly, I think the others have heard enough from me today."

"I can do it."

"Good." I wave a hand at the others. "Let's plan on meeting after the second meeting this evening to coordinate specifics. Go. Enjoy the sun." As they exit in different directions, I collapse back into the chair. *By the Lady, I need a nap.*

Chapter Thirty-Seven

Instead of heading to my bedroom, I make my way to the hospital room. Although I have been overwhelmed running the House of the Evening and trying to stay on top of the War Council, my background thoughts rest on my father. His condition has not improved much. Not that I can visit enough to notice. Elise and Neil visit him religiously and refuse to let me in the room with them. Elise can't stand me being there, particularly if I'm dressed like any kind of Lady. There is a fury in her eyes that can't be tamed.

And Neil… Neil's too brokenhearted about both the state of our father and the loss of the heirship that his anger lashes out much quicker than hers does. It doesn't stew in his chest. It comes out in a rush of words and occasionally, magic. I try to leave before it escalates to that. Last time, the glass in a cabinet next to me shattered and I had to shield my father from the falling shards. Analise at least gives me a little sad smile when she sees me, but Elise is always with her, so the same problems apply. I have only asked that the doctors keep me posted on his condition.

To my surprise, none of the other family members are in my father's room. My hand hesitates at the curtain. I haven't had a chance to truly look at him in his fragile state. I don't know how I will feel when I do. But there is no time to waste. I don't know when the others may come in again. It's now or never. Drawing my hand across, I pull the curtain away to reveal my father's hospital bed.

He looks so frail. His skin has an unnatural white hue that makes him look like a ghost. He looks too old to be a father, a grandfather perhaps. A wave of emotion overwhelms me, and I kneel beside the bed. I take my father's hand and squeeze. Then I bring it to my lips and lightly kiss the back of it. *By the Lady, I hope he wakes up.*

As I kneel next to him, I talk idly about what I have been doing for the House of the Evening and for the war effort so far. I tell him about how Aiden left and how Faolan has taken his place and how confused it makes me feel. All the while, I try my best not to cry. All this time, I have needed someone to tell me what to do right now. I need my father to tell me what to do. But eventually, my stepmother comes to visit him, and I have no choice but to leave the room and move on.

The War Council meets again, and Aira presents the issue of Kiara to the other members. There wasn't much debate over the recognizance mission itself, only who would go on it. Once it was proposed that Faolan and I would go, things got a little heated. But Aira spun it as a chance for him to prove himself to the rest of the Council with me taking over all the communication. I also offered up Talon as a third chaperone to oversee the utilization of such telepathy magic. We finally reached a unanimous vote, though I think that says more about their desire to get Faolan out of the palace temporarily rather than some newfound trust in him overnight.

When I head down to the stables the following morning, Talon is already waiting for me by my horse. "Thank you for agreeing to come on this mission, Talon. I know it was out of the blue."

"No problem." He waves off my thanks, handing me my saddle blanket. "I have to say, judging from what I heard around the palace recently, most of the other Lords and Ladies aren't happy with your choice of Lord Faolan as your second. I am somewhat inclined to agree. Why in the world are you trusting him?"

"I got some good advice from Lady Luna. We went through everyone on the Council, and frankly, she made some very good points about why Faolan should be my right hand. I'm keeping an eye on him, don't worry. I can handle myself."

"It's not handling yourself I'm worried about. I'm worried about you handling him."

"Talon..." I sigh in frustration. "I need to convince the other members of the War Council that he can be trusted. We need him on our side. I picked him to boost his credibility. Hopefully the mission will help as well."

"Well I hope you know what you're doing." He laughs. "However, I am happy to accompany you both. Besides, the telepathy you're attempting is advanced instruction. I need to keep an eye on you and your magic." His face grows a little more serious. "Just... be careful with Faolan, Grace. Don't get mixed up in something you're not ready for."

"My ears are burning," Faolan's voice chimes in behind us as he strides into the stables. "Are you two chatting about me?" I roll my eyes while Talon scowls at the Lord. "Hey Talon, have you decided to join us? Trying to keep an eye on me?" He raises his eyebrows teasingly. I stifle a laugh.

"I've been asked to come along as backup," Talon replies shortly. "Grace, when are we headed out?"

My lip curls up. "Now."

Once the men load up their bags, the three of us mount our horses and take off for the House of Peace. Faolan leads us down a twisting pathway through small villages, forests, and secluded countryside roads. It's difficult making our way over discreetly in the afternoon, even with the clouds, but Faolan seems to know what he's doing. We stop at a small village to rest before continuing into the next day.

When I see the House of Peace and its temples in the distance, we divert down a side road and end up riding through the forest. We venture deep into the woods before Faolan raises up a hand to halt us. "We're as close as we can get, Grace." I dismount quickly followed by Talon behind me. The men turn around slowly, surveying the area. They confer in hushed tones for a moment, before Faolan then takes my arms and steers me over to a tree to lean against.

Talon kneels beside me. "This is gonna take a lot of strength to do, Grace," he warns. "This is the longest distance telepathy you have ever attempted. Are you sure you want to do this? We can get the information to her another way."

"No, we can't," Faolan and I counter almost in unison. I whip around to look at him, and my confusion is reflected on his face. "Faolan's right," I quickly add. "This is the safest, most direct way to get her the information without high risk of being caught. Physical messages will be caught."

I close my eyes and lean against the tree. "Keep watch," I order quietly. "I may need help getting up when this is over." Both of them nod before stepping away from me, facing outwards. I notice that Faolan is staying a little closer to me. I don't quite know how it makes me feel. I tap into my sensing magic and let it wander out of my head, out of this forest, and into the city itself. It searches for the House of Peace daughter, winding through the streets and up into the palace tower. I sense Kiara's magic, and through there, I can attempt a telepathic connection.

"Kiara?" I tentatively put out through my mind. I feel an instant rush of startling surprise that causes me to grip the tree roots beside me. "Whoa, whoa, Kiara, calm down. It's Grace, Lady Grace of the House of the Evening. I'm a way outside of the House of Peace. Are you alone?"

There is a long pause, long enough that I wonder if I have lost connection. But finally, a cautious voice responds, "Yes."

CHAPTER THIRTY-SEVEN

"Good." I breathe a sigh of relief. "Can you hear me alright?"

"Mostly clear," Kiara's voice answers, a little stronger this time. "You startled me."

"Yeah, I'm sorry about that. We couldn't get a message to you through normal channels, so this is the best I could do." I feel her nod to herself. "We don't have a lot of time, so I need you to listen to me very carefully. We are coming to get you."

"What do you mean?" I feel a sense of apprehension start to rise in her chest. "Who is *we?*"

"The War Council is leading the opposition to the Houses of Darkness, Fire, and Sun along with every other House that we could get resources and people from. The Council is made up of the heirs this time around while the High Lords take care of their own Houses. Within the larger Council is a secret group of six of powerful noble children, me included. These are..." I gulp, unsure of how to express this. "How familiar are you with prophecies?"

"Um... I'm familiar with prophecies in general," she answers. "My father talks all the time about the prophetic books in our libraries. I've read most of them. Why?"

"Well, let me cut to the chase here. The six of us are part of an eight-person cooperative that has been prophesied to lead the realms into battle and save the world as we know it. And... we think you're number seven." There is another long pause as I feel Kiara's shock, panic, confusion, and underneath it all, curiosity rising to the surface. The push of emotions is almost too much for the telepathic connection to handle. It is almost painful. *I gotta rein this in.* "Kiara, you're overloading the connection; you have to take a breath, or we're going to be disconnected."

"You think I'm one of the prophecy's members?" Her voice is heavy with skepticism.

"Yes. I want to explain everything, Kiara, but we don't have much time. Each of the members has a moniker in the prophecy, the Enchantress, the Witch, the Soothsayer. One of the members is the Potioner. You have the strongest combination of plant and herb magic in the realm. It's just gotta be you. We are planning on breaking you out of the palace, okay? But I need to know exactly where you are located."

"I'm in the far-right tower facing the street. I'm pretty much trapped up here; food and sometimes books come in and out three times a day. I haven't talked to anyone for days. You're the first." Kiara's voice grows quiet. "Are you going to be able to help my family?"

I sigh. There is fear in her voice. I recognize it from my own thoughts about leaving my family behind when I came to this realm. "No. I'm sorry, there are too many soldiers. We can only smuggle you out. But if you come with us, you will have a much better chance of helping your family. Are you in?"

This time, Kiara answers with only a second or two of hesitation. "Yes. Yes, I'm ready to be rescued." She chuckles, but I can detect a hint of desperation in her voice.

The telepathic connection begins to pull heavily on my mind and my magic. I am drowning. It isn't likely to hold much longer. "I don't have much time before this breaks, so pay attention. We will be back in five days' time very early in the morning. Sleep during the day if you can and stay alert. Keep an eye out for me, okay?"

"Got it. Thank you, Grace." I feel her give a soft smile.

"You're welcome." I groan as the connection extends further. "Stay safe. Stay strong." I cry out as the connection breaks, and I slump forward. "Ah!"

Through blurry eyes, I can make out the outlines of Faolan and Talon moving toward me. "Grace, are you alright?" Talon's voice echoes in my head.

"She can't answer you," Faolan's voice gets quiet, but insistent. I feel his rough hand slide under my chin and lift it up. "This is a healing potion, drink this." The smooth glass of a vial presses to my lips, and I drink. The fuzziness clears slightly, but not enough for me to stop feeling woozy. "Strange…" Faolan's face appears directly in front of mine. "That should have done more than that."

"She's exhausted her magic supply," Talon speaks just above my ear this time. "She's barely trained; she never should have attempted this."

"Well, it worked, didn't it?" I mumble.

"Come on." Talon slides my arm over his shoulder and pulls me up from the ground. "I don't know if you can stay upright on your horse."

"You take care of the second horse, Talon," Faolan says to him as he gingerly slides a hand under my legs and lifts me into the air. If my head wasn't so out of whack, I probably would have reacted more. I see Talon swear under his breath but do what Faolan asks. He somehow manages to get both of us up onto the horse at the same time. He pulls me back against his chest. "Can you hold on at all?"

"Yeah." I nod and wince as it rattles my head. "Ow…"

Faolan chuckles. "I'll take that as a no." He wraps one arm tight around my waist. "Lean back," he orders. I begrudgingly do so. "Close your eyes. You need to focus on resting. Your magic is gonna take a little time to recharge. The less focus you use up, the faster it will go. I won't let you fall." I want to ask how he knows any of this, but he flicks the reins, and the horse trots forward. I close my eyes and lean back, resigning myself to the dizziness swallowing me.

Chapter Thirty-Eight

My recovery is slow, but steady. I notice a small difference in my exhaustion on each of the days that we travel back to the House of the Evening, but as soon as we arrive back at the palace, I head upstairs to sleep it off. Faolan helps me to my room. His concern is… nice. Unnerving still, but nice. Magical exhaustion is no joke. It's more than physical; it penetrates deep into my mind and my core. I feel completely drained of all energy in thought. My brain can't even form words to speak; all I can do is make vague gestures and nod a lot. Once I am asleep, Faolan and Talon take on the responsibility of informing the War Council of our success.

Hopefully, if my father wakes up, he sees this as a victory and not as a step back.

I finally heal from the magical exhaustion thanks to the potions I was brought by the palace doctors. I sleep off the excess in a little over a night, waking up around midday to a soft knock on the door. Rubbing the sleepiness from my eyes, I unlatch the door to find Faolan leaning against the door frame. When he turns to look at me, his eyes scan my frame. When I look down, I realize I'm still in my nightgown. "Ooh…" I blush. "One second." I hear a soft chuckle as I dart back into the room to grab a robe to put on. When I come back to the door, he's giving that smarmy half-smile. "What… did you need?"

"I wanted to come check on you," Faolan says. "See how you were after yesterday."

I smile. "I'm feeling better. My head is clear. My magic doesn't feel off anymore. I assume it's returned to normal."

"That's good." His expression is pensive, almost like he's hesitant to talk. "Do you think you have the energy to come down to the arena?"

I raise an eyebrow. "Are you finally offering to train me?"

"Come down and you'll find out." Faolan brushes a curl behind my ear before shooting me a wink and disappearing down the hall. I slip back inside my room and get dressed. I'm pleasantly surprised to find that Faolan wants to teach me something new. Whatever it is. As much as I hate to admit it, he's quite the mage. I rush out the back way by the kitchens and grab an apple on the way as I run down to the arena.

Faolan stands in the center of the arena and holds his arms out wide when he sees me. "The half-Fae prodigy returns! Get down here!" I roll my eyes, but jog down the stairs.

"So what exactly are you planning on teaching me here?" I ask. "I'm not sure what magic you have in common with me."

"Just flight, telepathic, and disintegration magic. And since we already managed to deal with a few of the problems in your flight magic, disintegration is the logical next step." He saunters over to me. "How far has Talon gotten with your training on that?"

"Not far," I reply. "He doesn't have that magic, so most of it is book knowledge translated into practical application."

"Ah… tsk tsk tsk…" Faolan clicks his tongue. "Nothing works as well as teacher to student instruction. Observe." He motions to a collection of structures standing across from us. Each appears to be created from a different set of building materials. Some are softer substances, like fabric and lighter wood. Others are more solid structures, like brick and stone.

"I've worked with all of those before." I turn to Faolan. "I've done these exercises."

Faolan smirks. "Okay. Go ahead. Try the fabric one."

I reach out with a hand and throw my will dead center to the block. To my surprise, it doesn't explode. Not even a puff of dust off the top. I throw my hand forward again, this time with a little more force. Again, nothing. "What is going on? That's fabric, it should be easy."

"You didn't feel it out at all. You didn't even try to sense."

"That wasn't in the books."

"Then you were reading the wrong books." Faolan scoffs a bit. "You can't just throw your magic out to the center and think your will is going to be enough to disintegrate it. That may work most of the time, but not all of it." He moves in front of me and lightly knocks my hand aside. When he uses his magic, the fabric disintegrates at the top edges and slips down the block to reveal a diamond core. "Appearances can lie. The material you see may not be the material that is found underneath. You can't always focus on the core. You have to take the whole object or person into account."

I shake my head absentmindedly. "Wow."

The man turns and shrugs at me. "Hey, I gave you a shot. Now we do things my way." He moves behind me and places both hands on my shoulders. I tense up a bit. I haven't been this close to him since the night in the cave-in. "Use your sensing magic. Reach out carefully at first. Don't just trust your eyes; feel the material like you're holding it in your hands. Study the whole piece. All sides. It's gonna take some time at first. But soon it will be second nature." One of his fingers is brushing over my left shoulder. It is distracting. "Go ahead. Try the second one."

I take a tiny step forward so his hands slide off my shoulders. *Better to get rid of distractions.* With a soft breath, my magic flows out to the wood block. My consciousness swirls around it slowly, taking in its size and edges. When I probe deeper and slide between the tiny gaps in the fibers of the wood, I find a solid stone core. I then know to send my disintegration magic through the entire object. The wood splinters around it before I push through to the center and send stone fragments across the arena.

I hear a quick clap behind me. "Yes! Good! Do it again."

We spend time identifying different objects, breaking them down, and then exploding them. Eventually, we leave the arena and make our way up the mountain. Faolan takes me to an abandoned derelict house, an old safehouse for his black-market crew. We both take part in a little demolition, tearing the structure to shreds. Faolan's magic and mine complement each other as they move about the rubble.

I have to admit, Faolan is not a bad teacher. He has the same direct nature that Talon has but isn't afraid to get a little crafty. I like his methods. If he's willing to teach, I might as well learn from him.

Chapter Thirty-Nine

After taking the next day to map out and plan our rescue mission, Faolan and I make the two-day journey again. We arrive on the outskirts under the cover of the fading sunset. I'm trying to relax in preparation for this stealth mission, but my heart is pounding. This is a significant mission, and I've got this new second to the right of me who I have never fought with before. I don't know what to expect. I glance sideways at my companion to find him alert, keeping an eye on our surroundings. "Should we go over the plan again?" I ask quietly.

"If you'd like. Though I still say you should allow me to kill anyone in the way if necessary. If it comes down to them or us. It's not like breaking out their imprisoned Lady will dampen their desire to kill us. Best to just remove the threat entirely."

I grit my teeth. "I told you, I want to minimize casualties. We may not know who the House of Darkness operatives are and who are House of Peace people being forced to guard places."

"Then we force them to tell us and kill anyone who argues or refuses," he argues. "It's not like they can stop us."

I sigh. "Cut me some slack, Faolan. I'm not comfortable with the idea of killing people that might be innocent."

"Neither am I, Grace. But if it comes down to it, I wish to remove as many threats as possible."

"Fine," I finally acquiesce. "We'll do it your way."

Faolan brings his horse alongside mine and leans over to get closer to my face. "This is the best course, High Lady. You chose me because this is something you know I have done and because you need my help. So I'm glad you've decided to come to your senses."

"I chose you out of necessity," I scold, although somewhat a lie. "The rest of them need to trust you." Faolan raises an eyebrow. I turn away quickly. "It was you or your sister. And I need to keep a closer eye on you."

Faolan laughs. "Oh, I am no danger to you. Because I don't want your position. Though I cannot say the same of my sister. I've already got mine and the head of the black market to boot. My power is absolute, and I am content."

I roll my eyes. "Well, Mr. Absolute Power, what do I need to know about your father's army?"

Faolan sobers up immediately. "They will kill you if they can."

I shiver involuntarily. "Point taken."

He nods. "As much as I love the games, Grace, when we get into the city, they end. You follow my lead, or we die."

"I understand."

Faolan rides a few lengths ahead and turns his horse in front of me to cut me off. "I want to make this clear. There will be some things you may not want to see. So please be prepared for that. These men have killed innocents. My father has a love for intimidation. It may sound foolish and garish, but there may be heads on pikes or bodies hanging off the wall."

"I can handle it." I try to convince him and myself.

Faolan nods and with a light flick of the reins, he starts off again. "Having said all that," he glances back at me, "you should hide your hair. The reddish color in your hair is distinctive; it will stand out."

I nod and wave a hand over my hair, changing to a darker brown with a light glamour. I also add a few freckles and patches to my face to change its appearance. "Will this do?"

"It will." Faolan slows his horse again and pulls over to the side of the road. I follow behind curiously. Climbing down, he plucks some leaves off a nearby tree. He faces towards the road again, towards me as he pushes his hands together. His eyebrows furrow in concentration. The leaves construct themselves into a small, fragile moth. I let out a short gasp in surprise, which grants me a pointed look from Faolan. But I couldn't help it. I have never seen this delicate side of Faolan's magic. The Fae man holds out his hands, and the moth flies out toward the city.

Faolan walks back over to me, his eyes slightly hazy. "That will go check the gate and report back. But it is a rather large strain on my magic, so we may need to wait. Imposing shapeshifting on something other than myself is hard."

"Let's stop here then." I rummage through my satchel and offer him a canteen. "Water?"

Faolan nods and takes it, drinking slowly. He takes a seat on the ground against the tree. Then he sets it down and puts his hands together, eyes closed. I can sense him sending out some powerful magic to connect with his moth. He grits his teeth, and his chest starts heaving with heavier breaths. I don't know whether to move closer to help him or stay back. When he drops the spell, he slumps forward against his knees. "Sixteen…" he chokes out.

I rush over to him and force the canteen into his hand. He drinks the water greedily. Clearing his throat, he sets the canteen down and leans his head back against the tree. "Sixteen guards total," he continues. "Eight in the guard house, eight on guard or on patrol. I may have missed some. Operate under the assumption of 20-24. We will need to go over the wall. I will fly us over, but I need to use that potion Cary gave me."

"I got it." I hop to my feet and open Faolan's satchel on the side of his horse. I grab the one red glowing bottle and hand it over. "Here."

Faolan pockets the vial. "We will have to use it right at the wall. Until then, I will need to focus on the magic needed to cover us."

"Can't I help you?" I protest. "I don't want you drained before we even get there."

"Seeing as you're planning on flying us out of the city yourself, I'd say this is more than enough. I will rest when I can."

"I hope you're right."

Faolan raises an eyebrow. "That's what we agreed on, me doing all the initial magic."

I shake my head. "No, no, you are right. Just… getting nervous."

"Good." Faolan chuckles softly. "Just don't start letting panic get to you. Nerves can be helpful, but if you're afraid, you're as good as dead. As powerful as we may be, these men are trained to fight. So to err on the side of caution is…" He cuts off suddenly and holds his hand up in a quieting gesture. He listens for a moment and then scrambles to his feet. "Take cover." I leap up and dart into the woods, taking shelter behind a large tree. Faolan disappears from my view. When I send a feeler out, I can sense an intense foreign energy.

When I peer out from behind the tree, I see quite a strange sight. A small child with short blonde hair wanders down the middle of the road. She stares with an unnerving, unbreaking gaze at our horses who buck against their tied reins under her eyes. She grins wickedly at their fear as her head tilts at a disturbing angle. My eyes widen, and my throat constricts. The evening shadows seem to cling to the child, and when she reaches out a hand, my horse strains as if being choked. The child's body twists, her mouth opening to show jagged teeth set again a black nothingness. No throat, just… a void.

I whip around and press my back to the tree, covering my mouth to halt any sound. I throw out my focus to sense where Faolan's magic is so I can find where he is relative to me. I feel his sending out of magic before it even leaves his hands. Faolan pushes his hands forward and sends out lights scattered throughout the forest like torches. The child reacts violently to it. She drops the horse as her body splits in half, a demonic entity pouring out from her broken frame. The child costume is then absorbed back into the demon's skin as it searches frantically for where the light is coming from.

Seeing what Faolan is going for, I focus on my hands and send out a few fireballs that roll out as self-contained balls of energy and more importantly, light. The demon is disoriented further. Faolan swings out from behind a tree a few paces ahead of me and throws up a massive wave of blinding light around the demon-child. "Grace!"

I spin out and sprint toward the demon, sending out a rapid wave of fire in its direction. I siphon a bit of power from his light spell to keep another one coming. The demon stumbles back, but lets out a sound of nightmares, a coarse shrill shriek that echoes through my skull. The sound forces me to one knee.

Faolan's voice barely breaks through the sound. "Grace! Kill it!" I panic. Concentrating as hard as I can on the creature and the trees around, I throw out a hand, casting a disintegration spell and exploding the roots of the trees around us. The trees collapse and tumble on top of the demon trapping it. Lighting my sword in flames, I charge forward and fly over to the creature, plunging the blade into its chest. To my horror, the head turns around its neck and opens its mouth, hissing at me before taking its last rasping breath. It moves no more. I fall backward on my hands, leaving the sword and scrambling back.

Faolan groans and comes out from behind the tree. He collapses at the edge of the road again, gripping his head. "By the Lady. We're planning on fighting more like that? I've used too much magic already."

"I've seen eyes like that," I manage hoarsely. "Demons. There are demons in the city."

"You think I can't tell?" He scoffs. "If that were a Fae child, its mouth would've been a damn mouth!"

"Don't shout at me!" I slap my hand down on my other wrist to stop both of my hands from shaking. Sighing, I turn my head and look at Faolan. "We gotta rethink this plan. If there are demons in the city, Kiara is going to be a lot harder to get out."

"I have an idea." Faolan breathes heavily. "But it will take a hell of a lot of luck."

I gulp as I slowly turn my full back on the dead demon. "What is it?"

"I have augmentation, and you have disintegration." Faolan leans forward with his hands folded. "We're going to blast the wall open in as many places as we can. It's highly unlikely there are demons in the city. I assume the living are kept there, and the demons are outside to keep us out and others in. But if we open the city, the guards will be forced to fight any demons for us. And we can get Kiara. It will sacrifice lives, but at this point, I think it's the only way not to sacrifice ours."

"O… okay. Let's do it." I try to get up, but my body is not cooperating. "Let me just… get to my feet, and we'll be out."

"After we blast the wall down." Faolan pushes himself up and walks over to me as he talks. "I will keep a shade over you, and you go to where Kiara is being kept. I will keep the horses safe. She will have to ride with you. Before this is done, we may need her power. I may not know all her magic types, but make sure she grabs any alchemy supplies or any potions she might have at hand. We're going to need them."

"Alright," I answer, slightly more assured. "I'll let her know what needs to be done." I push myself to my feet. Faolan steadies my arm as I stand.

"Also, if she can fly, have her fly her own ass out of here." I chuckle at his words. Faolan walks back over to where we started, combing through the disrupted leaves, and pulls out the glowing red potion. "Thank the Lady…" He breathes in relief.

"What did Cary give you anyway?" I ask.

"Blood magic. It's a potion attuned to me and my magic. It's a very high-level magic. Very rare. She had an alchemist create a potion using my blood to give me heightened magical capabilities. It's one of the most expensive potions in this realm. It'll last long enough to get us in and out of the House of Peace, but I'm going to be out of commission tomorrow. So I suggest you leave me be if I take this." He shakes the vial lightly.

"Is it dangerous?"

"Nothing so dramatic." Faolan gets back up. "Just complex alchemy. They break the blood down and strengthen it, I don't know. It's a heavily guarded secret. Only one or two mages that can pull it off."

I cross over and pat his arm. "Hey. Are you prepared to put yourself out of commission for this mission?"

He shrugs. "It's not the first time I've done it. First time, I was out for a week. It was not a pleasant experience, besides… if it puts a thorn in my father's side, it's worth it."

I bite my lip. "Is this gonna work?"

"You better hope it does. Are you ready?"

As ready as I'm going to be, I think to myself. "Yes. Let's go."

Chapter Forty

Faolan and I ready ourselves for the fight. He grabs one of the regular restoration potions out of his pack and takes it. He grins, and I sense the power flowing back into him. "Can I have a swig?" I ask.

"Go ahead." He indicates the pack. "You may have *one* of them," he emphasizes. "We need to save the rest."

I reach over and take a small vial. Popping over the cork, I throw it back. I shiver and stretch as the cold liquid sends a surge of magic from my head to my feet. "Oh, that feels good."

"Can we get going now?" Faolan looks over his shoulder at me.

I take a breath. "Yes. To the gate."

"First I augment, you disintegrate, and then I'll cloak you. Just like that."

"Done. Let's go."

We reach the wall in very little time. Its height is impressive and built from dark gray geometric stones. Every guard is still in their place as the moth described, if only slightly shifted. They stand strong and ready for anything. I can only hope they are not ready for us. Faolan gives me a pointed look before closing his eyes. When he opens them again, his eyes shine brilliantly in the night. I feel a strong, overwhelming surge of augmentation magic blanket me, and I smile at the heady feeling. Faolan then shrouds the entirety of the wall in darkness except for a few key structural points, mapping them out for me.

I close my eyes and mouth a slow, careful chant before slamming my hands forward and causing multiple explosions in the key points on the well. The entire structure blows to pieces, tumbling down behind and on top of the guards. They lose their minds, shouting and spinning around to try to figure out what happened. Faolan chuckles as we watch before putting a shroud over me. With a flick of his wrist, he summons shades of my silhouette that act as decoys to storm the wall. They take off, climbing through the holes in the defenses hoping to distract the guards away. "Good luck," he mutters to me. I hit his arm lightly in solidarity before jumping over the rubble and racing down the street.

While Faolan's shroud covers me, I sprint through the street and head directly for the palace. Guards and soldiers are running past me towards the gate to see what the commotion is. I spin, duck, and weave to avoid them. When I reach the palace grounds, I rush past two guards and unfurl my wings. Trying to remember what Faolan taught me, I launch into the air and use the wind to guide my body straight up to the balcony of the far-right tower.

With a full concentrated wave of my arm, I blow the doors off their hinges. "Kiara!" The woman in question whips around when I come in. Her purple hair whips over her shoulders, and I catch a glimpse of her violet eyes. She hesitates for a moment, then springs to her feet.

"Grace?" She asks tentatively, but her eyes are wild.

I bob my head. "Grab every potion you can and hurry. We're getting the hell out of here now." Not even minutes after I say that, there's a pounding at the tower door and fumbling with the locks on the other side. We shove a few vials into a bag, and I throw it over my shoulders. "Can you fly?"

"Yes."

"Good. Come on!" I shout. Hand in hand, we take to the sky. Kiara's wings unfurl, pale delicate purple wings that are much smaller than mine but much more powerful. We speed towards the forest. Her flight patterns are so much more assured than mine. By this time, we are finally being seen. I control the wind to move us away from projectiles and fight against other wind mages trying to knock us out of the sky. "Get ready!" I yell to her as we are near the edge of the woods. "We're gonna drop down there. Faolan is waiting. No time to rest; we gotta move our asses."

Suddenly, I see Faolan's signal: a brilliant blast of light that lights up the entire forest area. He's throwing it up to blind the archers who may be able to hit us on our way down. "Now!" Kiara and I tuck our wings in and spiral downwards. We are flying almost blind with the flash of light, but with a quick slash of my arm, a breeze carries us down. We tumble onto the forest floor. The breath is knocked out of me as I hear Kiara hit down beside me.

Faolan walks over beside me, the night going still and dark again in a moment as he drops his power. His eyes still shine white, laying out little suns on the forest floor. He grips my arm and yanks me to my feet before helping up the other Lady. "Let's go!" he whispers urgently. I push Kiara over to my horse before hopping up behind her. Faolan swings up to his and flicks the reins, pushing his horse to a trot and then to a gallop. He blankets the road in shadows to hide our movements.

We gallop off at full speed into the night. I force Kiara to grab onto my waist to hold fast as we go flying forward. Out of the corner of my eye, I see Faolan slump forward in his saddle. "Faolan?" I ask as I shift our horse closer to him. The man grits his teeth while fiddling with a rope that he's pulled out of his bag. It takes a moment to realize he is tying himself into the saddle.

He tosses me an additional rope. "Lead my horse along with yours. Take changes in pace slowly." He presses his head into the horse's neck and lets his body fully slump forward.

"Faolan!" I whisper frantically. He doesn't respond. "Faolan!" I reach over and touch his arm, but he does not move. "The Lady be damned… Oh, we don't have time for this. Kiara, can you ride?" She nods. I give her the reins, and she slows the horses down to a trot. I quickly make a tricky transition from my horse to his. "Pick up the speed," I say to Kiara. Both of us flick the reins to bring us back to a gallop.

I roughly pull Faolan up and grip him to my chest. "Come on Faolan, hang in there for me bastard." I hiss to Kiara, "Keep at full speed. We need to be as far away from here as fast as possible." I struggle to keep Faolan on as we move. It takes all my strength to keep him balanced.

I feel a soft rumble from Faolan's chest as he chuckles. "I'm resting," he says quietly. "Not dead. Fuck off and let me go to sleep."

I grit my teeth. "Just keeping us moving. You could say thank you."

"I tied myself on. I'm not in any danger of falling off."

Double-checking his tying work, I have to admit that he's right. *Well, now I feel embarrassed.* I swear under my breath. "Go to sleep." He collapses back against me and closes his eyes, drifting off. We ride on towards the House of the Evening, our freedom growing ever closer.

Chapter Forty-One

When we return with Kiara, we are welcomed back with cheers and plenty of congratulations. When Kiara recounts how the rescue went and what Faolan and I managed to accomplish, the War Council has no choice but to begrudgingly accept that Faolan has some good use. I pass Kiara off to Aira to get her up to speed with Council plans and prophecy matters. Faolan takes over explaining the demon that we encountered outside of the House of Peace. It alarms the rest of the Council and Lady Morgana. For the first time, I see her demeanor break. She is sincerely troubled, even more so than when her fellow High Lord of the House of the Earth was killed. We make plans to increase our scholars' studies into demonic magic. The next few weeks pass by rather uneventfully for war plans after that, though I have to take on more administrative duties of the House of the Evening.

That being said, I didn't expect one of those duties to be a Founder's Day dance.

I can't believe I'm about to go to a party in the middle of a war. But with our latest victory and the looming presence of Founder's Day, it has been made very clear to me that I am expected to show up to at least one of the clubs that is throwing a big party. My father's right hand has informed me, other officials have been asking me what my plans are for weeks, and the multitude of invitations to different establishments in town that I have been ignoring keep pressing for me to attend their party. Apparently, this is an important event to keep morale high among the people. So I am stepping up as best as I can.

I slip on a pair of formal black heels and fasten the straps around my ankles. I also slide a dagger into a new thigh sheath. *Never hurts to be prepared.* Then I face the mirror to give myself a quick once over. My handmaiden spent about an hour on my hair, setting the curls right out of my bath and pulling it up to sit high on top of my head. This white dress isn't something I would normally wear; it's too long and hangs high on my neck. From what I've been told, this is the standard dress for Founder's Day for a new heir. As a baby, it would have been cute. As a woman… not so much. I slip my amulet around my neck and let it fall against my skin. *I guess this will do.*

A heavy knock on the door interrupts my thoughts. "Grace! Open up!" The silky and oh-so-irritating voice of Faolan shouts through the crack in the door. I groan loudly and ignore the knocking. "Grace!" Unfortunately, my second is much more insistent than I am, and I lose my will. Begrudgingly, I unlock the door and open it.

"Faolan," I greet the man.

"Hello, High Lady. Don't you look formal?" The man strides into my room without an invitation.

"Isn't that how I'm supposed to look? And thank you for just walking in here," I snark as I shut the door.

"You look fine," he considers me, "but you could look better. Haven't you ever been to a Fae club?" Faolan chuckles to himself. "No, I don't suppose you have, have you? How about a mortal club then?"

"Not really my scene."

"Alright, let's fix this. Come here." He motions for me to step over to the mirror again.

"Oh no, you're not doing anything with me." I open the door quickly. "We are leaving."

Faolan darts over to me and grabs my arm. "Nope." He drags me over to the mirror. "Your hair needs to be down." He starts fiddling with the pins holding up my hair.

"Hey! Stop, what are you…" I try to protest and bat his hands away, but with a few quick motions, he dismantles all the last hour's work. "Seriously?" I shout at him and shut my eyes tight.

"Oh, relax." Faolan tsks. "You'll like this a lot better." His fingertips move gently through my hair and drape the curls lightly over my shoulders. He combs through my hair slowly to take out the frizz. He fusses a bit, ruffling one side and then the other. "Alright, don't move, or something really bad is going to happen." I open my mouth to tell him off, but a slight burning smell fills my nose and I freeze in place. When Faolan snaps his fingers, I feel fabric pull away from my neck and shoulders. I slam my hands over my chest to keep my dress up, but to my surprise, it's not falling off me. "Perks of magically woven fabric," he says. "I can make some modifications, and it won't fall." Faolan's hands then press into my arms. "You can look now."

I carefully open one eye before opening them both widely at what I see in the mirror. My curls are settled back on my shoulders, and they look and feel much more natural. The white dress has been cut at the top into an off-shoulder dress. Faolan's gone ahead and sliced off the bottom too, up to just above my knees. The seared-off fabric has fallen in rings around my feet. I feel a lot more like myself. "See?" Faolan breathes in my ear. "That's better."

I gulp and turn to face him. "Thank you." I take a brief scan of him decked out in a dark red button-down shirt and black leather pants. He certainly appears lordly, but that outfit is… tight. I turn away. "You don't look half bad."

Faolan laughs. "Shall we?" He saunters over to the door and opens it out into the hallway. When I step out, he offers me his arm. Amused by his antics, I take it. He escorts me down the hallway and down the stairs where a small crowd of nobles and their attendants are waiting for us. Everyone looks absolutely beautiful. Every dress has a characteristic style that fits the wearer and a bright color. With one look, one would know that tonight was a celebration. There is idle chatter echoing through the hall, and I am happy to hear joyous voices and excitement. There hasn't been a lot of that these past few months.

"Wow!" Luna darts up the stairs to meet us, her purple dress swishing around her thighs. She begins walking down backward as she grins. "You look so pretty, Grace."

"Thank you, Luna," I laugh.

"And Faolan! You look handsome."

"Don't I always, Luna?" Faolan gives her a little wink, and to my surprise, she blushes and scampers down the stairs. I glance over at Faolan and raise an eyebrow. He chuckles. "She used to have a little crush on me when we were kids. She's being courted now by a nice young woman, and she's very much over me. But I can still manage to make her blush every now and again."

Rolling my eyes, I tighten my grip on Faolan's arm as we descend into the crowd and through to the front. The doors open, and we lead the people outside. It's a beautiful crisp evening; the slight breeze sends the littlest bit of chill through me. The sun is hovering just over the horizon, sending a bright pink glow over the bottom third of the sky as it fades into purple and then to navy. There couldn't be a more perfect night for a dance. The carriages wait for us in a neat ring. Guards sit on horseback alongside each carriage to escort and protect us while we are in town. Faolan opens the carriage door and I step inside. Out the window, beautiful people follow suit. When he joins me, the whole line of carriages departs and rolls out of the courtyard.

I find myself smiling as we roll through town. Once more, music pours out from the windows and into the street. People are dancing inside the taverns and on the streets. There is not a single soul who isn't dressed in their best and going out tonight. It is such a refreshing atmosphere to the shit I have been going through this week.

When we come up on the club, I am surprised at its simplistic elegance. The music and the bass pouring out of the open doors would indicate that it's a new-age place, but the wood slat building pouring out onto a massive outdoor deck reminds me of those old places in the Middle Realm where I once played. Lights adorn the railing and all around the frame of the house. The driver opens the door, and I step out to greet the music.

Faolan and I lead the congregation of nobles into the club. I look to Faolan. "Do you know what happens now?" I ask. "Is there a speech or a… presentation or something?"

"No one briefed you?"

"I'm so tired, I don't even know what I had for breakfast this morning."

Faolan laughs. "All we have to do tonight, my lady, is dance."

The bass is heavy, the strings ring out, and I'm instantly in love with the vibe. Tonight, there is no separation of the classes. We all move into the thick of it, and the music sweeps us away. Mixing in with the crowd, we dance. I separate from Faolan and make my way around the room and dance through groups of people to spread the love. Drinks flow around me, tiny glasses filled up with the finest of wine. The band plays whatever the people ask for, smoothly sliding into each transition. Everyone here is happy, and oh, by the Lady, I haven't seen happiness like this in a long time. The night tastes like freedom, and I want to get drunk off it. I end up in the middle of Luna, Aira, and Kiara, living our best lives in one night.

I feel so… free.

Somewhere midway through the party, I lean against the wall at the back of the club taking it all in. Silver strands of lights are hanging down in vertical lines from the ceiling, sending shimmers across the dance floor. Aira and Luna are swirling around with each other, laughing. I don't think I've ever seen Luna happier, even though she is perky in general. I watch Talon spin Kiara in dizzying circles on the floor. She laughs loudly, and he grins before sending her into another spin. Everyone in this club looks peaceful and happy. One wouldn't think that there was a war going on outside these walls. Tonight is about living and living well.

A cleared throat interrupts my thoughts. I turn to my right, and Faolan is standing there, smiling at me with a coy, yet subdued smile. "May I have this dance, High Lady?" he teases.

I chuckle. "The last time I danced with you, Faolan, it was a trap."

"You were a mere lady then. Now you are a High Lady. I'm sure you can handle me for one dance."

My lips curl up as I offer him my hand. He grins as he whisks me onto the dance floor. His hands slide up my arms and pull them around his neck before sliding down to settle on my waist. The drumbeat is steady underneath the melody line as Faolan pulls me closer. We move together with the music in almost perfect sync. He takes my hand and spins me in a circle outward. I turn rapidly under his fingers before spinning back into him. He catches me, my back to his chest, and his hand stretches out to catch one of mine. We move forward and back, turning and swirling around each other.

Faolan suddenly lifts me up, and I lay back on his shoulders. There's something so freeing about being in the air supported by one person's arms. As we turn, I take in the ceiling, the lights, the music, the feeling of being free. I breathe it all in deeply before being brought down to the ground. Every move we make feels deliberate, planned, yet spontaneous at the same time.

I am breathless.

The music changes. It's a new song, but Faolan shows no signs of letting me go. And… honestly, I don't feel like stepping back. We slide into a slow dance, swaying and spinning with a swelling but steady beat. The lights shine down on us and light up the floor as we turn. There's something fitting about having this second dance in this setting. It's informal, but beautiful. It's a perfect place for a second chance. For this dance, Faolan and I don't speak to each other. But there's a look in his eyes that I am attempting to read that is telling me things I'm not quite sure I'm ready to hear.

"What are you thinking about?" Faolan whispers just above my ear as he shifts us closer to each other.

I smile softly. "How… nice this is."

"Yeah." Faolan smiles as he looks above my head at the scene behind us. "Makes you forget everything happening outside." He looks down at me with that pleased smirk of his, and I can't help but smile back. I lean in and brush my forehead against his shoulder as he chuckles at me.

When I raise my head again, Faolan's eyes have changed dramatically. They no longer reflect the fun happenings around us. Suddenly, he reaches down, grabs his dagger, and shouts in my ear. "Get down!"

Chapter Forty-Two

As a silver bullet flies towards my body, I cast a forcefield to contain it as Faolan whips me around and to the side. The dancers around me scatter. "Well, there goes the evening," Faolan snarks as he plunges the room into darkness. The lights above us and around the outside shut down, the moonlight being the only source of where the exits are. Colorful magic flies left and right while people rush for the exits. Screams pierce the air as fireballs engage with the walls, igniting. Luna and Kiara set straight away to putting it out with their water magic. Faolan and I are getting jostled left and right as people push past in a panic. I try to keep my eyes on the enemy, but after a disintegration spell sideswipes me and explodes the staircase behind me, I realize he wasn't alone.

"How many?" I shout over the chaos.

"I count three!" Faolan grips my wrist and pulls me out of the way of another man charging for me.

"Nope," a familiar female voice behind me as Cary slips in beside us. "Four." Within moments, we are joined by all our fellow heirs around us. We spring into action. Aira and I send blasts of wind to send spells awry while Cary sends waves of fire in an attempt to disarm. Talon joins Faolan in hand-to-hand combat against two of the men. Kiara has joined forces with Luna to get as many people out as possible with the least casualties. Though I am horrified to see at least two innocent dancers' bodies fall.

The war has finally made it inside.

This pisses me off. *How dare they invade this night?* That rage fuels my fire magic that glows brilliantly through Faolan's dark spell. It wraps around the assassin in front of me and tightens around his waist in a vice grip. With a flick of my hand, I send the man flying toward the wall. Another man charges me and takes my dagger to his shoulder. Faolan plucks him from me and throws him as far as he can. *Strength magic.* It doesn't take long for Aira, Luna, Kiara, and Cary to subdue the other attackers, working together. We corral both the captured and the unconscious in a corner. One of the men still kicking spits at me, and Faolan cracks him across the face with a hand. I grab his arm to stop him. "Not now."

As I look around the room, I am distraught. The walls are broken, the roof is caving in, and there are burn marks everywhere. There's an acrid smell of smoke with a tinge of blood that makes me scrunch my face. The level of destruction is wholly unnecessary. Now that the threat has been neutralized, medical personnel are rushing in to take care of those people who have fallen. Too many are injured. But at least they are alive. The casualties could have been so much worse.

"Grace." Faolan touches my shoulder. "We should go."

"I can't just leave, Faolan. People need help."

"We don't know if more are coming. We need to get you back to the palace."

"Grace," Talon interrupts gently. "I can stay and make sure things are taken care of here."

"We can stay too," Tristan adds as he and Jason approach our little group. They are cut up, but they have steely looks in their eyes. "We will let you know what happens down here."

In a rare moment of solidarity, Jason adds, "Hey, don't worry about it. It's protocol in many of the Houses to move the noble family as soon as possible when incidents like this go down. You guys take off; we can handle it."

Reluctantly, I nod, and the eight of us rush outside. Luckily, most of us have flight magic, so we can make a quick trip out of here. Faolan holds on to Luna as we all take off. Catching a breeze, we speed off toward the palace. Below, I see a town in turmoil. Magic from the battle gone awry has struck nearby buildings and taken out homes and businesses. People from the party are evacuating, flooding the streets and seeking shelter. Shouts and tears and curses run rampant, and I can't help but feel a deep pain at seeing the realm gone to hell so quickly.

When I reach the courtyard, I drop down like a bomb and hit the ground running. "Lockdown now!" I shout to my soldiers guarding the front entrance. "Spread the word; get everything together and send help to Silvervale. There was an attempt on my life and the lives of the other nobles. There are two casualties that I know of. The others are still in town taking care of the people. I want medics and guards down there immediately. Go now!" One man runs off to get the barracks prepared while the others usher me inside. The other heirs follow behind.

"Grace, what do you want to—" Faolan starts to say.

I hold up a hand as I sprint up the front stairs two at a time. "Not now. I'll be down in an hour. I need some time. Meet me in the throne room." Without waiting for answers, I rush towards my bedroom. When I lock myself inside, I put a force field around the entrance to ensure I am not disturbed. I fling open the balcony doors and storm outside. Only then do I finally take a breath.

There's this fury deep in my bones at this. I thought I had worked reasonably well to keep everything running smoothly, keeping the House of the Evening's affairs separate from the war effort. But I am now seeing that that was naive. This war affects all of us, not just when it is inside our walls. But how dare they. How *dare* High Lord Carron send this in on Founder's Day. I should have known he would do this, particularly today. Like Faolan said, he has a flair for the gut punch.

I have to do something to help. I can't just sit here and wait patiently for something to happen. When I see my violin lying innocently on its stand, I am hit with an overwhelming rush of magic in my chest. I seize the violin, knocking the stand off the table and onto the ground. It bounces with a distinctive *clang*. I storm back onto the balcony and whip the bow around to the string, drawing out a harsh, growling note. Then I just... play.

The bow flies across the strings quickly. It bounces and dips as I move my fingers in quick hops across the fingerboard. The song isn't a piece that I know; it's something I feel busting out of my hands like it just had to be played. As the notes play on, I find my eyes transported to the scene back at the nightclub. The heirs battling. The enemy trying to take everything I have. The people afraid, confused. Everything moves in slow motion. Every spell fires so brightly and exaggeratedly, I can almost pick out individual strands.

Then I sense it. A magic pouring out from me into the night. And when I open my eyes, I can see it. Long purple strands of pure energy stream out into the sky and make their way toward the town. Although I am confused by it, I am not afraid of its effects. It moves rapidly and dives from overhead down into the streets, weaving towards the rubble of the club and surrounding buildings. I can see the Fae's eyes looking at it, curious, afraid. The purple strands then plunge down into the wreckage. The music from my violin echoes through the magic and begins to repair. The actions are slow at first. Broken beams slowly stick together, and brick pieces merge.

That violin sings under my will like it has never sung before. I play with wild abandon in a strange state of free will and forced notes.

Every note feels predetermined, yet the movements feel like mine. I don't know who or what I am playing for, but I can tell something big is happening. And as I continue to play, I feel other individuals' magic join mine, empathetic magic like mine. New layers add to the music. A lone guitar catches my ear from a different part of the city. A steady drum beat. A cello. We make a small dent in repairing the city through magic and music.

I don't know how long I played. All I know is that the next thing I remember is Faolan breaking through the protection on my bedroom door lock and busting into the room. Startled, my bow slides awkwardly on the wrong note as my hand drops the violin from my shoulder to my side. The magic trail cuts off on my end sharply and slowly flutters towards the ground like a ribbon in the wind. We stare at each other, Faolan's expression an unreadable one. "Come downstairs," is the only thing he says before turning away and walking toward the hall. I move to the doorway to say something before he can walk too far, but no words come to mind. Instead, I just watch him leave.

Chapter Forty-Three

When I get downstairs, Faolan is not there waiting with the others. Instead, I see stares and awestruck gazes. Luna has a self-satisfied beam on her face while Cary looks up at me and shakes her head.

"What the hell was that?" Cary finally asks.

"What was what?" I breathe heavily.

"You did something." She climbs up the stairs to meet my level. "You did something, and there was this brilliant flash of magic."

"The magic signature was purple. Your shade," Aira adds.

"I told them it was yours as well," Luna chimes in.

"But we couldn't just take her word for it," Cary interrupts. "Was it yours?"

"I… I have no idea." I look out over the nobles' faces, and for the first time, I have no idea how to answer them. "I was… playing my violin, and I guess my empathetic magic kicked in. But I don't really know. I just played my music, and it moved down into the town. I had some sort of vision of that magic beginning to repair buildings. Then other people began to offer their magic and their music, and the reparations grew stronger."

"That is some impressive magic, Grace." Kiara shakes her head in awe. "I've never heard of empathetic magic that is able to create."

"I wonder what else it can do." Cary's eyes narrow at me, as if studying me.

"Where are the men who attacked us?" I try to change the subject.

"Talon took them to the barracks for interrogation," Kiara says quietly.

I nod. "What happened tonight?"

"Assassination attempt, obviously," Cary answers. "You know that. This is my father's classic play when things aren't going his way. He sends a small handful of very strong guys out to assassinate whoever stands in his way. Congratulations," she snarks, "you're officially powerful enough for my father to be concerned."

Well damn... isn't that something to wrap one's head around?

I feel like I have to say something to break the silence. "Everybody… go to bed. Just… go to bed and we'll figure all this out in the morning." I wave to a few servants standing in the wings listening, and they move to help everyone upstairs. I wait with the few heirs that remain, my prophecy group. "I want a meeting tomorrow. Early. In the library, I don't know when. No, no, after meeting. After the meeting with the larger group, prophecy group in the library." My stuttering isn't doing a good job of getting the point across, but they understand. The group dissipates shortly after.

I'm quite glad that I have waited until everyone else has gone away in one direction or another to move because I am having trouble staying upright. I have no idea what is going on with my magic. I don't want people to see me broken down like this. I make my way up to the hallway and take a roundabout route toward my room to avoid servants who might be doing rounds this evening. But before I can reach the second set of stairs, an open door to one of our balconies catches my eye.

I move to the door to shut it until I see Faolan's hair peeking out over the back of a chair. A tall decanter of wine sits on the table beside him with another glass. Faolan's arm raises up as he downs the drink he has in his hands and sets it on the table. He lets out a groan. I almost feel like I'm intruding on a private moment.

As I turn to leave, I nudge the door a little wider. It makes a soft squeak. But it's enough to catch the man's attention. He whips around quickly but relaxes when he sees me. "Ah, it's you." He settles back into his chair. "Care to join me?" I make a soft hum in affirmation as I walk over to him.

"Pour me a glass," I say simply as I sink into the chair beside him.

"You drink wine?"

"I do now." I sigh, closing my eyes against the setting sun.

Faolan chuckles. I hear the clinking of a second glass and the unscrewing of a glass top. Wine tumbles into the glass quietly like waves sliding over the beach sand. I open my eyes as Faolan hands me my drink. I smile softly in thanks before taking a long, slow sip. My head tips back on the back of the chair, and I just try to breathe.

"Hey…" Faolan's voice echoes in my ear. "What're you thinking about?"

"It's been a long week, Faolan. Smuggled one girl out of the House of Peace, took down crazy assassins, and we still can't move forward." I drop my head into my hands and rub my eyes. "And I have no idea what's happening here. My magic did something, and I don't know what to do with it."

"I don't know if I can help you with that."

"I don't expect you to." We sit in silence, the wind as the only disruption to our little space here. I could stay here forever.

"Hey," Faolan's voice gets a little softer. I feel a hand against my forehead. "You feel a little warm, Grace. Are you feeling alright?"

"I told you," I snap, "I'm tired." *Wow, that came out way more aggressive than I wanted it to sound.* I sigh. "Faolan, I'm sorry, I—"

"Don't worry about it," he dismisses me. "Come on." He pulls me to my feet and wraps my arm around his shoulders. "Let's get you to bed."

"Is this really necessary?" I'm trying to argue with him, but I am starting to feel a bit dizzy in my tiredness.

"Nope. But this is." He suddenly sweeps an arm out under my legs and lifts me up into the air.

"Hey! Faolan!" I whack him in the arm. "Put me down."

"Nope. I'm taking you upstairs."

"Faolan…"

"Nope. If you protest one more time, I'll stop dead in the middle of this hall and anyone who walks by will see you in my arms. Then you'll have a lot to explain."

I groan. "Fine." Faolan laughs and carries me up the stairs. Surprisingly, I don't feel the usual bumps of being carried; he's holding me in a way that we seem to just glide on up. Or maybe he's flying, I don't know. The next thing I recall clearly is arriving at my bedroom door. He swings it open with ease and sets me down on the edge of the bed.

"What kind of lingerie do you wear?" Faolan asks way too nonchalantly.

"You're not getting me pajamas, Faolan! Don't start digging around in my underwear drawer."

"You can barely move; just tell me which drawer's the right one, and I won't explore any other drawers."

I roll my eyes softly, but I realize I could probably use the help. "Third drawer, second dresser."

Faolan actually complies with my instructions and pulls out a shirt and some lightweight pants. He tosses them to me, and I manage to catch them. I raise my eyebrows at him when he doesn't move to leave. "I'm not changing with you in here."

"I'm not going until you're safely stuck in bed. But I will turn around for you."

Interesting. I keep my eyes trained on him as I change clothes, but he never turns around. I'm almost impressed. I give a little cough to let him know before laying down on the pillows. "Thank you, Faolan," I say as he turns around to face me. "For the ride and the clothes."

"You're welcome." To my surprise, he sits down on the edge of the bed. "Under the covers."

"By the Lady, you're not tucking me in." *What the hell is going on?*

"You're in no position to argue."

"How do I know you're gonna leave when I'm asleep?"

"I'll leave, I promise. You don't need to be afraid of me, darling. You should know that by now. Come on…" He pulls my blankets over my legs and up to my chest. "Sleep."

I roll over on my side away from him in a bold move of trust. "You can't just command me to sleep, you know." I yawn.

He chuckles before a hand lays on my back and rubs lightly. "Watch me," he whispers. Then I'm surrounded by that comforting warm darkness that caresses my cheek and pulls me into its warm embrace.

Chapter Forty-Four

Come morning, I wake up slowly. Opening my eyes feels like moving through a thick layer of fog. For the first time in a long time, I feel very refreshed. Judging by the light patterns against the curtains and shining through the entire room, it is late morning. I lay in bed against the pillows for a while, reveling in their softness. *Oh... I don't want to get up.* Lingering on my lips is the taste of wine with a hint of whatever dark magic Faolan put me under. *I need an entire case of bottles of whatever that was. I could become addicted to it.*

When I glance over at the table, I spot a single black lily laying among my things. I slide to a seated position and pick it up. The stem has been cut smooth with no thorns or bumps in sight. I finger the petals likely and sense a hint of the same magic I tasted last night. *Ah... Faolan... slippery bastard. What a specific choice in a flower.* A black lily symbolizes rebirth, life after death, and something unique and powerful. The gift is a small, but reassuring little boost, and a soft smug smile settles on my face. But it doesn't last long as I realize it's time to face the gravity of last night's situation.

The War Council is silent at the table the next morning. We all sit around idly looking at each other without anyone standing up and offering an idea or a plan. Even Faolan is quiet, tapping his fingers on the table. Everyone is still reeling from the events of last night. I passed around a report from our top generals on the damage in the town below us, and it looks like suffering was minimal. Three casualties in the crossfire at the club and four or five buildings in various stages of destruction. Repair efforts have already begun. Condolences have been dispatched and the House is providing a worthy funeral for each of the deaths. I wasn't going to leave them unprovided for as Leo was. No… we were going to get this right.

And now, we need to come up with next steps.

The House of Darkness needs to answer for this. And to me, there is only one clear way to accomplish this.

All eyes turn to me as I rise to my feet. "We need to make an offensive strike. We have been playing defense for far too long, focusing on keeping our territories and sending humanitarian aid to those who have fallen. It's time to show the House of Darkness we won't stand for this.

Bodies shift and lean forward. "Are you serious?" Jason asks. "We can't take them on."

"Not head-on. But a concentrated strike, a concentrated fight… will show them we mean business."

"That's not a bad idea." Faolan nods to himself. "We could use a victory. But where would we strike?"

"It needs to be somewhere critical enough to disrupt their operations, but small enough to be taken and held by us." Cary starts making notes. "We would have to pick extremely carefully."

"Where's a map when you need one?" I mumble under my breath. Aira hears me and rushes to grab one. When she returns, the nobles gather around and pour over it. Fingers point places out and then quickly pull away as they reevaluate our current supply level.

"What about Willowdale?" Aira presses her finger to a House of the Earth town in the east. "Right here along the Clary Mountain Pass on the outskirts of the House of the Earth. Intel shared the House of Darkness had set it up as a stop for refueling on their supply chain.

We could intercept their supply line."

"Let's cut it out of the equation entirely," I counter. "Let's take back the whole village."

"Oh, wouldn't that be brilliant." Cary chuckles as she leans back.

"I have contacts in Willowdale," Faolan offers. "I can have them join us when we step in."

"That would be good," I reply. "Tristan, Jason, Cary: I want you three looking at physical landmarks, best points of entry, and ways of transport. Faolan, you need to contact your guys. Aira, Kiara, take stock of what manpower and what supplies we have. High Lady Morgana, I need—"

Suddenly, the doors to the conference room fly open. I and several of the others shift into a battle stance. We're all a little jumpy after yesterday's events. One of my generals enters the room and makes a beeline for me. I move closer and lean in. "What's going on?"

"I'm sorry, High Lady Grace. There's news from the battlefield."

"What is going on?" Faolan comes to my side quickly.

The general looks around at the table and turns slightly to address all of us at once. "We have received word from our allies in the House of Light and House of Water." The heirs of said Houses look stunned. My stomach twists. "A few nights ago, the armies of the Houses of Darkness and Fire split up. The House of Darkness took the House of Light two days ago. The House of Water fell to Fire last night. Messengers were able to escape just before everything went to hell. But we are alone in this now."

Alena lets out a sob, and Aurora hugs her tightly, holding back her own tears. Tristan stares at the table blankly. When I glance over at Faolan, his jaw is tight. Quiet falls over the room as we all reel in the news. *We are alone in this. It's just us left.*

The doors slam open yet again, and this time, an entire congregation of officials and dignitaries move into the room led by Damien. Frankly,

I'm a little frustrated by it. *What could it be now?* "Excuse me? Is there a reason you are all interrupting this meeting? We are dealing with a crisis here." When Damien locks eyes with me, I know something horrific has gone wrong. His expression is a mixture of regret and resignation.

He walks over to me and leans in to speak in my ear in a hushed tone. "High Lady Grace, you are needed in the hospital room. Immediately."

The room falls deathly silent again. I rise slowly from the table. *No. Not now.* The other nobles are staring at me. Without saying a word, I walk around the chairs before brushing past Damien. Once the doors to the chamber shut, I practically sprint towards the hospital room. The men follow quickly behind me. All the while, my thoughts are racing. *Is he awake? Is he dying? Is he already dead? What happens to the war effort in any of those scenarios? What happens to me?*

When I throw open the hospital doors, Neil is already there with his mother and Analise. As soon as I see Neil's devastated face and the overwhelming tears of the women, I realize that... it is over. My shoes click against the tile floor as I move over to the bed. My father's pale face has been drained of the last bit of color, and his chest no longer moves. I softly take his hand and kneel beside the bed. I press his hand to my forehead as I try to hold back the overwhelming emotion that I feel right now.

I had just met him. I should have had more time.

I can't even bring myself to look at the rest of the family now. I don't have any words to say to console any of them. I'm at a loss. All I can do is turn to the hospital chief and ask, "When?"

"A few moments ago," he replies mournfully. "He just... went. Something shifted in his body, and his heart stopped. It was his time. He is at peace with the Lady now." I rock back and sit square on the tile floor. *My poor Father. To go so quietly like that... a peaceful end, but... without any family to see you off into the afterlife.* My heart aches.

"I will leave you all to your mourning." The man steps out of the room, and I am left alone with the others.

Analise walks over to me quietly despite her mother's soft sound and tentatively takes my hand. I immediately pull her into my arms. She cries into my stomach, and I lean down to hold her. She is so fragile in my arms. I worry that if I hold her too tightly, she may break.

"Please let go of my daughter," Elise's voice asks shakily.

"She wants to hug me," I answer. "I won't deny her."

"She is not your sister."

"She is as good as," I retort. With a deep breath, I continue, "There is no need for us to fight right now. Not over my father's body."

"What are you going to do with us now?" she presses on, much to my irritation. "Are you going to kick us all out?" Analise whimpers in my arms and I tighten my grip on her.

"No." I level my eyes at my father's wife. She seems to falter under my harsh gaze. "I will not be kicking any of you out. You will have a home here as long as you want one. You may have treated me like dirt, but I am better than that. Do not make me regret that choice."

"High Lady?" Damien's voice speaks from behind me. I whip around.

"Don't call me that," I hiss. "Not now."

"I'm sorry… miss. But we need to speak immediately on affairs."

I rise to my feet. "I don't think you understand me. I said—"

"Grace?" A new voice chimes in as the dignitaries part for the High Lady of the House of the Wind. "Can we have a moment? Perhaps in another room?" I look back at my stepfamily in their grief, and I nod slowly. Letting go of Analise and pushing through the officials once more, I follow the High Lady out of the hospital room and into a side chamber. As soon as the door closes behind the two of us, I push both hands into my hair and bend over. I can barely breathe.

"I am deeply sorry for your loss," the woman says quietly.

CHAPTER FORTY-FOUR

I gulp and blink slowly to hide my budding tears. "Thank you, High Lady."

"Call me Morgana, child."

"Thank you… Morgana."

The High Lady walks over and places her hands on my shoulders. "The realm is going to be looking to you now to take the lead."

"I… I can't. I can't, Morgana."

"Being a High Lady is hard enough." Morgana runs a hand over my head as I start to break down. "Being a High Lady in a ruling position is harder. People are always going to question whether or not you are strong enough for this." She shakes me lightly. "But you are. You will lead the House of the Evening forward, and you will lead the rest of us in victory. I wish that the world would give you more time to grieve, but I'm afraid, my dear, that you may only have today. But you will get through this." She pats my cheek. "Stay here. I'll ward off the men for now."

I nod once. "Thank you."

"You're welcome." The High Lady leaves the room. As soon as the door shuts, I just break down. Sinking to my knees, I let myself cry. This feels different from my grief for Leo. It's a grief of what could have been. It's a deep grief and one that pours out rather than settles. Perhaps because I have such limited time to grieve. There are so many people outside waiting for me. I can hear them talking and arguing and failing at trying to be quiet.

I just want to stay holed up here.

The door opens behind me once more. I don't pay attention to it. If anyone speaks, I swear by the Lady I'm going to blast them out of here. Before I can scream at them to get out, Faolan sits down quietly beside me. He doesn't say a word; he only puts his arm around me and lets me cry. And as I allow myself to cry for my father, I find myself grateful that he came in.

At least for a moment, I can lean on someone else.

270

Chapter Forty-Five

When I have dried the last of my tears and Faolan has helped me to my feet, I don't want to face the War Council right away. My legs shake, and I'm leaning too heavily on my partner. My mouth feels too dry to answer a million questions about my plan. Instead, Faolan shields me from their questions as I make my way back to the hospital room. My father is covered with a white blanket, stark white. I try to ignore the figure outlined underneath it. Elise has gone away with her daughter, but Neil is still there, holding his father's hand as if he could bring him back just with that action. "Neil." My voice echoes in the empty room. My half-brother sighs but doesn't move. "Neil."

"What do you want?" he finally answers.

I take a deep breath. "I am about to go downstairs and inform the War Council of the High Lord's death. However… I think we have to wait to tell everyone else."

Neil's head jerks up and he stares at me in disbelief. "What do you mean wait?"

I gulp before pressing on. "Our father's death is going to be a devastating blow to everyone. Not just our House. There are… multiple armies in this palace and outside these walls that I have to lead and take care of. And before I got the news about our father's death, I learned that we lost two more Houses to the House of Darkness." Neil's eyes flash in recognition and alarm. "We were in the middle

271

of planning a maneuver to take back a small but important village on their trade route when I learned of the High Lord's passing." I squeeze my hands into fists and release. "Our father's passing." I move closer to the hospital bed. "I need you to talk to your mother and your sister… about keeping his death quiet for one week."

"Are you serious?" Neil gets to his feet and drops my father's hand. "How can you—"

"How can I? Because I have to. Don't you think I want to mourn him too? We have to keep morale up if we are going to have a fighting chance at winning this thing. I am leading them into battle. You get time. I don't."

"You are leading them?"

"They don't know it yet, but I will be. If I die, you are next in line. You can step up and take control of all of this, the war, the funeral, everything. Bury me in a field for all I care. I am asking you as my half-brother… and as our father's son to consider doing what is best for the war effort. Help me just this once. Please."

Neil considers the offer for a while. His eyes stare off into space down somewhere towards my feet. I hold my breath. When he looks up again, I see the answer in his eyes. "Do what you need to do," he says before kneeling back to take our father's hand. I nod once to him and clear out of there.

As much as I don't want to, I call the War Council back into session. When I announce the death, I only give the others a moment to process before launching into what may be my fastest delegation ever. "My father would want us to soldier on. Therefore, the information I just told you does not leave this room. I want to keep the morale of our armies and our people up. We are taking Willowdale, and we are doing it in the next few days. Jason, Faolan, Cary, you three will be working on organizing the regiments that we are going to take. Faolan, I need you to reach out to your black-market contacts and find out how much aid we can get from them. The rest of you, Tristan, Aurora, Alena, Luna, Aira; I need you here overseeing the refugee crisis. And so you know, I plan to take at least two of you all with me when we storm."

"Refugee crisis?" Faolan asks, shooting me a confused look.

"Silvervale and the surrounding villages are about to become outposts for refugees from all kingdoms. I want messages sent out right now by any means necessary. To save your lorddoms, all our lorddoms, everyone needs to abandon them. Evacuate. We'll have soldiers funneling people through the House of the Wind for screening. The House of Water should be able to funnel out the fastest by the Balsard Sea; the House of Light can retreat via the Bhean Ocean. Tristan, I want you to get our navies on that as soon as possible. Talk to Captain Menkin. I don't know if we can accomplish all of this, but I want to see it done." I finally take a breath. "Any questions?"

When I look around the room, I find determined faces. I don't know if they are putting on a brave face for me, but I am grateful for it. The groups I assigned tasks to split off and begin their work. Faolan keeps his eyes on me for a moment longer, probably to make sure I'm feeling alright. I nod to him once before settling back in my chair to take it all in.

It's time to take back some ground.

* * *

On the morning of our strike, dawn rises as it always does with a slow shift from silence to sound. I should know. I have watched the last nine out of nine sunrises because I can barely stay asleep. I end up sitting on my balcony most mornings watching the night sky turn orange with the rising of the sun. Today, however, I'm long since out of my room. Instead, I huddle in the back of a covered wagon with one hand pressed tightly to my sword wondering if this plan was the right decision. Whether Willowdale is the right target or not.

Nine days of debates. That's what it took to get here. Nine days of people talking over one another and officials coming in with more paperwork and generals plotting out the best movement all to boil down to one moment. One singular moment where an ambush at the changing of the guards could prove to be our shot at gaining some ground. I have to hope that this is it. Because if it's not, this whole war effort could fall apart in one move.

Especially with the news of my father's passing that I have to share when I return home looming over my head.

As we rumble over the road, I look around at the people with me. There are a handful of soldiers with me in this wagon and another couple dozen in the wagons behind us. Jason and Aira stand on either side of me. Aira gives me a half smile when I look over at her, but she returns to nervously rubbing her fingers. I understand that feeling. It's her first time out in the field, but her magic is a great combination for this mission. Her sensing magic will be able to check if the numbers of House of Darkness soldiers we heard from Faolan's black market contacts are accurate. Her wind and flight magic also complement mine, and we are going to need the extra strength. My other pick, Jason, has the military experience that I am grateful to have along for the ride. Faolan tried to fight his way into the mission, but I told him that I needed him to stay home. If something happens to me, I need him to hold things down until Neil can make decisions. He'll do well at that.

My thoughts are interrupted by a steady slowing of the wagon. A sharp three taps echo above our heads. "We're coming up on Willowdale," Jason mumbles to me out of the corner of his mouth. "That's the signal."

"Alright, that's the signal. Everybody; get into position," I say a little louder to the soldiers around us. "Stan, Raphael, communicate with the others in the train behind us that we're almost ready." The two soldiers nod and immediately get to work with their telepathy. "Stand ready. Be prepared for anything. Pray to the Lady we got this right."

My heart pounds in my chest as we all shift. In the moments before all hell breaks loose, I think of Faolan. I hope the people he reached out to nearby will join us in time. I think of home. I wonder if we're overflowing with people by now or if no one will answer the call. *What if there is no way for the refugees to get out of their homes?*

Jason breaks my thoughts as he taps my shoulder. Hand on my sword, I crouch down as the wagon rolls to a stop. "Inspection, sir." I hear from the House of Darkness soldier outside. "What are you carrying today?"

Our driver answers him, "We've got food and medical supplies coming in from the House of Water."

"I'll need to look at that."

"Yes, sir."

Aira presses her back against the wall of the vehicle, knocking her shoulder briefly into mine. I tap her hand reassuringly before gripping tighter on my sword. My other hand readies itself with a wind blast. The regiment around me ready themselves as well, hands on weapons and spells. As I watch them quietly, I wonder if their faces reflect what Leo looked like seconds before a battle. I wonder if he felt all the adrenaline pounding in his ears like I do now.

The latch clicks.

The door opens.

With all my might, I push the wind gust forward. It sweeps through the wagon and straight out the doors, blowing the soldier a dozen feet back and taking him to the ground. "Go!" I shout.

All at once, we rush out of the opening and pour into the roadway. We are stopped right alongside the village, and several of our men rush into the square. Shouts from the enemy regiment milling around town call for backup as they rush to meet my soldiers. At that moment, three other wagons burst open through the roof as Fae fly out in all directions or leap out the back. I praise the Lady that Faolan's black market intel was right and it was going to be a fair fight.

There's no time to waste. I wave on Aira to get to the outpost tower as fast as possible while I lead the next group into the village. Taking control of the base of operations and knocking out enough of High Lord Carron's men puts the territory in our hands. We have to move quickly if we want to keep the element of surprise working for us.

I blast down soldiers with fire and wind. Sword in hand, I clash blades with the man in front of me. All around me, elements are flying in brilliant colors. Flames slip behind me, and I feel them singe the hair on the back of my neck. A disintegration spell to the man's feet stops the onslaught. The ground erupts underneath my feet as elemental earth mages on both sides battle it out and disrupt the general fight. I dance from location to location to stay upright.

More House of Darkness soldiers rush the courtyard in hopes to stop us. I claw my way through a few more of them before taking to the sky. A rush of pain stabs through my body as my left wing is singed by an enemy Fae behind me. I spin around him and use the energy of his spell to take the strength from his flight away. I feel a twinge of regret as he plummets down to the earth. But there's no time to feel anything as the onslaught of bodies and spells continues.

I have never seen so much chaos. The people of the village have caught on to our presence. While they don't move in to help the House of Darkness, they're not rushing to help us either. Not that I blame them. I don't expect them to help as long as they stay out of the way.

I follow Aira to the tower where she is battling it out with who looks to be the head general. Her magic works frantically to keep her aloft as the general slices at her with magically enhanced speed. I soar in through the broken window, intent on knocking him away from her. I throw a fireball at him, which he extinguishes with just one flick of a finger and a stream of water summoned from his mug. Aira and I tag team him, throwing spells left and right. Unfortunately, it's not working as well as I had hoped. The general fights with such rigor and spirit that I am starting to feel in over my head.

Suddenly, another figure busts through the door. I instinctively throw a disintegration spell at the man, but he ducks fast. "Hey, let's not take out our allies here," the man says before throwing a blast at the general. When his hood slips off his head, I recognize him. It's Mahlin from all those months ago, Faolan's right-hand man.

"Mahlin?"

He shoots me a half smile. "Faolan thought you could use some help. You have disintegration magic?"

"Yes!"

"Flight?"

"Yes."

"Then I need you to grip my arm and cast with me and be ready to get the hell out of here." The air shifts as Mahlin sends a spell out and forces the general to the ground. *Gravity magic.* He growls at us as he fights the pull.

"Aira, get out now!" I shout to her. She takes off out the window. Gripping Mahlin's arm tight, we both push out against the walls of the tower.

There is a glorious explosion as the entire building comes down around us.

I catch a glimpse of Mahlin's narrow wings bursting from his back as we take off from the crumbling floor. As excited as I am, there is no time to waste. The two of us fly back to the ground and join the rest of our regiment in fighting the enemy.

When the carnage dies down, we have won. As the people from

the village emerge from their homes, I see the same shock and awe in them reflected in my troops' eyes.

We made it.

Now we have a shot.

Chapter Forty-Six

Our group returns to Silvervale triumphantly with an impromptu parade through town. To my surprise, the people come outside to cheer for us and throw flowers. For the first time, I see wide smiles and hear a few shouts of Hail High Lady Grace. My heart swells with pride to hear the people finally show just a little bit of acceptance. When we arrive at the palace, Faolan, Cary, and Tristan come out to greet us. Tristan gives each of us the biggest hug, and we all have this little celebration in the front courtyard. Faolan presses a hand to my lower back as he congratulates me on a successful battle. The War Council holds a little feast in our honor, and I feel a little seed of hope plant deep in my chest.

Unfortunately, there is no time to bask in that glory because I have to announce my father's death. I can't hold on to that secret forever. What was an all-out victory becomes a bittersweet change of pace as I go down into the town to be with the people when I announce my father's untimely death. Thus ensues a several-week mourning period. I wear dark formal clothes at almost every meeting and event I attend. The people play soft sad music nearly every night to commemorate him.

I make final arrangements for my father's funeral. It was a beautiful ceremony, the kind of ceremony I wanted Leo to have. My father was lowered into a jeweled iron coffin with carvings of his life story.

Well… most of his life. His life in the Upper Realm anyway. Though I did sneak down one night and magically etch the initials of my mother in the very back corner under the lid. To me, it is important that all stories be told, not just the ones that make a man look proper.

Even still, there is little time to rest. There is now a steady influx of refugees flooding into the city. We have been having a hard time housing them all. Luckily, most of them have been strong and healthy and have been able to aid us in building, creating, and generating more supplies for the war effort. On top of that, the Council must plan their next move, and the prophecy group must find our final member.

I am woken up early one morning by a loud short knock at the door. "One second!" I slide ungracefully out of bed, grab a robe from the wardrobe, and slip it on. Stumbling over to the door, I unlock it and pull it open. Luna smiles at me.

"Good morning, Grace."

I rub my eyes. "Hello Luna. No offense to you, but was it necessary waking me up at this hour? I did just return home."

"Oh, that's right, I'm sorry. Faolan tried to warn me that you would want some rest, but Aira thought you might want to be involved."

"Involved in what?"

"The prophecy group is trying to make headway on that last member. A couple of us have been up for a few hours now, and the rest joined us shortly after. Come join us when you can." She smiles as she turns and practically skips down the hallway.

By the Lady, I will never understand that woman.

When I'm out of bed and peer in through the library doorway, I can see the others have been hard at work for a while. Kiara, Aira, and Luna are pouring over some sort of chart while Cary and Faolan argue heatedly in the opposite corner. I take a moment to lean back against the door frame and watch them. There is a level of intense concentration that I don't want to break.

Eventually, Faolan happens to glance over and see me. "Hey, you're up."

"Regretfully," I counter to which Faolan chuckles. "What are we looking at here? Someone fill me in."

"I finally heard from a few of my father's officials still in the House of Peace." Kiara beckons me over to show me the message. "Instead of guarding the outside of the city, High Lord Carron started calling the demons into Craine. There are demons in the palace now with him and with my family." Her voice wavers and I can tell that she's barely holding it together.

I pat her shoulder firmly. "I'll see what we can do to get them out as soon as we can."

"Thank you, Grace," she answers quietly. "I understand if we can't divert people, but… I'm really worried about them."

"I understand." I reach over and pat her arm lightly. Then I lean over the table to look at the large document Aira is working from. "Aira, what am I looking at here?"

"This is a list of heirs and powerful mages across the different Houses that we could come up with. We're still missing one prophecy member, and the clock is ticking on that. Look."

I walk around and peer over the Lady's shoulder. The group has put together a comprehensive list of names from a variety of houses. All the other times, we have had pieces of a list; everyone has had their own. This is what we should have done before. "Has everyone looked at this?"

"Not the full version," Cary answers.

"Everyone gather round," I say. "Scan over this and tell me if anyone jumps out at you." We all fall silent as we scan through the multiple pages spread out across the table. The only sound in the room is the occasional sliding of pages from one side to the other or the occasional shuffle of one of us to get a better view.

"We are missing one of the Houses," Cary interrupts. The table turns their heads to look at her as she leans on her hands flat on the table. "We haven't considered the wild card."

"And who exactly would the wild card be?" Kiara asks.

"The House of War," Cary says plainly. The room is silent for a moment before bursting into several hushed discussions happening in pairs and across the table.

I tilt my head in thought. "The House of War…. Why haven't we considered them previously?"

"They're a pain in the ass," Faolan leans back in his chair. "And they don't play well with others. We better hope to the Lady it's not one of them."

"Faolan's right," Aira adds in a vote of confidence for the House of Darkness heir. "The House of War hasn't allied themselves with another House for centuries. Even their tentative trade partnership with the Alliance of the Lily is in name only. They never come to anyone's aid. You expect me to believe that our final prophecy member is one of them?"

"It would be poetic, wouldn't it?" Luna muses. "The House of War finally lending a hand to stop what may be the biggest war in all of Fae history?"

I rub my hands through my hair. "Poetic…" I chuckle dryly. "That's it. Last known ally, final hour. This is where we're at. The House of War is the very last House that has not chosen a side in this fight. We need to reach out formally."

"You know what that means though, right?" Cary looks around at the group of us. "We have to tell the War Council."

"No," Faolan groans. "Why?"

"Because if it's a formal request of alliance, they need to be in on it. And trust me, Grace, the heirs are not just going to fall in line with the thought of reaching out to the House of War."

"Why not?" I ask.

"Because it's not done," Faolan answers. "Most messages to them go unreturned. The only missives they answer are primarily related to trade. Or to reject an invitation to a Solstice, which they do regularly. We're lucky if they make even one a year."

"And because of this," Cary continues, "the other Fae in the Realm take offense at having to reach out to ask them for anything. *Especially* help. It's a pride thing. They think it's beneath them. Or that the House of War is too proud. Usually a little of both."

"Well…" I stand up straight. "I'm not too proud to ask for their assistance."

"We're gonna need a good excuse," Aira warns. "The War Council won't accept just anything."

I gulp. "Will the truth suffice?"

Everyone turns to me in shock. Kiara is the first to recover. "You mean the *truth*, truth?"

"Yes. The prophecy. It's time."

"Are you sure, Grace?" Faolan shakes his head. "That's a big move." When I look into his eyes, I see uncertainty, but also a willingness to move forward with me if I ask. I wander over to the window and look out over the town as I consider what I'm offering. Sharing the prophecy is risky. It moves a secret from a small few to a little larger few. More people means more chances for this to get leaked. But I feel like it has to be time. I feel like… I just can't go any further without having the Council's support. I'm tired of keeping information from my allies.

"Yes. I'm sure."

Cary whistles. "Wow… you've got guts."

I smirk softly back at her. "We call a meeting tonight."

Chapter Forty-Seven

When the War Council gathers that evening, my nervousness is at an all-time high. This is the first time we have to reveal the prophecy in an official capacity to anyone. I'm not prepared for the potential consequences of this. I told the others I only plan to pull this out of my back pocket if necessary. Hopefully, we will be able to convince them reaching out to the House of War is a good call. Once everyone is settled, I stand once again to address them. "Good evening. Once again, I have called everyone here because Aira, Kiara, Luna, Faolan, Cary, and I would like to present a possibility to you that we came up with this afternoon."

"What were you all doing this afternoon together?" Jason asks with narrow eyes. "Do we need to be concerned about a faction in the War Council?"

"If you shut up, we would tell you," Faolan retorts.

"We came up," I interrupt the two of them, "with a proposal when we were idly chatting and throwing around ideas. It happens."

"What is the proposal?" *Thank you, Alena, for cutting right to the point.*

I look over at Faolan briefly for reassurance who gives me a little nod. "We would like to reach out to the House of War and ask for their assistance in the war effort. They are the only House that has not put their two copper coins in on this, and if we get them on our side, we stand a chance militarily."

"We can't ask the House of War!" Tristan shouts.

"What an interesting idea," High Lady Morgana muses. "What reasoning do you have for this?"

"If we could get them on our side or secure any kind of aid, it could make all the difference. A volunteer regiment, weaponry, crops, medical supplies. Any of it could turn the tide of this war."

"They haven't helped anyone in literal centuries," Alena protests.

"All the more reason to give it a shot," her sister counters. "These are unprecedented times."

"There is no way they will send us any assistance," Jason says.

"We won't know until we try," Aira points out.

The conversation goes around in circles like this for a while. There are equal points for reaching out and equal points for not daring to try. But as the minutes go by, we are nowhere close to an agreement. The Lords and Ladies are split on the issue. When I look up at Luna, she gives me a little nod. Her eyes are telling me the exact thing I didn't want to hear. *It's time to bring out the big guns.*

"There is another reason we want to speak to the House of War," I say quietly, but firmly.

Everyone turns to look at me. "What other reason?" Jason asks with a raised eyebrow.

I look around the table at the other prophecy members. Everyone's eyes look apprehensive, but there is an underlying layer of determination to succeed that I have to step back and admire. If they can be ready for this, so can I. "As all of you undoubtedly know by now, I journeyed across the entire realm in search of answers about my brother. What you may not know is that my journey took me down to the Lower Realm." There is a smattering of murmurs and shocked noises that spread across the table. The High Lady looks taken aback, but intrigued, nonetheless. I had left this part out of my journey to find out more about Leo's death when I spoke to her.

"While I was down there with Aiden, we came across the fabled Half-Fae Coven," I continue.

"Wait," Tristan interrupts. "You're telling me you actually spoke to the coven?"

"You couldn't have. They're just a legend." Jason stares at me. "Right?"

"They're real," I answer. "They're as real as you and I are. And while we were with them, they revealed a prophecy to us." Now the word prophecy gets more shock. The room practically erupts into questions before Faolan waves a hand over the room, causing the lights to flicker. That silences everyone. I look at Luna. "Will you do the honors, Luna?" Luna nods and gets to her feet. She recites the prophecy in a powerful, echoing voice. The other Lords and Ladies lean back in their seats. I keep an eye on them to gauge their reactions. I see shock, confusion, awe, and concern. I feel them in my own heart. I feel it every time I listen to that damned prophecy. When she finishes, not even a breath can be heard.

"So that's why you all have been spending so much time together," the High Lady finally breathes, shaking her head. "And why you wanted to speak to my daughter directly when I took you to the House of Wind."

"I'm sorry we weren't able to reveal this information sooner, High Lady," I apologize. "I couldn't trust just anyone. The House of Darkness was searching for black obsidian in anticipation of such a prophecy like this, and they didn't know I would be the ringleader. It was too dangerous. I'm not sure they know yet. But now we think the eighth and final member will be found in the House of War. That's why we need to reach out."

"Why ask us for our input?" Tristan asks, quieter now.

"What do you mean?" Cary chimes in.

"Why ask us to weigh in on the War Council at all? Particularly on the issue of the House of War? You don't need us anyway, do you?"

"You're wrong." I sigh. "I need all of you here. I needed you before we found the remaining members, and I need you now. Jason, you're stubborn, but you take care of business. Alena, you and I haven't always seen eye to eye, but you have been a huge help organizing healing aid here. Aurora, same to you with your work organizing the local people and food donations. Tristan, your ideas have been sharp since you got here, and I value your input. You all represent what is left of this realm, and you will be the people to help rebuild when all this is over. That's why I want your vote. You may not think it matters, but it does."

The War Council considers my words, and I can see that I have managed to convince them. There is genuine respect in their eyes, a respect that I haven't seen fully before. Even Jason seems to be softer than I have ever seen him. "Can we have a vote now?" I ask. There is no hesitation. When we go around the room, the vote is unanimous. For the first time, I feel a small beacon of hope blossom in my chest. *Ready or not, House of War. Here we come.*

Chapter Forty-Eight

The journey to the House of War is a solemn one. Despite knowing that the last prophecy member must be there, no one is excited about approaching them with the information. Firstly, I don't feel comfortable revealing the prophecy to them without some sort of promise to keep it a secret or a promise of aid. But High Lady Morgana informed me that the House of War never makes a decision without considering all the facts and options available. And secondly, because we don't even know which son it is. It's not like we're going to get the opportunity to speak to all three alone, especially since this is somewhat of a surprise visit. Lady Aira did send word ahead of time, but we never received a reply.

We make our way down the mountain range to the Calypso River. It is a several-day journey that gives us all the time in the world that we would need to talk and plan out what we wanted to say. But no one can find the right words. Instead, we chat idly about how things are going back in the House of the Evening, what plans need to be made next for the war effort, and the state of our inventories. Occasionally, I hear Aira and Luna discussing what they would like to do when it's all over… the lives they want to get back to.

I'm not quite sure what life holds for me after this. I am the High Lady of the House of the Evening now. I can't go back to… playing my violin and running across the realms. I have to focus on policy and rebuilding and taking care of my people before myself. Whether or not there's anything else in the cards for me, that's something I can't bring myself to think about yet. Whether or not Aiden returns. Whether or not I cut love out of my life for now or forever. Whether I see my mom again or not.

When we reach the river, Faolan arranges for one of his black-market contacts to ferry us to the House of War. The man doesn't speak much; in fact, he will only speak directly to Faolan, adding to the mysteriousness of it all. He guides us with a slow and steady pull of his magic as we float across. Seeing the House of War again is different this time around. The atmosphere is more serious if one can imagine that after that pass-through I made with Aiden. Looking over the fog on the river, I see scores and scores of signal fires burning on top of every building. Figures stand guard there, watching, waiting. It is eerily quiet. I can only imagine what kind of army has been building up on the inside. After all… this House has legendary preparation for battle, and it's no secret that this realm is indeed at war.

When we disembark and make our way to the front gate, we are instantly surrounded by a congregation of soldiers. More than I expected honestly, almost two dozen to cover our little party. As soon as we step off the boat, the general halts us right at the shoreline. "Ma'am, I'm going to need to stop you right there. You and your party will need to turn back. The House of War is accepting no visitors and no refugees."

I quirk an eyebrow at the 'no refugee' comment. "This party is neither visitor nor refugee. I am High Lady Grace Faelie of the House of the Evening, and this is a diplomatic mission accrued by representatives of several of the Houses of this realm. We sent word of our arrival to the High Lord, and we are going to the palace."

"I'm sorry, but without notice from the High Lord, I can't let you enter the city."

"Without notice?" Aira pipes up angrily to my surprise. "I sent him a letter!"

"This is ridiculous," Cary mumbles behind me. I shoot her an angry glare. The last thing I need is for her to escalate this. I'm not getting into a brawl with House of War soldiers on their ground.

"Send word to the palace, and let them know that we are here," I insist. "We will not be moving from this spot until we are admitted." The general and I engage in a little standoff before he finally sends a soldier toward the palace through the gates to the city. We stand waiting for quite a while before he returns, pushing his way back to the front of the group of soldiers.

"Sir?" He hands the general a scroll. "Message from the High Lord."

The general opens the notice and scans the text. He then looks up at us. "It appears your request for an audience has been accepted by the High Lord. We will escort you to him." The ranks part and fall into two lines on either side of us. As we move through them, the general takes the lead and brings us to Main Street.

I was right about the city preparing for war. More soldiers line the streets than several of our armies combined, if not more than all of them put together. They march in such neat, precise lines with swords or daggers hanging off their belt. *The House of War doesn't fuck around.* The buildings around us seem as rigid as the people who enter them and walk beside them. Everything is stone and dark wood. There is very little color to them besides the occasional flash of a rusty red.

When we reach the palace, it stands tall and harsh, ready to keep out all that it doesn't want inside. Its stone structure intimidates as does its big iron door. Our group is delivered by the regiment on the palace's doorstep. The doors are pulled open by people on the inside, and we step inside. It is a straight shot down the hall to the throne room. We enter the room to find the noble family of the House of War standing at the ready. High Lord Caddell sits high on his throne next to his High Lady. They both look at us with calculating eyes and grim faces. Behind them stand their three sons, each with their own similar stare. All of them have wide frames and broad shoulders.

"Grace?" Luna whispers behind me as the general who led us here speaks to the High Lord in a hushed tone.

"What is it?"

Aira speaks under her breath, "A lot of power coming off Gideon. The middle son." I turn back around and look up at the lineup, focusing on the middle child. He stands tall by his eldest brother's side, looking as though this is his natural position to be at attention. His brown eyes stare at me with the same intensity as his family, but there's something that feels slightly forced about it. When I send out a feeler of sensing magic, I am nearly knocked off my feet. Out of all the magical signatures up on that platform, Gideon's burns the brightest. It is a powerful wave of magic, a sturdy kind of magic that I have not felt before when feeling out for any of us prophecy members.

The general leaves the room, and the group of mages assembles in the middle of the stone floor with me at the head. I lead us in a bow to the High Lord.

"High Lord Caddell, it is an honor," I say. The others echo my sentiments.

"Why have you come to speak to me?" The High Lord's voice cuts sharply across the room like a knife. "High Lord Caddell, I would like an audience with your son, Lord Gideon." I see a flicker of something pass over Gideon's face.

"Anything you have to say to Gideon, you can say in front of us," the man's voice booms.

"The matter is delicate, High Lord," I protest.

"Not so delicate that you cannot disclose it to this hall."

Faolan steps forward beside me. "It's a matter of life and death, High Lord. We need resources from you, ones only your son can provide."

The eldest brother chimes in. "My brother is not in charge of any resources; that would be me."

"He leads your army," Faolan fires back.

High Lord Caddell slams his staff into the steps. The rest of us fall silent. "No one is getting a private audience with my son! You will state your case here, or you will be escorted out of the House of War."

Internally, I am fuming. *How dare this man expect to know everything when we have been fighting on our own for months without their support? I have been trying to keep this under wraps, keep the War Council out of this decision, and now I'm supposed to lay out the prophecy at this man's feet without reciprocity and hope it doesn't travel any further than this room?!* I ball my fists by my side, but a telepathic nudge from Kiara stops me from saying what I want to say. "Come on, Grace," she whispers to me in my mind. "We need their help. Give them what they want, and we'll figure it out later."

I take a deep breath in and step forward, separating myself from the group. "For months, we have been locked in a war to stop the House of Darkness, the House of Fire, and the House of the Sun from taking over the Upper Realm. We have been struggling to pull resources together, to pull men and women together to fight to preserve this realm and the next. There has been evidence of demonic interfe—"

"We know all of this information," the High Lord interrupts. "Skip to the part why you need us and particularly my son to get involved."

I blink. "I'm sorry, you're aware that demons are ravaging the Upper Realm?"

"Yes," he repeats simply.

I struggle to contain my anger. *How can a High Lord that is supposedly for the noble cause of fighting the good fight be so callous with other people's lives? How has he not stepped in before now?* Through gritted teeth, I continue. "We have reason to believe your son is part of a prophesized group along with the six of us to lead us into battle and right the balance of the realms." I turn back and acknowledge Luna and Aira with a nod. "Lady Luna and Lady Aira have confirmed this with divination and sensing magic, and I have just corroborated that belief with my own sensing magic. I am asking for your son to join us in the House of the Evening and combine your resources with ours, so we have the opportunity to win this war."

I raise my eyes and metaphorically lock horns with High Lord Caddell. He looks back at me with a solemn face. "No."

I hear sounds of protest from the nobles behind me, but I hold up a hand to stop them abruptly. "Excuse me?"

"I said…" The High Lord rises to his feet. "No."

"You don't want to hear any more? That's all the information you need to make a decision?" I raise my voice incredulously.

"Lady Grace, I have no interest in getting involved in your little war. I don't care what role you think my son may or may not be destined to play, but I refuse to get involved. That's my final decision." He steps in front of me and heads for the door.

I explode.

"That is High Lady Grace to you, Brandon," I snap. Out of the corner of my eye, I see Faolan's jaw drop. Cary lets out a short laugh. Caddell's sons have no idea how to react although the heir has risen to his feet.

The High Lord stops short and slowly turns his head. "What did you just call me?" He storms over to get in my face. "You have no respect for…"

"You're right!" I shout at him. He takes a step back in surprise. "You're right. I don't have any respect for you, High Lord. Despite clearly understanding what's going on outside your four walls, you have chosen to ignore it instead of sending aid. You have the biggest army in the Upper Realm, and you appear to have no desire to actually use it!" I lean closer to him. "Part of being a good warrior is knowing when you need allies, and you, High Lord, are really going to regret your choices when the House of Darkness comes knocking at your door.

"We can handle any threat to…" The heir lord Duncan tries to speak.

"Oh really?" I whip around to him and storm away from the High Lord.

"Guards!" High Lord Caddell calls out.

I ignore the call. I get in Duncan's face. "What are you going to do when the rest of the Houses have fallen down around you and you are on your own against the demons? Do you think your people can handle a hundred demons in a constant onslaught of battle for days and days with no relief? Cause that's the world you're looking at if we fail."

The doors burst open with soldiers, and I know I only have a few moments to act. I dart over and grab Gideon by his arms. He startles, but he doesn't move out of my grasp. "You have an opportunity to fix this. You are the Deliverer, and you belong with us." I am roughly grabbed and pulled backward by my arms. "We need your help! Without you, this realm will end in flames!" I struggle violently as I am physically dragged out of the Great Hall. My companions are pushed out with far less rough treatment as they were not resisting. We are escorted all the way outside before I am literally thrown from the palace steps. Faolan stops me from landing face-first on the pavement.

"That…" Cary starts. "Was amazing."

I raise an eyebrow and face her as Faolan sets me on my feet. "What?"

"Do you know how many times I have wanted to go off on a High Lord? And by the Lady, you just reamed out the High Lord of the House of War." Cary smirks. "I'm so proud of you."

I roll my eyes and turn around to look back up at the palace doors that are now closed to us. "But at what cost?"

Chapter Forty-Nine

When we exit the courtyard, the group tries to keep their heads high. But looking at the other faces around me, I can tell that everyone feels defeated. There's a slump to Kiara's shoulders. Even Cary has a little fatigue lingering at the corners of her eyes. Faolan's jaw is tight. I can see the ache in everyone.

I don't know what happened in that room. I didn't mean to lose my head, but the way he was talking to me felt so disrespectful. I may be a new, half-mortal ruler, but no one deserves to be spoken to like they are beneath the other person. How could High Lord Caddell not see what his decision is going to do to the rest of the realm? Of course, the House of War could sustain themselves if the rest of us were conquered, but how are they so confident that they could hold up against a demon attack?

"Do we stay the night?" Faolan asks me. "Or do we cut our losses and leave?"

"I'm not sure." I look around the town. "I want to stay and try again, but I have a feeling that we wouldn't be welcome if we tried."

"I say we cut our losses and go," Cary interjects.

"We can't go," Luna counters. "We need their assistance."

"Screw them," Cary scoffs. "They can battle it out with the demons by themselves. The arrogance is astounding."

"We need to regroup and come up with another—" My words are

interrupted by a shaking underneath my feet. It's subtle at first like a small tremor, but it quickly grows louder and more violent. "Does someone feel that?"

Before I have time to hear the answer, a booming explosion sends a jolt of panic through me. The seven of us immediately hit the ground. Without hesitation, I throw up a shield to protect us from multiple fireballs that land where we are laying. They bounce off the shield one after the other. My ears ring intensely.

"What the hell…" As I look out, I am floored. Down the street, the front gates have been blown off as a large thick cloud of smoke pours in from the outside. The entire wall has crumbled down, and there's rubble everywhere. A small, yet mighty force of the House of Darkness storms through it and floods into the city. The soldiers spread out like wildfire, and before I can blink, they are tearing the place apart. Disintegration spells knock down walls like they were pillows. The cries of the people inside shriek out into the open air, and I can feel the sound in my core. Hellbent on destruction, the regiments move through and sweep the area, stabbing or blasting anyone that they can see. Too many haven't had a chance to protect themselves before being mowed down by the House of Darkness.

Kiara lets out a sharp gasp as overhead, a group of six winged demons flies into the city. I feel the power shift in the air as they soar overhead. Each takes on a different shape and size, and my sensing magic is going crazy trying to identify their power. With a flick of their hands, fire and rock rain down from above. They hit buildings nearby and much further behind us leaving a path of destruction in their wake. The smell of blood becomes too much for me.

"Get up!" Cary shouts as she yanks Aira to her feet. Luna and Kiara take cover on either side of a tavern's doors as Fae pour out to see what the commotion is. When they spot the invasion, instead of screams of panic, I hear cries of battle. Weapons come out of sheaths, and magic begins circulating from hands as the general populace joins their House army in a charge. Faolan yanks me up from the ground and pushes me to safety behind a building. But I don't stay still for long; I rush to the corner to take stock of what's happening.

"How many soldiers are we looking at?" I call to my second.

"Several dozen at least. I recognize a few of them. This is my father's secondary force. Strong enough to wreak some havoc, but not necessarily expected to take the city. But with the addition of the demons, I could be wrong. What's the plan?"

I hesitate. I know I shouldn't, but I do. No matter how powerful the Fae of this House are, six demons in one concentrated space are no small task to take on. Plus the foot soldiers? The city will be razed within the hour. But they refused our request for assistance since they thought they could handle the impact all on their own.

"We fight."

When I lock eyes with Faolan, he doesn't hesitate. His eyes flash red, and he moves out from behind me. With a grab of his hand, I watch the panic on two nearby soldiers' faces as the light is snatched from their eyes and they fall blind. We rush forward and knock them both to the ground with a well-placed kick to the chest. Faolan knocks them both out while I rush over to the other women. "Spread out," I instruct. "Do what you can. Keep the city from being seized."

Cary rushes into the House of Darkness army and sends out a circular wave of flame. Engaging in hand-to-hand combat with one of the generals, she lands a knee on his ribs before disarming him. Kiara and Aira launch into the sky towards one of the winged demons who is lagging and combine forces to try to force him out of the sky. The demon isn't going down without a fight though. His dark power radiates like black watercolor bleeding out on a canvas to send the two of them spiraling in opposite directions around him.

I reach out and latch on to some of that power and absorb it into my own. This magic is unruly, and it does not like me. It fights me every step of the way and once it's mixed with my power, it is incredibly unstable. I can't hold onto it for very long. "Luna!" I manage to shout. "Help me." Luna grips my arm and together, we push a wind blast up toward the demon. With the demon's own magic, it spirals wildly before striking hard enough to break one of the creature's wings. I cringe as I hear the bone snap. He tumbles out of the sky head over heels. When he hits the ground, he burrows into it, causing a small explosion.

"Help them." I motion her to follow the others after another demon while I rush into the crowd of warring armies. Pulling out my sword, I clash blades with a House of Darkness man. My magic flows into the blade, and my frustration at the situation of still being here and fighting to save a place that won't help me and mine fuels a fire in me. Being in the thick of it means people are trying to kill me on all sides. I do my best to divide my concentration between Weapons Amplification magic and other forms to keep those around me at bay. I wish I could say that I knew what to throw when, but it's completely random. Fireballs, gusts of wind, pulling from other spells to convert into energy, telekinesis to send weapons haywire: I'll do whatever I have to to stay alive.

In the back of my mind, I'm paying some attention to how the House of War fights. Every movement is sharp; it's calculated. One can practically see the thought process behind their plan reflected in their eyes. When I watch their magic move through the crowd of warriors, there's a clear force backing it. Spells are pointed directly at their target, and they never miss. No one takes a shot without knowing where it is going to land. It's quite incredible to watch.

Out of the corner of my eye, I see Luna split off from Kiara and Aira to help put out the fires that the foot soldiers are lighting. Water draws in from the harbor nearby into her hands. It twists into a massive wall of water that she's right behind. She doesn't seem afraid that it will come down and drown her. Instead, she blows it through the streets, wiping out flames left and right. It soaks the people but doesn't drown them. The magic control is amazing.

I quickly realize that the demons are the most pressing issue, not the soldiers. My wings unfurl as I hit the sky. Thank the Lady for a windy day. While my friends continue to attend to some of the smaller demons, I head for the clear leader of the pack approaching the palace. This demon is built differently than the others. He is a massive winged and horned monster with eyes that glow orange and pierce flames into the heart of the stone tower defenses with one glance. I have no idea if my magic is going to be strong enough against his to knock him out of the sky, but I fire off a fire spell at him anyway.

The spell hits him in the back of the head, but instead of causing damage, it seems to just nudge him. He turns around and stares at me with an intense gaze. A creepy smile grows across his face. "You're her," he says in a gravelly voice. Without hesitation, I grab every ounce of wind that I can feel and direct it toward his wings hoping to pull them in opposite directions and make him fall. But they pull only a fraction. It's like I made him stumble.

I'm waiting for him to throw something at me so I can absorb and convert it, but he doesn't. I fire off a few more fire spells before following up with a huge ball of air that spins in the center. Everyone I have tried that on has been sent spiraling to the ground, but to the demon, it's like a summer breeze.

He laughs loudly. It echoes deep in my chest. "I see you, child. You're the Enchantress."

His words hit me so hard, I nearly drop out of the sky. My wings stall, and I spiral down for a while before getting my bearings. I rocket back up to him. "What did you just say?" I send a wave of fire his way.

The demon laughs at me. "You know what I said, Enchantress. Just look at you squirm." We circle each other slowly in the air. "That's right, Grace; I know everything you know."

He's just trying to throw me off. I have to believe he's trying to throw me off. I cast another spell, but he deflects it instantly. "You don't know what you're talking about," I shout to the wind.

"Prophecy girl. Half-mortal child. Daughter of High Lord Alexander and Amelia the artist." Every phrase falls from his tongue and sears into my skin. I feel a magical force behind every word he says, drawing me closer into his eyes. "You were the one your brother fought to save when he destroyed the black obsidian mine. But he couldn't protect you from all of it now, could he?"

"Who the hell are you?"

"They call me the Ancient One, Malik. I was born before this realm was made, and I will be alive long after you are dead, little girl. High Lord Carron has made me a very generous offer to let me and my kind roam free in exchange for access to my black obsidian collection."

My breath catches in my lungs. "He knows."

The demon's teeth glisten in the sunlight. "Yes…" he draws out the words. "He knows…" It is then I realize I'm directly in front of the demon. I should have paid more attention to the force drawing me closer to him. His breath smells like poison fumes as it bears down on me. I am frozen.

Suddenly, in a flash of black feathered wings, something knocks me out of the sky away from Malik. Two arms come around me, and I am wrapped in Faolan's wings. We spiral towards the ground where the fighting is still in full swing. My head clears. "What the hell were you doing, Grace?" he shouts in my ear.

"He knows," I gasp. "Your father knows about the prophecy."

"Are you sure?" Faolan quickly turns serious. I can only nod. Faolan doesn't hesitate; he only continues down rapidly and lands us on the ground. I look back up to see if the demon is headed back for us, but to my surprise, the creature is gone. Turning around, I watch him soar out of the city at breakneck speed with two others by his side.

"Where are they going?" I mumble to my partner.

"I have no idea," he answers in my ear.

Down below, I see Kiara and Aira took out another one and the House of War took out one of their own. Faolan and I race back toward the front entrance to help the army beat off the last few remaining soldiers. Weapons in hand, we manage to drive the last of the regiment out.

With heaving breath, the prophecy members and I regroup. Cary looks scratched up to hell. Kiara is sporting two prominent bruises on her cheek and left shoulder. I take stock of the injuries of my people before moving out into the field to help. Most of us help lift soldiers onto stretches while Luna and Kiara move to help heal those in need of immediate attention. Pride swells within me as they step up. This is a good group of mages. I'm honestly… proud to be working with them to get through this war.

"Lady Grace?" The High Lord's voice comes up behind me. I turn around to see him, Gideon, and the eldest brother. They look as rough as we do with a few burns and sweat dripping down their faces. "What are you still doing here?" He takes notice of our disheveled state. "Are there any major injuries?"

"We're fine," I say very calmly. "We were on our way out when the attack happened. We weren't going to abandon you to the demons."

The man simply nods, as if it were a simple matter of fact. "Thank you for your assistance."

"You're welcome." The two of us stand and look at each other. I feel like the man is finally beginning to see me for the first time.

"I hope you don't expect us to change our minds after this," the eldest interjects.

His father cuts him off with a sharp motion of his hand. He then turns to me and bows his head slightly. "We will possibly reconsider." With that, he exits. The heir says nothing and glares at me before following his father.

I nod to myself as I watch them leave. I wave to my group of fighters and motion for them to follow me. Nothing more needs to be said.

It's time to go home.

Chapter Fifty

When we trudge back into the castle after a long quiet journey home, I am not feeling particularly well. The journey was an utter waste of time, and frankly, I don't know what I'll do next. Without the House of War on our side, there is a much higher chance of the realm falling. My heart sinks when I turn to the others, and their faces are looking at me expectantly. Just waiting for me to say something inspiring or useful. I don't have anything to give them.

"What's next, Grace?" Aira finally asks.

"Do you have a plan?" Cary chimes in, arms crossed. I see Faolan motion subtly to her to cut it out. If I wasn't so damn tired, I would appreciate his efforts.

"Tomorrow." I wave them off. "I'll answer everything tomorrow. We're all too tired to sort this out now, and tomorrow's a new day. Conference room directly after breakfast." I don't bother to hear whether they have any other questions. I drag myself up the front stairs, tuning out the low voices talking behind me. The hallways and the endless line of doors blur as I stumble my way across the third floor. Bypassing my own room, I head to the end of the hallway towards the library.

The balcony doors are open, and the hall is doused in moonlight streaming in from the night outside these walls. When I reach them, I stand in the doorway and look out over the landscape beneath me, bathed in purplish light. The lights are still on in the town streets, and I hear soft fiddle music still playing from a tavern's window. Only when I grip the balcony's railing do I allow myself a heavy sigh. My eyes shut as I reel in the events of the last couple of days.

I don't know why I got mixed up in all this. I have no idea how to lead like this *all the time.* No matter what I do, there is always a setback. And no matter how hard I work, I can't seem to catch a break. I barely sleep, and those very few moments I get to myself, I can't relax. Being so… out there all the time takes a lot out of me.

Two arms suddenly slide their way around my waist. "Well, that could have gone better."

I start violently and curse when I turn around. "By the Lady, Faolan, will you stop sneaking up on me?" I slide out from under the hold.

"And lose my charm? Never." His smirk has a bit of softness to it tonight. But I am still not in the mood.

"I'm not in the mood for your games tonight, Faolan. What you could do is help me figure out a Lady-damned plan, which is your job as my second." I lean forward against the balcony. "That was horrible."

"Like I said, it could have been better."

"Gideon won't move without his family's say-so, and without him, we're screwed." I throw my hands up. "I tried. I don't know how to get him to see that we need him." I rub my eyes. "His brother's a menace."

"If you let me do it my way," Faolan says as he raises his eyebrows. "His brother wouldn't be a problem."

"We do not need to be in a three-front war by accosting the heir to the House of War. We need them on our side, which we have repeatedly spoken about. I don't care how you feel about him, and I don't care if he owes you money; we are not blackmailing, assaulting, or kidnapping." I groan. "Have I covered all the bases?"

"So killing is on the table?"

"Very funny." I turn my head back to the doorway.

Faolan nods and takes my hand firmly in his. It's surprising, but not unwelcome. He pulls me to the edge of the balcony beside him, bracing himself on the railing with his other hand. "You just can't accept that they won't recognize you unless you can speak the same as they do. And they only speak with their muscles."

I grit my teeth. "That is…. beside the point."

"No, it isn't," Faolan counters in a soft tone. "You're taking this on by yourself, again. And you want help, you ask for it, but you struggle to implement it because you're so stuck trying to prove to yourself that you can handle it. But a leader needs to take her team's opinions into account and implement it too."

I chuckle wryly before saying, "I have asked your opinion on every matter since I asked you to be my second."

"You have," Faolan acknowledges, "but you struggle to actually make a plan with it because you're caught up in the moment." His eyes stare into mine. "You ask my opinion but don't always use it."

"All eyes are on me, Faolan. What am I supposed to do?" I let go of his hand as I pace the balcony. "I am the half-breed heir to the House of the Evening," I half-scoff. "I've been thrust into the role of head of the War Council. And I'm supposed to lead the prophetic eight into battle. How does one not get caught up in the moment with that?" I sigh and turn my back permanently to the town. "I can't breathe most days."

Faolan chuckles. I turn to him to be cross, but I find him up on the railing of the balcony, walking its length. *I suppose I can't push him off, can I? He's... too agreeable today.* "You stand here. On the edge. You're scared cause you don't know what's down there," he teases as he wobbles over the edge. I reach out to grab his shirt before he falls, but he dances out of my grasp, recovering seamlessly. "You don't want to fall, but you're letting all that fear control you."

He hops off the railing and stands in front of me. He shrugs. "All you need to do is walk. The rest of us, we're here to help. Your strength is only so much. You gotta rely on someone else sometimes. You gotta let someone in."

A small smile crosses my lips. "Maybe you're right."

Faolan slides a hand over mine again. "Of course I am."

I look down at our joined hands and then slowly back up. His amber eyes glow softly against the dim night. "Why do you stand beside me? Why do you... take my hand?" I ask quietly. I'm almost afraid of the answer.

He chuckles. "Can't you tell, Grace?"

Things are moving too fast here. I pull away and make my way toward the palace again, backing away. Faolan watches me with a raised brow. I feel warm, but I can't look away. For a moment, I wonder if he's invading my mind again, but his presence feels cool, not warm. "I... I don't trust you yet," I finally settle on.

Faolan steps forward away from the balcony, moving closer to me with every step. "Why not?"

I am mesmerized by the man in a way I can't quite place. "I..."

"All this time, I've been your second." Faolan shakes his head and chuckles. "And yet you don't trust me?"

His expression looks almost a little melancholy, and I feel the need to assure him. "No... I..." My voice drops to a whisper. "I do trust you." My back hits the column by the next doorway to the hall. A couple more steps and I'll be free. I'll be away from this man who's still slowly moving closer to me. But my body won't move any further. Faolan watches me expectantly. *Am I supposed to say something more?*

I barely get out the next words. "That's what scares me."

Faolan smiles and slips in closer. "Don't be scared," he breathes against my face. My eyes slip closed as his lips brush mine softly.

Then there's no stopping the inevitable.

Faolan kisses me suddenly, pressing me hard into the column. His lips are insistent and demanding, and I cannot help but let him in. My hands slide up and into his hair and tighten, pulling softly. I kiss him with wild abandon. He lifts me up and pulls my legs around him without disconnecting our lips. I have no fear of being caught.

There is something so wicked about kissing Faolan. Relief, certainty, control flood back into my body. For months, there has been this tension between us that I have been trying to ignore. But this... this feels right. Despite my trust issues, it hadn't been very hard at all to trust the man. And he has always given me those ridiculous eyes that just...

Faolan's lips slide down and nip at my neck softly, and I lose my train of thought.

When he pulls back from me, his eyes are so fierce. We don't say a word to each other as we both breathe heavily. He reaches out and tucks a strand of hair behind my ear. To my surprise, however, Faolan sets me down and begins to move back. Without hesitation, I reach out and grab his arm, stopping him. "Don't go." My voice sounds strange and echoey against these empty halls.

He freezes where he is before slowly turning back to me, a simple smile crossing his lips. His eyes still contain that hint of danger and excitement though that I love to see. "I wouldn't dream of it," he whispers to me before catching my lips again, a little softer this time.

There is something that is forbidden about this kiss. A House of Darkness Lord, an enemy, an unlikely ally against a House of the Evening Lady... High Lady... a half-Fae, half-mortal bastard child. But I don't care about breaking all the rules of this realm if he doesn't step back. His hands are soft, yet insistent and rough as he pulls at my hair. He presses kisses to my cheeks and my neck like fire against my skin. I've never been so overwhelmed with sensations in my life. There is no time to speak.

When he reaches the hem of my shirt though, I am jerked back to reality. I grab his hand to stop him as I pull away. My head hits the column behind me, and my breath heaves in my chest. "Don't…" I say softly. He watches me as I duck my head. "Not tonight. I… I can't…" I want to communicate how I feel, but the words just aren't coming out. How much I want to say yes, but with everything happening around me, I can't just… go… and…

Faolan presses a finger to my lips gently before kissing them once more. "You don't have to say it. I know." I step forward and press my head to his chest. He wraps his arms tightly around me and hugs me tight. One of his hands lightly strokes my hair and draws through my curls. The other brushes its knuckles softly across the small of my back. It feels so careful, so peaceful. I could fall asleep here. But too soon, he lets me go. "Tomorrow then." He smirks at me as he kisses my hand before fading into the night.

"Tomorrow," I call to him when he disappears. Then I am left alone in the cool night, wondering how I could let him walk away.

Chapter Fifty-One

When I wake up, the first thing I notice is that I can still feel Faolan's kiss on my lips. I don't think that should be allowed. Not a full night's sleep later. Not when I am trying to push my feelings aside. My heart pounds in my chest, and there are too many emotions that flood my chest. Fear, loneliness, a deep pang in my heart that is lodged so deep. Since Aiden left, I have been all out of sorts with myself. Faolan has made life easier, sure, but am I really falling for him? Am I reading too much into this? I groan and roll over under the covers, hoping to forget this whole thing.

Bang! Bang! Bang!

A loud insistent knock comes on the door. "Grace! I need to talk to you now!" Cary's loud voice echoes from the hallway. "Can you open up?"

Oh great, this is exactly what I need. "Not now!" I shout as I pull the blankets over my head. "I'm not dressed!"

"Well, get dressed!" she yells back. "This can't wait. Either you're opening up, or I'm coming in anyway."

I begrudgingly get up and pull on some clothes, cursing that wretched Lady all the while. When I throw the door open, she practically storms in. She gives me a once-over. "Everyone is looking for you. Faolan said you were asleep."

"I was asleep."

"Well, you need to come downstairs. There's an issue in the House of Peace. My father has gotten in way over his head. Something is… not right."

I wave her out into the hallway and follow close behind as we rush towards the stairs. "What's not right?"

"Intel from some of Kiara's friends and servants have suggested that High Lord Carron isn't himself. His power has increased significantly, and his voice has changed. And… there are more demons from the Lower Realm now entering the Upper Realm."

"More? How many more?"

"Dozens. No one can figure out why. He may be calling them somehow or casting a summons, I don't know. But we need to get downstairs and figure out what to do. Everyone is in a panic; they are all waiting in the throne room. We haven't even had a chance to tell them about how things went in the House of War. You've got your work cut out for you."

We rush towards the stairs. I'm desperately trying to process this information. *So the High Lord of Darkness is now calling demons from the Lower Realm and they are responding. He's acting strangely. Physical aspects have changed...* I'm not sure I want to extrapolate what I'm thinking. When we reach the bottom of the front staircase, Cary makes a beeline for the throne room. I move to follow, but a sound catches my ear from the doorway outside.

Cary looks back over her shoulder. "Aren't you coming?"

I hold up a hand. "One second. I hear something."

"What is it?"

"I'm not sure…" I strain my ears and put out a little sensing magic. I feel something unfamiliar, a significant amount of magic coupled with a low rumbling noise.

"Is it Faolan?" she asks. "He went outside earlier on a walk; it could be him coming back."

"Hey!" I hear Faolan's voice shout from outside. "We got company!" His voice is steady, but there's a sense of urgency in his tone.

"Cary, get everybody over here now," I order as I rush towards the front door. She doesn't hesitate and takes off in the other direction. I join Faolan in the courtyard, my eyes darting all around the perimeter to check for danger as I race to the walled-in edge. "What's the problem?"

Faolan's eyes are trained on the town beneath us. "Look," he says simply as he gestures downward. When my eyes adjust, my jaw drops. The largest army I have ever seen is marching through my town. Scores and scores of horses with soldiers on their backs make their way down Main Street and towards the road entrance to the palace. Each of them is armed heavily with staffs and swords. Following along behind them are dozens of carriages stocked full of supplies. As they come over the ridge, I see the House of War's gray and red banners flying. When I send out another wave of sensing magic, I recognize Gideon's magical signature.

"By the Lady," I breathe. The House of War has arrived.

I turn around quickly as Cary brings out the rest of the War Council and a handful of soldiers that must have just come from breakfast. "Wait, wait!" I yell as I rush over to stop them from rushing into battle. "Stand by! Fall in line and stand ready but stand by!" Our men and women fall into line, weapons and magic at the ready. I slide alongside Faolan again. We lock eyes, and he takes my hand as we move to the front of the courtyard as one. The others fall in behind us. We are ready for whatever is coming, battle or alliance.

Gideon rides up over the hill only a few moments later, his army marching and riding in perfect formation. I hold my breath. He comes up to the courtyard and stops about ten feet in front of us. His head is held high, and I can't quite read the expression on his face. When he hops off down from his horse, Faolan starts beside me. I stop him from charging forward with a hand on his arm. Gideon strides up to me. I take a tiny step forward.

There is a standoff happening here. Stubborn man to stubborn woman, one prophecy member to another, and both not quite fully accepting their roles in things. The look in his eyes is both apprehensive and determined. I feel like I'm in a staring contest for my life, and neither of us will make the move to blink first. Finally, Gideon reaches out his hand to me. I grasp it, waiting. Those fateful words tumble out of his mouth. "You've got yourself a Deliverer," his voice rumbles as the corner of his mouth curves up into a partial smile.

The rush of relief that washes over my shoulders has never felt so good. Faolan smiles and turns away, chuckling happily, while Aira lets out a loud whoop. The army behind us celebrates as the army in front of us blends into ours to join us. I shake Gideon's hand firmly. "Welcome aboard, Lord Gideon."

"Glad to be here, Lady Grace," he replies as he lets go of my hand and runs it through his hair. "Here," he offers me a tightly rolled scroll. "A missive from my father," he explains as I unroll it and read. "He believes that we should be joining you in this. He sent about half the army with me while the rest recover from the House of Darkness attack. Then another portion will join us here."

"That's only half the standing army?" Cary says.

Gideon chuckles. "Yes, Lady Cary. We can pack quite the punch when needed."

Faolan nods and shakes Gideon's hand. "We are grateful for the support. Might actually have a fighting chance now." I grin at the two of them and turn around to join in with the other celebrating nobles.

But not too long after, we are interrupted yet again by the sound of the rumbling of carts and the long strides of horses. They fly no banners, and I can see no crest displayed. "What the hell…." I turn around and hold up my hand to stop the conversation. *What is it now?* Faolan squares up behind me and waves a signal to the people gathered around us to stand ready. I nod to him as I unfurl my wings and leap up to get a good look at who is on the way.

Then the familiar blond man leading the charge breaks my concentration and sends me spiraling down to the pavestones. Faolan catches me from landing on my knees. "Who is it?" he demands from me, prepared to strike if necessary.

But it's not necessary. Not now at least.

"It's Aiden," I manage to get out before shouting to the group around us. "It's Aiden!" The War Council erupts into cheers as do most of the other prophecy members around us. They run towards the hill to meet them and accept them back into our fortress. Faolan, Gideon and his army, and I stay behind. My heart pounds in my chest, almost faster than the heat of battle. I dare to glance over at Faolan to try to gauge his reaction, but his expression is unreadable.

When Aiden's steed rounds the corner with an influx of soldiers, regiment after regiment, part of me is thrilled. Two armies added to our numbers may be enough to turn the tide of this war. And of course, I always logically knew we would need to bring Aiden back for us to complete the prophecy. But… mentally, I'm not sure I'm ready for this. Aiden's eyes lock on mine, and they do not look away as the group makes their way up the road to the courtyard. They come to a dead stop right in front of us.

Aiden hops off his horse and stands in front of me with this strange expression on his face. I don't move an inch. There's something welling up in my chest; I can't describe it. Suddenly, he moves in and hugs me, spinning me around. His lips press to the top of my head over and over again. I'm in shock. My arms rise and under his arms to return the embrace. "Thank the Lady," I hear Aiden whisper.

"Why are… how are you here?" My lips move, but the voice I'm hearing doesn't seem connected to my brain.

"I tried to do so much, Grace; I have so much to share with you," he gets out all in one hurried breath as he pulls back enough to look into my eyes. "But none of that matters right now, you need to know this. I am here." He shakes my shoulders a little. "I am so sorry. I didn't think any of this through and leaving you behind was just… a terrible mistake. And…" Suddenly, his lips are on mine, and I have no idea how to respond. He tastes familiar, but foreign at the same time. To be honest, I have no idea if I'm leaning into the kiss or trying to pull away. "I'm here now."

Aiden pulls me into a hug again and spins me around a little, which puts me in front of Faolan. He's moved to lean against the courtyard wall over the hill now. Our eyes lock. I see a hint of darkness under his eyes, but his face is otherwise inscrutable. He raises his eyebrows ever so slightly, and I am instantly reminded of how it felt to be in his embrace. It sweeps through me in a brief second, but it leaves me with the same breathless feeling as when his lips were on mine last night. Then Faolan's mouth curls into that familiar smug smile. He barely moves his lips as he blows me an undetectable kiss.

Fuck.

Now what?

"Grace?" Aiden is looking at me with those blue eyes, expecting me to say something. Expecting me to fall into his arms and welcome him back with love. When my eyes shift to Faolan, he looks expectant as well, though I can't tell for what. It's driving me mad. A slow sense of anger wells up in my chest. "Grace, are you alright?"

That question triggers an explosion in me.

"How dare you," I hiss, "waltz in here with your army and a sweet smile and talk about how much you missed me." On instinct, I reach out and shove Aiden back hard. "You abandoned me, you bastard. You left without a trace; I haven't heard from you in months."

CHAPTER FIFTY-ONE

The lord is taken aback. "Grace, I—"

"My father is dead," I interrupt. "I became the High fucking Lady, and you were gone. Not a letter, not a message in a ball. You didn't even try to communicate. Your sense of duty may be strong, but your priorities are fucked." Aiden is at a loss for words; his mouth keeps opening and closing, but with no sound.

I move up close to him, jabbing my finger in his chest. It lingers there as I see the pain in his eyes. "You… you need to earn my trust again. Don't come to me like I am your lover. I am your leader, and I want you to treat me as such." I look sideways at Faolan who is watching me with an odd fascination. With my eyes locked on his, I continue, "I am not ready to be anything more than that to anyone now. Not until this whole damn thing is over." Aiden doesn't catch my change of glance. He looks crushed, nonetheless. "I'm sorry. I am happy that you are here. But you can't waltz back in and be my second. I have what I need now, and I don't need anything more than that."

Looking around, the other nobles are having mixed reactions to my outburst. Some are showing apprehension; others like Gideon are more mildly amused. Maybe even impressed that I would dress down Aiden in front of everyone. All of them, however, are looking to me for the next move. As I survey the people around us, the nobles, the soldiers, the attendants; everyone has a role to play here. And it's my job to make everything fit together.

I turn towards the palace and curl the corner of my mouth upwards. "Get inside. It's time to take back the realm."

Acknowledgments

As another book closes, I want to take the time to thank the people who helped pull this sequel together and make it a reality for me. First and foremost, my production team has been absolutely incredible. My editor, Angela R. Watts, and her suggestions took Chasing War the last few steps that it needed to be something readers would enjoy, and my cover designer, Milan Krstevski, created a cover that I am so proud to add to my collection of stories.

Truthfully, I would not be here without the support of all of the people who purchased books from my presale campaign, who I would like to recognize here:

My family, Julie Hammer, Morgan Hammer, Todd Hammer, Trisha and Jim Blanchard, Jill Hammer, Andy Hammer, Jane Gargett, Matt Gargett, Brennan Gargett, Joan Ohlweiler, and Jack Ohlweiler.

My boyfriend, his family, and family friends, Daniel Sage, Amy Boyd, Derek Lewis, Cindy Lewis, and Stephanie McClung.

Fantastic family friends, Michelle Czajkowski, Kathryn Ward, Jane Philion, Emma Coriveau, Randy Holloway, Lisa Finlayson, and Prentiss Cooper.

My friends and classmates, Caroline Cox, Maddy Mulder, Cassie Wiltse, Alexa Regnier, Liberty Bassett, and Diana Honey.

My amazing high school physics teacher, C. W. Stacks.

Lovely writing friends and readers, Jessika Rucker, Dartanyan D. Johnson, and Olivier Martin.

Finally, I would like to say to my readers: thank you for joining me on this journey. I have never been happier to put my work out there and share it with all of you. You have been incredible with your feedback and your words of kindness. I read every single comment and review that I receive, and I have been thrilled by your response to Chasing Fae. I really hope you enjoy this one as well. Much love to you all!

About the Author

Cady Hammer has been a writer for most of her life. From the time she was eleven years old writing her first novel between classes, she always looked to the world to bring inspiration. She was often teased for being in her own world, but never hesitated to invite others along on the adventure. She now spends her time at the College of William and Mary pursuing a Bachelor of Arts in History and minoring in Anthropology.

Cady is the author of Chasing Fae and loves to create stories that take people away from the world for a while. She creates her universes with inspiration from her studies, trying to create a place that feels so real that readers have to explore it. These stories explore the complexities of relationships crafted around the idea that love, friendship, and grief are all interwoven. She hopes to one day become a bestselling author alongside her desired career in museum work.

You can connect with me on:

- https://cadyhammer.com
- https://twitter.com/CadyHammer
- https://facebook.com/cadyhammerauthor
- https://instagram.com/cadyhammerauthor
- https://pinterest.com/cadyahammer

Subscribe to my newsletter:

- https://chasingthepast.ck.page/dee7464b51

Also by Cady Hammer

Chasing Fae

Grace Richardson is a young mortal woman whose only concerns are providing for her family, playing her violin, and spending as much time as possible with her brother, Leo. When Leo goes into service in the Fae's world as a mercenary, she expects him to return with the honor that he deserves.

When Leo suddenly dies in an unspecified accident, not a word, medal, or penny comes down from the higher-ups. Suspecting foul play, Grace disguises herself as a Fae and sneaks into the Upper Realm to get some answers. She anticipates being in way over her head, but the Fae soldier who discovers her true identity only a day in? Not so much.

Now Grace is forced to drag Aiden along as she tries to work out exactly how and why her brother died. Along the way, she has no choice but to confront her prejudices against the Fae as she attempts to sort out the difference between the honest and the dishonest. Political conspiracies, demon realm escapades, and family secrets will all lead Grace to the answers she's looking for… and some that she isn't.

Chasing The Past: A Chasing Fae Collection
From the universe of *Chasing Fae,* this short story collection highlights three characters from the House of the Evening, a lorddom of the nightlife, music, and art. Each of these characters represents an important part in Grace Richardson's past and future.

A Chance Meeting: When Amelia, Grace's future mother, meets Alexander for the first time, she is intrigued by his mysterious appearance and his disdain for the art she loves so much. She works to teach him the joy of creating and ends up learning a little bit about seizing life herself.

Taking My Place: Elise may not be as high ranking of a girl as the other daughters of the men her father works with, but she plans to find and take her place in the House of the Evening no matter who gets in her way.

Coming To Terms: Grace's half-brother, Neil, has never had to compete for anything. As the heir to the House of the Evening, he will inherit everything to make his own. But when his father brings home a bastard daughter, his world gets thrown into a tailspin.

The Ivy Labyrinth

Cady Hammer

The Ivy Labyrinth

In a world of magical instability, four high school students are chosen every year to enter the Ivy Labyrinth and attempt to break its hold on the planet. Four go in, but none come out. Now, it is Kristy, Kai, Brianna, and Ash's turn to enter the maze and solve its challenges and riddles in hopes of making it out alive. This magical realism serial will be written from four perspectives and take readers on a quest through physical and magical obstacles as the students struggle towards the center. Available on serial fiction platforms!